MW00790090

twisted
collide

USA TODAY BESTSELLING AUTHOR
AVA HARRISON

Twisted Collide
Cover Design: Anna Silka
Editor: Editing4Indies
Content Editor: Readers Together
Proofreader: Proofing Style, Crystal Burnette

twisted
collide

chapter one

Dane, 18

THIS IS NOT THE BEST PARTY OF THE YEAR.

This isn't even the best party of the month.

Despite the blatant false advertisement, Nick followed through on the endless booze. It leaches from every inch of the living room, wafting up from the couch I'm sulking on.

Coach will kick Nick off the team the minute he finds out about the party—he always does—and he will be out.

It doesn't help that the "small" gathering spiraled out of control fast. I don't know half these people.

In front of me, some chick I've never seen catches her boyfriend cheating. She winds back her arm, a red Solo cup clutched tight, and launches the stale beer at him.

Of course, she misses.

Of course, it lands on me.

And that's my cue to leave.

I make my way up the stairs to wash it off. Technically, Nick announced earlier that his room is off-limits. But technically, I don't give a fuck. I protect him on the ice. If he wants that to continue, he'll shut the fuck up.

It's quieter up here and much more tolerable. The hall mutes the music downstairs enough to make out words coming from somewhere nearby.

Nick will lose his shit when he discovers that someone other than me came up here.

I'm about to dip into his room when I hear it.

"Get off me."

I freeze, wondering if I heard it wrong.

Then, she says it again, and I'm taking off in the direction of the voice. I prowl down the hall, unable to make out who or where she is.

"Get off me!"

The cracked voice sounds too much like fear to ignore.

The thumping bass quakes the floor beneath me. The assholes downstairs are all too drunk to notice anything.

I strain to listen again, but it's just far enough away that I'm not sure if I'll be able to.

Eyes narrowed, I peer around the space, but the hazy smoke blurs my vision.

Can't hear. Can't see. *Just fucking great.*

Best guess—it's coming from a bedroom nearby. The problem is, Nick's parents are filthy rich, which means there are half a dozen on this floor alone.

My instincts lead me toward the north wing. The closer I get, the more I'm certain the plea wasn't my imagination. With each step, the telltale signs of a struggle rise. Muffled shrieks. Soft thuds. Heavy grunts.

The second I identify it, I toss open the door.

It takes half a second for the scene to sink in and another half for me to react. I fly across the room faster than I would on skates and land a punch right at the asshole's elbow.

He releases the fist that's wrapped around the hair of a girl I don't recognize. His free hand, working its way beneath her underwear, falls with his shock. She slumps down the wall, free from his hold, and scrambles across the carpet in the opposite direction.

"What the fuck?" the asshole barks, but I don't answer.

I have him by the throat. He isn't going anywhere. Now that she's safe and out of the way, I unleash my anger. *All* of it. Years and years of pent-up frustration. From being forced to do things I don't want to do. To being fucked over. To being raised by a shitty father.

I'd never met a piece of shit more worthy of my wrath. A grin dances across my cheeks as I form a fist. With a dark chuckle, I do something I know I shouldn't.

I throw the first punch.

My hand makes contact with a sickening crack. It isn't his victim I see. It's Molly. My little sister. The mere thought is enough to send another surge of protective instinct through me.

I hate bullies. I hate people who pick on others and make them feel small.

And I especially—more than anything—hate any scumbag that would lay a hand on a woman without permission.

It doesn't matter that this girl isn't Molly.

I continue to punch, over and over, until he drops to the floor like an anchor. He writhes in place, begging me to stop. I barely register his words, following up my fists with a kick of my feet.

Everything is hazy. I don't even notice the screams around me. I don't notice anything. Not the hands pulling me off him. Not the kids yelling that the cops are coming.

All I can do is feel. The chaotic thumps of my heart as adrenaline surges through my veins. The delicious satisfaction each punch and kick brings me. The sight of this handsy fucker on the floor—and the knowledge that I'll scare him so badly that he'll never do it again.

"Thank you."

It's barely more than a whisper, but it thrusts me back into reality. I turn to the girl this fucker took advantage of, spinning my head away when I notice she's in the middle of straightening the skirt bunched around her waist.

The situation comes to me piece by piece like a flip book, each flashing at me one after another. The sirens blaring. The footsteps pounding up the steps. And the feel of two cold hands as they jerk my arms around my back and drag me away.

"Thank you," the girl says again, louder this time.

It's enough to make the officer pause. I nod once to her as the cop clicks a heavy pair of cuffs around my wrists.

Slowly, the realization begins to settle in.

I might've taken down a guy who deserves it, but that doesn't mean I won't pay for my good deed.

I can't believe this is happening.

Actually, I can.

If luck were a spectrum, I'd sit somewhere above Tsutomu Yamaguchi (who survived one atomic bomb only to be killed by another) and below Roy Sullivan (hit by lightning seven times, but at least he survived). Life dealt me a bad hand. So, I barely flinch when the cops shove me into a patrol vehicle to wait as the girl gives her account of what happened.

Ten minutes later, he pulls me out of the car and frees me from the cuffs. I rub my wrists, well aware I'm fortunate to not spend the night in jail.

The guy I beat up agrees not to press charges, a miracle considering I mangled that asshat. I got lucky tonight, that's for sure. (See? Above Yamaguchi and below Sullivan.)

I can't even imagine what would have happened if I had been arrested. Coach would bench me, and my father . . . Fuck, I'd never live it down.

But that doesn't mean I won't experience my own form of prison.

The cops make me call my father. They ignore every argument

I can think of. That I'm eighteen and, legally, am not obligated to call my parents. That I have my phone and am more than capable of finding a ride. That Nick would let me crash here for the night.

None of it passes their litmus test, and who am I to fight it? Alas, small-town politics rear its ugly head yet again.

I make my way to the front, waiting for my father's arrival and subsequent disapproval. He sounded pretty fucking pissed that he has to pick me up tonight, but I'm sure it has less to do with the errand and more to do with the stain on his image.

I know how I look, standing outside Nick's house, hands tucked in my pockets, with a police officer babysitting me. That'll send dear old dad right over the edge.

I purse my lips but don't speak another word to the cop beside me. Instead, I tap my fingers against my upper thighs as we wait.

I'll never hear the end of it. Not now. Not ever. Dad has never been one to keep quiet about his plans for me. He expects me to become a hockey legend. Wayne Gretzky, Bobby Orr, and Gordie Howe rolled into one. If I somehow manage to screw that up, I'll be tossed aside. Disowned. And he'll absolutely see this as a move that could've fucked that future up.

After this, my father will make my life a living hell until I'm finally off to college.

I can't wait for that day.

It's the fastest way out of this joint.

I pace back and forth, waiting for his wrath.

It's wishful thinking to hope that the drive here will cool him off. Nope. On the contrary, it gives him time to simmer in his rage. He's probably thought up every insult he can possibly throw my way.

Ungrateful.

Incompetent.

Idiot.

Then, the speech will come. Jonathan Sinclair lectures like he's the keynote speaker of a TedTalk. I expect it to be twice as bad, since I pulled my parents away from a charity event and their important friends. Surprise. Surprise.

There's always something more important. A reason not to be home with me and my kid sister. It doesn't really affect me these days since I'm almost out, but Molly is stuck in that house for at least seven more years with that dickhead.

I can see the light at the end of the tunnel because college starts in the fall. But Molly's only eleven, which means years of neglect are still in her future.

That's the one thing that makes moving away from Ohio hard. Leaving her behind.

Knowing that, once I go, no one will be here to take care of her.

I shake my head, pulling my mind away from its usual depressing thoughts. She'll be okay. I peer up at the night sky and take in the darkness that bathes me from above.

The stars are bright tonight, and if it weren't for my pissed-off father headed to pick me up right now, I'd give anything to just sit and get lost in the peaceful moment.

Where anything is possible.

A life far from here.

One where my life isn't controlled.

One where I can just be me.

What I would give not to have my father's voice in my ear. In my head. Telling me what a failure I am.

The only place I excel is hockey, and even then, I'm still not good enough.

I start to pace.

This is taking too long. Where is he? With each passing second, my anxiety grows.

Time moves slow, though.

It creeps over me like grains of sand.

I'm not sure how much time goes by, but eventually, I see a car heading toward the house. My body tenses as I prepare for what's to come.

It's not the car I expected, however.

Nope.

It's yet another police officer called to the scene to help disperse the crowd of underage drinkers.

Luckily, I'm not one of them, or I'd be in the back of one of the cruisers on the way to the precinct.

The car slows down and parks right in front of where I stand.

Once the officer is out, I expect him to head around back, but instead, he looks over at the officer a few feet away from me and heads in his direction.

I watch them from where I stand. They speak for a minute, both glancing in my direction every other word. They can't be changing their minds about taking me downtown, right? The two men walk in my direction, and my back straightens.

Maybe I'm less Sullivan and more Yamaguchi. Fuck. I knew better than to celebrate my freedom prematurely. Coach always warns about that. *It's not over until it's over*, he shouts every half.

Still, I'd be shocked if they arrest me, since the girl involved threatened to press her own charges if her attacker goes after me.

The officer removes his cap, holding it between two white-knuckled hands. "Dane Sinclair?"

"Yeah."

I wait for him to speak.

And when he does, I know my life will never be the same.

chapter two

Josie

Thirteen years later . . .

THE EARLY MORNING SUNLIGHT BEATS DOWN ON ME FROM above. I squint my eyes, fighting the brightness, along with the groan that's dying to release. The last thing I need is for Mom to wake up. I'm not even past the front door, but the walls are thin and she's a light sleeper.

Today will suck.

Well, not necessarily.

If Mom's still asleep, I'll probably slip in unnoticed. That would be ideal. Then I'll be able to catch some sleep for a few hours. Which I need. Desperately. It's a well-known scientific fact that I turn into a gremlin when tired.

I tiptoe up the small set of stairs to the door. The ancient lock struggles to accept my key. I cringe, hoping it doesn't choose today to act up again.

Please be quiet. Please.

No such luck.

The second I twist the lock, the metal screeches loud enough to resurrect the dead. I slam my eyes shut, resisting the urge to bang my head against a wall. The squeak has nothing on the wood as it scratches the floor after I crack the door open.

I must've betrayed my country in a previous life.

Unless my penny-pinching mom is sleeping with the TV on full blast at six in the morning, there's no way she won't wake up from the noise.

The moment I step past the front mat, I know my prayers have gone unanswered. Mom stands utterly still in the center of the living room, not even turning to greet me. It's just over seventy-five degrees in here, but she's still in her flimsy pajamas, her eyes fixed on the old clock above the broken fireplace mantel.

Finally—*finally*—she turns to me, and I wish she never did.

Boy, does she look pissed.

It feels like the temperature rises ten degrees in an instant. I wish she'd let us use the air conditioner. We're better off financially than we used to be, but that single-mom, every-dollar-counts mentality has never left her.

Well, fuck.

We're silent as we face each other, neither of us daring to speak first.

I force out a breath, knowing I can't smile my way out of this one. "Morning, Mom."

"Where the hell were you?"

Chills race down my spine. I've never heard her speak this loudly—and certainly not at this hour. I wouldn't be surprised if the neighbors could hear her. I pull my shoulders back, readying myself for the tongue-lashing I'm about to get.

"Mom—"

"Don't *Mom* me. I asked you a question."

And just like that, Mom reminds me that, in her eyes, I'm a constant disappointment.

"I'm twenty-two years old—"

Her hand flies up, and the words I'm about to say die on my tongue.

"Stop right there, young lady. I don't care if you are twenty-two or thirty-two. This is my house. My rules are law, and coming home at six o'clock in the morning is not allowed in my home."

For the millionth time since I moved back home, I curse the job market. This is the hardest part of this setup. In college, I got used to being on my own—not having a curfew or my mother to track my every move.

"You knew the rules when you decided to move back in. Right?" she asks, but she knows I know the answer.

We've had this conversation many times. Practically once a week. But Mom is the queen of rhetorical questions.

"I mean, as soon as I find a job, I won't be able to go out anymore, so I just figured . . ."

"And when exactly will that be?" She arches a brow in challenge.

I cross my arms in front of my chest. "Well, without experience, it's hard."

Her jaw tightens. She looks like a cartoon character ready to explode. "And when exactly do you plan to do that?"

My brows knit together. "Get experience?"

"Yes. That. Because I'm having a hard time believing you're trying. I haven't seen you do anything that remotely looks like you are even attempting to get a job."

I release a long sigh. This again. She says this every day, and every day, nothing changes. I'm trying. I am. I've emailed over one hundred résumés and contacted a recruiter, but nothing has panned out. I'm told the same thing every time—you need experience.

But how am I supposed to get it when nobody wants to give me the opportunity?

"No one wants to hire me. I don't know what to tell you, Mom."

She's quiet for a second, most likely taking in what she deems as my lame excuse, then she shakes her head.

"It's enough. No more." She throws her hands up. "I'm done."

This is typical of her. She excels at drama.

"What do you mean?"

"You know exactly what I mean, Josie. You come and go as if you have no responsibility. You don't work. You act like you're still in college. You aren't even trying to find a job." I open my mouth, but she shakes her head. "No. I don't want to hear any more of your excuses."

Finally, she sits, only to begin drumming her fingers on the woven armrest. I feel like I should do something, but I'm frozen in place, waiting for her to throw down the gauntlet of whatever she plans to say to me.

I bite my lower lip. Right now isn't the time to speak, but I'm finding it hard not to stand up for myself. Maybe if I give myself a little pain, I'll be able to refrain from angering her even more. The pressure of my teeth isn't enough to break the skin, but it's enough to keep me from saying something I'll regret.

"I saw it."

Her words pierce the veil of my pity party.

"You saw what?"

She doesn't blink as she stares me down, not breaking eye contact. "I know all about your little extracurriculars."

"What are you talking about?"

"Deny it all you want. You won't change my mind. I've been patient enough." She shakes her head, and a lone tear slips down her cheek so fast, I'm not sure I saw it right. "This isn't the woman I raised."

I stare at my feet, unable to meet her eyes. "*Mom.*"

The wail is guttural, and ugly, and so unlike me, but something changed in the past minute. I don't know what, but suddenly, it feels like nothing will ever be the same.

"I made a few phone calls . . ." Her words trail off, and my head snaps up so that our gazes lock.

"Who did you call?" My voice cracks.

"A few people."

"Okay," I whisper, finding it hard to get the word out. My stomach tightens as if something bad is about to happen. Even the air in the room feels heavier.

"I called your father."

My knees wobble. I'm barely able to hold steady. I brace my hand against the wall to keep upright. Did she just say what I think she said?

"What do you mean, my father? I don't understand. You know who he is?"

"Yes, I know who he is." She sighs heavily, eyes never wavering from mine. "But right now, we need to discuss—"

"What the hell do you mean you won't discuss this with me right now? I deserve to know. Have you been lying to me my whole life?"

Despite knowing that I obviously have a father, she's never mentioned him before. I mean, sure, a few sentences in passing, but I've always known that the subject was a nonstarter.

Any time I've asked in the past, she's changed the subject. Either that or reminded me that she was the only parent I needed.

Father? She'd laugh, shaking her head. *I raised you myself. I provided for you when you got sick, when you found a new book you wanted to read, when you needed a laptop for school. You don't need a father. You have me.*

I stagger against the wall. Her words shock me into silence. I don't know anything right now—how to think, speak, *feel.*

Most of my childhood, I thought I was the product of artificial insemination. Not that anything is wrong with that; I just didn't think anything would keep a father away from his kid . . . so, I must not have had one. Mom, of course, nipped that thought in the bud as soon as I was old enough to ask her.

But a part of me still held on to the hope that she lied to me. The part that wanted to believe that my father would never leave me of his own volition.

In my mind, something stopped him.

In my mind, it was never about me.

He always wanted me.

But now, as I stand on Jell-O legs, feeling like the world will swallow me whole, I have to accept that everything I've thought of all these years was a lie I told myself. Something to protect my fragile heart.

"I had a father all this time, and you never told me?"

I have a father, and he never wanted me.

"Josephine, I will not get into that with you right now."

"Wow." My eyes go wide. "Really, Mom?"

Did she actually just drop this bomb on me and then say she can't talk about it? Seriously. Am I in the twilight zone?

What the hell is happening?

"Enough." She tips her chin up, using that no-nonsense voice she ordered me around with for decades. "All you need to know right now is that I spoke to him, and after a long talk, he agreed to help you."

My head shakes back and forth, and now I'm sure I will pass out if I don't sit. I cross the room and plop onto the ottoman across from the couch.

"Help me? I don't need the help of a man who abandoned me." I laugh, but it's humorless. I can't believe she had access to him this whole time and waited until now to contact him. "In fact, I thought you were on the same page. What happened to the woman who insisted she raise me herself?"

"I *did* raise you." She shrugs. "We didn't need him."

But I did.

I needed him, and he didn't want me.

Without even knowing my father, I already hate him.

I scoff. "And now I do?"

"I will not sit still as you waste your life away as a…as a…"

"As a *what*, Mom?" I shake my head, raising a hand up. "You know what? I don't want to know. All my life, you've made decisions for me without ever considering what I want. What's best for me."

She crosses her arms at her chest. "There's a lot you don't know—"

"And whose fault is that?" I raise a brow. "None of this was your call to make."

"As your mother, everything regarding you is my call, including this." She stands, plucks an envelope off the coffee table, and tosses it in my lap. "I expect you out of the home by the time I return from work."

"Excuse me?"

The envelope tumbles to the carpet, along with every jagged piece of my heart.

"You're lost, sweetheart. You need change." She shakes her head, sighing. "He agreed to let you live with him."

"You-you're sending me away?"

It's one thing to know my father doesn't want me—he's never met me. Who is he to judge me?

But my mother?

She's known me my whole life. She held me when I lost my first tooth, when my best friend moved to Canada, when I discovered boys are assholes who break hearts like candy. We've never had the best relationship, but still…she's my mom.

Mom ignores my question. "You'll finally get the work experience you've been going on about."

"You want me to work with the man who abandoned me for twenty-two years?" I shoot up to my feet, crushing the envelope beneath my heel and twisting it for good measure. "I refuse."

"That's up to you, Josephine. You're an adult, after all…" She pats the crown of my head. It takes every ounce of self-control not to close my eyes and lean into her touch. "…but you're no longer welcome in my home."

And just like that, she leaves without even glancing back.

It's true what they say…

Parents teach kids the most important lessons.

Mine taught me that I don't need anyone.

chapter three

Dane

WITH ONE STEP INTO THE ROOM, I ALREADY KNOW THIS IS the last place I want to be.

Normally, I'm not one for crowds, but today or, rather, tonight isn't just about the crowd, it's so much worse.

I hate what all this stands for. Don't get me wrong, I love playing hockey, but I hate that even years later, my father's voice is still in my ears. This is not the time or place to think about him.

Who am I trying to kid? *It is.* I'm only here because of him. I can't even enjoy this win because my father takes up too much of my headspace.

Also, I know winning the Cup is a monumental moment, but how many times do we need to celebrate? This is the fourth party I've been dragged to. Can't I just enjoy my summer break without having to celebrate something that happened almost two months ago?

A harsh sigh escapes my mouth, and I know I can't stand here forever.

The sharp sound of a woman's laughter cuts through the air and pulls me from my thoughts. I look over in the direction of the noise to find another one of Hudson Wilde's groupies. Her shrill cackles make the hairs on the back of my neck rise.

I don't know how he deals with that bullshit, but this is Hudson we're talking about. My teammate lives for the pussy. His words, not mine.

A shiver courses its way down my spine at the crass thought.

This is going to be a long night.

I tilt my head in the opposite direction and take in the room, trying to determine which way will be less painful.

Hudson will be harmless but annoying.

To my right, I see Mason Goode speaking to our coach. There's no appeal to that either. I don't care to hear about everything we did right, followed by what we fucked up. Coach Robert might be like a father to me, but when it comes to hockey, his lectures can be tedious. *They never end.* We can win the biggest game of a coach's career, and the man would still have some feedback.

Scanning the space, I look around for Aiden and Cassidy, but they're nowhere to be found. Not surprising. They always sneak off to be alone. Too bad because hanging with them would've been my preferred option.

My gaze locks with Molly, and she takes me in for a second. Her brow furrows with concern, and she steps in my direction. I quickly turn away.

Nope. Not tonight.

She knows me too well and will read right through my false bravado that everything is all right.

Instead of dealing with my sister, I head to the lesser of all evils.

"Hudson it is," I mumble under my breath.

As I navigate the loud and boisterous crowd, I try my best not to make eye contact with anyone I pass. Conversation and laughter fill the air, and I know if given an opportunity, any one of my teammates will stop me. I'm not in the mood for celebrating, let alone small talk.

I weave my way through the clusters of people until I make it to the bar, where Hudson is cozied up to a flock of girls vying for his attention. I halt my steps, leaning my back against the bar and crossing my arms over my chest. I'm hoping to make it clear I'm not to be approached.

My presence has Hudson pivoting in my direction and jerking his chin up. "What's up, man? Glad to see you joining the festivities."

"Nothing," I grunt out. A better man would pretend to be happy. Too bad I'm not that man. Hudson stretches his arm out and places it around my shoulders. "Come on, bro, smile."

When I don't, he rolls his eyes and laughs loudly. It's not that I don't love the guy, but I'm not in the mood for his juvenile antics right now.

"Dude, we just won the Cup. Why do you still look fucking pissed?"

"I'm not fucking *pissed*." I step out from under his arm, giving me the distance I need right now.

This is my fault. I set myself up for this. He didn't approach me; I went to him. I shouldn't be an ass to Hudson. It's not his fault I'm here.

"Could have fooled me." He turns to look at the blond girl beside him, the one who clearly finds him to be the most entertaining human in the world since she cackles at everything he says. "Don't you think he looks miserable?"

She bobs her head. "He does."

"Maybe you can help cheer him up." He grins at her, waggling his eyebrows.

Great, just great.

Now I'll have to put up with Hudson trying to get me laid. This night keeps getting better and better.

At his words, the blond girl takes a step closer to me, raising her right hand to touch me. I take a step back, avoiding her.

"Not interested. But thanks."

Hudson barks out a laugh before lifting the glass in his hand to take a swig. Once done, he lowers his hand, then shakes his head. "Can I at least convince you to have a drink with me? You know, for celebration."

"I'll pass on that too."

Someone bumps into me as they're walking by, and I turn to see who just knocked into me. It's a pretty redhead, and when she catches me looking, she smiles seductively. If I were Hudson, I'd take her up on that offer, but unfortunately, no desire stirs. Maybe I'm broken. She's gorgeous, but I'm just not in the mood tonight.

Not for her, and certainly not for this place.

"How long have you been here?" Hudson asks, and I turn back in his direction and shrug.

"Five minutes."

"And how long are you planning on staying?" His mouth twists into a knowing smirk.

"Not sure."

He turns to the blonde with a shake of the head. "That means he's leaving. Guaranteed by my next drink, he's gone."

"Don't kid yourself. I'll be gone way before that," I fire back.

As if my comment is a challenge, Hudson raises the glass to his mouth and takes the rest of the contents in one gulp. "Challenge accepted." He then lifts his hand to get the bartender's attention. Once he does, he signals that he wants another.

"On that note . . ." I turn on my heel, not even allowing them time to object before I give them my back, migrating toward the exit.

A few friends nod at me as I head out, but I give them my usual blank stare. Sure, they all think I'm an asshole, but it doesn't matter. I need to get out of here.

I'm a few more steps toward the exit when I practically run into a disheveled Aiden and Cassidy.

No need to guess what they were just doing. The muscles around my heart contract for a beat, but I shake off the feeling. The only way to have something like Aiden and Cassidy is to let someone in. Letting someone in is not in the cards for me.

Cassidy says something to me, but I can't make out her words. The music is too loud, and the people milling about are even louder.

Instead of responding, I grunt, nod, and keep walking.

I'm sure I'll hear shit about it later from Aiden, but right now, I can't find it in me to care.

I need air. *I need to get the fuck out of here.*

Finally, I make it to the back entrance. I push the door open, and the warm summer air slaps me in the face as soon as I do.

The Château is located on a small vineyard twenty miles outside of Redville, and it's the perfect venue for a wedding or, in tonight's case, a celebratory party.

Not only are there multiple restaurants and bars, but there's also a hotel on the premises.

I walk around the back of the building until I'm on the main street that leads toward the hotel. It takes me about five more minutes, but then I'm standing in front of the large glass doors of the boutique hotel on the property, hoping this is the sanctuary I've been looking for.

This is what I need—somewhere to have a drink where no one will talk to me.

I'll be able to let go a bit without anyone I know being around to judge me and, worse, wonder what's wrong.

I open the door and meander down the hallway that leads to the lobby. Once there, I head to the hotel lounge, ready to let go for a few.

Sighing in contentment, I slink into the nearest seat and raise my hand. I've never been more ready for a drink.

chapter four

Josie

ONCE I WALK THROUGH THE DOOR, EVERYTHING IN MY LIFE will change.

I stand outside the address I was given, but my feet won't move.

There's no choice but to go—I promised my mom I would—but no matter how many times I tell myself to walk, I don't.

I'm not ready.

The moment I cross the threshold, I won't be able to pretend that my father simply doesn't exist. The evidence that he didn't want me will be thrust in front of my face.

With my body weighted in place, I allow myself to look around the property.

From the corner of my eye, I can see a beautiful building on top of a small hill. The valet mentioned that it was the vineyard's boutique hotel.

The original game plan for today was that once I arrived in town, I'd head to the party, and from there, I'd get the keys to the small guesthouse on my father's property. The thing is, I'm not mentally prepared to meet him, let alone crash at his house. The fact that my mother even thought this was a good plan should be criminal.

A tiny piece of paper with the name Robert and a number is all she gave me. *Talk about walking into the unknown. I didn't even have a last name to stalk him.*

Not cool, Mom.

From where I'm standing, I can hear the loud music blaring inside the banquet hall. I have no idea what they're celebrating, but lord, they're having fun if the roars of laughter are any indicator. Then there's the couple dancing in plain view from the large windows.

My stomach feels tight.

This is my father's life.

All these years that I've been living with my mom, a woman who could barely make ends meet, a woman who had to work multiple jobs to pay the bill, and my father has been living a life of luxury.

I'll never fit in.

I'm not like these people. They'll take one look at me, and despite being put together, they won't think I'm good enough.

Maybe I'm not.

Maybe that's why he never came for me? None of that should matter now, but it does, because as I stand here by the door, it feels like a crossroads of life.

In one direction, the party . . . in the other, a hotel. An escape from reality for just a bit longer.

My body decides for me, and I find myself striding in the opposite direction of the party.

I take the winding street, and as I'm walking, I notice the vines are everywhere.

They line the drive. It's hard to see them under the darkness of the night, but I see enough to know this is a smaller patch of grapes.

I wonder what type of wine these particular grapes make.

If I'm being honest with myself, a sort of excitement comes with the potential of this place and this job that was presented to me. My sperm donor aside, I'm already itching to know everything I can about this vineyard and the wine created here.

It would be fun to get a closer look. Maybe later. Right now, my main priority is to see if I can get a room for the night. Somewhere to buy me time before the inevitable.

It doesn't take me more than five minutes to walk to the front doors of the hotel, and once inside, I walk straight up to the reception desk.

The beautiful young lady behind the counter could be my age—early twenties—with perfectly straight black hair and deep brown eyes.

"Hi." I beam so brightly that my cheeks burn.

Mom always says to kill them with kindness, and that you get more with honey than you do with vinegar. Ironic, if you ask me, since she doesn't take her own advice, but I digress.

Let's hope this works.

If not, I'll have to turn tail and go to the dreaded party. This woman holds my destiny in her hands.

Here goes nothing. "I was wondering if you have any rooms available for the night?"

"Tonight?" Her voice rises in question.

This establishment probably doesn't often get last-minute requests like this.

"Yes, I know it's last minute, but my other accommodations fell through." I rummage in my purse to find the credit card my mom gave me a few years back for emergency use only.

This is an emergency, after all. Besides, I'm about to embark on a new job. I'll pay her back, with interest, proving I'm not as worthless as she's made me feel lately.

I place the card on the counter and meet the woman's eyes.

Her brow is furrowed. She looks confused but doesn't say anything as she types on her computer screen.

Maybe I'm not the first random girl to show up asking for a room at eight o'clock at night.

I bet my story isn't even the craziest.

"It's your lucky day. I do have a room. I'll just need your license and credit card, and you'll be all set."

I slide the credit card across the marble, then reach into my purse and wade through my wallet until I find my license. Once I hand it to her, she goes back to typing.

Time seems to stand still as I wait for her to get me sorted.

Eventually, she must because she looks back up at me with a large smile on her face.

"Here you go, room 602."

I thank her with a smile before taking back my cards and the room key. I walk toward the elevators when I notice the lobby bar. It beckons to me from across the space. The loud chattering of the patrons having fun calls my name.

My luggage is still in the trunk of my car, because I thought I was going to my father's house after the party, so I have nothing to drop off. Might as well let loose.

Just for tonight.

Escape for a second.

Enjoy the moment and celebrate the new start, no matter how awkward or terrible it could turn out.

I start moving in the direction of the bar. The closer I get, the dimmer the lights become.

It sets the ambience—mysterious and seductive, just the way I like it. It reminds me of a bar you would see in a movie, where anything is possible. It's the kind of lighting that makes a person loose and free.

When I'm beside the large lucite bar, I slide onto a stool and nod to the bartender. The woman seems to have a resting bitch face. Either that, or she doesn't like me after a single glance.

Perfect start.

"Tequila, extra chilled," I say because nothing will do the job better than that.

I peer around the room as I wait, taking in the other patrons.

It's not like the usual bars I frequent. There are no rowdy college kids here. Nope, the frat boys are replaced by businessmen, or at least that's what they look like with their gray suits, boring white shirts, and drab ties. These types of guys are trying to escape the monotony of their lives.

A few feet away, a table of women sit, sipping on fruity drinks in pretty glasses, most likely moms gone wild out and about for girls' night. I lean back in my seat and wait for my drink to arrive.

Once it does, I take a tentative sip. Cautious to confirm it's chilled to my liking. It's perfect, which I should've expected from a place like this.

From the corner of my eye, something snags my interest. I turn my head just enough to see a man who commands the room's attention.

He doesn't look like the rest of the crowd. With disheveled brown hair, he has a freshly fucked look. The type of look that's my own kryptonite. I'll never know why I find it so attractive in a man, but lord, do I like it.

His face is chiseled to perfection with a five-o'clock shadow dusting it. He's stunning in a male model sort of way, yet still rugged at the same time.

He doesn't seem to notice anyone as he makes his way to the bar. Once he's beside me, our gazes lock, and I swear the breath is knocked out of my body by the striking color of his blue eyes. They shimmer with a cold depth that reminds me of glacial ice.

Holy hell.

This man is perfection.

I can't even take my eyes off him.

There's no question I need to. It's becoming obvious that I'm gawking, but he doesn't seem affected at all by my pathetic display.

Nope, instead of acknowledging me, he signals to the bartender to order a drink.

"Whiskey, neat." His gravelly voice makes chills run up my spine.

Now closer, I clock his age as older than me. Much older.

He's got to be in his early thirties, and at barely twenty-two years old, I must look like a baby deer trying to walk to him.

It doesn't matter because I've already decided this man will be my distraction for the night.

I tip the shot back and take it all in one smooth gulp, savoring the burn.

Here goes nothing.

chapter five

Josie

"COME HERE OFTEN?" I ASK AS THE GORGEOUS MAN SLIDES onto the stool next to mine.

The line is absolutely ridiculous, probably one of the worst pickup lines ever, but in a situation like this, ridiculous is necessary.

As I said, I need a distraction, and he's perfect.

"What?" His voice is smooth like honey, a sound that makes your mouth water with the promise of how good it will taste.

"I said, come here often?" I rest my chin on my fist, tilting my head to the side. He blinks at me, mouth opening and shutting. "It's a pickup line if you must know," I retort, not even trying to hide my sarcasm.

His chuckle is a deep, rich sound that makes my knees feel weak. "Now that's one way to do it."

I shrug, taking a sip from my drink. "I figure I can cut to the chase. That way, we both know what I'm angling for."

Who am I? I've never been quite this forward. But when in Rome or, in this case . . . my version of hell.

"Are you even old enough to drink?"

I'm not sure how I feel about that comment. It sounds like a brush-off if I've ever heard one.

"Well, seeing as I was already carded, it would appear so." I lift my glass to get my point across.

He studies me closely, but I can't read him. It's unnerving.

"Are you always this blunt?" he finally responds.

I roll my eyes. "Are you always this grumpy?"

He just stares at me, and I wonder if he'll respond when he finally does. "Actually, yes," he admits.

It makes me giggle. Great, not only did he just call me young, but here I am, giggling like a schoolgirl. Talk about cliché.

"Wow, was that hard to admit?"

He cocks his head as if to think about his answer and then says, "Not really."

That makes me full out laugh this time. "Now that we have that out of the way, and we've yet to establish if you come here often, I think I'll change direction and see if I can get some answers from you."

His lips purse, but he allows me to continue. "What brings you here?"

"What brings you here?" he fires back.

I smirk. "Oh, avoiding my question with a little deflection. I can tell I'm going to like you." I turn toward the bar and wave down the woman for another drink. "I came for the expensive booze and the minibar snacks in my hotel room. Now it's your turn."

"I needed a distraction." His low voice reminds me of a storm brewing in the background. A feeling I know all too well.

"Rough night? Or rough day?" I ask on a sigh.

"Both, and you?"

I nod in understanding because, same. "Me too, actually. A better word might be soul-crushing." I shrug. "Maybe we're kindred spirits."

"It does seem that way." He lets out a grunt.

Silence engulfs us, and perhaps my night of distraction isn't meant to be. It appears that I got ahead of myself. Just as I'm about to order another drink and then duck out, disappointed with my tail between my legs, the bartender returns with another drink for the broody stranger.

"I hate crappy days," I murmur, mostly to myself.

He raises his glass and takes a swig. "I'll drink to that."

I raise mine in the air, not one to leave another hanging, and take a gulp. "I also hate spiders."

He looks at me out of the corner of his eye, likely thinking I'm insane. This whole night, I've been nothing if not random. But why not? I don't know this guy. I'll likely never see him again, so I might as well be myself—something I don't do often.

I hide behind a massive wall that I've built to protect myself. I'd rather live in my bubble, convincing myself everything is wonderful. The world might be on fire on the other side, but in here, I'm safe.

"I think every person hates spiders," he muses, inspecting his glass before taking a pull of the amber liquid.

"I hate waking up in the morning. God, do I love sleeping," I say, continuing with the random bits of information. Might as well get the small talk out of the way, just in case he's game to take this somewhere else.

He runs his hand through his hair. "I'm indifferent."

"Interesting," I say, pursing my lips, trying to appear unimpressed.

"Not really all that interesting." He turns toward me, face pinched as though he's about to impart the biggest secret. "I *hate* pickles."

"Blasphemy," I say, barely a whisper.

He chuckles, shaking his head.

"I hate charm bracelets that have no charms." I wiggle my wrist, showing him the empty silver-plated chain to prove my point.

"Any reason you're charmless?"

I shrug. "It was a gift, and the original charm fell off. I guess I've never gotten around to replacing it."

He peers from my wrist to his own. A beautiful and very expensive watch clings to his. "I hate watches."

"Story there?"

"They're pointless. Everyone has a cell. They're basically a way for men to show off their wealth."

He does have a point, *pun intended*. There's really no reason for them at all.

My eyes lift to the television above the bartender's head, a clip of some hockey game playing on the screen. I've never been a fan. I find it boring, if not a bit violent.

"I hate hockey," I say, looking down into my half-empty glass.

The stranger next to me chokes. "Hockey?"

My finger runs around the rim of my glass, wiping the liquid away absently. "Yes. I find it to be a stupid sport."

"Stupid?" he says, one side of his mouth tipped up.

"Stupid." I nod my head for good measure.

"I'm not much of a fan myself." He looks at me. "I'm curious why you seem to loathe it. You appear to hate spiders less."

I chuckle. "No. Spiders top the list, but hockey is a close second."

"Why?" he presses.

"It's the dumbest sport ever."

"I'm not sure I'd go that far—"

"Nope. It's terrible," I say, cutting off his defense of the sport. "All you do is watch a bunch of grown-ass men chase rubber around a ring. Pretty lame if you ask me. And don't get me started on the fighting."

"Don't knock the fighting. That might be the only thing worth watching." He grins, and I return it with one of my own.

"I'm not a Neanderthal," I say, motioning for the bartender, who appears to be ignoring me.

"Wow, you really do hate it."

I lift my shoulders. "What? You said you hated it too."

"No, I said I'm not a fan."

Not like that's abnormal. I feel like hockey is an acquired taste. People tend to love it or leave it; much like golf.

"Semantics." I roll my eyes. "I also hate baseball."

"Is there a sport you like?"

I think about that question for a moment, not wanting to speak without thought. In the end, I realize sports are just not my thing.

"Not really," I say. "But hockey takes first place for the most hated sport of all time."

"Noted."

I tuck a strand of my hair behind my ear. "Anything you hate as much as I hate hockey?"

He sucks on his teeth before sighing heavily. "Parties."

My eyebrows knit together as I try to unravel this man. "Is it the crowds? Or the socializing?"

"A little bit of both."

"You're a grumpy introvert."

He lifts his wrist and looks at his watch. "Wow, ten minutes, and you already got me pegged."

"You're practically an open book."

He's quiet for a second before finishing his drink and gesturing to the bartender for another. "Another of whatever she's having, too."

"Would you like to start a tab?" she asks with a little too much honey in her tone, considering she's been lukewarm at best with me.

"Yeah, let's do that." He turns back to me. "If that's okay with you?"

"I'm all in. I'm definitely okay with hiding out and drinking right here for the rest of the night."

"Now that seems like a long and complicated story."

"It is. I imagine it's about as long and complicated as whatever brought you here."

He chuckles a bit darkly. "If that's true, then we might as well get the bottle."

I lean closer to him, my lip tipping up into a smile. "Now that's a good idea. Which one do we get? Whiskey or tequila?"

The stranger lifts his glass and takes another swig of his whiskey. He grins. "Whiskey, of course."

"Wow, you're either hardcore or just old." I grimace, and he laughs, so I start to laugh. The bartender returns with my fresh drink, not whiskey, and I take a sip. "So, how about an agreement? No talking about what brought us here."

He thinks for a moment, then nods. "That I can do. Anything else off-limits?"

"Sports."

"Well, we already established you hate them all. Anything else?"

"Not unless you have something to hide," I respond with a smirk.

"No mention of real life."

"Real life? What does that mean? Doesn't that fall under the previous off-limits number one?"

"Not really. Number one is more or less the catalyst to arriving here. I mean, no talking about work."

I raise my glass, moving it closer to him in a cheer. "Now that I can agree with. No talking about work or anything serious. And no sports." My glass collides with his before he pulls back and lifts his brow.

"Well then, what can we talk about?"

"We don't even have to talk about anything if you don't want. I'm more than happy to just keep you company. Drown my emotions, and then . . ."

"And then what?" he says with a note of challenge.

I shrug. "See if I can make you less grumpy."

He throws his head back and laughs. "I like the way you think . . ." His eyes narrow. "I don't know your name."

"Isn't that more fun?" I tease, not really caring either way.

He stares at me, and I feel like butterflies erupt in my stomach. The way he looks at me is unnerving. Like he's undressing me with just the way he looks at me.

"Okay." His one-word answer gives me pause for a minute, but then his lips spread, and damn. Lord, is this man handsome.

I tilt my head and take him in.

I shouldn't do this.

But I want to.

Come tomorrow, my life will change. I'm not stupid. I'm well aware I won't be able to hide in this hotel when the sun rises.

I'm surprised my mother hasn't already called me. Actually . . . I reach into my purse and grab my cell, then touch the side until it powers off. No distractions. No mention of the real world.

The stranger narrows his gaze at my phone.

"I don't want to speak to anyone tonight but you."

For a second, he continues to watch me, then he removes his own phone from his pocket. Once he's powered it down, he puts it away and lifts his glass to clink it to mine again.

"And what were those cheers to?" I ask before biting my lower lip.

"To an interesting night."

"To an interesting night," I agree before adding my own. "To putting aside the past and the future and enjoying this moment." He meets my glass again with his.

Both of us drink.

I'm not sure what brought either of us here tonight, but it doesn't matter. I'm excited for the first time in a long time, and that's all that matters.

Tomorrow, I'll deal with the consequences of my actions. I'll take whatever my mom throws at me, and then I'll go to my father's, but for tonight, I'll be free.

chapter six

Dane

T HE ONE BIG PLUS OF BEING A HOCKEY PLAYER IS THAT, MORE often than not, no one recognizes you.

Take this moment right now. The woman beside me has no clue who I am, so in turn, this is the most relaxed I've been in a long time.

She doesn't want anything from me, and it's nice. Different.

I can be myself because what will it hurt? By the time she figures out who I am—assuming she ever does, considering her loathing of hockey—I'll be long gone. Could she sell the information I shared? Maybe. Doubtful, though, because I still choose the things I share carefully.

I take another swig of my drink and study her.

She's gorgeous. A bit young, but again, I'm not exchanging numbers or trying to make this more than it is.

We've talked about everything and nothing. Our favorite seasons—hers is fall and mine, summer. Our favorite vacation spot—she enjoys exploring a new city, while I love to get out and experience nature. She loves to read Greek mythology. Me, not so much.

For the past ten minutes, we've sat in peaceful silence, each lost to our own thoughts, sipping away at what has to be our fourth or fifth drink each. Neither of us is feeling the effects as we've been smart enough to chase every drink with two glasses of water.

"I think that's it for me," she says as she places her drink on the bar. "If I want to walk out of here without making a fool of myself."

Maybe I spoke too soon.

"Drunk?"

She shakes her head. "Nah, but I will be if I keep up this pace."

Her gaze locks onto me, and I watch as her upper teeth bite down on her lower lip. The move instantly makes my dick hard.

Fuck. I'm not ready for the night to end, but I'm also not in the place to pursue her if she says she's going to bed.

I don't have that luxury.

She looks innocent right now. Her previous bravado fading away to uncertainty. Although we have been tiptoeing around the idea of hooking up, this is the moment of truth, and she's suddenly unsure.

"Cue?" I ask, narrowing my eyes at her.

"Your silence is deafening." She chuckles awkwardly.

So damn cute.

"This is clearly where the night ends." She offers me a small smile.

"Yeah." I lift my arm and signal for the bartender. "Close out our tab, please."

The girl beside me sits up straight and stops chewing on her lip. She puffs up her chest, pushing forward the confidence from before. "You don't have to buy my drinks," she declares.

"I do," I respond, not leaving any room for rebuttal. "For a night of mystery."

At my tone, she smiles. "Thank you. It was nice meeting you."

I nod my head. "See you around," I respond as I wait for the bill.

I watch from the corner of my eye as she stands. I'm not exactly sure where she's off to, but I know I've made the right decision.

I can't afford to be reckless in my life. I need to concentrate on my career, making sure Molly is okay, and that's it. It's for the best.

A girl like that, well, she would've been a distraction. An amazing time for the night, but that's all it could ever be.

Nope, it's better this way.

After about five minutes, my tab is settled, and I stand from my chair and head to the door. I place my wallet in my back pocket, and when I look up, I see a familiar figure swiftly moving toward the back entrance.

It's her.

Where is she going?

I keep my eyes on her, intrigued by this mysterious girl. She looks left and right before she pushes the door open. It feels so clandestine.

Interesting.

Wherever she's going, she doesn't want anyone to see her.

What's this little hellfire up to?

From the brief time I spent with her, I already clocked her as reckless and bad news, but still, despite this knowledge, I can't help but follow her. I'd love to say it's simply curiosity, but in truth, my protective nature rushes to the surface. I might not know this girl, but if she were Molly, there would be no way I'd let her walk off outside by herself at this time of night.

Especially when I know she's itching for an adventure.

The warm summer air slaps me in the face as I step outside. I take a moment to look up, appreciating the stars twinkling overhead. That's not something you see in the city. The full moon shines brightly, providing the minimal light out here tonight.

This property is gorgeous. One of a kind.

I'm sure half of my team is in rare form already, itching to Uber back to the city to continue the night at one of the local clubs. That's where I differ from my friends. I want quiet, but not until I uncover where she's off to and make sure she arrives safely to wherever she's headed.

Step by step, I follow her. I'm practically right beside her, but she doesn't even realize it, which is a tad concerning. She just continues walking on along without a care in the world. With each move she makes, something in her right arm reflects the light.

What is that?

A bottle?

Did she really grab a bottle and go outside to keep drinking? I shake my head, completely mystified by this woman.

It is a nice night, so I guess anything is possible.

"I know you're following me." Her soft voice cuts through the air. It makes me smile because, despite the low sound, there's no denying her sarcasm.

Even tipsy, she's giving hell.

I like it.

"I wasn't trying to keep it a secret."

"Well, that's good 'cause you were doing a horrible job of blending in."

I chuckle, my chest shaking in effect. "What are you doing out here?"

"I wasn't ready to go to sleep yet." One slim shoulder lifts before she starts to walk. Each step is slow and deliberate. She moves forward in a straight line and then back, then she moves a few inches and does it again. It's almost like she's doing it on purpose. Like she's making a pattern.

"Why are you walking like that?"

Better question—why do you care?

Warning bells go off in my head. I don't do social attachments. I don't do anything but sleep, eat, and skate. And I certainly don't ask pretty girls why they do the things they do when I should be in my room, keeping my head down. Like always.

She continues with her odd steps, unaware of the war I've just waged with myself.

"Walking like what?" Her balance slips as she glances down at her feet. "Oh. That. I'm tracing the shape."

"What shape?"

"Down there." She points at the ground.

I shake my head. "I'm not following you."

"The fork."

"The fork?"

"Yeah. Don't you see it? It's made from the rocks."

I follow her line of sight, studying the way worn yellow stones pop against the otherwise gray pavement. The design could use another edit or five, but I make out three sharp peaks stemming from a large stick. If that's a fork, the Eiffel Tower is a cottage.

"A fork?" I repeat, wondering if she has her head screwed on straight.

Probably not. Yet another reason you should turn around and leave.

"You don't see it?"

Maybe I would've, but her lower lip juts out, and suddenly, I can't see anything else.

"A fork designed for a sadist, perhaps." I tap where the stone forms a jagged spike with the tip of my toe. "It's a trident. Or it's trying to be one, at least."

"A trident?"

"Yes."

She frowns. "I liked it better when it was a fork."

"It was never a fork." Oddly, I don't feel good about bursting her bubble. Still, I double down. "It's a trident. Poseidon's trident."

A sudden smile sweeps up her cheeks, wiping away her frown. "Poseidon's trident," she repeats with a nod, as if the idea satisfies her.

I expect her to say more, but instead, she finishes her journey around the trident and jets off in the opposite direction.

I follow.

Of course I do.

"Now, where are you going?" I ask, growing more curious by the second and hating it.

"The vines look lonely." She doesn't bother looking back at me, stampeding forward at her signature clipped pace. "Duh."

It's quirky, odd, and exactly something she'd say, I'm starting to realize.

It should annoy me that she knows I'd follow.

I didn't even know I'd follow.

At this moment, she feels bigger than the moon above us. Than the Earth we're standing on. Like she has a gravity of her own, and I'm lucky to be in her orbit.

I take a look around. Even with the moon and stars, it's dark out here. Not exactly the best time of day to see the vineyard.

"So, you decided that this is the right time?"

"Tomorrow, I can't." I wonder what causes the sadness to her voice.

"And why not?" I press, not giving a fuck if I sound nosy. I am.

"Tomorrow, I report for duty."

"Duty?" I ask, feeling like I'm going to have to drag this information out of her.

"Yes, my job. But we can't talk about that, right?"

We had agreed not to discuss such things, but I really do want to throw that rule out, just to know a little bit more about her.

I shouldn't care.

I should just turn around and go.

"Yeah. That's right. No talk about our jobs."

She takes a few more steps and then stops. I just about run right into her back. "Found them," she says.

"Found what?"

She looks over her shoulder at me. Under the moonlight, her features are barely visible, but it doesn't stop her from looking ethereal.

Like a goddess sent down from heaven to test my patience and tempt me to sin.

"The vines, silly." A laugh bubbles up from her throat.

"Silly? That's not something I'm called often."

She shrugs but doesn't elaborate.

I take a step closer, making my way to the space beside her.

Now, this close, I can see what she's holding is a wine bottle, an already opened one.

"Think the grapes are ripe yet?"

I purse my lips, knowing the answer to that question. "No."

"Why not?"

"Everyone around here knows grapes are harvested at the end of summer, early fall. I don't think they're even edible yet."

"Only one way to find out." She takes a step forward, her free hand extended.

"You wouldn't dare."

"Wouldn't I?" Even in the dark, I can see her smile. Her lips tip up into a mischievous smirk.

"You're a hellfire. Has anyone ever told you that?"

"Hellfire? No. Trouble? Yep."

I narrow my eyes, not that she can see. "Who says you're trouble?"

"My mom and she would know." She groans. "But again . . . we can't talk about that." She looks up at me and smirks. "On that note." She reaches forward and picks a grape right off the vine.

"I don't thi—"

"That's your problem, grump. You think too much."

Before I can say anything else, she pops the grape into her mouth. A second later, she's spitting it out.

I smother my grin, watching as her face twists up at the bitterness. "Not what you expected?"

"Not even a little. That was gross. It's like . . ." Her shoulders shiver, and she raises her hand, putting the open bottle to her mouth to wash out the taste. She makes a sound, smacking her lips together. "Better. Want some?"

39

I take a deep breath, knowing I should pass, turn around, and head home. But that's not what I do.

"Might as well."

I raise my arm and grab the bottle, taking a swig of the wine. The smooth liquid travels down my throat, pooling in my belly. It's not exactly what I wanted, but it still does the trick.

"Guess winemaking won't be the job for me," she murmurs.

"No talk of jobs, remember?" I infuse enough teasing into the words.

"I'm not talking about my current job; I'm talking about what I want to do. Totally different."

"Looking at changing career paths already? You made it sound like you haven't even started yet."

She turns to me. "That's an awfully personal question." One side of her mouth lifts.

"How old are you?"

"I'm twenty-two, if you must know," she says, placing her free hand on her hip.

"Have you even finished college?"

She purses her lips. "Yes. Just. This will be my first job, and I'm not looking forward to it."

"Winemaking is an interesting first job," I muse.

"It's something, but apparently, it's not for me because I already seem to suck at it."

"Do you have a backup plan?" I ask.

"By backup plan, do you mean crazy idea?"

I laugh at that. "Why am I even surprised? Sure, that's exactly what I meant." I wave a hand out. "This I have to hear. What's the plan?"

She turns to face me fully, keeping her hand on her hip. "I can be a tightrope walker," she announces like it's not the craziest thing she's said all night, which is saying a lot at this point.

"Oh, can you now?"

"Yep." She pops the *p*.

She has to be more than a little tipsy, but you wouldn't know it. She seems completely fine and dead-ass serious.

"And what do you know about tightropes?"

She tilts her head. "I know you put one foot in front of the other."

"Easier said than done," I comment, thinking about how much balance and core work that would take.

"Watch me."

"You're going to do it now? Right here?"

"Why not?" she shoots back.

I can think of a million reasons. The biggest being that even if she's on the ground, she's had too many drinks to successfully attempt this. Although she did manage to trace a trident, so who knows. Plus, a part of me wants to encourage her to try.

"All right then. Let's see."

I watch as she places her hands to her sides, mimicking the correct stance I've seen many do before. She puts one foot in front of the other, taking one step, and that's as far as she makes it before she tips to the left side where I am. I reach out to steady her as I force down my laughter that's bubbling to the surface.

With the ground uneven and the fact that it's dark out, she keeps slipping, but eventually, with me by her side, she makes it across to the next row of vines.

When she stops walking, she looks over her shoulder. Our faces are practically touching with how close we are.

"See, that wasn't so hard," she practically whispers.

I bend down so that our noses are almost touching. "Because I helped you."

"Exactly." She smiles even bigger before closing the space between us.

I take it from there, fixing my mouth over hers, sealing our lips together as my tongue plunges in.

Her arms wrap around me as she pivots into my body.

The kiss is hot and fast. Desperate and needy. She tangles her fingers into my hair, and I pull her flush against me. Fusing our bodies until no space separates us. I kiss her faster. Harder.

Tongues clashing, hands roaming.

I'm lost to this woman right now. Her reckless behavior and antics make me feel alive for the first time in I can't remember. She moans into my mouth, and I take the opportunity to lift her into the air. She wraps her legs around my waist as I walk us deeper into the vineyard.

I have no idea where I'm taking her, but I need her.

Being with her, inside her, is all I can think about.

"Where are we going?" she asks between kisses.

"Anywhere I can have my way with you."

"Right here is fine." The words come out breathy and full of need.

"Here?" My voice is rough and husky, the desire mounting with every second.

"Yes."

With that, I drop her back down to her feet and pull my jacket off, placing it on the ground.

"Lie down," I command.

I expect her to object, but she doesn't. Instead, she sits on my jacket and leans back on her elbows, staring up at me.

With the soft glow from the moonlight, she looks like pure, innocent temptation. The kind I'm going to love to corrupt.

I drop down to my haunches and push her legs apart.

Her skirt lifts, and I'm met with a small scrap of material covering her.

Reaching my hand out, I remove it, leaving her bare to me.

"I want you," she says.

I smile. "Patience." I move closer, placing kisses on the exposed skin of her legs. I trail my mouth and tongue up her skin until I reach her pussy.

"Please," she moans. I give her what she wants, closing my mouth around her clit, and sucking her.

It's not long before she's writhing beneath me.

"Please."

I pull away from her. "Please what?"

"Please fuck me."

"Whatever you want, Hellfire."

"Why do you keep calling me Hellfire?"

"I don't know your name, but it seems fitting," I say, discarding my shirt.

"If you only knew how right you were." She laughs.

Moving off her, I unzip my pants and free my dick from the confines of my briefs.

I look down at her, meeting her eyes. "Are you sure?"

"Never been sure about anything in my life."

I hold her stare. "This is the one time you really need to be. So let me ask you again, are you sure?"

She takes a deep breath. "Yes. About this, I'm sure."

"Thank fuck."

Reaching into my back pocket, I pull out a condom, rip the foil, and then slide it over my dick.

Running my hand from root to tip, I get myself ready before moving back between her legs.

I align myself with her core and don't hesitate before I push in.

Just the tip at first, but then her hips angle up, and she takes more of me, signaling she wants me to move.

Nothing has ever felt this good.

I'm not sure if it's the location or the craziness of the moment, but I can't get enough of her.

I slide in deeper until I'm fully engulfed in her heat.

"Fucking perfect." I groan.

"Move," she orders, and I laugh. "I need more." She groans.

I give her what she wants, driving my cock into her. My hips rock, and I start to fuck her in earnest. She meets me thrust for thrust, perfectly in sync with every move I make.

She's close, and I'm just as close.

Her eyes close on a moan, and I watch her closely. Her mouth is agape, and her chest heaves. I lift her shirt and bra, baring one perfect breast to me.

I wish I could take my time with her and devour every inch of this woman. But I can't. We're in the middle of a vineyard where anyone could come across us, even at this time of night.

"Harder," she begs.

As I stare down at her, I can't help but feel connected to her. A sense of familiarity washes over me. Opposites may attract, but like calls to like. I can see the same brokenness. The same rebellion I feel some days written all over her.

"Please," she says, and it helps to bring me back to the moment.

Reaching between us, I rub her clit furiously until her body quakes beneath me, and she's falling over the edge.

Electricity runs through my body at the feeling of her pussy clamping down on my dick. The look on her face as her orgasm crashes over her is a thing of fucking beauty.

"Fuck," I groan as I fall over the edge with her.

chapter seven

Josie

THE SOUND OF MY PHONE BLARING IN THE DISTANCE HAS ME peeking my head out from under the blanket draped over my face.

Ouch.

How much did I drink last night?

Too much, that's what.

I regret turning the phone back on when I got to my room early this morning.

A smile spreads across my face.

Even though my head pounds, I don't regret it. Not one minute of it.

That man was delicious and exactly what I needed. Now, I have to face the music of my choices, but at least I'll have a wonderful memory to get me through the grueling days ahead.

Again, the loud and obnoxious ring from my phone goes off. Whoever is calling will not take no for an answer. That means it's one person . . . the one person I am not in the mood to speak to right now.

I'm not ready to deal with her. Not when it feels like I just closed my eyes.

On the fourth ring, I push the blanket off my body and grab my phone.

Yep, it's her, and as much as I don't want to answer the call, I'm very well aware that if I don't, she won't stop annoying me.

I press the button and wait.

"I'd ask where you are, but I know damn well where you are."

"Hello to you too, Mother."

"How could you?" Her harsh voice echoes throughout the room.

"You're going to need to be clearer on what I'm being yelled at for." Something tells me this will be a long conversation filled with lectures and threats, which means I probably should make myself comfortable.

I prop myself up in my bed, rearranging the pillow behind me.

"You know what I'm talking about. Booking a hotel room. Imagine my surprise when your father texted me last night and told me you never showed up at the party. Then I check my email, and I had a notification from the credit card company that a hotel was paid for on my credit card."

"Oh yeah, about that—"

"I'm not done speaking, Josie." She lets out a long, audible breath. "This has to stop."

"If you'd allow me to speak—"

"Nope. I'm done listening to you. I have worked myself to the bone my whole life to provide for you, so now you will listen to me."

Funny, because in all my life, that's the one thing my mother has never done. It's always been her speaking and me listening. I've never had the chance to voice my concerns because anytime

I've tried, I've been gaslit or ignored entirely. Maybe that worked when I was a child, but if she wants me to grow up, then she needs to start treating me like an adult.

"First things first, I expect you to take my credit card out of your wallet and cut it up," she orders.

"Fine," I say.

Cutting up my credit card is extra, even for her, but she's right. I need to figure it out for myself.

"I expect you to then drop it in the mail. I want you to send it to me to prove it's been done."

"Okay."

"Good, and then after you do that, I expect you to head over to your father's place. You are too old to be a freeloader. You will work for him. You will do what you need to make connections."

"I don't need your lectures anymore. I'm an adult."

"Too bad, young lady. You've made it really clear you can no longer be trusted."

"Mom—"

"You're behaving like a child. You are twenty-two years old, and it's time for you to start acting like it. You understand me?"

"Mother," I snap. "Can I talk?"

"No," she barks back, and I'm seconds away from losing my cool for the first time ever. "Josephine . . ." What now? What more can she say to me? It's bad enough she shipped me to live and work with a man I've never met before . . . someone she's purposely kept out of my life. Now she's just piling it on thick. "I'm doing this because I love you."

My heart feels tight in my chest. It's always the same. Berate and then declare it's all done out of love. She constantly trivializes my feelings. The older I get, the more I see it for what it is. She gaslights me, and I stonewall her. I should respond, but all I can get out is "Okay." Then I hang up. There's no point in trying; nothing will change my mother's mind once it's made up. Now, it's time to face the music.

I'm not sure what I expected, but it certainly wasn't this. This house is much nicer than how I pictured it. In my imagination, living in his *guesthouse* didn't make sense, but now it does. The property is ginormous, and the house even bigger. Must be nice to have had all this yet have no relationship with your kid.

Even now that I'm moving in with him, I'm not sure he'll have any interactions with me. The man won't even know I'm here.

I take it all in and find myself feeling wholly insecure. Who is this guy?

The house is a large colonial with red brick and white pillars. It's the type of house that reminds me of a Christmas movie. The type of house where a happy family lives.

It seems a little large for one person.

My stomach plummets . . . is he alone?

I never asked, and now that seems like a very important detail.

He might have a whole family. I might have half-siblings.

I feel sick.

Bile crawls up my throat, and my hand lands on my stomach as if that can stop the ill feeling.

What will I do if he does? It's been hard enough dealing with the fact that I had a dad I didn't know about, but what if I have a whole damn family?

I take a step up to the front door and pause for a moment, wondering if I'll ever be ready for this introduction. No part of me wants to knock, but I've already stalled long enough.

It's time to put my big girl panties on and face whatever's to come.

Just as I raise my hand to knock, the door swings open, and there he is.

I know it's him right away because, like me, he has eyes the color of a tropical ocean. So blue they are almost translucent.

My mouth opens and shuts as my hands shake at my sides.

Is this how it feels when your whole life changes?

"You must be Josie? I'm Robert, your father."

So formal. So awkward.

My hands go behind my back, and I rock on my feet, unsure of what to say or do.

"Come in," he says, stepping aside and motioning for me to enter.

The place is even grander inside. I can't imagine kids have ever lived here. Everything is marble and expensive. So contrary to where I grew up.

It makes me wonder if this is why Mom kept me away. Did she feel inadequate compared to this man? I surely do, and I've hardly spoken a word to him.

"I know this is a bit . . ." He sounds almost unsure himself.

"Overwhelming? Weird?"

He chuckles awkwardly. "We'll go with overwhelming." He offers me a smile, but I can't even force one of my own.

"I know this is a lot. It is for me too," he admits. "But for what it's worth, I'm glad you're here."

I'm not sure how to feel about his words. Surely some warmth or happiness should envelop me, right? Wrong. I feel nothing but uncertainty and insecurity.

"Let's take it day by day, shall we?" he says, and I nod.

That's as much as I can offer. Because no matter how glad he is that I'm here, in twenty-two years, he's never once came for me. And that's something I won't forget.

"About this job. What exactly will I be doing? Because I have to tell you, I don't think I'll make a very good winemaker."

He quirks a grin. "No winemaking in your immediate future."

"Oh, thank God," I say with a massive breath of relief.

He cocks his head to the side. "Didn't your mother tell you why you were coming here?"

I rock back on my heels, suddenly uncomfortable hearing him speak about my mother in any capacity. I don't know anything about their relationship because she refused to talk about it. As far as I can guess, I'm the product of a one-night stand that was never going anywhere.

That makes me think of the stranger from last night, but I tamp that down because I do not want my mind to wander to comparisons when my mother is part of the equation.

Yuck.

"I need assistance in marketing for the hockey team I coach," he says, and I can't help but groan.

"Hockey," I mutter. "As in sticks and black rubber."

He perks an eyebrow. "Not a fan of hockey?"

This feels like déjà vu, and I wonder if the universe is truly out to get me. Regardless of my less-than-fond thoughts on the homicidal sport, I need this job.

"I'll admit I don't know much about it, but I'm a quick study and ready to learn."

He nods his head. "Great. That's what I like to hear. Team player."

Something tells me he wants me to smile, but I can't. Everything feels twisted and wrong. What have I gotten myself into? Can I do this?

Yes.

I don't have a choice. Getting work experience is what I need. Without it, I'll never get a real job. I will make this work, and I will prove to my mother that I'm not a lost cause.

Universe, please be kind.

chapter eight

Dane

Hudson changed the name of the chat to "Hockey stick up Dane's ass."

Mason: Not cool, Wilde.

Dane left the chat.

Mason changed the name of the chat to Redville Sinners.

Mason added Dane to the chat.

Hudson: Aww, he's back.

Mason: Stop acting like a douche.

Hudson: Just keeping it real.

Hudson: He did in fact have a stick up his ass.

Dane: Fuck off.

chapter nine

Dane

AN IMPROMPTU MEETING WITH THE TEAM AND OUR COACH wasn't how I wanted to spend my day.

Not only am I still hung over from last night, but I'm not in the mood to be lectured that I bailed out early on the party.

And Coach will lay into me. Rightfully so, of course, but my head is killing me, and the truth is, I'd very much like to linger in the high I'm still feeling from bumping into the little hellfire in the vines.

Fuck.

There are no words to even describe how much I needed that.

She was everything I didn't know I needed at the exact moment I needed it.

Pure perfection.

A silly goddess, *one with a trident*, but a goddess, nonetheless.

When she started walking the "tightrope," I knew she was like no one I had ever met before, and for the first time since my parents died, I felt anything was possible.

Too bad it couldn't last longer.

Luckily, the memory is mine, and I'll be replaying it in my mind for a long time.

My phone rings, and I know who it is without even looking at it. By now, Molly has found the little surprise I left for her at her front door.

I grab it from my pocket, swiping the screen to answer it.

"What the hell did you do?" Her high-pitched voice is a bit much after last night, but I understand that she's excited, so I'll give her a pass for practically blowing out my eardrum.

"You'll have to be more specific?"

"Don't be an ass. You know what I'm talking about. The ticket. The trip."

"No one in the world deserves it more than you."

"It's too much, Dane." A crashing sound echoes through the phone. "Shit. Sorry. I'm fine, just dropped my cell." Her voice sounds far off, and I can't help but laugh despite the pain it causes me in my hungover state.

"You good?"

"Yeah, sorry. But seriously, Dane, this is too much."

"Nothing is enough for all you do for me." I halt my steps, not ready to walk into the arena yet.

"But this is over a month. I don't get back until the first game of the season. How will you live?"

That's my sister, always cutting right to the chase. "Do you think I'm totally helpless?"

"Yes."

"Ouch, I'm wounded." I'm not. She's right. I am helpless, but I won't admit that, or she may actually not go.

"No, you're not. You know it's true."

She has me there.

"Fine. I am, but I promise I'll be okay."

Molly takes a deep sigh. "If you say so, but just in case, I'm going to call a temp agency. I love you, Dane. I wish—"

"Listen, Mol, I have to go. Coach called a meeting, but text me when you get to the airport."

"Will do. Bye."

"Bye." I hang up the phone, then swing open the door and walk into our practice facilities. I head in the direction of where Coach said to meet.

When I arrive, I'm not the first one there.

Actually, by the crowd formed in the middle of the room, I'm most likely the last.

Coach isn't around when I walk in, so I look for Aiden Slate. He's typically in the know of what's to come. Aiden takes the sport seriously. He loves the game, and it shows.

Aiden's standing next to Hudson and Mason. Hudson says something, and Mason slaps him in the gut, drawing a harrumph from Hudson.

I head in their direction, preparing myself for the questions. And there will be questions. Hudson can't help but pry.

"Look who decided to finally grace us with his pres—" Hudson starts, but Aiden cuts him off.

"Oh, give the guy a break." Aiden nods in my direction. That's why I appreciate Aiden Slate; he knows when I need space. He can read the room, unlike the idiot Wilde.

Don't get me wrong, I love Hudson—he's one of my best friends—but the guy has a lot of growing to do.

"I'm not doing anything." Hudson raises his hands. "I just wanted to see what happened last night and why he's late today."

"Am I late? Because from what I can see, the meeting hasn't even started. Any idea why we're here?" I ask, directing the question to Aiden.

"I'm actually surprised you don't know. Coach likes you best," Hudson chides playfully. Normally, if someone said that, I'd think they were jealous, but not Hudson. He's just keeping it real. Coach does like me best.

Probably because he's known me the longest out of all the guys.

When I first started playing professionally for the Saints, it was the coach's first year with the team as well.

The man is more like a father than a coach to me.

He knows about my past . . . well, most of it.

Some things I wouldn't tell him or anyone, at that. Those secrets will go to the grave with me.

Not even Molly is privy to them.

"Guess we'll find out now. Coach just walked in," Mason says from beside me.

I shuffle my weight from one foot to the other and then wait. Time goes slower as the room becomes quiet. Even though we just won the Cup, this man won't go easy on us; knowing him, he'll actually push us harder.

His footsteps echo through the space until he stops dead center in the room and lets out a cough.

"Men, I'll make this short and sweet. I'm sure you all have a lot to do, and by do, I mean training, right?"

A few men start laughing.

I look over at Hudson. Everyone in the room knows he plans to spend the next few weeks making his way through every bar in Redville and most likely fucking every female in the town. He's a notorious player.

"We'll have some staffing changes next season. I figured I'd tell you now rather than drop this on you guys on the first day back. That way, if you have any questions or concerns, we can discuss them beforehand. Not that I anticipate any issues."

Coach speaks, but his words sound blurry in my head. A killer hangover will do that.

He's rambling on about marketing. Some social media shit. Maybe I should have made Molly come to this meeting. This is more her speed because lord knows I'm not listening for shit.

"—meet my daughter." I don't catch any of his words but those, and that makes my head snap up.

What did he just say?

Daughter?

I didn't know Coach had a daughter. How did I not know he had a daughter?

I take a step forward, pushing my way through the crowd so I can figure out what the hell is going on.

With all the time I've spent with this man, I should have known this, right? Apparently, we both have secrets.

My chest feels tight. I lift my hand to rub at the spot, but something tells me the pain isn't from a tight muscle.

I stand in the front of the crowd directly before him. My brow is lifted when he catches my gaze. He gives me a nod. From my knowledge of this man, this is his way of telling me there's a story, and it's a story he'll tell me later.

Interesting.

"Here she is," he says as he pivots his body toward the door. My head turns in the direction with him, and the moment his daughter saunters through the door, my heart stops.

What the hell is this?

Her footsteps are barely audible, but in my head, they echo like a freight train. Actually, that might be the sound of the blood rushing through my veins or the pounding headache that is now threatening to knock me unconscious, and the reason stands right in front of me.

Hellfire.

The little hellfire is the coach's daughter.

Fuck my life.

chapter ten

Josie

A DEER CAUGHT IN HEADLIGHTS, *THAT'S WHAT I AM.*
The moment I stopped, I saw him, and now I can't pull my gaze away.

It's him. Holy shit. It's him. How is this possible? The look on his face is one of pure shock. And how could it not be? Last night was random. No names and all our talk of hating hockey . . .

Wait.

He said he hated hockey.

Was that real? Or an act.

No. I'm good at deciphering how people are feeling. I can read people well and take in their emotions. That was all real.

He hates hockey, yet he plays for my father.

"Josie," the man's—who I now know as the sperm donor—voice cuts through my thoughts and forces me to pull my gaze away from the handsome and sinfully sexy stranger from last night.

I step up to where he is forcing me to turn away from my

one-night stand turned awkward first day at work, and look up toward the man I only just met.

Should I call him sperm donor? Dad? Coach? Robert? Mr. Harris?

All of the above.

Since it's a job, I'll call him Coach Robert.

Yeah, that's easier.

Coach Robert nods down at me. "Josie will be interning with us this season."

A bunch of the guys start to speak at once, and despite my best efforts, I can't make out what anyone is saying.

How long do I have to be here today? Will he try to speak to me?

My heart rattles in my chest. I hope not . . . yet I do. I want to speak to him.

"Now, listen closely. . ." Coach Robert takes a step forward and looks right at some younger, handsome player. "No one, and I mean no one, will cross me on this. Josie is off-limits."

His words drop like the bomb that they are. The stranger in front of me goes ramrod straight. If I didn't know better, I'd mistake him for a statue. His jaw is stiff, and he stares at me like he hates me.

A chill runs up my spine.

What the actual hell?

Does he think I did this on purpose?

Does he think I knew?

Well, if he does, then he has a thing coming for him because I didn't.

After a few more minutes of the coach yapping about God knows what . . . yes, I know I should be listening, but alas, I have more pressing matters at hand, like why the hottie is giving me death glares.

Finally, the meeting concludes, and the stranger walks. I follow him.

I'm not sure where he's going, and I'm sure my sperm donor is expecting me, but when I turn my head over my shoulder, I see he's already preoccupied with the young guy he was staring at during his speech. This must be the team "player."

Too bad he's not the one my "father" should be worried about.

"Hey," I whisper-shout, and surprisingly, he stops.

With slow and wary steps, I make my approach. He turns around to face me. Large blue eyes that only yesterday made my knees weak are now narrowed and hard. Decadent lips are set into a straight line, and the hard-set jaw I'm staring at makes my hands tremble.

He crosses his arms over his chest. "Did you know?"

"Know what?" There are a few different topics he could be speaking on.

"Cut the shit. Did you know who I was?"

I shake my head. "No."

"I find that hard to believe," he snaps. My shoulders straighten, and I stand tall.

I open my mouth, then clamp it shut as I think of what he's implying. Does he really think I planned this whole thing? I take a deep breath, calming down the storm brewing inside me with the words I want to say before I'm calm enough to speak.

"It's the truth." I inhale again. "I had no clue who you were. If you remember, I'm not a fan of hockey?" I lift my brow in challenge. "If anyone was lying last night, it wasn't me."

"You want me to believe this is some sort of coincidence?"

"Or fate."

"Cute," he chides. "But I don't believe in that shit."

"Listen, it is what it is. No harm done. Unless—" I step closer to him, lip tipping up into what I like to consider a sexy smirk.

"There will be no unless," he says, voice hard and unyielding. "Coach is like a father to me."

"Must be nice," I mutter under my breath.

If he hears my comment, he doesn't let on. Instead, he places his hands in his pockets and is silent for a moment; a second later, his chin lifts, and he meets my stare.

"Nothing happened. You don't know me."

"Whatever you say—I don't even know your name."

"Good."

"Wow, if I thought you were grumpy yesterday, it has nothing on this new version." I shake my head. "I should know your name, so I know who to stay away from."

He lets out a breath. "Dane."

"And do you have a last name, Dane?"

"Sinclair."

"Very well, Dane Sinclair, I'll avoid you like the plague. Wouldn't want Dad to know his 'son' fucked his daughter."

"Stop." He lifts his right hand and runs it through his hair, pulling at the locks. "Are you always this reckless?"

"Isn't that what you liked about me?" I wink. "I'm a *hellfire*, after all."

I'm baiting him. Purposely going against what he's asked of me. I'll pretend I don't know him in front of my father, but right now, I want to make him feel as off-kilter as I am.

"You're something all right," he says, shaking his head.

"Don't forget, I'm also a tightrope walker."

If looks could kill, I'd be dead. "Do you ever stop?"

"No. Not really, but don't worry, I'll get out of your hair." I turn on my heel but look over my shoulder. "For now."

"Maybe you can go trace another *trident*."

Despite my previous words, I change my mind.

I won't be leaving him alone.

Not when he's so much fun to play with, and right now, I need all the fun I can get.

chapter eleven

Dane

IF IT WEREN'T BAD ENOUGH THAT THIS HAS BEEN A SHITTY WEEK, starting with the impromptu meeting on Monday where I found out I fucked the coach's daughter, now today, Sunday, it's raining.

Of course, it is.

Why wouldn't it be?

Today is the day *I* get the Cup.

It also means I have the damn Cup ambassador tailing. I'm not in a pleasant mood, let alone prepared to be social. Oh well, sucks to be him because where we are going, he's going to get ignored and soaked.

Not my problem.

I've been drinking since seven o'clock. I can't care less if I'm a drowned rat. I'm so goddamn numb; maybe a chill will do me good.

I have refused to consider what has me more prickly than normal because I know, and quite frankly, I prefer to just stick to ignoring everything.

When we arrive at the location, the car stops, and I don't wait for the driver to open the door for me. Instead, I throw it open and hop out. Right before exiting the car, I grab the Cup.

The driver I hired to chauffeur my ass around is most likely not impressed by me, but I can't find it in me to care. He made money off me, so how I act is not his concern. Nothing is wrong with his car, and I don't pay him to like me.

My foot slips a little from the rain, not the booze, although I doubt the Cup ambassador or my driver probably agree with that assessment.

Nonetheless, I trudge through the mud. With each step I take, my clothes cling to my skin, and my hair sticks to my forehead.

How cliché can I be?

I'm the lead actor in a made-for-TV film, where the drunk hero visits the grave of his dad.

But I'll have a great epiphany in the movie version, something I'm sure won't happen here today.

The grass is muddy, and my shoes have taken a beating by the time I finally make it to the bastard's grave.

From my back pocket, I grab the flask, and then I pour the contents directly into *Stanley*.

We're on a first-name basis now that my team won.

"Bet you never thought this is how I'd spend my day, huh, Dad? Actually, I bet you never thought this day would come at all."

I lift the Cup and take a swig. The whiskey burns as it travels down my throat, but I welcome the feeling right now. It reminds me I'm here.

"Cheers, Dad," I slur as I wave the cup in the air. "This is the moment you've waited for. Sooo . . . did it live up to the hype? Oh, wait, you're dead. How could it?" I laugh bitterly. "Not much of a talker, are you? Funny how things change. You always were back then. Always endless lectures about goals. Funny how you never took your own advice."

I plop down on the ground, my wobbly legs no longer willing to hold my weight.

Now, sitting, I can feel the mud seeping into my jeans. Fuck it. Fuck it all.

Anger swells inside me. Of course, this is how it would be. "What a fucking joke this all is. But you know what? I have no one to blame but myself. It was my fault, after all. I'm a fuckup. Isn't that what you said that night on the phone? But look at me now with a championship under my belt."

My arm collapses by my side, the Cup almost tipping from my grasp. I catch it at the last moment.

I'm not worried about the Cup; it's been through worse. Stories of the Cup's escapades are legendary. A little mud won't hurt it. Nope, I'm worried about the contents. That's some pretty good whiskey.

"You know the worst part . . ." I run my hand through my soaked hair, grabbing at the strands and pulling to the point of pain. "You killed her. She trusted you, and you killed her."

My mother was the glue of our family. The day she died, our family died too.

"And Molly. Don't get me started with Molly. The fact that she's so amazing has nothing to do with you. The fact that I'm here, Cup in hand, has nothing to do with you. It's all because of Molly. She's the reason I'm here. How does that make you feel?" I hiss as I lift the Cup and take another swig. "The funny thing is, here I am, not so much unlike you. How's that for irony? You killed me that day too. Killed the fun-loving guy I could have been and left this—" Another swig, another burn. "I guess this is the Sinclair legacy. Angry drunks."

"So here's to you, Dad." I laugh, but it's a hollow, empty sound. "Here's to the bastard who only wanted one thing—a famous son. Whelp, you got it. Even if you had to kill everyone to achieve your goal."

I look at his headstone. Jonathan Sinclair.

The words dance in front of me because my vision is blurry. Is it the rain or my tears that blind me?

Maybe my hate.

With one final swig, I finish the whiskey and push myself back to standing.

"I hope you rot in hell, old man. It seems I'm right behind you, so you might as well save me a seat."

chapter twelve

Dane

IT'S BEEN A FEW WEEKS SINCE I LAST SPOKE TO COACH. THE OFF months have everyone scattered about, and with no official training in the books, I don't usually see him, so when the text came from him asking me to have dinner at his house, I was taken aback and a little nervous about the reason for this dinner.

Not long ago, we had dinner often, but he's had a lot going on lately, so the dinners stopped. Now I wonder if *she's* what has him so busy.

Robert is like a father to me, and during the offseason, I often spend time with him and his wife, Sherry.

They've been there for Molly and me since the beginning of my career.

Robert knows how important my sister and her well-being are and why I've never gone very far from Redville.

Dinner shouldn't feel weird, but it does because of her.

Josie . . . aka Hellfire, could not have been in his life until recently. I would've known about her. Right? Would Coach have kept her a secret from me?

I find it hard to believe that he's never mentioned he had a kid in all these years, especially since he's been so instrumental in helping me raise Molly.

I'll need to ask him because none of this makes any sense.

I'm starting to sweat, a cold panic taking over.

Will she be there?

Does he know about our night at the vineyard?

Fuck.

I pull the car to a stop and then throw it in park.

My hands are still on the steering wheel when the front door opens.

Coach stands in the frame with a perplexed look on his face as he watches me.

What does he see? A kid about to lose his shit? If only he knew how close to the truth that is.

Still sitting here, car off, unmoving.

The lines on his forehead are more pronounced as he stares at me. He doesn't speak or say anything, but the questions on his face are clear.

Are you getting out?

What's taking so long?

I let out a long sigh and throw the door open.

"You okay over there, Sinclair?" he asks.

"Sure am. Was just thinking about something."

"Must have been pretty serious."

If he only knew.

Based on his teasing lilt, I don't think this has anything to do with Josie and me. He doesn't sound mad, and if he knew, he'd be more than pissed.

Thank God.

What he doesn't know won't get me killed, so now I just need to keep it that way, and the best way to do that is to hope that she's nowhere near me.

I know Josie will be working for the team, but I didn't pay enough attention to ask what that meant.

Now I can't.

I'll just need to wait until official practice starts at the end of September.

I take the steps two at a time until I'm standing in front of him.

Robert looks like he's aged ten years since the last time I saw him. Which is crazy. We've been on break. What could be worrying him?

Her beautiful face pops into my head. *She's what's aging him.* I don't even have to ask to know. There's a story here, but as much as I'm desperate to know, I need to mind my own fucking business. Especially if I want a place on this team and in his life.

Banging his daughter will not win me any points with him.

"Come on. Sherry is waiting to say hi." He moves back and opens the door farther to let me pass. Every time I come to his house, I feel at home. I still remember when I first went pro. I was so young, but I needed the money. Molly was only thirteen, and raising a kid while still being a kid was hard work.

That's where Sherry stepped in. I'll never repay that debt. Which is why Coach can never know what happened that night with his daughter.

I follow Robert as he leads me to the dining room, and the moment I step into the room, my breath leaves my lungs.

Fuck.

She's here.

Sitting at the table, beside an empty chair that's set for dinner for me, is Josie.

Sherry moves to stand, but I shake my head. "Stay, I'll come to you."

I need to move. Need to expel some of this intense energy flowing through me.

I cross the room until I'm by her side, then bend down and kiss her on the cheek.

"Have you formally met Josie yet?"

"Can't say that I have," I respond. Not a lie. Josie and I never exchanged names. But I think I told her mine the next day. It's blurry. My mind was going a million miles a minute, and I barely remember what all was said other than the fact that I was royally fucked.

"Josie, this is Dane Sinclair. He's a defenseman for the Saints."

"Hi, Dane." Her eyes narrow, and then she scrunches her nose. "A hockey player."

"Yep." I incline my chin down. "How do *you* feel about hockey?" I ask, knowing damn well how she feels. If my memory serves me, she has an intense opinion about the sport.

"I don't," she chides.

Robert shakes his head, and his skin has gone pale; he looks mortified by her comment. "That's not nice, Josie."

I lift my hand to him. "It's fine. I could tell by the way she said hockey player that she wasn't a fan." I chuckle, trying to dispel some of the awkwardness that's fallen over the room.

"And what about you, Dane?" She says my name in a teasing way, as if I'm privy to some inside joke, which I am, but does she have to be so damn obvious?

Pot meet kettle.

"Obviously, I love it." Needing this conversation to stop.

Coach gestures to the table. "Why don't you take a seat."

As I pull back the chair, the wood scraping against the floor sounds like nails on a chalkboard, but it beats the awkward silence as I finally sit and wait for the reason I've been summoned here.

"I'm sure you have a lot of questions, Dane," Coach says, and I turn to look at Josie beside me.

Is she uncomfortable with him talking about this in front of me?

"It's really none of my business," I tell him as I pull my gaze away to look back at the center of the table.

I don't mean it, and based on the look he's giving me, he knows it too. I'm only saying it because the tension in the room is thick, and I would like to avoid conflict as much as possible. I also don't need nor want to know more about Josie, and I know that going down this road will only lead to that.

"It might not be, but I didn't want you to think—"

"It's fine, Coach." I stop him. This is already too much talking for me. I hate this shit.

"Okay, well, if you ever want to talk."

I nod. I won't. He knows it. I know it.

Coach leans forward, placing his elbows on the table. A habit I know Sherry hates. I peer over in her direction, and not surprisingly, she's biting her cheeks in. It makes me want to laugh. She's working really hard not to say anything to him, and it's obvious. Maybe not to his daughter, but it is to me.

"The reason I want you here is actually about Josie," he says. It feels like a bowling ball is dropped in my stomach. What the hell does he want to talk about? "I'm concerned about the guys."

My hands under the table go stiff. "The guys?"

"That one might try to take advantage of Josie. She's young, after all, and my daughter."

Bile rises in my throat. Little does he know that I'm that bastard who already has. I might not have realized it, but I knew she was young.

"I'm sure everyone knows better than to make a move on your daughter." I turn to her when I say this, trying to let her know that I never would have done what I did had I known.

"Be that as it may, I want you to do me a favor."

"Anything," I respond. After everything he's done for me, I'd do anything for him.

"Keep an eye on her. Watch her like you would Molly."

The weight of his words hits my chest. I can feel the pain with every breath I take.

How will I ever look at this man again, knowing what I did to his daughter? I feel sick to my stomach, but I can't let on. I can't say anything; what's done is done, and I just have to move forward.

As if she can hear my words and decides to do the opposite, I feel something touching my foot from under the table. It takes me a moment to realize what it is.

The little hellfire is trying to fuck with me, and her method of torture is playing footsie with me under the table.

My jaw goes rigid, and I turn and glower at her.

She's smiling innocently at me, then turns back to her father, her lips flattening into a thin line. "I don't need anyone to look out for me," she responds. "I get that I needed a job, and you're the only one hiring, so I'm stuck here, but I'm twenty-two, which is hardly a baby. I can take care of myself."

"You might think that, but you don't know my players. It would mean the world to me if Dane here would—"

"Protect me." Although she isn't facing me, I can see her roll her eyes, then the corner of her lip tips up. *Shit.* What is she up to now? My question is answered when her foot travels higher, and I nearly choke.

"Yes."

"Very well. Dane, will you do it?" she says, but by the way she says it, protecting her isn't what she's talking about anymore.

She's trouble with a capital *T*, and I don't think she's the one who needs protection.

chapter thirteen

Josie

I T FEELS LIKE I'M IN PRISON.

While my father's house is the nicest place I have ever been to, the walls feel like they're closing in on me.

I've sequestered myself within the guesthouse for days, refusing to leave.

I freeze, realizing the source of my sour mood. It's Sunday Date Night.

Growing up, my mom worked eighty hour weeks, yet she *always* managed to put aside Sundays for our mother-daughter date nights. Even if it meant switching shifts. Or missing out on overtime. Spaghetti, movies, online shopping for things we never bought. I miss it all.

On instinct, I press the first speed dial on my phone. It doesn't even ring before I end the call, realizing what I almost did. I refuse to be the first to break.

I can't be here anymore.

The air feels stale and stagnant. I can't breathe, and to be honest, I ran out of food last night.

I'll have no choice but to walk to the main house today. That is, unless I want to starve to death.

I wonder if I can order delivery to the backyard?

Nope. Not an option, considering my mom shut off my credit card and I have no money. Never mind that it's a ridiculous idea to even think about.

The truth is, I'm pretty much up shit creek unless I square my shoulders, put on a brave face, and deal with the cards dealt.

They want to get to know me . . .

I have reservations about that. Why? Because I don't know how to act.

How does one pretend they don't have trauma from feeling abandoned by my father? I had to convince myself I was a product of science just to deal. The truth is, I didn't convince myself of shit. I knew deep down all along but refused to acknowledge it. If Mom couldn't, why did I have to?

I know the day will come when I have to be an adult and talk to him, but getting to know my estranged father is not how I want to spend the remainder of my summer. I've chosen to ignore the huge elephant in the room, and despite him asking if we can talk, I've brushed him off every time he's tried. I'm being a baby, and I know this, but right now, being in a new place, I need to protect my heart.

Before I can second-guess myself, I walk to the guesthouse door and peer outside.

Just go.

The main house is far away. It doesn't even feel like I'm on the same property.

If they wanted, they could rent this out to someone and never see that person. Kind of like me hiding out, a renter could easily go unnoticed for months. It feels disconnected.

It's a good thing and a bad thing.

Good, because I don't have to be confronted by real life, real life being I'm living on the property of two people I only met days ago, and one of those people is my biological father, who I have no relationship with.

Yet.

That little girl in me whispers, making promises she has no business making.

Promises of hope.

Of happiness with a father that I get the chance to know.

Josie, put your big girl pants on and get out of here.

I have to go to the main house. I can't stay hidden forever. I've been lucky. Although I've started working for the Saints, my father has been on summer break, but that will end soon. The team will be back, and I'll have no choice but to be around him.

The problem is, seeing my father makes me feel sick. My whole life feels like a lie, and it has everything to do with my mom. Why did she refuse to tell me about him? Why didn't he come for me? He obviously knew about me, so where has he been?

The fear that he'll reject me again is something I can't shake.

I'm sure it has everything to do with my feelings of lack and worthlessness, and a couple of days, and the fact he did eventually "come for me" doesn't erase all those years.

I reach my hand out and turn the knob. Taking a deep breath, I push it open.

The grass crunches under my flip-flops, and I just hope the rain from earlier doesn't prove to have hidden muddy puddles. That would be my luck, showing up for the first time covered in mud.

The only problem with the location of the guesthouse is there's no path or driveway leading to it, so if it rains, you're basically shit out of luck.

It takes me a minute to make it up to the main house, and when I do, I open the back door which leads to the mudroom, head moving back and forth around the area, searching for signs of life. I find none. It's quiet.

Maybe I'll avoid the awkward run-in after all.

Since my shoes aren't wet, I head straight for the kitchen.

As soon as I step inside, I regret my decision to come here. I'm met with the dark brown eyes of the woman married to my biological father.

"Josie!" She smiles so broadly I wonder if her cheeks hurt.

I give her a half smile. One that doesn't lie. She probably sees how little I want to be here.

"Can I get you anything? Tea? Water? Something to eat?" I have to hand it to her, she's really going for the doting mom feel. I hate it.

And I hate that I hate it because I don't know if it's about her or my issues with my own mom. If I really dig deep, I bet I'd find that it has everything to do with resenting how this stranger can be so kind when my mother never was. *Sometimes she was.*

I'll dissect all my issues in private. I just need to get what I need and get out of here.

"I'm fine." My voice is flat. I turn away from her, trying to decide whether I should leave the house or suck it up and stay in this kitchen while she's here. It would be easier, but I also don't want any more awkwardness.

Maybe what I really need to do is get to know her.

Would it really be that bad?

Despite the fact that I know there must have been a reason, and I should probably find it out, my heart hurts too much when I think about it. I'm not ready to forgive either one for their absence. I'm not sure I'll ever be ready.

"You sure? You must be hungry." Her voice cuts through the air, reminding me that I'm just standing here like an idiot, trying to decide my next move.

As if my body refuses to obey, my stomach chooses that exact minute to make the loudest gargling sound.

"Yeah, you're hungry. Come on, Josie. Let me get you something."

I pivot back around. "We don't need to do this."

Her eyes go wide, and she takes a step back. "Do what?"

"Serve me. Force a relationship you don't want . . ." My chin dips, but I don't miss the way her jaw trembles.

"I'm not pretending."

"Then why did it take my father twenty-two years to ask to see me? Why now?" The words rush from me, and my cheeks heat, embarrassment taking root.

I never meant to say those things out loud.

"I'm sorry." I sigh heavily. "I didn't mean to unload on you."

She takes a tentative step toward me, reaching out but pulling back, unsure what to do. "I'm serious, Josie. I want to know you. You're part of this family." She takes a deep breath. "Talk to your father. There's a lot you don't know."

"*Your mother lied to you.*" Of course, she never said those words, but that's what my brain concocts, and just like that, the anger surges.

"I'm good, but thanks." I turn on my heel and rush back out the way I came. I know she's watching me, probably thinking I'm an immature brat, but I don't want her to see how broken I am.

I thought I was ready to know the truth, but I'm not.

My appetite is gone, and all I want to do is lock myself away. To be alone in my misery.

When I get back to the guesthouse, I start to pace. Hot tears prick my eyes, and then they fall.

I can't be here.

I can't care this much.

Yet I do.

The little girl who always wanted to know her dad cares.

Too damn much.

chapter fourteen

Josie

TODAY IS MY FIRST DAY WORKING WITH THE *PLAYERS*.

Sure, I've been working for the team for the past month, but since there's been no official practice, my sperm donor thought it would be a good idea for me to rotate positions within the organization. That way, I could experience different jobs, and when my internship ended, I'd have a better grasp of what I wanted to do with my life.

The mailroom was fun. Accounting, not so much. Now, I'm working at the practice facility in a floater position until the season starts in three weeks.

Things are about to get real.

I'm going to see Dane again.

Something will go wrong. *It always does.*

Whenever I start something new, it's usually awful. I've never gotten lucky enough to have things go right. All of my life, I've been destined for first-day failure.

Like when I started high school. I wore two different shoes

to school, and if that wasn't bad enough, my shirt was inside out. Double oops.

Then there was the time I started college and fell flat on my face in the middle of campus.

Of course, a group of hot frat boys were all watching. While I was mortified, I wouldn't let them know, so instead, I stood, back straight, and bowed.

It was legendary.

So today, while I know I'm destined for something awful to happen, the plan is to wear the embarrassment with pride.

I take a step inside the practice facility, and I'm instantly met with the smell of ice. I never realized ice had a scent, but it does. It smells crisp and cool and like Christmas morning.

I don't know what I was expecting, but certainly not this. Maybe stinky jerseys and sweat—something to make me hate hockey even more.

Eventually, after they play, I'm sure that will linger in the air, but for now, I close my eyes and imagine a big cup of hot cocoa and sigh.

That would be nice right now because this place is freezing despite the warm air outside.

Guess I shouldn't be surprised. It's an ice rink, after all.

I wonder what I'll be made to do today. I was informed by Laurie, the woman who's technically my boss, that I'll be doing errands for now, but what does that even mean?

Will I be carrying smelly jerseys around? Or maybe I'll have to clean the skates.

No, that seems like a job for someone who knows what they're doing.

"Hey! Coach's kid," some player shouts, and I narrow my eyes, trying to see if I can figure out which one called out to me.

When my attempts end up fruitless, a grunt breaks from my lips.

"Over here," he calls again, waving his hand in the air, and I head toward him.

I lift my brow. "Coach's kid? Seriously?"

"Wow. That's a whole lot of attitude for an intern." He chuckles.

"What can I do for you—"

"Hudson," he says, cutting me off. *Ah, the player.* Coach, aka sperm donor, aka Dad, warned me about him.

Placing my hands on my shirt, I push the material down. "Hudson, what can I do for you?"

He eyes me up and down before returning his gaze to my lips. "Got any water?"

I tilt my head. "Am I a water girl?"

He smirks, lifting his shoulders. "You might be."

I pinch my lips together while I try to think of a witty rebuttal, but I'm saved by another voice. One I know far too well.

"Leave the girl alone." Dane's husky tone makes my knees feel weak, but then his words filter in through my brain, and my stomach turns.

The girl.

He knows just how to rile me up. I'm so damn sick of him acting as though I'm a fucking child. I'm a grown-ass woman. One who certainly caught his attention.

If steam could come out of my ears, it would.

He wants to be an ass, fine, but that just means I'll have to come up with my own brand of torture.

My lips tip into a smile. This will be fun.

"It's Josie. Or Josephine. Not 'the girl.'" I turn my attention back to Hudson, batting my eyelashes and laying it on real thick. "Coming right up, Hudson." I draw out his name seductively, knowing full well it will piss off Dane. I look at Hudson. "Anything else?"

"I'm good. What about you, Dane? You good?"

"I'm fine," he grits out through clenched teeth.

"Doesn't seem that way." I smile broadly. "You seem awfully tense. Or maybe . . . constipated?"

Hudson barks a laugh. "She's got you there."

"Cute," he mocks before turning toward Hudson. "I said I'm fine."

"Very well. I'll be back." I walk off in the opposite direction, making sure to swing my ass and give the boys a view.

There. Take that.

One point to me. Once I'm in the back, I find the stash of water and then return. The moment Hudson sees me, he smirks, skating over to where I am. I walk to the edge of the ice and hand him the bottle.

From the corner of my eye, I watch as Dane skates around the ice.

He is so gorgeous. No one should be that handsome.

With his helmet on, I can't see his hair, but I can see his jaw-line. Damn, he's like a Greek god.

Poseidon.

Technically, Boreas is the god of ice, but Dane Sinclair is not cruel enough for that moniker. No, I prefer Poseidon, grumpy by nature but not outright evil. *Plus, he has a trident.*

Too bad he's off-limits and an ass.

Sperm donor's number one rule. No dating my daughter. Okay, he didn't say date. He said no anything with my daughter. A wide net was thrown on what these guys can't do with me.

I stare ahead, wondering if there's any way around that rule, when I hear Laurie.

"Josie! Need help."

"Coming," I shout back, pulling my gaze away from the ice and ignoring Hudson.

I head to where Laurie is, and she's holding a stack of towels.

"We're short-staffed, and the guy who usually puts these in the locker room isn't here." She reaches out, and I raise my arms to grab them. "Do me a favor and bring these to the locker room; it's empty now, so it's a good time."

I nod and head toward the locker room of the training facility.

Looking around, I clock a table and place them down on it. I'm not sure where they're supposed to go, but seeing as this isn't actually my job, it will do.

"That's not where they go." Dane's gravelly voice takes me by surprise.

"What are you doing here?"

What is he doing here? Wasn't he just skating on the ice?

My heart rattles in my chest. Did he come here for me? I can feel the apple of my cheeks warming at the thought.

"That's none of your business," he practically growls.

"Your personality, maybe?"

His head tips in question.

"That's what you must be looking for since you obviously can't find it."

Nothing. Not a smile. Not a laugh. This man is wound up tighter than a broken clock.

The night I spent with him, he was moody, grumpy even, but this is next level.

Is it me? My presence.

No.

This is more. This is him, but for a second that night, he wasn't like this.

God, he was beautiful when he laughed.

An idea pops into my head, something to make him smile.

I hop up onto the bench.

"What are you doing?"

"Since I can't do this job right, I guess it's back to the tightrope," I tell him while I place one foot in front of the other, moving slowly. I try to balance. It's a narrow bench, and I can feel myself slipping.

"Stop."

"No. Since the last time I saw you, I've done research. This is my calling. If you walk in a straight line—"

"You're going to fall."

"Then help me," I challenge.

"No."

I place my hands out by my side. My foot slips a little, but I don't have to worry about falling because Dane crosses the small space with lightning-fast reflexes.

His one hand wraps around my upper arm, while his other holds my waist.

I turn my head, and my pulse accelerates.

Our faces are so close that I can see the small ring of green surrounding his blue eyes.

Wow.

I never noticed that before, but how could I? It was dark that night.

"Get down," he grits out, his jaw locking after.

"Lighten up, hockey. I'm just having fun."

"That's your problem. You can't take anything seriously. You're acting like a child."

I blink, and my mouth parts on a quick inhale of breath.

The only person in my life who has ever had the ability to make me feel small is my mom, yet here's Dane, doing a damn good job of it.

I hop off and then scurry away. Not wanting him to see the embarrassment I'm trying desperately to hide.

Once out in the hall, I let out a breath, slumping against the wall and trying to hold back the tears welling in my eyes. It's not about him; it's about me. About this place and everything it stands for.

I'm overwhelmed and out of my element without one person to confide in. And the only person who could've fit that bill is bound and determined to be a giant asshole.

Well, good for him. He wins. I'll keep my damn space.

chapter fifteen

Dane

Hudson: Fuck. Coach's daughter!

Mason: I know man.

Hudson: The things I would do her.

Dane: Watch yourself, Wilde. She's off limits.

Hudson: Do you know me at all?

Aiden: Hence him warning you.

Hudson: Oh, Aiden. You're here.

Aiden: No, I'm not.

Hudson: Umm . . .

chapter sixteen

Dane

W HAT A GODDAMN DISASTER.
        I knew having her near would be too much to handle,
but I had no idea just how bad it would be.

The way she looked at me before running off.

I really fucked up.

She looked seconds away from crying, and that's one thing I
can't handle.

I'm finally walking out of the training facility, doing my best
to put as much distance between Josephine and me as possible.

I'm meeting the guys at some dive bar Hudson has been rav-
ing about.

Why he's obsessed with it is beyond me, but something tells
me there must be a female involved, or many, knowing Hudson.

I pluck my phone from my back pocket and press call on my
pinned contact. The call goes straight to voicemail. Disappointment
stabs at my chest. There's only one person I want to talk to right
now: my sister, and her phone is off.

"Hey—Um, call me." I hang up, tucking my cell back where it belongs, and continue my trek to the bar.

It takes me five minutes to drive there, and the only cars in the parking lot are the ones my teammates own.

This place actually holds promise. If we're the only ones here, I won't have to deal with the bullshit of people wanting to talk to me. Or worse . . . ask for pictures and autographs.

Throwing my car into park, I open the door and head inside, dragging my feet even after seeing the near empty lot.

The place is dark; only a few lights hang over the bar, and besides that, maybe one or two recessed lights illuminate the space.

My shoes stick to the dirty floors as I head to the bar, where I see Hudson, Mason, and Wolfe.

Aiden isn't here.

That's not a surprise since he spends most of his free time with Cassidy.

"Sin, didn't think you'd show up," Wolfe says, holding a fist out to bump.

"Here I am," I deadpan. Everyone here knows I don't want to be here, but Hudson was laying it on thick that I needed to hang with them tonight, so I came.

"What's your deal, bro? Coach looked ready to kill you," Hudson says, getting right to the heart of this little get-together and his insistence I show.

Guess I should have known what this was about. Practice was especially brutal, and not because Coach did anything differently. I was just off my game, epically.

The guys insisted I come here so they could figure out why I'm skating like shit. It's written all over every one of their faces.

Not going to happen.

Fuck no, am I telling them that the team's new intern is the reason I'm distracted. The reason I'm playing like a newbie.

Hudson nudges me with his elbow. "A drunk penguin has better balance than you had today."

"You're such an asshole," Mason says, shaking his head. "But really, man, you good? You seem off . . . and not just at practice."

"I'm fine." My fingers drum on the bar. This was a bad idea.

I don't talk about feelings and whatnot. Not with Molly, if I can help it, and definitely not with these jokers.

"You know you can talk to us," Mason says, with far too much concern for my liking.

"I said I was good," I practically growl.

Mason raises his hand in surrender. "Okay, I'm done. But if—"

"Thought you said you were done?" I fire back, leveling him with a look that says he better shut the hell up.

"Jeez, get this man a drink." Hudson raises his hand, and the moment he does, I see why this is his favorite dive bar. "Whiskey?"

"Yep," I mutter, reaching into my back pocket to grab my wallet.

"There will be none of that. Drinks are on me." Hudson looks at the bartender with a smirk.

Great, I'm here to watch him flex for this girl. That is the last thing I need.

I'm already pissy for playing like shit at practice, and now I have to watch Hudson shoot his shot and inevitably win whatever game he's playing.

"Oh, there she is," Mason lifts his hand to wave someone over, and I pivot to see who he's waving to.

Fuck.

As if this night couldn't get any worse, Josephine strides over toward where we are standing.

She smiles broadly as she approaches, but her steps falter just a bit when her eyes land on mine.

"What's she doing here?" I lift my brow at Hudson.

"I invited her." He shrugs.

"And that's a good idea, why? You heard Coach."

"'Cause she's hot," Wolfe says, and I turn on him.

"You know damn well she's off-limits." My teeth are bared to him like a wild animal's. He furrows his brow at me.

"And what Coach doesn't know won't hurt him . . . or me." He smirks.

I open my mouth to respond but quickly think better of it. I want to fucking kill him for even implying that he would touch her. I want to remind him again about Coach, but I know damn well he doesn't give a shit about her father. He doesn't hold the same respect for Coach that I do.

The closer she gets, the wider her smile becomes. Great. Just fucking great.

As usual, she looks gorgeous. My heart rate picks up as my fists clench at my sides.

"What are we drinking?" Her voice sounds sexy as hell.

She needs to leave.

I look over at Hudson, who's ogling her. The hot bartender is long since forgotten.

"Are you even legal?" I snap more harshly than I intended. She flinches slightly.

"I don't know, am I?" She raises her brow in challenge.

I walked right into that one, and the only thing I can do is smash my teeth together.

Of course, she's old enough since we've had this conversation before. I was being an asshole, and it backfired.

"Man, lay off her. There's no need to be an ass," Wolfe says.

I let out a groan while I rub my temples.

"The proper thing to do is apologize," Hudson mocks, and I scowl at him.

"It's okay," she says, not bothering to look at me. "He doesn't need to apologize. After the practice he had, I wouldn't expect anything from him."

"Oh man . . . she got you there," Mason says, grimacing.

I'm not sure why her jab hurts as much as it does, but it hits its intended mark.

Straight into my chest, where it stings the most.

I hate when I let people down, and the way I played today let Coach down. It let my whole fucking team down.

Fucking his daughter also let Coach down, but I'm not going to go there.

Not now. Not ever.

It was a mistake, one I won't make again.

Even if I want to.

chapter seventeen

Dane

ANOTHER DAY, ANOTHER HEADACHE, AND TO TOP IT ALL OFF, I'm distracted. It's all her fault. Avoiding her is nearly impossible.

She's everywhere.

At practice.

At the bar.

In my head.

The worst part is she's temptation on a stick. She strides around this place wearing the thinnest T-shirts I've ever seen. How Coach doesn't scold her is beyond me.

Her fucking nipples are always visible.

I'm not the only one who notices either. Everyone does, everyone other than her damn father, who clearly has his head in the damn sand.

Also, what's with the skirts? Who wears a skirt to an ice rink . . . ? Hellfire, that's who.

Last night, when I went to the bar to meet up with the guys, and she showed up, I thought I was going to lose my mind.

After our little barb session, I ended up sitting in the corner alone and drinking my sorrows as she laughed and had the time of her life.

The shrill sound of Coach blowing his whistle echoes like a freight train, pulling me from my thoughts.

"Head in the game!" he shouts, and I know he's yelling at me. I skate harder, muscles burning as I chase the puck.

Need to focus.

Stay in the play.

Don't think about her.

My lungs burn as I take my aggression out on the ice. I feel like a caged animal, ready to break free.

I grit my teeth and charge.

Aiden skates by as my stick connects with the puck, cutting me off.

"Fuck!" I bellow.

"Hit the showers!" Coach hollers, signaling that practice is finally done.

He's pissed, and rightfully so. I'm pissed.

I move to skate off the ice when I see Josephine. Lord knows what grunt work she's doing now, but her presence alone pisses me off further.

I pull my gaze away and continue toward the exit.

A few minutes later, I'm back in the locker room, and I yank off my helmet and throw it into my locker with a loud clatter.

"You good, man?" Aiden sidles up beside me.

"Yeah."

"Doesn't really seem that way. You sure? You looked like you were about to murder someone out there."

"Guess I was hungover," I mutter, untying my skates.

"I take it that means you don't want to go out with Hudson tonight?"

My stomach roils just thinking about it.

"Nope."

"You want to have dinner with Cass and me? You know we'd love to have you." His offer is genuine, and while I appreciate it, the last thing I want to do is play the third wheel, no matter how much I like Cassidy.

"Nah, man, I'm good. I promise."

He narrows his eyes at me, holding my stare. "Do I need to call Molly?"

I sigh, rubbing my hands over my face. "I said I'm fine. Just drop it. Please."

He nods and pats me on the back.

"Then get your shit together, man. I don't mean to come off harsh, but we need your head in the game." And with that, he walks off, leaving me alone.

You know you've gone and fucked up when Aiden calls you out.

Great. Just fucking great.

Thirty minutes later, I'm hitting Aiden's contact button on my phone.

"Hey, Dane. You good?" he answers.

"I've changed my mind. Is dinner still an option?" With my free hand, I hit the button on my key fob, and then, once the door is unlocked, I get in my car.

"Dinner is always an option. See you soon."

"Thanks." I hang up the call and start my car. Aiden and Cassidy don't live too far from where we practice. It only takes me about fifteen minutes to get there and find a parking spot before I head into the apartment building where they live. I ride the elevator up and then get off on their floor.

It's a nice place, but I can't imagine living here. Sure, my house is too big for me, but when I bought it all those years ago, I got it for Molly. It was the right *home* to raise her in.

I stroll up to the door and knock.

The door flings open. "Dane, I'm so happy you're here." Cassidy smiles brightly at me as she steps out of the way to let me in.

"Thanks for having me. I came straight from practice, or I would have brought something."

She shakes her head. "Dane, you're family. You don't have to bring anything."

Her words are exactly what I need right now. With Molly gone, the past month has been weird.

I didn't realize how much I depended on her, and I don't just mean for my day-to-day activities.

There's also the fact that Hellfire is living with Robert. That's throwing me off.

Normally, I spend a lot of time with him and Sherry, but currently, I'm trying my hardest to avoid Josephine, so my trips over there have been nonexistent.

"Go sit down, and I'll get you a drink." She points at the couch in the living room, and I start heading in that direction.

"You're one of a kind," I call over my shoulder before taking a seat on the couch.

Not even a second later, Aiden strides into the room, head wet from a shower. He might dunk his head at the arena, but showering there isn't part of his routine.

He sits on the smaller couch across from where I'm sitting. "Hey, man. Happy you came."

"Honestly, thanks for inviting me." I recline back, making myself more comfortable.

Aiden shakes his head at me. "You know you don't need an invitation, right?"

"Yeah, you've said that, but who knows what you guys are up to."

A laugh sounds from the entrance of the room, and I peer up to see Cassidy making her way with my drink in her hand.

When she reaches where I am, she hands me the glass, and I take a swig.

"Okay, spill. What was up with you today?" Aiden asks right before Cassidy leans down and places a kiss on his lips before walking off to the kitchen.

"My head isn't in it."

"Is something going on? You know you can—"

"I know, man. And I appreciate it, but there's nothing wrong." Except for the fact that I had sex with Coach's daughter, will most likely get fired for it, and the only person I would normally talk about this with is . . . Coach or someone on his team, which I obviously can't do.

His eyes narrow, and I know I need to throw him a bone. That's why I'm here, for them to try to help me, so if I don't tell him something now, I run the risk that Cassidy will start in on me too. The problem is she's damn good at seeing the big picture, and I can't risk it, so I give him the only thing I can.

I sigh loudly. "Molly."

"Got it. You miss her, and rightfully so."

"Is this the first time you've been away from her for this long?" Cassidy asks as she reenters the room. "Dinner's ready, by the way. No rush, just figured I'd mention it."

I start to stand, ready to eat. "It is."

"That's rough. Well, if you need a stand-in sister, I'm your girl." A soft smile curls her lips. It's warm and caring, like her, and it does what it's meant to do . . .

It makes me smile too.

chapter eighteen

Josie

THE EARLY MORNING SUN GLEAMS ACROSS THE SKY, AND I take a moment to appreciate the scenery.

Normally, I don't come to work this early, but I have to help with a social media campaign today. All I have to do is take pictures of the guys during practice. Action shots are one thing I can do.

Easy enough, I think, as I grab my phone from my bag and head in the direction where I might find the team.

As I step inside and head toward the rink, skates slicing through the ice and pucks clinking against sticks echo around the arena.

They're already practicing, which is a relief. The last thing I need is Dane's attitude when I'm just trying to do my job.

I nod to Hudson, who skates by me, and then I take pictures rapidly. Hudson does exactly what I hoped he would—putting on a show for the camera. The man is nothing if not a showboat.

He spins around, looking more like a figure skater than a hockey player, and I snort.

Idiot.

Although I've never taken pictures of the guys before, they don't seem bothered by me. They are used to me doing weird tasks. Although most odd tasks are for the guys, Laurie sometimes asks for my help doing grunt work. Luckily, those times are few and far between because I don't love moving equipment or collecting towels. Social media marketing is more my speed.

The last task was to essentially interview the guys, asking questions about how the Red Tails posted on their Instagram an old game where the guys were *off*, and wondered if the guys could pull off another championship this season. Needless to say, the answers were colorful.

Laurie then had me get inside information about each player to post to our socials. Dumb questions like their favorite food and the greatest movie of all time.

Dane's answers were clipped and not genuine. I don't know how I know this, but I just do. Hudson, on the other hand, kept to his typical flirtatious answers. Favorite food? Exotic fish, followed by a wink.

My nose scrunched at that one. I was not surprised that he would have some inappropriate response. It earned him a tongue-lashing from Aiden and a gut punch from Wolfe.

Today, when I look over at Dane, he looks more serious than usual. Which isn't crazy 'cause the man rarely smiles.

Not true.

I've seen him smile.

A strange feeling lingers in the air whenever he's around, and today, it's worse. More tense.

Maybe it's that he's avoiding me. Or maybe it has absolutely nothing to do with me at all.

That's more likely what's going on.

My stomach twists at the thought, but I keep snapping away,

hoping I won't think about him if I take enough pictures of the other guys.

No such luck. No matter how hard I will myself not to look, I do. I can't help it.

I'm obsessed, and I have to wonder if it's actually him who has my attention or the fact he's ignoring me, and I have some childhood issues about not being enough.

That's something to unpack another time.

From across the ice, I see him look up. I'm not able to see his eyes clearly, but it doesn't take a rocket scientist to tell he's not happy. I click away, taking as many shots as I can.

Without even thinking, I head in his direction, swallowing hard to calm my racing heart as I continue to take picture after picture.

He glares in my direction, and as my hand hovers over the shutter, I look up from the camera and directly at him.

What did I do now? I'm just doing my job. Something I was ordered to do.

Why is he extra grumpy today?

My brain filters through the past few days. Have I done something to piss him off?

I haven't really spoken to him since the bar.

He tears his gaze away, going about stretching. I force myself to take shots of the other guys, pushing Dane and his apparent irritation far from my mind, but before long, my eyes wander back to him.

He skates, and I watch as he does a few drills with his teammates. When he skates in my direction, I move in close.

"What are you doing?" he snaps, and I look up, a bit startled. "Sorry?"

"Why are you taking pictures of me?"

I tilt my head. "I'm taking pictures of everyone. It's my job."

His eyes narrow, and he must realize he's being ridiculous because his hard gaze softens.

"Are you okay?" I ask, not expecting him to answer me, but he moves closer to the ice's edge.

"Yeah. Fine."

"You sure? You look . . ." I try to find the right words. "Extra. Um, grumpy?"

His eyes go wide, and now I'm close enough to see the blue of his irises.

He really does have beautiful eyes. A stormy ocean turning and shifting with the wind and waves.

"Wow, you went there, Hellfire."

I purse my lips and lift an eyebrow. "And you went there."

He shrugs, looking not at all fazed by this interaction. "I did."

"So . . . what's the problem?" I ask, holding his stare.

"You."

My mouth drops open, and I swear I look like a fish out of water struggling to breathe.

"Are you serious right now? Me?" My hand is wrapped tightly around the camera.

"I am," he says so nonchalantly that slapping him seems like the best course of action.

But it's not, and I can't. Not if I want to keep this job.

"Okay, well, on that note." I move to walk away, and a part of me thinks he will stop me, but he doesn't.

Asshat.

I head in the direction of Hudson, hoping to rile up Dane in some capacity. Not because he cares about me but because he cares about his beloved coach's warning to the team.

"Drinks tonight after practice?" I practically bat my eyelashes, laying on the flirtation a little more than I ought to.

He looks like the cat that ate the canary. "You got it."

I offer my best smile, winking for good measure. "Great. See you later."

I'm playing with fire, but it can't be helped. The need to get a reaction from Dane, any reaction is so strong it's damn near crippling.

If Dane can't get his head out of his ass, it's his problem. Not mine.

The days of locking myself in the guesthouse are over. If I'm going to make this situation work, I'm going to get a life.

Screw Dane and what he thinks.

I'm looking out for me from now on.

chapter nineteen

Josie

A HOST OF ERRANDS FOR THE TEAM HAS KEPT ME BUSY THE past few days. My tasks seemed more grueling today, so I'm happy work is over. I'm exhausted and ready to fall into bed.

It's hard to concentrate as I drive back to my father and Sherry's house. I keep having to shake my head to wake up.

Probably isn't safe for me to drive, but I have no option as long as I live and work with the team.

You could always ride to work with your father.

The man has offered this to me every chance he's gotten, which isn't often since I'm basically avoiding him like the plague.

A huge part of me knows I'm being a baby over this whole thing. I should just sit down with him and ask him all the damn questions I have, but the small voice inside of me that says, "You won't like his answer," is too scared to broach the topic. My time here is too long to risk it. What will I do if he tells me that he knew about me and chose not to meet me until I was fully grown?

That's the thing that terrifies me the most. It's very easy to acknowledge a daughter once she's no longer a child and thus not a burden.

I barely survived knowing I was a burden to my mom; how would I survive knowing he thought I would be a burden too?

The low volume of the music in my car is so loud as I drive that I realize when I roll to a stop at the light that I missed a text.

Looking around, I figure I have a few more seconds before the light turns, so I decide to check who texted.

It's my father. *Speak of the devil.*

Sperm Donor: If you're free for dinner, we'd love to have you. Dane is coming.

Of course he is. Why am I even surprised? Sperm donor's golden boy.

I'm torn.

The stubborn part of me doesn't want to go.

But the part of me that stays up at night thinking of him doesn't want to pass up the opportunity to see him.

Tired or not, I could rally for that.

I wish I had someone to talk to. Anyone.

But I don't.

All my friends have gone their own way, and my mom . . . well, we don't have that type of relationship. Never have.

Sure, I love her, and she's been the only parent I've ever had, but she's strict.

The only time we ever talked about boys went something like, me joking that it was time we talked about the birds and the bees and her reluctantly agreeing. When I was in middle school, I thought it was time. Her response was to keep my damn legs shut.

Good talk.

Yeah, needless to say, that was the last time I ever brought up anything having to do with sex.

I think it should be obvious that I was traumatized by that one statement.

Now, older, I've never been able to confide in her, and it's sad.

I guess her answer makes more sense now that I think about it.

She probably regrets getting pregnant with me, seeing as my father was never around, and that's the only thing she's ever said about sex. I have to assume she wishes she had made that choice for herself.

And with that thought, my mood plummets, and all those nasty insecurities bubble to the surface.

Before I know it, I'm pulling up to the house. I still haven't made a decision on whether I'm going to dinner or not.

Is this a regular thing?

Dane at dinner?

I did notice they were really close the last time he was here. That, coupled with the dad comment, makes me think they are, but they barely speak at practice. Then there's the whole part about him being made my *keeper*.

But I guess it makes sense that they don't talk in public. There can be no favorites on a team. He needs to ensure he comes across as impartial.

As I sit here in the driveway, my heart hammers heavily in my chest. Like a shot of adrenaline, I'm no longer tired. Energy courses through my body.

Normally, when I come here, I go straight to the backyard and head to the guesthouse, but today, I'll enter from the main door.

I didn't bring the key my father gave to me, but it's fine. I'll simply knock.

What's tonight going to be like?

Awkward after our last interaction? Maybe he'll be nice. He'll have to be, to a certain degree, in front of my father.

The sky has become dark, and the air feels heavy. It almost has an ominous feeling.

Great, that doesn't bode well for the evening.

I'm about to knock on the door when I hear the sound of a car over the gravel driveway and then footsteps a few seconds later.

I don't need to turn around to know who it is, not just because it makes sense but also because I can smell his delicious cologne.

The scent is crisp and decadent. All male perfection.

The door flings open, and my father stands there looking out at us with a strange expression.

His gaze darts back and forth between us, but he doesn't seem disturbed. More along the lines of . . . happy? Why would he be happy? If only he knew the truth. Things would be very different for Dane and me.

I'd probably be shipped right back home, no job and no experience, never to see him again.

"Did you guys come together?" he asks, a bit of uncertainty in his voice.

"What? No." Dane steps to the side and points. "See both cars."

Jeez, can he sound any more sus?

This man is basically holding a sign that says, *I banged your daughter, and I don't know how to keep a lid on it.*

If I weren't worried about how tonight was going to go, I'd find this whole thing funny.

But I'm actually worried.

The more I think about the ramifications of being found out, the more nervous I become. I'm bringing on even more anxiety, and if I don't reel it in quickly, I'll have a panic attack.

I don't want to go back to my mom's.

I need this job.

You want to know your father.

Ugh . . . I'm not going there right now.

I try my hardest not to spend time with Sherry or Robert, but no matter what I tell myself, I have to face the facts. It's out of self-preservation. If I don't let them in, they can't hurt me.

We all walk into the house together, and my father leads the way to the dining room.

The table is already set. The last time we were here, I sat next to Dane. It appears I'll be doing the same tonight.

Fun for me.

Most likely hell for him.

The idea of torturing him brings me a little joy today, and I'm happy about it because it means I'm not thinking of the big elephant in the room, and I'm not talking about the fact we had sex. I'm talking about the fact that I've been living here for over a month and have yet to speak with my father about the things Sherry told me I should talk to him about.

I guess I'm scared. No matter how strained my relationship is with Mom, what he says could cause an even bigger rift. Then who would I have?

Nobody.

I'd be completely alone.

Sherry walks over to the table and lifts a bottle in the air. "Who's drinking?"

"Me," I say, lifting my hand like an idiot.

"I'll have a glass, please." This comes from Dane, and it's said with an edge that annoys me.

As if the only way to get through this night is with alcohol.

You're not any better.

She pours each of us a glass. Once mine is filled, I take a sip. The taste hits my tongue, and I welcome it.

This *is* what I need to get through tonight.

Or maybe another distraction. Maybe I should stick to my original plan and make Dane pay attention to me.

A distraction named Dane Sinclair seems like what the doctor ordered.

Not a good idea, Josie.

But the train has already left the station. I'm all in, even if it's going to crash and burn.

chapter twenty

Dane

FOR THE LIFE OF ME, I HAVE NO IDEA WHY I KEEP TORTURING myself by seeking Josephine out.

Last night, for example, going to dinner, yeah, that wasn't my smartest idea. I need to put distance between us, but I find myself doing the opposite instead.

The whole damn meal, she watched me, and I'm pretty sure Coach saw her doing it. Now I have to hope he didn't notice anything because *fuck*. I couldn't handle that shit right now.

"Dane." Coach's voice echoes through the practice facility the moment I walk in. He sounds pissed. Yep. I'm screwed. *He noticed.*

Here it comes, the inevitable. I'm about to get my ass handed to me.

"What?" I ask him as I move closer to where he's standing.

"You missed the interview you had scheduled."

Oh, thank fuck. This has nothing to do with Josephine.

I lift a brow at him. "What are you talking about?"

"This morning. You were supposed to talk to the local paper about the charity event the team is throwing."

"I didn't miss it." Fuck, did I?

I mentally try to remember what I had today, but I'm barely functioning with Molly away.

After winning the Cup, followed by one to many celebrations, I thought it would be a good idea to send Molly on an all-expense paid trip to Europe. *I was wrong.*

"You did." His voice is full of reproach, and I know I messed up.

"With Molly gone . . ."

"Don't even say it. I hired you a temp while she's away for the summer, and you fired her on day one."

"I'll make sure—"

"Dane, you also fired the second one." Well, when he puts it that way, he might have a point, but I had my reasons. I just need to tell him.

"She fucked up my—"

"Again, stop. I understand you rely heavily on Molly, but if she's not going to be here, you need to have someone manage you, and if you're going to fire every person who comes into the room, we'll keep having issues."

"I'm not going to fire every single person." As the words leave my mouth, I know it's a lie. I will because no one can replace Molly. For the longest time, it's always just been us, which is why I'm struggling now.

After my parents died, I fought for custody of her. She was only eleven, and I was eighteen, a senior in high school.

My uncle, the scumbag who I wouldn't let watch my fish, wanted to take custody, probably because of my parents' estate and the money he would be in control of if he raised her, but I fought tooth and nail. Since then, it's been us against the world.

Molly is the reason I live in Redville. We grew up here, so when the time came to play for the NHL, and she was still in school, it was a no-brainer.

The moment she graduated, she started to manage my life. Again, it was her and me against the world.

So, as much as it sucks for her to be gone for the next month, she deserves the three months I gave her to travel.

Unfortunately, it also means I'm lost without her.

"Well, this shit has to stop. And I have the perfect solution."

I have no idea what he's talking about, and if he means bringing Molly home, that's not going to fly.

"Laurie!" he shouts.

"Yeah, Coach," I hear her shout back, head peeking around the corner.

"Bring Josie here."

Shit. Wherever this is going, I don't like it. This is a bad idea, and he hasn't even said what the idea is.

"Sure thing." She offers a toothy smile, one that looks like more of a grimace than anything else.

My back is rigid as I wait, and fuck is my jaw tight. If I didn't know better, I'd say I was about to lose my shit just at the concept of what I fear is about to come out of his mouth.

Anything that puts Josephine in the same room as me is a bad idea.

Horrible.

A few seconds pass, and then she comes bouncing along.

She looks young today. Still beautiful, but in an innocent way.

Something I know she is not.

That's what makes being near her so hard. She's temptation. The sweetest sin.

Her long blond hair, normally down, is pulled up into a high ponytail, and she's wearing black leggings and a skintight cropped white T-shirt.

How her father allows her to walk around all these men in that outfit is beside me.

It's practically indecent with the way her nipples pebble under the thin material from the cold.

And don't get me started on the skin of her flat stomach.

She's walking fast, practically jogging here, and her breasts bounce with the movement.

Is she even wearing a bra?

If my jaw was tight before, now it feels like it might snap in half from how tightly I'm grinding my teeth.

"You needed me, Coach?"

For a second, I'm taken aback. Coach? Does she not refer to him as Dad? I scour my brain, trying to remember if I've ever heard her say it.

I've tried to avoid her as much as possible, and ninety percent of the time I've seen her, he hasn't been around. But now that I think of it, she didn't call him Dad at dinner either.

And now I'm certain that she hasn't ever called him Dad. I know there's a story there, and while I wonder what it is, I won't ask. I told him the first night that it wasn't my business, and I intend to stick to that.

"Please feel free to say no to what I'm going to ask you; you are in no way obligated to say yes, of course. While your job here is as an intern, this will fall a little outside the parameters I set."

"Okay . . ." She's clearly confused.

While I'm not confused about what he's going to say, and hell to the no am I going to allow this, what I am confused about is why he talks to her like this. Like he doesn't know her at all. Like she hates him. Like it's a huge imposition to even speak to him, and he's treading carefully.

I know I shouldn't care, but I find I want to know everything more and more by the second.

No, you don't.

Despite my inner voice telling me I don't, I do, and it pisses me the fuck off.

"I was wondering if you could spend the next few weeks before the season starts helping Dane out." He stops for a second to watch her. When she doesn't say or do anything, he nods and then continues. "Dane's sister, Molly, handles everything for Dane."

"She's his assistant?"

"More like life manager," he corrects, and I have to hand it to him. That title is the most accurate description of Molly. Life manager and keeper of sanity works too. "Molly is away for another month, and Dane here needs someone to help him. Of course, I would understand if you wanted to say no. It's not exactly the experience you came here for—"

"Yes." She cuts in.

Fuck.

What the hell is she up to?

Clearly, she's out to make my life hell, and can I blame her? Not one bit.

chapter twenty-one

Josie

"THANK YOU SO MUCH, JOSIE. YOU HAVE NO IDEA HOW HELPFUL this will be," the sperm donor says before turning to Dane. His face changes the moment he looks at Dane. While he was smiling when he spoke to me, his lips have sagged back down and now resemble a straight line.

He's all business now, and by the looks of things, he's not happy with Dane.

His whole demeanor feels off from the family dinner a week ago. There, they spoke like father and son, but now, he looks at him like he's ready to scold him. Dane's face is rock hard, lines forming between his brow, and man, his posture is unnaturally straight. He looks like a stubborn child ready to throw a tantrum.

The interesting thing is he doesn't. He grinds his teeth but doesn't speak.

"I'll leave you two alone to hash out your schedule. Josie, you should get in touch with Molly if Dane gives you any problems—"

"There won't be any need for that," Dane assures.

My father nods, his face still showing little emotion, but I see a small line form in his cheek. He's pleased with himself.

It's obvious that Dane doesn't want an assistant other than his sister. It's also obvious that my father feels triumphant that he pulled this one over on him.

If he knew the history between us, he wouldn't be smiling. However, that thought alone makes me want to smile.

Dane hates me for no reason. He chose to sleep with me, so that's on him. He needs my help, and that makes me feel in power for the first time in a while where he's concerned.

When I'm around, he seems a little more relaxed. Okay, maybe not now, but that night in the vineyard.

He seemed so free, and if I can bring that out in him again . . .

"Seeing as I have no choice, give me your phone number," Dane grunts out, and it reminds me I just got lost in my thoughts and wasn't paying attention.

I lift my head and notice my father has left. It's now just Dane and me, standing alone. This man needs to lighten up.

"You do have a choice," I remind him. "You can have Coach call your sister and make her come home."

"No. That's not a choice," he responds. "She deserves this time. I won't mess it up for her."

"Where is she anyway?" I ask.

He scowls as though I just asked the most intrusive question. "That's none of your business."

I take a step back; it feels like I was verbally slapped.

"Excuse me." I place my hands on my hips, squaring my shoulders and stand a little bit taller. He doesn't get to talk to me like that. "First of all, it is my business. It seems, in case you forgot, that I was just promoted to your personal assistant. Life manager, if you will."

"You could never be my life manager." His tone is unnecessarily cold.

"Fine," I huff. "Personal assistant, whatever. But seeing as that is my new position for the next month until your sister returns, it is, in fact, my business to know where she is. In case you missed the part where your coach specifically told me to call her if I needed to."

He cocks his head to the right. "That won't happen."

"You don't get to decide that, Dane. Believe it or not, I might need to reach her."

He shakes his head. "I don't think so."

I lift my hand. "Listen, you might not like me—"

"I don't care enough to like or dislike you."

Ouch.

"Okay, but not the point." My hand rubs at my chest, needing to shield me somehow.

"What is the point? Please get to it, as I have to start practice."

I let out a long-drawn-out sigh. This man is infuriating. I can practically see why no one but his sister wants this job. If I weren't hell-bent on making him thaw to me, I'd probably tell my father no as well. But I don't like that he doesn't like me. The truth is, I hate when people don't. I recognize that I don't always make it easy, but that's because my wall is up to protect me. I have enough reasons to be on guard at all times.

When the people who are supposed to love you most in the world either act like you don't exist or that you're their biggest nuisance, it's easy not to trust anyone.

The fact that he feels so strongly about me in a negative way has me spinning my wheels to change his tune.

It's definitely not a well-thought-out plan because I'm also hopelessly attracted to this man and dream of his hands touching my body every day, but I figure I can knock both things off with one task.

Make him not hate me and convince him that the vineyards shouldn't be a one-night thing.

I'm not looking for him to fall in love with me, but he'll make living with my father and his wife tolerable for the next few months.

Also, I'd be lying if there wasn't some appeal to the fact that this man is like a son to my father, and it feels like banging him again would be sticking it to my dad.

It will get him where it hurts.

Then I can go back to my life and not have to deal with him.

After I get the experience I need to land a job, that is.

Yeah, this might not be a well-thought-out plan, but it'll have to work.

Do I sound like a petulant child? Probably. But such is life.

"I might need to contact her. I'm sure there are things on your schedule that you might not even know about."

"She left a link to share everything relating to me. It's well organized, and if you open it, you won't need to reach out to her."

"You really don't want me to talk to her, do you?"

He inhales deeply, and I wonder if he's going to answer me or if I've just pissed him off more, but then he shocks the shit out of me when he meets my gaze.

There is so much emotion in his blue eyes. The iris is practically gone, and I feel like I'm drowning in the black abyss of his soul.

"Josephine."

"That's a change. It's not often that anyone calls me by my full name, especially *you*."

"Would you rather I call you Hellfire?"

"Well, no, but . . ."

He shakes his head. "I know you wouldn't, but it does suit you."

"How do you figure? You don't know me."

"I'd say I know you pretty well."

His intense stare and blatant mention of our night together makes my knees quake slightly.

"I don't care if the sun falls and the Earth is on fire. Molly has taken care of me ever since she graduated from college. She has asked for nothing in return. She deserves a break from me. She deserves a piece of her own happiness."

I bob my head, understanding where he's coming from and

having so much respect for his sister and all she seems to do for him.

"If it were up to me, she would stay far away and live her life, but it's not, so this is the best I can give her."

His words and tone have my mouth glued shut. There's so much to unpack in one sentence, and I don't know how to, but I know I eventually want to.

The sadness there is a beacon to me, and I just want to make him shine again. Like he did that night.

Maybe because I don't like to see my own sadness reflected in others.

"I'll send you the link." Then he's gone, leaving me more confused than when this started.

chapter twenty-two

Josie

THE FIRST THING I DO WHEN I WALK INTO THE ARENA THIS morning is look for Dane. Yesterday, I went through everything Molly had lined up for him. Today, I'm ready to hit the ground running.

As I walk toward Dane, my father waves. "Josie, do you have time to talk?"

That's the last thing I want to do right now.

"Actually, I need to speak to Dane. He has something."

I don't stay long enough to hear if he has anything to say about me blowing him off. Instead, I stride to where Dane is.

"It's time," I say as I make my way to him.

His brow furrows. "For what?"

I roll my eyes. Shouldn't he already know this? "Time for your interview."

"What interview?"

"The one Molly had scheduled, but the assistant before me

dropped the ball on. Or maybe you fired her. I can't remember all your assistant drama."

"Fired her."

"Got it. Yep, I've rescheduled it, which reminds me, why did you fire her? She didn't seem to be too bad. I mean, she wasn't even the one who scheduled the interview in the first place. It's not her fault you fired her before she could tell you that Molly had set it up, thus making you miss it." I lift a brow, and he covers his face with his hands.

A few seconds go by before he drops his hands, and then he leans his head back.

"Oh, just spit it out. It couldn't have been that bad."

"It was."

I laser him with a look that should scream bullshit. "A fire-able offense?"

"Obviously, or I wouldn't have fired her."

I move closer, which is probably a bad idea because of how good he looks right now, but still, I'm like a damn moth to a flame. I can't help myself. "Now I need the tea."

"What do you think this is?" He sounds annoyed.

I smile broadly. "Teatime?"

"We aren't friends, Hellfire."

I puff out my lower lip. "You are *no* fun." Rolling my eyes, I continue to press. "Just tell me."

"You don't want to know."

"Of course I do. I work for you now. What would get me fired . . . ?" Because I'd do it just to piss him off, knowing it would take a lot more for my father to allow him to fire me.

"Tell me, tell me," I chant.

Mr. Grumpy lets out a sigh, obviously annoyed at my per-sistence, but hey, maybe I'll get what I want.

"She hit on me."

His words wipe the smile right off my face, but not for the rea-son you'd think.

Hitting on him would be easy. I'd happily do it, and not even to get fired, but that's not what pisses me off. It's the fact that she did it.

Now the questions start to swim in my brain . . . and I can't shut them up.

Did they sleep together?

Are they an item?

Does he like her?

Wait, he fired her, so that means he didn't do any of the above, right?

"Interesting. Is this your thing?"

His brow rises. "Thing?"

"Hooking up with your assistants."

"First of all, no. Second of all, fuck no. My sister is my assistant."

My stomach drops. My dumb jealousy. When will I learn to keep my mouth shut? I always do this.

Not only am I a klutz in life, but I'm also notorious for putting my foot in my mouth.

I look up at him sheepishly and try to think of something, anything, to break the tension threatening to suffocate the room.

Dane Sinclair is extra surly right now. If looks could kill, I'd be dead. There is no warmth in his gaze.

I need to defuse this moment, but how?

"Help me walk the tightrope," I sheepishly mutter out in a pathetic attempt to make him smile and right his mood.

It's not going to help. If anything, I've probably pissed him off with my little joke, but I had to try something.

It's not that I care if he hates me, but accidentally insulting his sister? That's not okay.

Dane hasn't spoken, but his lips tip up a smidge at my words. *Interesting.* Maybe he doesn't hate it that much after all.

"I'm sorry about my comment," I say after a minute of silence.

"It's fine. Now why don't you tell me where I need to go for the interview so I don't screw it up again."

The big elephant in the room, why I'm here, because he missed a huge interview, and I had to fix it.

"I've set it up at a coffee shop in town. Is that okay?" For some reason, I feel awkward, so I look down at my hands. The material of my shirt is bunched up, and I push it down for something to do with my fingers.

"Are you coming with me?" His voice drops low; it's a different sound than I'm used to. Tilting my head up, I meet his stare.

His blue eyes seem softer today. There is a vulnerability in the way he looks at me.

I might not know him well, but I can tell he wants me there. I'm not sure how I know, but I do, so I make my decision. "I am."

His reaction is everything I need to confirm that my assumption was correct. It's not that it was obvious. No words are said, he simply nods, but I see how his back muscles relax.

I nibble on my bottom lip as I process the fact that I'm now going to be spending time with him outside of the practice facility. I have never been with him outside of this place since I started working here. My stomach feels like butterflies are flying. Nerves? Or excitement.

"Do you want to drive separately?"

Please say separate. I'm not sure I can handle the small confines of a car.

"Together."

Shit.

I smile broadly, pretending I'm not affected by this news, but I am.

My hands slightly shake by my sides as we walk, making our way out of the building. If I'm this nervous walking with him, what will I do in the car?

How does this man make me so unhinged?

It's not that I'm normally calm and collected, but with him, it feels like I'm holding a balloon, and I can't stay tethered to the ground.

Once outside, he leads us to his car.

A shiny navy-blue Range Rover.

It's not what I expected from him, but I guess I don't know what I thought he would drive. He's not reckless like Hudson, who I picture in a sports car, and Aiden is down to earth, I guess I expected a tank. Something extremely safe. Like a Hummer.

A natural protector.

I wonder if something ever happened to me, if he would protect me too.

chapter twenty-three

Dane

S HE'S TOO CLOSE.
Despite the size of my car, she's too damn close. The soft
smell of her floral perfume accents the air, making me hyperaware
of her presence and reminding me of how she tastes, how she
moans, and, the worst, how she feels.

All I can think about is tasting her again.

I want to lose myself in her body and never be found.

Having her work with me is officially the worst idea Coach
has ever come up with, and obviously not for the reason he would
think.

I need to get rid of her, but if I told him this wasn't working
out, she would feel the brunt of it. He would assume, like the rest
of the temporary assistants I've fired, she did something wrong,
but the only thing she's done wrong is existing because her presence is too much.

My need and desire for her are all-consuming.

It's all I think about.

I need to taste her one more time.

Maybe sending Molly away was a bad idea. No. She deserves it. She's put up with my shit for years. She claims she owes me, and it's the least she can do after I raised her. She claims I gave up my life to take care of her, but that's the biggest bullshit I've ever heard.

Sure, I had to make sacrifices, and yes, some things I did to keep her were not my finest moments, but in truth, Molly gave me a reason to live.

The guilt from my parents' accident will live with me forever. My penance was making my life about her, and it still is about her.

The fact is, she's been through hell. My father's reckless drinking and driving not only resulted in the accident that killed our mother, but it nearly killed Molly too. Now, she's left with survivor's guilt, and that isn't fair. She was an innocent child, and he took that innocence away from her.

My hands on the wheel grip tight enough that my knuckles have turned white.

"Everything okay over there?"

"Just fine." I stare intently at the road ahead. My anger is still simmering on the surface; I need a distraction, or I'll head into this interview with fire in my veins. That won't bode well for the charity. "Where's home?"

She fidgets in her seat. "Indiana. A small town. Doubt you've heard of it."

"Try me."

"Harbor Woods."

I drum my fingers on the steering wheel, trying to place the name. Nope. Nothing. "Yeah, I never heard of it."

"Told you."

An awkward silence fills the air. Why is getting information out of her like pulling teeth? She's closed off, and I don't like it. *You're one to talk.*

"You like working for the team?" Can I be any more cliché with my questions? At this point, I'm better off riding in silence, but for some reason, I can't stop myself from asking her mundane questions. What the hell is wrong with me? *You want to get to know her.* I'm pathetic, that's what.

"It's fine." She flicks the radio on loud enough to drown out my questions. *Smooth.*

I lower it. "Fine?"

She lets out a sigh. It might be dawning on her that I won't back down easily. "Yeah, I guess. Some parts I like more than others."

"And those parts are?"

Josephine glances out the window. "I like the marketing aspects. Don't love the cleaning after smelly players."

"We don't all smell."

She turns back to face me. "Yeah, you do."

"Ouch."

From the corner of my eye, it looks like she rolled her eyes at me, but I can't be sure. "I never said you smelled bad."

I tap the brakes and come to a stop at the light before glancing in her direction. "And how exactly do I smell, Hellfire?"

She shakes her head. "Not going there."

We both go silent. The hum of the engine is the only sound present in the car. What is she thinking? She's probably thinking she wishes I would stop asking her questions. Sorry, Hellfire, no such luck today. I'm on a roll.

"Tell me more about you."

"Jeez." She tilts her head back. "What is this, the inquisition? You already know the important things."

"Come on, Hellfire, throw me a bone."

"I already told you things about me. Such as my fear of spiders."

My right hand leaves the wheel and runs through my hair. "You aren't going to make this easy, are you?"

"Would I be a *hellfire* if I did?"

She's got me there, but she still won't win this battle. "What's your favorite color?"

She taps her left-hand fingers on the center console. "Blue."

"Food?"

"You're intolerable." She lets out a deep sigh. "Fine, donuts. Happy?"

"No, what did you study in college?"

"Greek mythology," she answers, her tone clearly annoyed.

"Seriously?"

She squirms in her seat. I wonder if she's considering bailing on the ride. "Seriously."

"No wonder you couldn't find a job."

"Now you're telling me." This time, she definitely rolls her eyes.

"Who's your favorite god . . ."

She barks out a laugh, and I turn to face her, catching the smirk that lines her face. "Poseidon." Clever girl. I stepped right into that.

"How did I know you would say that?"

"'Cause you're smart. You remind me of him."

I try to keep my face serious, but it's no use. My lip curls up. "Do I now?"

"Yep."

"And how exactly do I remind you of Poseidon?"

"He was grumpy too, but he meant well. Not a full asshole like Ares."

"Good to know . . . and who are you in this equation."

"That's yet to be seen."

"Why don't you talk to your dad?"

"And on that note . . ."

From beside me, I see Josephine reach over the console and start fiddling with the radio again. This time, I don't stop her. It was worth a try. Then a song that I don't know is playing. She seems to know exactly what song it is by the way she sways in her chair.

I try to keep focused on the road, but it's hard as her shoulders move seductively.

At the red light, I slow the car down to a stop and turn to look at her. Her eyes are closed, and her mouth is softly singing the lyrics.

This girl is trouble.

She doesn't even realize it, but she is the sexiest woman I have ever seen, and she's not even trying.

The way her lips move with each sultry word has my dick hardening in my pants. No one should be this sensual. Especially when she's merely singing in the car.

Her voice is low, and I can't make out the lyrics, but fuck, does she sound good.

Luckily for me, the light turns green, and I have to go back to paying attention.

We only need to drive for about five minutes more before we pull up to the little coffee shop, where I will have to answer questions I don't want to. But I wouldn't put it past Molly to come back if I don't, so I'll suck it up.

The next few minutes are painful.

All I want to do is get out of the car. If Coach only knew what I wanted to do to his daughter, he'd kill me.

Hudson would have no problem with any of this, but fuck, why does she have to be Coach's kid?

I remember the day I knew Robert would change my life. The rink was cold, the air thick with the scent of ice and sweat. Coach Robert, with his clean shave and country club look, pulled me aside after practice.

"Dane," he said in his gravelly voice, *"you've got potential, kid. But potential isn't enough. You gotta work for it every damn day. You've got to want it more than anything."*

I nodded, hanging on his every word. It was more attention and guidance than I had ever received from my father, who preferred to simply push me to live the life he always wanted and couldn't have. An angry, stoic figure in a sea of cheering parents.

Coach continued, his words sinking deep into my core. "Hockey's more than just skating and shooting. It's about heart. It's about sacrifice. You wanna remain at the top of this level? You gotta give it everything you've got. No excuses. Especially for you, Dane. You have your sister to consider."

His advice wasn't just about hockey; it was about life. About perseverance, about pushing through the tough times. It was about believing in myself, something I struggled with when Dad's distant nods were the closest thing I had to approval.

"Listen to your instincts, Dane," Coach said, clapping a hand on my shoulder. "Trust your teammates, but trust yourself most of all. You've got what it takes."

Those words stuck with me through every game, every practice. They became my mantra, driving me forward even when the odds seemed stacked against us. Coach believed in me and saw something I struggled to see in myself.

Looking back now, I realize that moment with Coach was more than just a pep talk. It was a turning point. It was the moment I realized that I didn't hate hockey; I hated what it meant to my father. But I wasn't living for him. I was living for myself, and hockey was as much a part of my life as the air I breathed. I didn't know any different, and in reality, father aside, I didn't want to.

He's been there for me through some of the toughest years. Always encouraging me in ways my father never did.

The distance evaporates, and I make the turn and then throw the car in park.

We hop out and walk inside.

A woman in her early thirties walks right up to me, hand stretched out.

"Hello, Mr. Sinclair. Can I call you Dane?"

No. You can't, is what I want to say, but something tells me that won't go over so well.

This woman doesn't know me, but by the way she looks at me, I think she thinks she will.

"Sure."

She beams at me and then turns to Josephine, her smile now a straight line.

"Thank you for bringing him . . ."

Josephine takes a step forward and extends her hand. "I'm Josie."

The woman looks down at her hand like it's diseased. "Cute," she says in a patronizing voice.

Is she for real right now?

"Josephine is my temporary assistant while Molly is out of town. She's Coach Robert's daughter."

That wipes the snide smirk right off her face. It also makes Josephine look like she might throw up.

Instantly, I hate that I said it.

The reason I did was to tell this bitch to treat her with respect, but I realize now, more damage was done to Josephine than to the reporter.

"Let's make this quick," I say, pointing at a free table. "We have another appointment after this."

I turn toward Josephine to see if she'll back me up despite the fact that we don't have anything after this, but she plays along.

"Yep. Sorry, oh, I forgot your name."

"Natasha."

"Yeah, sorry, Natasha, Mr. Sinclair's schedule is jam-packed. Busy man. So you guys might want to get to it."

"No problem." Natasha scurries behind me as I walk to the table.

The moment we get away from Josephine, Natasha is back at it, fluttering her lids at me and licking her lips.

Not acting at all professional.

"She's a bit young. Don't you hate nepotism?"

"My sister works for me," I deadpan.

Her mouth opens and shuts like a guppy.

It takes her a few minutes to right herself before she takes out her recorder.

"So, tell me about your involvement with Saints and Starling

Foundation. From what I heard from Coach Robert, this charity is near and dear to your heart."

It is, more than he knows, more than anyone knows.

I take a deep breath and tell her the watered-down version of why I help raise money to assist people with legal fees.

How I want to make sure that people who don't have access to funds can still get the representation and advice they need.

Even without money, they don't need to sell their soul to ensure they are looked after.

They don't have to do what I did when I had no one to help me.

chapter twenty-four

Josie

I DON'T THINK I'VE EVER WANTED TO PUNCH ANOTHER PERSON as badly as I did that reporter. Her condescending demeanor was so unprofessional, but having Dane come to my defense was worth the insults she threw.

He cares.

Whether he admits it or not, he does care about me in some capacity. Our night together mattered.

I matter.

"What's going on in that head of yours?" Dane asks, peeking out the corner of his eye at me.

"Nothing. Just thinking about where we might be off to since we have a jam-packed day." I air quote, repeating his earlier words.

"Anywhere far from her."

I laugh and nod in agreement. "She was awful."

"She was, but I guess a necessary evil, or at least that's what Molly would say." He grunts. "If that woman had talked to her like that, I would've come unglued." He shakes his head as if imagining the scenario in his head.

"Molly sounds pretty great," I say, wondering what she's like. Is she broody like him, or the sunshine to his dark clouds?

"She is," he says, and his voice is lower and softer.

So that's what his voice sounds like when he loves someone. I wonder if anyone loves me like that.

My heart tightens in my chest.

Despite my mom being cold at times, I know she loves me. She's the only person I know who cares for me. I don't really have anyone else.

I had a few friends in college. Obviously, the girls I partied with, but the sad truth is since I was shipped off to live with my father, not one of them has called me.

No one cares.

I was a fun girl to hang out with and get drunk with, but when push came to shove, they weren't real friends. There were never phone calls just to check in or chat. Every call came with a motive, and it was always attached to a night on the town and me acting as the wingwoman for one of my more flirtatious friends.

I also realize that I was the one initiating the friendship. I always went out of my way to remind the girls that I was there and ready to hang out.

And it's even more obvious that I was a last thought, being as though none of them have bothered to check on me.

"She's nothing like me."

I look up, eyes narrowed in on Dane. "Huh?"

"Molly. I was saying she's not like me."

I'd been lost in my thoughts and had forgotten what we'd been talking about.

"Can you tell me about her?"

I doubt he will, but when he pulls the car up to the now empty practice facility, he pivots in his seat and looks at me.

"She's incredible. Smart, funny. Full of love." He smiles warmly, thinking about his sister. "She'd give a stranger the shirt off her back. She's just that way."

"Got it. The opposite of you." I wink, but I see a flash of hurt and immediately regret the bad joke. "I'm sorry. I was just—"

"Don't apologize," he says more seriously. "She is my opposite, and I don't mind admitting it. She deserves so much more than this life has given her so far. I intend to ensure the rest of this life is different for her."

I can tell there's a long story there, and I hope he tells me. That's all I wish—for Dane to open up to me. To trust me with his secrets.

I'm not sure when it happened but over the past few weeks of working with the team, I realize I wish he would confide in me. I wish I could get him to open up. *Truly open up.* Sometimes I do, giving him little glimpses into my life. I know in my heart that I can trust him completely with my truths, but I want that trust reciprocated. I'm greedy and hungry for it.

"Growing up—" He starts and stops, and I reach across the console, taking his hand in mine. I give it a reassuring squeeze.

He will pull away any second, but when he doesn't, I feel lighter and happier than I've felt in weeks. Instead, he keeps holding my hand, and in my mind, it feels like he's pulling the energy out of me to find the strength to open up to me.

"Growing up, it was just us. Well, that's not true . . . It was just us when I was eighteen and she was eleven. I'm not sure how much you know about me, but I raised Molly."

"You did?" The word comes out reverently, shock and awe taking root.

"I didn't have a choice and wouldn't change it for the world. Our parents died in a car accident, and my sister almost died with them. It was just her and me, and there was no way she would live with anyone else. Not when I was old enough to care for her."

I swallow, thinking about how young and brave he was.

With every new detail I learn about him, I grow even more desperate for more.

"Will you tell me the full story?" I ask, voice barely a whisper.

He takes a deep breath. "Maybe one day. But not today."

And with that, the conversation is over, and broody Dane is back in full force.

chapter twenty-five

Dane

Hudson: Hear me out I think Danes got the hots for Josie.

Dane: Shut up.

Hudson: That's not a no. So tell us, what's she assiting you with . . .

Dane: You're really not funny.

Hudson: Do you see me laughing?

Dane: I don't see you at all.

Hudson: You know what I mean. Okay, but seriously, you banging her?

Dane: I'm not above murder.

Mason: I'll be your alibi.

Aiden: Children.

chapter twenty-six

Dane

THE ONLY THING I WANT TO DO TODAY IS GO HOME.
Coach pushed us hard. It's not that he doesn't normally push us hard, but this is harder than normal.

Not one of my teammates would understand. Hell, I barely understand, but winning the Cup has been bittersweet.

It shouldn't be. I do love playing hockey. I'm smart enough to admit my emotions are misplaced, but it feels like a win for him, and even years later, he doesn't deserve it. But what makes it even harder is I know what I did to get here.

Don't go there. That road of thought is a dark road, and if I cross into that territory, I might not come back.

I head out of the locker at a slower-than-normal pace.

There is no question that Josephine will be waiting for me the moment I close the door.

"Where are you off to, man?" Hudson says.

"Not home, that's for sure."

"I can't believe Molly loaded your schedule like this and didn't have the decency to stay in town to help you through it."

"It's not her fault I surprised her with a trip."

He bobs his head. "That's true. And she probably did you a favor. I'd love to be waited on hand and foot by Coach's daughter. Fuck, she's hot."

I stop dead in my tracks and pivot my body to look at him. Smug little shit.

Despite the two years of friendship, I'm finding it hard to re-member why I even like him right now. *Fine, I liked him much bet-ter before Hellfire showed up.*

Currently, the only guy on the team I like is Aiden. *He's the only one not making a pass at Josephine.*

There's also the fact that he's the most like me out of all the guys. He has ghosts.

Secrets he doesn't share.

Yeah, now I know a few of them, but because of the way he was raised, he knows not to ask me questions about mine.

I move closer, staring Hudson dead in the eye. "Stay the fuck away from her."

He lifts his hands. "Jeez, man, I was just kidding. What's got your panties in a bunch?"

"What's got my panties in a bunch? Are you fucking kidding? That's Coach's daughter, and she's off-limits. How many times do I have to remind you of that?"

He narrows his eyes. "It's more than that, though." Then, as if he's had an epiphany, his eyes widen, and a Joker-like grin spreads across his face. "Ah shit, you do like her?"

"What? No." That didn't even sound convincing to me.

"That protest sounded weak even for your grumpy ass," he says.

"Fuck off, Wilde."

I turn away from him and storm out of the locker room, bar-reling right into the one person I don't want to.

My body collides into hers, and I reach my arms out on instinct to steady her.

"Watch—" Her words dry up, and I'm not sure why, but then I realize I have her wrapped protectively in my arms. Our chests touch, and my hands are on her back.

We are so close. I bet she can feel the way my heart beats against hers.

I drop her as if she's a hot tool, and my hands are burned.

"Watch where you're going," she finally says as she rights herself.

"Sorry about that."

"What's got you so moody?"

You. "Nothing."

"You're lying."

"Why don't you speak to your father?" I challenge. One uncomfortable question for another.

"Wow. We aren't talking about me."

"Maybe we should be."

"I see what you're doing, but I'll let you in on a little secret: I don't give up easy. So . . . let's try this again, what's got you so moody?"

That's what I'm afraid of. "If you must know."

"I must. In my new job, I need to know everything about you." She practically purrs the words, and I want to growl at her.

"It's Hudson," I blurt out.

"Sure it's not me? Maybe you're excited to see me."

"I can promise you, Hellfire, it's not you."

She rolls her eyes. "Do you really need to call me that?"

"Do you really need to follow me around?" I deadpan.

"Yep."

With a deep inhale, I go to turn around. "Find another job."

She lifts her arms to her sides as she walks, one foot in front of the other like she's walking a tightrope. "But then who will help me on the tightrope?"

"Jeez, enough of that shit."

She shakes her head adamantly. "Now, why would I do that? Every time I do, I see it."

"See what?"

She lifts her hand and points at my face. "The way your lip twitches."

"I'm not following you."

"You want to smile." She grins back at me and continues to walk.

She keeps moving, and I can feel it happening despite not wanting it to.

She's right.

I do, and I'm even more annoyed now; not only that she is right, but that she could read me so easily.

"Come on, we don't have all day," she calls over her shoulder.

"Where are we going?" I speed up my pace, catching up to her in only a few strides.

"You need to get fitted."

I furrow my brow. "Fitted for what?"

She stops short, turns to look at me, and then her mouth drops open. "Did you even look at Molly's spreadsheet? Or Dropbox?"

What's she going on about? This girl needs to get her expectations in order if she thinks I'm going to spend my time trying to figure out how Molly color-coordinated my life. I shake my head at her. "Why would I do that? That's your job."

"And before me? Forget it. You don't have to tell me; I know, I know. You didn't look, hence how I got the job."

Are we really having this conversation right now? In the middle of a damn hallway. Apparently so, by the way she glares at me.

"I had others before you," I tell her because now I find the need to defend myself to my damn assistant. *What is wrong with me?*

"And let me guess . . . you never even gave them the sheet."

My arms find their way across my chest. "Well—"

Hers land on her hips. "You didn't, did you?"

"No."

"How did you ever expect them to work out if they didn't have her sheet?" She looks at me, narrowing her eyes. "Oh my God, you didn't. Those poor, underpaid temps—you didn't even give them a fighting chance."

"I didn't want them," I respond.

"You don't want me either."

"That's true." I shrug, placing my hands in my pockets.

"Then why do you bother with me?"

Isn't that the question of the month? Because you're beautiful, funny, and make me smile. *Fuck.* "I don't have a choice."

"Of course you do." Her eyes challenge me to respond. Dumb move. *You won't like what I'll say.*

"Nope. You're the coach's daughter. I'll never have a choice." Her face turns pale at my words, and the moment I see it, I regret my words right away. She backs up a step. "Jos . . ."

"Hellfire. Remember."

She turns her head and continues to walk. "Let's go. Chop chop. We're going to be late."

Two things occur to me.

One: If I want to piss her off, just mention that Coach is her father.

Two: The most shocking, I don't want to.

chapter twenty-seven

Josie

I'M SURPRISED WHEN HE FOLLOWS ME. EVEN MORE SURPRISED when he doesn't bitch, moan, or complain.

I expected something to that effect, but nope. There's nothing.

It's not that he's void of emotion, but he seems different. Not friendly or anything, just quiet.

Maybe he's deep in thought. If only I had a mind-reading device, then deciphering his moods wouldn't be so difficult. I thought I was confusing, bouncing from one emotion to the next, but this guy might give me a run for my money.

I try to think back to when his demeanor changed, but nothing jumps out. The other day, he got weird after he mentioned I'm the coach's daughter, and today, he asked me about my relationship with my father.

I wonder why he's thinking about this.

Maybe it's been on his mind since the reporter. Maybe he's probably bothered by my birth status due to the fact that we hooked up.

That's it. I bet he thinks I'm upset about that too. He couldn't be further from the truth. Whether we slept together has nothing to do with why I'm upset.

Which makes me wonder, what does he know? It's obvious he and my father/sperm donor are close, but did he tell him anything? Does he know we only just met? What about my mom? Does he know I was practically kicked out of the only place I've ever known to live with a man and woman I've never met? I bet he doesn't.

He told my father he didn't want to know, and something tells me he wouldn't ask after that.

I bet good ole Dad isn't dying to tell him anyway. He probably wants to keep our family reunion a secret.

Guess they aren't as close as Dane thinks. However, it's not surprising that the faux son isn't treated much better than the blood daughter.

It sucks to be us.

Leading Dane to the room where I have the tailor set up doesn't take long. I knew that getting him to leave the premises would be a challenge, so I arranged for the man to be brought here.

Didn't take much convincing. In a smaller city like Redville, fitting the star defenseman for a championship-winning hockey team is a big deal.

Once we're down the hallway, I throw the door open.

"Right this way," I tell him, stepping in and then out of the way so that he can move ahead.

Inside is an older gentleman. I'd put him around sixty or sixty-five years old. He's got salt-and-pepper hair and a matching speckled beard. He's not very tall, taller than me, that's for sure, but that's not saying much since I'm petite at five foot three.

"Dane, this is George. He'll be fitting your tuxedo for the event."

Dane walks over and extends his hand. For as grumpy as he is, he's being a perfect gentleman. My eyes widen, and a barely audible sound leaves my mouth. What is happening?

Mr. Grumpy doesn't look so grumpy right now. Wow, I was not expecting this level of agreeableness.

I guess I shouldn't be shocked. He was very charming the first night we met, so he obviously has it in him not to be an utter ass.

"I was booked by your assistant, Miss Sinclair, to make a custom tuxedo. Would you first like to try on a few fits and see which style you like?"

"Sounds like a plan," Dane says, not even sounding sarcastic one bit.

"I set up a makeshift changing room. I hope that's okay. I can step out if you want more privacy." I point at the curtain I set up in the corner of the room.

"I'm fine."

I lean up against the wall to give them room and not to be in the way when Dane lifts his black T-shirt over his head.

What is he doing?

Then he starts to unbutton and unzip his jeans, and I realize he intends to try on the tuxedo in the main part of the room.

My cheeks feel flushed, and I can only imagine how red they must be. Great, I probably look like a tomato. Can someone put me out of my misery now? Think of something unsexy . . . spider. I grimace. Good, that's better than drooling.

"Um, do you want me to, um, leave?" Please say yes. I can't see this man naked or at least practically naked. I'll never survive that. It's bad enough that I want him fully dressed, but if I have to see him in his briefs, hell, I might combust.

"You're fine. Nothing you haven't seen before." At his words, I cough, and he smirks.

Great. Now he's playing this game. And in a very public place. How does he know this man won't talk outside these walls? He might be older, but money talks. Then again, keeping in Dane's good graces also pays well.

I cross my arms in front of my chest and smile back. "Yep. You've seen one, you've seen them all."

That wipes the smirk right off his face.

Point to me.

George walks over to the rack and hands him the first shirt.

I've been trying not to look at his body, but my curiosity about which shirt is in his hands has me pulling my gaze down.

Damn.

I shouldn't have done that.

His arms flex as he stretches it out to grab the material, and when he pulls back, his whole chest is on display to me.

When we spent the night together, it was way too dark to see anything, but now that I have a clear view, I wish I didn't look.

I knew in my heart he'd be perfection, but perfection has nothing on this man.

His body is just . . . wow.

That's it. No other word comes to mind. Wow.

With perfectly cut muscles, he's tall and lean and just—did I say wow?

I need to pull my gaze away because if I don't, he'll catch me, but I can't.

This man has a gravitational pull, and I'm stuck in it.

My eyes continue to travel south, trailing down his torso until I'm met with the most phenomenal V I've ever seen.

Stop looking, Josie.

"Josephine."

Is it hot in here? I swear the heat has turned on, but I know it's not the case since we're in an office outside a hockey rink.

It's freezing in here; I'm just burning up because of the way he looks at me. His stare sets an inferno in my belly. It lights me up.

What I'd do to have one more night. One when I can experience this man in all his glory, not just a quick little romp on the grass.

To take my time with him.

Kiss down his chest.

I'd lick the dip in his V—

"Hellfire."

That has me snapping my head up, and I meet the smoldering blue eyes that haunt my dreams. The way he looks at me makes my knees feel weak.

"You okay over there? You look a little flushed." Then he gives me a knowing smirk.

Like a bottle of cold water poured over a candle, the fire is snuffed, all trace of the flame gone.

Bastard.

chapter twenty-eight

Dane

SINCE THE DAY OF MY TUXEDO FITTING, I'VE PUT AS MUCH distance between Josie and me as possible. The girl is getting under my skin, and it's dangerous.

She's everywhere.

A damn temptation begging for me to sin.

She's too damn close.

The vision in front of me is what I've been hoping to avoid, but by some sick twist of fate, I can't.

I don't allow myself to touch the dangling fruit, despite the way it torments me, and in turn, I'm a grumpy motherfucker.

Oh, who am I kidding? I was always an asshole and have been since my parents died, but this is next level. I've had to build walls.

She walks past me to enter the house, and the vision should be illegal from this angle.

Did she change? There is no way she was wearing this the whole day. I would have lost my shit. I wouldn't have missed this outfit.

I trail my gaze up her body, from her tanned and toned legs past her skirt.

Fuck, an inch of her torso shows beneath her cropped shirt.

Why does she have to be his damn daughter?

I don't want a relationship, but I'd love to lose myself in her one more time.

Her trimmed waist begs me to reach out and touch her.

This is my own personal hell.

This is bad.

"After you," I grit out as Sherry gestures to the table.

"Thank you, Dane." She smirks. It's mocking, coy. It makes me think that despite all my best efforts, she knows how much I want her and wants to toy with me.

Little minx.

A cough escapes my mouth, and I pull my gaze from her. It lands on her dad, who's staring at me in an odd manner.

Does he see it too?

I hope not.

Josephine takes the chair on the left, leaving me sitting on the right, closer to Coach.

The sound of me pulling the chair back echoes around, making my descent seem much longer than it actually is.

"I'm so happy you're both here," Sherry says as she reaches across the table to grab the bottle of wine. "Wine?"

As if this hasn't been the norm lately. I've felt like it's back to normal, with the exception of Josephine's presence.

Josephine says nothing, so I do. "Yes, I'd love some."

Sherry walks over to where I'm sitting and pours me a glass. "Josie?"

"Sure. Thank you."

There's no missing the tightness of her voice. She doesn't want to be here, and it obviously has nothing to do with me.

Once Sherry pours herself and Coach a drink, Coach raises his glass. "To a job well done," he says to his daughter.

I look over at her, and her eyebrow is raised. "Job well done?"

"Molly will be back soon, so I think it's safe to move you back. Dane, she'll still help you of course. Congrats, you're officially back interning for the whole team."

Her face is serious, and she nibbles on her bottom lip.

My jaw feels tight.

Is she happy or sad about the news? Her reaction seems odd.

Not my problem. I grab the now filled glass and lift it. It's exactly what I need, like a refreshing pool on a hot day.

"Dane," Coach's voice rings through the dining room, and I turn my head back toward his direction. "Do you have anything to add?"

No.

What can I possibly say? Thanks for helping out. I almost threw you down on the floor three times a day to eat your perfect pussy, but I figured your dad would kill me if I did that, so I decided not to.

"It was great having you step in for Molly. You were very helpful, and I really appreciate it," I grit out.

Coach smiles, and I know he bought it. I glance at Josephine, and the little hellfire is having none of it. She's currently trying to stop herself from rolling her eyes.

"You sure?" she says, shocking the shit out of me.

"Of course," I answer.

"Well, it's not like you ever smile, so how would I know?" She lifts a mocking brow.

"I'm not that bad. I smile."

She shakes her head. "Lies. And we both know it."

"Josie," her dad reprimands her, and she shrugs.

"What? It's true. The man never smiles. Hell, I'd never smile either if I had to work with him all day." She inclines her chin toward her dad.

There's an awkward silence before Coach's chair scrapes against the floor. He stands up and leaves the room. Sherry gets up too, following on his heels.

"Ugh," Josephine groans, eyes closing in frustration. Or maybe something else?

"What was that about?" I snap, not understanding why she would insult him at his own table. "He's a good man," I tell her.

"I wouldn't know." There's sadness in those words, and now I really have questions.

I might've said it was none of my business, but now that I've witnessed this, I change my mind.

I'm about to ask her to clarify, but then Sherry strides back into the room. This time, holding plates. She doesn't look at either of us.

"Time for dinner." She places the two dishes in front of Josephine and myself before leaving, most likely to get her and Robert's dinner.

"While this looks delicious, it's not really what I'm in the mood for."

I don't respond. Nothing good will come from talking to her. Not when she most likely is going to say something to drive me crazy.

"Don't you want to know what I want?" she asks.

I continue to pretend she's not speaking.

"Oh, so you're ignoring me? That's not very nice, Mr. Grumpy. Don't you want to know what your little hellfire has to say?" Her voice drips with innuendo, and I'm hyperaware that I shouldn't engage.

What is she doing?

I shouldn't look at her or speak to her, but like a moth to a flame, I can't help it.

I pivot in my seat and meet her stare.

Her mouth opens, and her tongue slowly peeks out from behind her red lips before she runs it seductively over her plump skin.

Something is really off here. I know we have chemistry, and

I have no doubt she does want another round, but the way she's acting right now . . . there's more to it.

"I want you."

Fuck.

My dick hardens in my pants, and I grit my teeth. Not the time. *Not the fucking time.*

"That won't happen, Hellfire. And if I were you, I'd keep your voice down."

"But wouldn't it be fun if it did?"

God would it ever.

What I would do for just one more taste. Why are the forbidden ones that much sweeter?

After the longest dinner of my life, it's finally over. I managed to keep my eyes off Josephine throughout the rest of the meal by some miracle.

"Come on, Dane, let's go outside by the pool and have a glass of whiskey," Coach says, entering the room now that Josephine is nowhere to be seen.

"I should probably be going home," I say, glancing down at my phone.

"Don't be ridiculous. One drink. We need to talk shop."

We have more to talk about than shop, but I'm not about to say that out loud.

"Lead the way," I say.

He turns back around. "Meet me by the pool. I'll grab fresh glasses."

Since I've been here more times than I can count, I head toward the glass doors leading to the patio.

When I step outside, I see I'm not alone. A few steps ahead of me, Josephine is walking toward the guesthouse.

So that's where she's staying.

I assumed she was staying in the main house, but I guess, given her age and relationship with her dad, this makes more sense.

She keeps walking, and I take a seat at the table.

If she noticed me trailing her, she didn't acknowledge it.

The cool night air feels good right now. I inhale deeply, allowing my shoulders to uncoil. It's not that I'm always uptight, but it's hard to let my guard down.

Here, under a canopy of stars, it's easy to forget my troubles for a minute, even if one of them has just walked out of sight.

chapter twenty-nine

Josie

I COULDN'T HAVE PLANNED THIS BETTER IF I TRIED. WHILE I had no idea this opportunity would present itself, I like the thrill of thinking on my feet about how to drive him crazy.

It's probably reckless. Oh, who am I kidding? It's one hundred percent reckless, but this is what makes me feel alive.

As I open the door to the guesthouse an idea pops into my mind.

I'm going to go swimming.

That will not only drive him mad, but it will most likely piss my father off too.

Which is a wonderful bonus.

Making quick work, I throw my bathing suit on, the smallest and most indecent one I own.

It's barely a bathing suit. It's more like lingerie; with black lace and tiny strings keeping it together, it leaves nothing to the imagination.

I don't bother grabbing a towel before I head back outside.

The temperature tonight is chilly, but Sherry likes to swim in the early morning, so the pool is always heated to a balmy ninety-eight degrees.

They don't hear me at first, but when I make it to the edge of the pool, Dane sees me. His head jerks up, and my father follows his movement, turning to look at me.

"Josie? What are you doing out here?"

I cock my head. "Isn't it obvious? I'm swimming. Is that okay?" I challenge.

"Of course, you can. I've just never seen you swim since you've been here."

"Tonight, I felt like it." I shrug, and at that, I dive into the water and start to swim the length of the pool.

Beneath the water, I can't see anything. Almost like my future, its depths are unknown, but that's what I like.

Not knowing.

Just living.

Once I'm done with my lap, I pop back up and look toward where they are sitting.

My father is talking, hands raised in the air as he describes in detail and gestures God knows what, but it's not him I care about. It's Dane, who has yet to take his eyes off me.

He watches me intently, like a man possessed.

He's not moving. Hell, it doesn't even look like he's breathing.

Not remotely subtle, Dane.

His perusal lights me on fire.

He burns me from the inside out.

I need to have him.

And just like that, my father says something, drawing Dane's attention away, leaving me cold and a bit annoyed.

Whatever my father says to him makes him laugh, and a sharp pain radiates in my chest.

It hurts.

Why can't he look at me and laugh?

When he stares at me, sure, I know he wants me, but I can also tell he hates me for it.

He looks so relaxed at this moment.

Younger too.

It's evident in the softness of his brow, the lack of lines marring his skin, and even his shoulders are less tense, but it's his laughter that does me in. Every time the sound escapes his mouth, I can't help but grin, remembering our time in that bar and the way he acted just like that for me.

Then, a thought hits me in the gut.

I want to be the person to make him laugh, to make him smile. I want to be the reason he lights up a room with his presence.

I dive back under the water, continuing to swim. I go another lap before I emerge again, but this time, I see my father stand from his chair, place his glass down, and move toward the house.

I choose that moment to strike. The pool's ladder is only a few strokes away, so I head in that direction and then make my way back up onto the ground.

I stride in his direction, feeling like a panther stalking her prey.

"Where did my father go?" I ask, wanting to gauge how much time I have.

"He went inside to help Sherry."

"So, it's just us?" I run a finger over my clavicle, drawing it down toward my cleavage.

Small lines crease his face.

"Yes." He's angry. He doesn't want to be left alone with me.

Pool water drips off my body as I make my way closer to where he is.

Finally, I close the gap, standing so close to where he's sitting that my leg touches his thigh.

I look down at him, hungry and wanting.

He's watching me. His eyes are stormy, and there is a harsh look in them. It's hard to see in the dark of the night, but his eyes look black. Like all of the blue has been eaten up and replaced by darkness that matches his mood.

"Hellfire." A warning.

One I fully intend to ignore.

I reach forward. "Sinclair. Or maybe I should call you Sin?" I smirk.

My hand finds his hand, and his eyes fly to that spot where we touch.

"What are you doing?"

"What we both want me to do." My words hang in the air, and I wait for him to object, to say this isn't what he wants. That I'm not what he wants, but he doesn't speak. He holds my stare, watching me intently.

I take his hand in mine, when our fingers touch, a wave of heat spread through my body.

It's cold out, but I feel no chill.

Instead, the feeling of skin touching skin sends an electric current through my body.

I move my hand, and he lets me.

My eyes are trained on his, watching him watch me. I can tell he's wondering what I'll do. He knows he should stop, but he won't. He's too curious. Too caught in my spell.

He swallows, his Adam's apple bobbing.

I can almost feel the way his chest rises and falls with every heavy breath he takes. The anticipation is doing the same thing to him that it's doing to me.

I place his hand on my thighs, and his fingers trail up my leg. As he does, he wipes away the tiny crystals of water that cling to my skin. Soon, he's made it to the material of the bikini. His finger traces the thin lace, eyes bouncing between the thin fabric and my eyes.

I take a deep breath. "Do it."

His finger dips beneath. My heart rattles fiercely. Just as I think he will touch me, he drops his hand and stands abruptly.

"No."

And with that one word, the air suddenly chills to arctic levels, and I'm left standing alone and utterly disappointed.

chapter thirty

Dane

THE CHILL OF THE ICE SEEPS THROUGH MY GEAR, GROUNDING me in the familiar feeling I've grown to love and hate in equal measures. Wolfe and Aiden flank me, their presence a reassuring force amid the sound of skates slicing and sticks clashing.

As the puck slides toward us, instinct takes over. I dig my blades into the ice, pivoting with controlled aggression. Wolfe surges ahead, deftly flicking the puck to Aiden, who swiftly maneuvers around Hudson, who's our opponent for this drill.

I circle back, eyes fixed on Aiden as he weaves through the defense. Time slows as I anticipate his move, a split-second decision that could tilt the odds in our favor. With a flick of his wrist, Aiden sends the puck soaring toward me.

I intercept the puck in one fluid motion, skating hard toward the goal. Wolfe streaks alongside me, ready for any rebound.

Aiden's shout cuts through the rink, guiding me with pinpoint precision. I feint left, then right, drawing the goalie off balance.

I release the puck and watch it sail past the goalie's outstretched glove.

"Hit the showers," Coach yells, signaling the scrimmage is over with that point and so is practice.

Thank fuck.

My legs are burning. Coach seemed different today.

Like he was exorcising a demon.

What's up with him? Is this about dinner last night?

It makes me wonder if I'm missing a big part of the puzzle on his and Josephine's relationship. I know there's a story there, and I know I've said multiple times that it's not my business.

But for some reason, even though I tell myself that, I find that what she does is my business. It doesn't quite make sense, and I don't like the feeling, but I just have this sense that everything she does is important.

It makes no fucking sense.

One by one, each team member slowly files out of the rink, leaving it eerily quiet and empty.

I'm not ready to go yet, so I don't. Instead, I pull my arm back and slap another shot.

I need to get my head back into hockey, and sometimes, when I'm alone on the ice, it's the best time.

Coach knows I like to stick around on the ice and let the guys get a head start before I head back to the chaos of the locker room, so he doesn't even question it anymore. In the past, Aiden was the last off the ice, but recently, that's changed. *Now he rushes off.*

Today, even Coach hurried off the ice, seeming irritated.

At one point, he said something about not getting lazy since we won the Cup this year.

After seeing how much Hudson has been partying and how MIA Aiden has been, I think he's probably on to something.

I'm certainly not giving it my all.

If anything, I'm barely functioning these days.

I need the little hellfire to leave. I just haven't figured out a way to tell Coach she has to go without getting her in trouble.

I'm torn.

I need her gone, but I don't want this to look bad for her.

She didn't do anything wrong, but she's too damn tempting, and the more time I spend with her, the harder it is to remember why I can't just grab her in my arms and kiss the ever-living fuck out of her.

I head toward the edge of the rink. My teammates are long gone, leaving the showers open. I had been in my own little world, skating around and thinking about Josie, and I completely lost track of time.

I see movement to my left and skate around to see who's here, and when they come into view, my jaw tightens.

Can't this girl just stop with the bullshit? Is she trying to push me overboard?

Yes . . . yes, she is. She's tempting me on purpose.

"What are you doing?"

The question comes out harsh, and I immediately regret it when I get close enough to see her face. There's no mischief there. None of the typical bullshit she's been pulling to seduce me.

No. She looks almost . . . sad.

"I've never been on the ice before. I was just waiting until everyone was gone to get closer."

My mouth drops open. "What do you mean you've never been on a hockey rink?"

"I've never been on the ice." She lifts her hands and gestures around. "Any ice."

"How is that possible? Your father is one of the best NHL coaches in the world. Surely, you grew up on the ice."

She stiffens, not answering me, but fuck is my mind going crazy.

"Didn't your father—" I start, and she lets out a dry laugh.

"No." She shakes her head. "That would imply I knew my father before I came to work here."

I widen my eyes, and the ground beneath me feels like it's quaking. Did she just say what I think she did? Little puzzle pieces start to fit together and make a pattern.

"You didn't know your dad?"

"Nope."

She tries to make it sound like that doesn't bother her, but I know better. I can see the sadness in her eyes. I know that look all too well. I've seen it too many times on Molly not to recognize it for what it is.

"So, how did you end up here?"

"Isn't that the question we all want to know?" Her voice sounds stranded, and I take her in. Really take her in.

Her hands are by her side, digging into her leggings, and her features seem strained and tight.

There's no way she's going to tell me anything right now, and the truth is, I'm not even sure she knows.

She looks heartbroken, and usually, from past experience, it means you have too many questions and not enough answers.

"Come on." I extend my hand.

Her brow rises. "What?"

I wiggle my fingers. "Give me your hand."

Her eyes narrow in on first my hand and then my face. "Why?"

I roll my eyes with a sigh. "Do you ever stop asking questions, Hellfire?"

"Nope. And I don't think you would like me as much if I did."

"You think I like you?" I tilt my head down and smirk.

"You must, or you would have told me to fuck off."

I throw my head back and laugh, shaking my head. "The night is still young."

"That's true," she says.

"I won't be getting any younger if you make me wait," I grind out, trying to put as much irritation into my words as possible, but it doesn't land.

"Wait for what?"

I lower my arm and lift it once more for effect. "Again . . . give me your hand."

She grins, clearly enjoying the moment between us. Finally, after a few more seconds, she reaches out, and I take both her hands in mine.

"You don't have skates, but you don't need them today."

"Today?"

I pull her forward out onto the ice. She starts to slip, but I wrap my hand higher up her arm and grip her around the waist with my other hand.

"Next time, I'll come prepared and give you your first lesson, but for now, I'll do it this way."

I start to slowly push her backward and watch as her eyes widen. Is that fear I see?

She quickly clamps her lips together and straightens a little, but it throws off her balance, and she starts to slip. The silence of the rink reminds me that we are alone together, so I pull her closer, my eyes locking with hers.

Her breath hitches, and I wonder what she sees at this moment. What is she thinking?

She's fucking gorgeous. Quiet and timid on the ice. It's the first time I've seen her this vulnerable, and something about it is so damn endearing.

The need to protect is so strong, and I can't understand it.

I let her go for a second, reaching my hand out to gently brush a stray strand of hair from her face. Beneath my other hand, I feel her shiver, but I know it's not from the cold.

I move closer, tempting fate.

She's close enough now that our faces are almost touching.

"Hellfire, what are you doing to me?"

"I don't know," she whispers, her cold breath caressing my lips.

Just as we are about to kiss, a loud sound thunders through the space.

Probably a blessing. I skate us back to the edge of the ice, dropping her waist and helping her out.

"Oh, good, I was looking for you." Laurie stands just off the ice, looking right at me, not seeming to be fazed by the current situation.

"Well, you got me," I say, lifting both hands. "I was just showing Josephine the ice because she's never been on it before. I caught her trying to head out there on her own."

Laurie looks at Josie. "You'll break your neck that way."

"That's what I told her."

Laurie shakes her head. "Good thing you were here, Dane. Your father would kill me if something happened to you on my watch."

Josephine stiffens at the mention of her father, but I don't have long to think about it because Laurie points in the direction of the offices on the other side of the building. "I need you to choose a jersey and sign it."

I look toward the locker room and then gesture to what I'm wearing. "What? Now?"

"Yeah. It's being auctioned off at the Saints and Starling charity event next week. We need to get the item up on the website so people can start bidding."

The Saints and Starling event is the biggest fundraiser in the area. The money raised goes to help with legal fees for people who don't have the resources to get the representation they deserve.

Starling company is the local law firm that represents the Saints and has teamed up with the team to put the event on.

"There are a few different options," she says.

"Why don't we auction off more than one?" Josephine asks, and Laurie's eyes widen as though she hadn't thought about that.

Laurie quickly masks the fact that she was bested by the temp and places her hands on her hips as if she is annoyed. Laurie isn't cut out for this job, but her father knows the owner, and that makes

Laurie's position pretty sound, even if the team could use some young blood.

"I have a meeting I need to get to. Can we please get this done?" Laurie says, checking her phone.

"I can do it," Josephine says. Laurie purses her lips but looks back at her phone and sighs.

"Fine. The jerseys are in the locker room on the table. Just sign them," Laurie directs to me, turning her attention to Josie. "When he's done, take photos of each of them and email me a high-res JPEG. I'll add them to the auction site tonight."

Josephine nods, turning to me and giving me a look that basically says *is this woman for real?*

"I'll see you later." Laurie rushes off.

When she's out of sight, I turn back to Josephine. "Do you think you can handle those directives?"

I'm surprised she hasn't rolled her—strike that; she just did.

"Did you just roll your eyes at me?"

"Yep." She pops the *p*. "You're being an ass."

"Tell me something I don't know."

"Hmm," she says, tapping her chin. "I think onions are only good in salsa."

"What?"

"Onions don't belong in salad, on burgers, and absolutely, under no circumstances, should they ever be eaten like an apple."

"I can't be around you," I tease, shaking my head and doing my best to look serious.

"Too bad. You heard the woman. We have work to do for charity," she singsongs, and the sound is somehow beautiful and grating at the same time.

Because she's wearing me down.

"If this weren't for something important, I'd say no." I work to remove my skates, not wanting to wear the bulky footwear all the way to the locker room. "But this is for charity, so I'll play nice."

"Laurie explained what the money went to, and I think it's

incredible. So many families get the help they need despite their financial situation."

"It does change things. Everyone deserves the same resources."

"Yeah." It's all she says, and I wonder if she knows about my situation at all.

I don't want to know. Instead, I change the subject and spit out the first thing that comes to mind.

"Did you play any sports?"

She scrunches her nose. "No. I thought that would be obvious from our first talk."

"So, what were you interested in?"

She purses her lips. "We have work to do." And with that, she walks off.

I let out a long-drawn-out sigh. This girl is a pain in the ass. Maybe I should change her nickname to that.

Something tells me that won't go over well.

I follow her as we head to the locker room. Once we're inside, I start the long process of removing my uniform.

Josephine decides to take a seat on the bench.

She's bored, obviously, but she should count herself lucky that I'm even allowing her to stay in here. It makes it even more difficult to keep my hands to myself.

We're in an empty locker room, completely alone. Nobody would know if I caved.

Not happening, Dane. Get your head out of your ass.

I might not touch, but that doesn't mean I can't play her own games.

Once I'm naked from the top up, I turn to face her.

The moment she notices me, I need to refrain from grinning.

I can't give this girl an inch. If she thinks there is a chance I'm interested, she will pounce, which is not something that can happen, but it doesn't mean I can't enjoy the way she looks at me.

She stares as though she's parched, and I'm the glass of water she needs to survive.

It's been a long time since a woman has gotten me interested, and it's a fucking crime that it has to be her.

Because I am interested.

If I could, I would take her right here and now.

The way her pouty lips part. There is nothing more I'd like to do than separate those lips and feed her my cock inch by inch.

Shit.

And now my dick is hard at that thought.

Think of something gross.

Something to turn me off.

I close my eyes for a beat, taking a long, deep breath. My mind goes blank. Nothing can penetrate the image running through my brain of her on her knees in front of me, sucking my cock—

"Dane."

I shake my head and meet her gaze.

"Yeah, Hellfire." My voice sounds lower, huskier.

"Oh, now I'm hellfire again?"

"Well, you're making me late to my appointment, so yeah, you're a hellfire."

"What appointment?"

"The one I'm about to make," I say, admitting that there is currently no appointment.

"For?" she drawls out, circling her hand as if to tell me to get on with it.

"I need a massage."

She swallows. "What?"

"I need to book a massage. My shoulder has a knot."

She takes a step closer, and I see that her nose is scrunched, and her cheeks are pinched in.

"You okay?" I ask.

"Just concerned about you. Can you put the jersey on so I can take pictures of you wearing them and then I'll grab the signed pictures after?"

"While I appreciate your concern, I just want to sign these

jerseys and get on with my day. But if I must wear it for a photo op, let's get it over with."

She tosses the first one to me, and I lift my arm to slide into the jersey. Just as the shirt is being dropped over my head, I let out a groan of pain.

I stop moving, and so does Josephine.

"Are you okay?"

"Hence the needed massage. I pulled a muscle."

Josephine rushes to me until we are close enough that I can smell the lavender in her soap.

Before I know what's happening, her hand lifts up, and her warm fingertips are on my skin.

"What are you doing?" I growl. My brain short-circuits from her touch.

"Trying to help you. I thought—"

"That's the problem, you didn't think . . ." I'm about to say more, but I wince in pain this time.

"That's it, let me see." Placing her hands on my shoulders, she sits beside me.

Even though I know I should object, I don't. Her touch feels too good as she massages the tight muscles.

The locker room is quiet except for the puffs of air I'm expelling.

The more she kneads, the more labored my breathing gets, but the knot is almost gone, and it seems she won't stop until the knot no longer exists.

With each second that passes, I can't help but wonder why I'm pushing her away so hard. Maybe it would be easier not to.

But then I remember her dad, the way he helped in those early years, and how much I needed him.

Being good might be more painful than the pulled muscle.

chapter thirty-one

Dane

HATE IS TOO STRONG A WORD, BUT MY CHEST FEELS TIGHT whenever I have to attend a fundraiser.

Even though we're here to raise money for a cause near and dear to my heart, I'm not too fond of these functions.

It's a necessary evil, but it reminds me too much of the past.

Especially when I look at my reflection in the mirror. Currently, my jaw is locked, brow furrowed, and not one hair out of place, but if you knew me enough to know what to look for, you'd know I wasn't happy. The reason I don't belong is because the man I am tonight screams that I belong and, worse, that I want to be here. Spoiler alert: I don't.

These nights always remind me of my father. Of the night when my life changed. It reminds me of him walking down the stairs, dressed in a tuxedo, my mother with him, and how he said he'd see me later.

How my mom gave me a kiss and told me to be good. I wasn't, and she died because of my mistake.

So even though I wasn't driving the car, and I didn't kill my mom, whenever I look at myself in the mirror, I see my father.

All the parts of him I hate.

I lift my hand to my tie and center it, then adjust my tuxedo jacket. Once everything is in place, I take a deep breath and walk out of the bathroom.

Tonight is already in full swing. The grand ballroom looks opulent, adorned with large chandeliers and rich burgundy table-cloths. Sheer drapes add to the timeless luxury, and it makes me want to roll my eyes.

None of this is needed. It's so extra.

I peer around the room and my hands fist. The who's who of Redville elite are all here, milling about, glasses raised, praising themselves like they did something important. Sure, they helped raise money, but in my mind, no one needed to take credit for their good deeds. The moment you do, it loses its soul.

The women in attendance are decked to the nines, dripping in jewels, dolled up, and begging for attention. All the guys from the team are here, scattered around, doing their best to work the room.

I should be mingling too, but I'm searching for one person instead. I'm having no luck finding her, but as if the crowd can hear me, they part, and she's there.

Josephine is always gorgeous, but today she looks like a goddess. She's wearing a stunning red gown that clings to her curves in all the right places. Her blond hair is swept up, exposing the graceful line of her neck.

What I wouldn't do to touch that neck. To caress her soft skin. But that's not in the cards, and I've been trying my hardest to stay away from her since she came to work for the team. The problem is, no matter where I go, she's there.

She haunts my every thought and my every dream.

It's a real problem.

Astonishingly, for the first time since I've known her, I don't even care.

I'm not the only one drawn to her either. My gaze drifts around the room, and a bunch of my teammates are staring, most likely thinking the same thing I am.

A drink will help tamp down my need for her.

With a new goal in mind, I stride to the nearest bar.

Once there, I rest my hand on the sleek marble, then lean forward to get the bartender's attention.

"Whiskey, neat."

My new location is even worse. Now I have a clear shot of the little hellfire, holding court and laughing away with random men who would love nothing more than to bring her home for the night.

Must be nice for them not to be burdened with the desire to have something you can never have. Soon, a drink is in my hand, and I lean up against the bar, nursing it, and try my best not to watch her. All is lost, however, when Hudson gallops up to her, like a prince in a fairy tale who would happily slay the beast for a moment in her bed.

It's too bad I like the guy so much because I'm having a hard time not wanting to kill him for how close he's currently standing next to her. I have no business being jealous. She's not mine, but it doesn't stop the fact that I want her, and I can't stand that my friend isn't burdened by the guilt of what Coach would say if I had her.

Hudson and Robert don't have the same relationship that we do. Robert has been the one stable person in my life despite Molly.

I shouldn't jeopardize that relationship. *Right?*

He reaches out a hand, and she takes it; then, before I can even blink, they're on the dance floor.

Fuck it, I'm going to kill him.

Fine. I won't, but I watch him dance with my girl. *She's not your girl.*

She should be, though. She should be in my arms, not his.

Breathe.

Nothing has happened to warrant kicking his ass, it's not like— goddamn. His hand is practically touching her ass.

Friendship be damned. I'm putting an end to this. I hate how jealous I am. It bubbles up inside me like a volcano erupting, and before I can stop myself, I'm striding across the space until I'm beside them.

They're still dancing, but Hudson stops when I playfully shove him.

The bastard has the audacity to smirk at me. "How can I help you, Daney-boy?"

I shoot him a look that would scare a lesser man, but Hudson is too rambunctious to sense a threat. "I'm cutting in."

Now, his smirk is a full-fledged smile. "Are you now?" He's loving this, loving my weakness. Hudson has been hinting for the past few weeks despite never letting on my history with Josephine. Despite his playboy persona, he's observant as all hell—a genuinely good trait unless it's aimed at you.

I suck in a deep breath. "Yes, asshole, I am. I need to talk to Josephine."

"Josephine?" He turns to look at her, but look isn't the right word. He undresses her lazily with his eyes. "Is that your *full* name?" His voice has dropped an octave, the pitch he has reserved for his future conquests. *Is this asshole for real?* I cross my arms at my chest, trying my best not to strangle my friend.

"What the fuck do you think Josie stands for? Michelle?" I bite out. I should really rein it the fuck in. I'm losing it, and I'm usually more stoic than an ancient rock.

Josephine, on the other hand, seems to be eating this shit up. "It is." She beams up at him, cheeks flushed.

"I like it, although I like *Josie* better."

"Hudson," I practically growl.

"Oh, you're still here." He lets out a sigh. "Fine. But, Josie, you better save a dance for me."

If it were possible for smoke to billow out of my ears, it would. Turning in her direction, I look at her face to see her answer. A small smile tips her lips, but she doesn't say anything. *Smart girl.*

Hudson fucking bows in Josephine's direction, and she goddamn giggles, and then it's just the two of us.

From this close, the image in front of me is even more beautiful than I could have ever imagined.

So fucking breathtaking it hurts.

Her features seem softer, and her blue eyes sparkle like the ocean.

What has this girl done to me? Here I'm the grumpiest asshole on my best day, but one minute in her presence, and I'm practically waxing poetic.

This whole line of thought has me unhinged, my mind moving a million miles a minute until the only thing I can do to shut my brain off is pull her into my arms.

Shit.

The moment I feel her pressed against me, it hits me like a ton of bricks. *I'm fucked.*

I don't think I have the power to continue to push her away.

"Are we going to dance or not?" she chides, and her words set me into action. With my hand on her lower back, my fingers caress her bare skin, and I start to sway her body.

"Can you be mindful of my hair?" she asks. "It's full of pins."

I arch a brow. "What do you mean?"

"You know, when you drag me back to your cave." And then, taking a deep breath, she asks, "What the hell was *that*?"

I try to find an excuse but sigh. I'm too tired for this shit. "I didn't like him touching you," I admit.

Josephine glares up at me. "So . . . you decided—what? Only you can touch me? Um, I don't like taxes, but I don't go around killing IRS officers, jeez."

My hand tightens against her back. "I didn't get that far. But seeing you together made me . . ."

Her feet stop moving. "Made you what?"

Despite the music flowing around us, the air is tense with our silence.

I clear my throat. "Angry. Jealous. Take your pick."

Josephine's eyes soften. "You can't act like a caveman in public. My father—"

I nod. There's no denying she's right. "I know."

Josephine lets out a sigh before she starts moving again, and we continue to sway our bodies together, my fingers tracing small circles on her back.

For a moment, the knots in my shoulders uncoil, and it feels like anything is possible, but then the song ends and transitions to a different one.

I halt my movement, feet now frozen to the floor. "This dance is over."

Silence engulfs us before she shakes her head. I look down at her, noticing a tight jaw and eyes that seem to burn into mine. "Wow."

"Wow, what?"

She draws in a deep breath. "That didn't take long at all."

I have no idea what she's talking about. "What didn't take long?"

"For you to become an asshole again." She takes a step away from me, and I miss the comfort I find in her touch immediately. Josephine smooths down her dress, and once it's back in place, she turns on her heels without another word, heading toward the exit.

I trail her. "Where are you going?"

She doesn't answer, and I follow her, even when she walks down the wrong hallway, going God knows where.

Her steps are wobbly, either from drinking too much or from anger, but I'd put my money on the latter. She stumbles forward, and for a second, I think she's going to fall, but I'm quick on my feet, reaching my arms out to catch her before she does.

Once in my arms, I pull her close to me.

She feels perfect in my arms. When I look down at her, I want to kick myself. Her big blue eyes are locked on mine, but the way she's biting down on her lower lip makes my heart beat faster. They look so fucking plump and kissable right now. I want to bite that lip, suck on her skin.

I should let her go now, but with our bodies entwined, I don't want to. I like how she feels in my arms. I lean in. She exhales, and we're so close I can almost taste the mint on her lips.

I want to. Her lids flutter shut, and I pull her even closer.

"What are you doing?" she whispers.

"I don't fucking know?"

The sexual tension crackles through the air. I don't think, I just act, crashing my lips to hers. The kiss is desperate, and with each swipe of my tongue, she holds me tighter, fingers digging into the back of my neck.

I might die if I'm not inside her—now.

"Fuck," I grit out; my throat feels rough, like I've swallowed gravel.

The buildup to this moment has been excruciating, but now that we are finally here, I don't want to stop. I pull back for a second before I descend again . . .

The kiss intensifies. We both need more. I glide my fingers down the exposed skin of her neck, dipping down her collar and trailing over the swell of her breast.

"I need you. Now." I pull away from her, take her hand in mine, and set off. I'm not sure where I'm going, but I need to find a place for us to be alone.

Finally, I spot a door and throw it open. I'm lucky it wasn't locked, and I'm even luckier when I see a table in the middle of the room.

I turn toward her, pick her up in my arms, and place her on the table.

My hands lift the hem of her dress until it bunches at her waist. She wraps her arms around my neck, and I close the small distance between us and kiss her, then I deepen the kiss. Our mouths collide in a frenzy of passion. "Fuck," I say against her lips as I stop kissing her.

"What's wrong?" Her fingers tighten in my hair as she tilts my face down to look at her.

"I don't have a condom."

One hand drops to caress my jaw, her soft fingers trailing across my skin. "I'm on the pill and have never had sex without one."

"Me either," I admit before lifting my brow. "You sure?"

"Yes, please. I need you," she rasps, and with my free hand, I unzip my pants, stroking myself from root to tip.

The sound of the party drifts across the air, reminding me I don't have time to worship her.

That's a shame because I would give anything to take my time with her, enjoy every second, and make her come as many times as I can.

My heart jolts in my chest as I press myself against her heat. She's so goddamn wet, I can't wait to sink inside her.

Soon, but not yet.

I swirl the head of my dick on her clit, then at her entrance, collecting the moisture.

"More," she begs, and I push forward, just the tip, torturing both of us. "Fuck me already, Dane."

I slam into her hard and fast, and she gasps when I bottom out inside her.

Tilting my head forward, I admire the sight before me. My cock buried to the hilt.

"Look at us," I groan, and she drops her chin to see what I see. A moan escapes her mouth as I pull back, my cream-covered cock gleaming.

Her mouth drops open as I thrust back in, every nerve ending in my body rejoicing. With my free hand, I find her clit, and rub in rhythm with my thrusts. She cries out, and I stop my movements.

"Hellfire, I'm going to need you to be quiet. Unless you want your father to hear us?"

Her hand reaches up to cover her mouth, and I move again.

I'm not sure if it's the idea of being caught or finally being inside her again, but it doesn't take me long to feel my balls tightening. I need her to come. I flick her clit harder and fuck her deeper.

"Yes," she mutters behind her fist. "Just like that."

I grab her hand from her mouth and seal my lips over hers. She tastes like champagne and strawberries. She's the most decadent forbidden fruit, and I can't get enough.

A moan escapes her, and I swallow the sound, fusing us closer until our tongues meet in a frenzy of soft strokes that soon become nips and bites.

Josephine's fingers find purchase in my locks, pulling at the roots until the point of pain.

It doesn't matter, though; her need fuels me. I swirl my tongue in her mouth and clutch her tighter, picking up my pace.

Her walls tighten around me, and in turn, my dick jerks as I fill her up. Moans escape us both, and our bodies tremble together.

For a moment, we just catch our breath, but then reality sets in. We aren't safe here. We need to leave.

I pull out, and she sighs as I do.

"Now what?"

"I really don't know, Hellfire."

And I don't. All I know is I don't want to let her go yet.

chapter thirty-two

Dane

Hudson: @Dane, broke your hockey stick on accident... : (

Dane: You WHAT?!

Hudson: Who knew those things don't bend like that?

Hudson: Kidding.

Hudson: But look who finally resurfaced after stealing my date last night.

Dane: She wasn't your date. You danced for two seconds, and I relieved her of your two left feet.

Hudson: Ouch. : (Someone is grumpy. I take it you didn't get laid?

Dane Sinclair left the chat.

chapter thirty-three

Josie

NERVOUS ENERGY COURSES THROUGH ME AS I ENTER THE practice arena.

How will today go?

My stomach churns as thoughts I shouldn't even be having twist through my brain.

Will he be an asshole? Will he ignore me? And the worst one of them all . . . will he tell me it was a mistake?

I'm not sure how I'd deal with that one. Knowing me, I'd probably go to war with him, first move, swap his shampoo with bleach.

Dramatic much?

With my shoulders pulled back and all the false bravado I can muster, I proceed to the rink. The sharp scent of ice filters in through my nostrils and causes my jaw to chatter.

Okay, the trembling is from nerves, not the temperature. Although it is chilly, I always wear a sweater or hoodie when I'm working here.

Today, I'm wearing a tight-fitting, long sleeve black V-neck shirt that leaves absolutely nothing to the imagination. My black fitted jeans also were carefully picked to cause Dane to drool.

I need to be prepared just in case he rejects me. Revenge outfit for the win.

The closer I get, the louder the jeers of the guys become as their skates cut through the ice as they practice their drills.

I'll inevitably have to talk to him, so it might as well be now.

It's funny how much things can change in twenty-four hours. Yesterday, my main concern was making sure his tuxedo would fit, and today, I'm worried if he'll acknowledge what we did yesterday.

I'm not sure which scenario is worse.

Probably the one where he acts like it didn't happen, seeing as I, on the other hand, have replayed every detail of last night over and over again in my mind.

Every moment.

Every touch.

Every breath.

They're all seared away, and even if I wanted to pretend it didn't happen, I wouldn't be able to.

What's also etched into my brain is how he reacted right after.

From where I'm perched on the table, I watch under hooded lids as he tucks himself back into his pants.

For a moment, I think things will be okay, but then, like a curtain dropping over him, the possessive man who couldn't get enough of me only moments ago is replaced, and the man standing next to me is someone else.

The haze from his orgasm is long gone, replaced by a tight jaw and hollow blues that won't meet mine.

Great.

One step forward and fourteen steps back, apparently.

This is exactly the situation I didn't want. Anxiety clings to my exposed skin like sweat on a hot day. I take a deep breath and push down the feeling of rejection clawing its way through my bones and fortify my walls.

Hard and no longer penetrable, I pat down my dress and stand from the table, taking great care to steel my spine at the same time.

"Never let them see weakness." Words Mom always said, and now I wonder if her disposition has to do with my father leaving her. Am I doomed to be like her too?

An angry shriek has me looking over to the far side of the ice. The reason for all my current problems, my father, is there barking orders at the guys.

I continue walking as Dane moves to the bench, and Wolfe, the other defenseman, steps onto the ice to take his place. When I'm finally a few feet away, he sees me.

My stomach feels tight, and my knees are wobbly.

Dane, of course, looks as grumpy as always, and I can't tell if that's a good or bad thing.

"Josephine," he says, his voice husky. This man could read the dictionary, and I'd listen. In his uniform, helmet off, he looks even more delicious than normal. His dark hair is slightly damp from playing, and his eyes sparkle in a way that gives me hope.

"Dane," I reply, struggling to keep my voice steady. "I, um, is there anything I can help you with today, or should I find Laurie?"

There's an awkward silence, and I shift my weight from one foot to the other.

"Yeah, I think it's best you talk to Laurie."

My heart hammers so violently in my chest I fear it might explode.

"About yester—"

I raise my hand to stop him from speaking. I can't take the rejection—*again*. Last night was more about not getting caught, but this, this is different. To top it off, it's bad enough that only ten feet away is my father, a man who most likely knew all about me and never wanted anything to do with me, but now this. "It's nothing. No biggie. Forget it even happened."

Dane's jaw tightens, and for a second, he looks like he wants to say something, but he doesn't. The silence stretches between us again.

This time, it's heavier and more uncomfortable, if that's even possible.

From the left-hand side of the rink, I can hear the distinct sound of laughter and look over to see Hudson basically tackling Mason.

For someone who doesn't know these guys, it would look like a fight is about to break out, but I know them, and this is just some friendly roughhousing.

"I should go," Dane says, moving closer to the ice.

"If you need me, let me know."

I turn and walk away, blood still pumping heavily in my veins. Finally, when I make it to the hallway near the offices, I let out the breath I've been holding.

That wasn't so bad . . . oh, who am I kidding? It was awful.

Why do I have to be so damn awkward?

I lean up against the wall, taking deep inhales to calm myself.

You know what? Who cares? Dane Sinclair doesn't want me. Big deal. It's fine. That's his loss.

I need to focus on what's important. Getting the job done, building a résumé, and getting the fuck out of Dodge.

That's it.

I don't have time for a handsome defenseman. No matter how skilled he is, on and off the ice. I have too much on my plate for his shit. Despite my reservations about coming to work for the Saints, I see the opportunity it brings, and I'm going to use it.

I'm going to kick ass and make a life for myself.

chapter thirty-four

Josie

YESTERDAY SUCKED.

I'm not hopeful that today will be any better.

Lord, I'm late.

Something I try not to be. I might not be here of my own volition, but I intend to do the best job I can. I want to get a good reference and get out of here before things implode. Which should be very soon, judging by my dynamics with Dane. *And* sperm donor.

I turn the corner to head toward the locker room when I stop dead in my tracks.

"So, did you miss me?" A soft voice giggles.

My back goes ramrod straight, and every muscle in my body feels tight, like a rubber band ready to snap.

Who in the hell is this girl?

And a better question: why are her arms wrapped around Dane's neck?

Breathe.

Throwing a shit fit won't go over well. Kicking her ass won't get me any brownie points either. This doesn't change the fact that I want to rip her off him, bang my hands on my chest, and tell her he's mine.

Wow. I'm pathetic.

What has gotten into me?

One kiss—okay, it was more than a kiss—and I'm already gone for this man.

I take a step forward from the shadows, where I'm hiding, and make my presence known.

This is a good thing.

He rejected me yesterday, and now he's moved on. That means by the time the season starts at the end of the week on Friday, I'll be over him.

The first game is an away game, with the Saints playing the Chicago Warriors. I'll be going with the team, and since I wouldn't know what that meant for Dane and me, I'd be worried and nervous all day. Yeah. This is a good thing. Now I know where I stand.

Time to rip the Band-Aid off on this awkward moment. I cough, and the girl turns to look at me. Her eyes narrow.

Shit. She's gorgeous. With dark wavy brown hair and sun-kissed skin, she looks like she just left a beach. Probably to pose for a magazine, seeing how tall she is. Bitch. Well, what did I expect? Of course, Dane would date a supermodel.

A giant knot forms in my stomach, and I swear I can feel sweat forming on my brow. Is this his wife? Wait, he doesn't have a wife. I'd know if he did, *right*? She's also too young for him.

Actually, she looks my age. Double shit. Pot meet kettle. She's perfect for him.

"Are you Josie?"

"Josephine," Dane corrects, and I look from her to him. I feel like a fish out of water. I'm not sure how to answer.

"That's me," I try to put on a cheerful tone.

Then, the girl moves away from Dane and approaches me. Her

arms are raised, and I brace for a slap, but that doesn't happen. Instead, she launches herself at me and hugs me.

"Josie, it's so good to meet you. Thank you so much for taking care of my brother when I was away."

"Molly?"

"Duh. Who else can love this big, grumpy asshole?" She laughs.

Okay, heart, time to regulate. Passing out while in front of Dane's sister won't be cool.

I take a deep breath, willing myself to calm before I cough and then speak. "You have a point there. I didn't think you were coming back until Thursday." According to Dane, she wouldn't return until then. Wonder what changed.

"My brother needed me—"

I look up at her, and she shakes her head. "Not that you did anything wrong. He just can't start the season without me. Tradition and all." She shrugs like it's no big deal.

"Got it," I mutter. Even though her excuse makes sense, something tells me it's a lot more than that. It feels almost like her brother wants to stay far away from me.

That idea sounds more probable. It also makes me want to vomit.

"Let's go grab coffee and chat, then I'll tell Coach I'm back."

I wonder what that will mean for me. Sure, I've been doing work that's for the whole team, but the majority of my time has been helping Dane.

I follow Molly toward the back office, and when we get there, my father sees her. His face lights up, eyes soft, and he's wearing the largest smile I have ever seen on his face. He's never looked at me like that. My stomach hollows.

He looks at her like a daughter. Like when she's around, his life is complete.

I'm his actual biological daughter, and he doesn't look at me like that.

It's soul-crushing.

A weight presses down on my chest, and it feels like I can't breathe. It feels like a hand has reached into my chest, squeezing my heart.

I need to get out of here, but for some reason, I can't will my legs to move. The longer I stay, the more I will shatter, yet I can't turn away. Can't stop the pain that's filling my veins.

"Molly, you're back early," my father says as he pulls her in for a hug.

"Between us, I missed home." Her words sound muted and distant next to the loud ringing in my ears.

I look at her and take in her soft features. "I'm not used to being away from family that long."

My last bit of strength slips away.

"I can understand that." He nods as he steps back. A sad, pathetic sound squeaks out from behind my closed lips. My father turns in my direction, and his mouth drops open the moment he sees me. I think he just realized what he said and how it would affect me, or maybe that's wishful thinking.

My heart thumps violently, and I fear it will break in half.

Can that even happen?

Mom once told me that you can die from a broken heart. Maybe she was referring to my father. Maybe her former self perished from his rejection.

Tears form in my eyes. I want to weep with jealousy, with how unfair this all is, but I can't. I need to stay strong. With each second that passes, more liquid collects, and I know without a doubt that if I don't get out of here right now, I'll fall to the ground and sob.

I turn back to Molly but don't meet her stare. "I'll meet you in a few minutes. I just forgot something."

Without waiting for her to object, I dart back in the direction we came, looking for an exit, for somewhere to go.

Finally, I see a door and throw it open.

It's a closet. A large one, but still a closet. This one houses equipment.

The moment the door closes behind me, I start to breathe heavily. I think I'm going to hyperventilate.

My lungs feel heavy, and it's hard to pull air in. I lean forward, placing my hands on my knees, and try to gulp in air. The sound of the door opening filters in through my ears, but I'm too lost in my mind to turn to see who's walked in. Then a hand touches my back.

It's comforting.

"Shh, you're okay." *Dane.*

He moves in closer until his presence feels large around me.

My shoulders shake until Dane envelops me in his arms, pulling me close. The warmth from his embrace calms the tremors working their way through my body.

"Take a deep breath, okay?" I follow his orders. Inhaling slowly. Then exhaling.

"You're okay," he coos, and I want to believe him. Want to cling to his words as if they are a life raft that will protect me and keep me safe.

Life doesn't play out like that, though.

Even if, for a moment, the world outside ceases to exist while in his arms, it will all come rushing back to drown me the second I walk out the door.

I'd still have no answers from my mother.

I'd still be living with a father who didn't want to be part of my life.

And I'd still be desperately attracted to a man who would never fight for me.

Dane brushes away a tear on my cheek with his thumb.

I can't imagine what I look like. My eyes sting, and my nose most likely is red and puffy.

A real picture of perfection.

It takes a few minutes of following his breathing prompts, but soon my heart is no longer racing, and I'm feeling more myself.

His hand reaches out, and his fingers lift my jaw.

"What happened?" His voice sounds gruff.

I try to pull away, but he won't let me. "I don't want to talk about it." Resting my head on his chest, I listen to the steady rhythm of his heart. The sound grounds me, keeps me present in the moment, and allows me a brief second of solace before reality crashes back in with the sound of his sigh.

"Talk to me. I know all too well about keeping stuff inside you, but sometimes it does help to let it go."

"And you know this how? You talk about all your issues?"

Dane inclines his head down, forcing our eyes to lock. "Hellfire . . .Talk to me."

"I'm not a hellfire now. Am I?"

"You will always be a hellfire. Even if you don't think so."

I search his eyes but don't know what I'm looking for anymore. "Because I'm always trouble?"

"No."

"Then I don't understand."

"You're a hellfire. You're strong. Powerful. Independent. You take no shit from anyone. March to the beat of your own drum. You walk the tightrope."

I shake my head. "I take more shit than you can even imagine."

He pulls back, placing his fingers under my chin, not allowing me to look away from him. "Then tell me what's going on."

"It's not your burden. We aren't anything. We just fucked, *twice*." My snarky attitude probably pisses him off, but I don't care. Right now, I'm allowed to act like a petulant child.

He scrubs at his eyes. "What am I going to do with you?"

"Fuck me again." I shrug.

He shakes his head at my suggestion but having him this close has me all types of confused. His presence calms me, and I want him. I want to touch him and feel him. "I can't."

"Please." I place my hands on his chest and trail them down. I dip one hand inside his sweatpants.

"Fuck. I can't think when you do that."

I run my other hand over his now hard dick. "Do what?"

181

"Touch me."

"Oh, does this bother you?" I slip my hand under his waist-band, then under the material, and palm his hard dick in my hand. Stroking him. He tilts his pelvis up.

"You have to stop."

"Make me." I drop to my knees in front of him.

chapter thirty-five

Dane

WHEN I FOLLOWED HER, I DIDN'T KNOW WHAT TO EXPECT, but it certainly wasn't her dropping to her knees with my dick in her hands.

The sight before me has my brain short-circuiting. Her small hand grips my cock, the soft pad of her finger feathering over the crown. If her tongue touches me, I'll lose my shit.

I'm liable to come from that alone.

Get yourself together, Sinclair.

It takes a second, but finally, I snap out of it.

Looking down at her, I see a Josephine I've never seen before. The vision has my chest tightening. The hellfire I have come to know is long gone, replaced by a broken woman.

Sure, she looks the same, trying to sling a false bravado of being strong, but as she looks up at me, trying her best to make me think she wants me right now, I can see past it all.

Her eyes are hollow. Despite her straight spine, she looks fragile.

I hate it.

Josephine should never look this way.

I don't think before I act. Grabbing her by the arms, I yank her up to her feet and wrap myself around her, cradling her to my body.

The moment her face collides with my chest, the sobs start again. "It's okay, I have you."

She hiccups through another cry, then tilts her head up. Her crystal-blue eyes are wet with tears. They look almost iridescent. "No. You don't."

Her small hands push against my chest, separating us. I open my mouth to stop her, but I'm too late.

She's already walked out the door.

chapter thirty-six

Dane

W HAT A FUCKING DAY.
Being near her was torture. Watching her cry was fuck-ing awful.

The only good part of the day is having Molly back.

Which is the only reason I said yes to Hudson's invite to go to the bar. Molly and the rest of the team are here. The only problem is, it's not just them.

Hellfire is here too.

So what am I doing? Drinking alone at the opposite side of the bar.

I'm not much better than my father, am I?

"Are you ever planning on coming over and saying hi, big brother?" I turn over my shoulder to see Molly right behind me.

I arch a brow, and she furrows hers. "I don't think so."

"You can't always be this antisocial, Dane."

"Sorry, do we know each other?"

Molly's lip twitches, then she shakes her head at me. "I'm going to go hang out with everyone. When you get your head out of your ass, join me." She stalks off in the direction of the rest of the team, and I lift my drink and take another swig.

To my surprise, no one else comes over to coax me to join them, which is fine by me. I'm more than happy doing my own thing.

Once my glass is empty, I stand from the barstool, and one thing hits me right away. I'm pretty drunk. Not shit-faced, but definitely feeling good.

The good news is I don't have a game tomorrow.

The bad news is, I do have one later this week, and being drunk even a few days before can fuck up my game.

The depressing news is that I couldn't muster two shits to save my life. And therein lies the problem.

I look toward where *she* sits with Hudson and the other guys on the team.

Come out, they said. *It'll be fun,* they said.

Bullshit. Not being able to touch her isn't fun. Instead, I'm just pissed.

Needing a moment to myself, I move toward the back door of this place. I don't want to talk to any of them, and I certainly don't want to see her having the time of her life, so instead, I choose to head out the door.

Once outside, the brisk October air hits me in the face.

It does help sober me up. Maybe it was the haze of the bar and the company that had me feeling so fucked up, but now in the darkness of the night with the wind blowing in my face, I'm no longer feeling like a weight has been dropped on my chest.

Eventually, I'll have to go back into the bar and settle up with Hudson. I don't need him buying my drinks, but I need some distance right now to get my head on straight.

I walk a few more steps until I see the small park adjacent to the bar. Since I have no desire to socialize, this is perfect. It's empty. No lights, no people, just calm.

I take a seat and close my eyes, inhaling slowly and then exhaling. What is it about her that has me tied up in knots?

It's her presence.

I want her near me, and when I can't have her, it feels like I'm drowning.

This is why Coach should never have offered her to me as an assistant. Now that I've tasted what life would be like with her in my presence, I don't know how I'll go back.

I take another deep breath, and when I exhale, I hear a sound beside me.

"Why are you out here all alone?" The voice I dream about says from behind me. I turn over my shoulder and peer up at her.

"The better question is, why are you out here? Shouldn't you be inside, laughing at Hudson's jokes?"

There's no hiding the jealous tone in my voice. If she hears it, she's gracious enough not to make any indication. Instead, she gives me a small smile. "I saw you leaving, and I wanted to say . . ."

"Say what?" I cock a brow, interested to know what she came all the way out here to say.

"Thank you for today." She bites on her upper lip, looking a bit uncomfortable.

I shake my head. "You don't have to thank me. I'm here for you if you need me. I know we're a bit of a trainwreck—"

She arches her brow. I smirk. "Okay, a whole lot of a trainwreck. But I care, you know?"

"I care about you, too." She reaches out but stops herself before she touches me. "Want company?"

I shrug, which seems to be an open invitation for her to lower herself onto the bench beside me.

"What's going on with you?" she asks.

I lift my hand and scrub at my face. "I don't know what you're talking about."

"You're extra grumpy," she clarifies.

"Wow. I'm grumpier than normal? Is that what you're saying?"

"It is. What gives?"

I pivot in my seat to face her, which is probably a stupid idea. It's easier to pretend it's not about her when I'm not looking at her, but when I see her under the moonlight, I can't deny the pull she has over me. She looks angelic, her golden hair like a halo floating around her.

I clear my throat. "Again, I'm not following. What did I do now?"

"You just look miserable. You never smile."

I cock my head. "I smile."

She rolls her eyes. "Yeah? When?"

My chest rises and falls. "Whenever your around and I forget myself." The words slip out of my mouth before I can stop myself.

She bites her lip, and her eyes look bottomless, vacant, and sad. "I also make you frown."

I tilt my chin down, a small movement but an agreement. "You do."

"Why?"

"Because I can't have you," I admit. I'm not sure if it's the darkness or the alcohol, but my tongue feels looser with my secrets. Her eyes go wide, clearly shocked that I've told her this.

Then she reaches out her hand to touch me. I shouldn't let her. It makes me feel too much, but now that we have, I can't find it in myself to push her off.

"Why can't you have me?" Her voice is barely a rasp.

I want to laugh, but I don't. The truth is too depressing. "You know why," I grit out, my mouth dry like the desert.

Her features are hard, yet so soft. "My dad."

"Among other things."

Josephine's eyes glide over my face, looking for answers. "Such as?" she asks.

"You deserve better."

She gives me a small smile. "And here I think you're perfect."

I can't look at her, so I turn away, focusing on a tree in the distance. The leaves slowly sway in the wind. The sound almost calming. "You don't know me," I mutter. "Or the things I've done."

"Then let me in."

I frown. "I want to."

"But?"

"But . . . I can't." I wouldn't want to burden her with my secrets. "I'm fucked up."

"Pot meet kettle. If you're fucked up, what does that make me?"

I turn to face her. "Perfect."

Her hand reaches up and twirls a lock of hair. "I'm hardly perfect."

"To me, you are. You're a perfect sunshine on a dark day."

A soft smile plays across her face. "I thought I was Hellfire."

That makes me laugh. "You're that too."

"Then why can't we?" She puffs out her chest, a deliberate move to keep me from thinking straight.

It almost works. "I already told you—"

"My father . . ." She huffs. "Who cares about him? Not me."

"I do," I say. I want to tell her about my relationship with him, but something tells me it wouldn't go over well right now, and to be honest, I'm so goddamn tired of pushing her away. I don't want to now.

She leans into me. "He doesn't have to know . . ."

I'm not sure if I'm just not in the right state of mind. Maybe it's the booze, or perhaps it's just her . . . maybe she's cast a spell on me, but I can't object.

I don't want to.

I'm not ready to let her go, so I won't.

Under the moonlight, she looks ethereal. A goddess sent down from heaven to tempt me, and fuck it, I'll let her.

I cross the small amount of space that separates us until our lips are only an inch apart.

She exhales, and I inhale her. I lift my hand and run the pad of my thumb against her jaw until I lift her gaze to meet mine. All I see is want.

She licks her lips, and my eyes drop to watch. Her lips are full and plump, waiting to be kissed.

I cup her face and decide to give us both what we want.

At first, when our mouths touch, it's slow and soft, but then I deepen it. I kiss her faster, harder, and rougher.

I need her to know how desperate I am for her. To be inside her again.

I know our time together is fleeting. No way can this last, so it makes me want to enjoy every second I have with her.

She pulls away from me, and our gazes meet. "I want you." Her words tickle my lips.

"I want you, too."

Her hand drops to my pants, and the sound of my zipper lowering echoes through the air.

I look around, making sure we are still alone, and when we are, I lift my hips, allowing her to free me from the confines of my pants.

In the distance, I can hear a car honk. I know this is risky, and we shouldn't do this here. But once her hand wraps around my shaft, all objections die on my tongue.

All logic is gone.

My need for her outweighs everything. "Get on top of me."

She moves to stand and slowly kicks off her panties. Then, with her skirt as our only coverage, she straddles my lap. Leaning forward, I trail my lips down her neck and across her collarbone.

I lift one of her breasts out of her top and suck her nipple into my mouth. She squirms against me.

"More."

I pull back on a pop. "You sure?"

"Yes."

"Rub me against your pussy. Get me nice and wet."

She lifts, and I feel her damp skin against the sensitive crown as her essence coats me. "Put me inside you. Fuck my cock, Hellfire."

She moves an inch, and her walls give way as I enter her. She's too fucking tight. I bite my lip to stop the moan from escaping as I slowly fill her.

I lift my hips until she's all the way seated on me.

"Pull your skirt back. I want to see you taking my cock."

She moves her hands, pulling the material back, and when she does, my dick jerks at the sight in front of me.

Her pussy tight around me.

She rocks backward, and it feels so good, but it's not enough.

Placing my hands on her hips, I lift her almost off me, my cock dragging through her wet skin, and then I pull her down, thrusting all the way back inside.

The view is fantastic.

Watching my dick covered in her juices has me working my hands faster. As I pull her off, I groan in satisfaction, and when I thrust back in, she does.

"Fuck, you feel good," I say, observing as my cock sinks back inside her.

I could watch us all day.

She tightens around me, and her breathing gets choppy. She's almost there.

"Touch yourself," I groan. "Make yourself come on my cock."

She follows my orders to perfection, reaching out and rubbing at her clit.

I watch as she works. Rubbing furiously.

A tingling feeling spreads across my body as her walls grip me.

"Just like that, Hellfire." Her fingers move faster, and then her whole body spasms around me. I thrust up once more and follow her over the edge, my dick jerking inside her as I coat her walls with my come.

As soon as I return from my high, reality settles in. I just fucked Josephine in a park where anyone could see.

Fuck.

I lift her up, and as my dick falls out of her, my come follows.

Fuck, why does she look so hot with my come inside her?

I can't be thinking this right now.

We could have gotten caught, and we're lucky we didn't.

She moves to standing and straightens her skirt.

"Now what?" she asks.

"We leave."

"Together?" Her voice sounds soft and unsure.

"As much as I want to parade you around looking thoroughly fucked, knowing you smell like me, I don't think either of us is ready for the consequences."

"But . . ."

I take a deep breath. "I don't want to, but I think we need to."

"So that's it?" I can hear the disappointment in her voice.

I stand, tucking my dick back into my pants, and step up to where she is. I tilt her head up. She looks so lost, and I hate it. What I would do to make her smile. To be the person who makes her feel alive. How does that even look? She makes me feel alive, but can I be that for someone else?

I don't deserve her.

My whole life is a lie, and if she gets involved with me—guilt churns in my belly.

I should let her go.

Tell her that this is done. She deserves better than to be my dirty little secret. Because that's all she can be.

If her father finds out, my whole hockey career would be at risk.

Would that be the worst thing?

Yes. *You love hockey.* I don't have to play professionally.

Molly.

You play for Molly.

She needs this job.

I keep trying to get her to do something else, but she refuses, so until she finds something that she's passionate about, I can't take this away from her. This means there's no future for me and Josephine, not while I play for her father.

"For now."

"And that's a bullshit answer." The lost girl from moments ago is gone, replaced with one filled with resolve.

I lift my hand and run it through my hair, pulling at the roots. "I don't have an answer for you right now. I want you, but—"

"No buts. You want me. And I want you. We are both adults. We'll just be careful." She walks away and turns to look over her shoulder at me. "Starting right now."

Then she's gone.

Leaving me wondering what just happened.

I'm pretty sure by not objecting, I just agreed to have a secret romance with the coach's daughter.

chapter thirty-seven

Josie

DESPITE WAKING UP IN THE SAME BED AS I HAVE FOR THE PAST month, today feels different. I'm excited. Something I haven't felt since being here in Redville.

It's him.

I know it is.

He makes me excited for what's to come.

With the game tomorrow, the Saints aren't on the ice today. Instead, they had off-ice training, so I didn't have to go to the practice arena.

I got lucky and have the day off, which is why I woke up at lunchtime instead of my usual seven o'clock.

It feels good to be lazy.

I stretch my arms over my head and groan. I can still feel him touching me.

It's ingrained in my memory, and I hope it never fades away. Last night felt like a dream, but it wasn't. Instead, it was the hottest fantasy that had come to life.

Apparently, sex in public places is our thing. A soft laugh bubbles up from my mouth. I wonder when I'll see him next.

Now.

I want to see him now.

I reach my arm out to the table beside my bed and grab my phone.

Should I call?

A groan escapes. Just do it. Text him.

Do I even have his number?

Duh, when I worked for him, I took it down, even though I never contacted him.

Josie: Hi

Short and sweet.

I stare at my phone, but nothing happens.

I throw my phone across the bed.

Stop watching it.

A watched pot never boils, after all.

A full thirty minutes pass, and despite throwing my phone across my bed, I reach for it to see if he's responded. He hasn't.

Josie: Is texting NOT okay?

Shit. Why did I just text that?

I hover over the delete button, but if I delete it, he'll know I deleted it. What's worse, looking pathetic? Or looking like a wishy-washy, pathetic person.

Why did I think this was a good idea? Why do I have to be so damn impulsive?

I pass time on my phone, checking my emails, texts, and missed calls, not sure what I'm searching for.

Okay, I do know. Some verification my mother remembers she birthed me. When I don't get it, I move on to double tapping every thirst trap of Dane on Insta.

Why hasn't he responded yet?

Another five minutes pass, and I cover my face with my pillow and scream into it.

The phone finally chimes, and I throw the pillow across the room and jump to grab it.

Dane: I guess that depends.

My heartbeat picks up, and my hand shakes as I hold my phone, trying to decide how to respond.

Josie: Depends on what?

Dane: Depends on why you're texting . . .

My breathing comes out in heavy pants. Now what do I say? I stare at the message. Does he want me to say something innocent? Or is he angling for something else? Something daring.

Or I can just lay myself out there.

Josie: I want to see you.

The phone rattles in my hand. I can't believe I put myself out there like this. Now I have to wait and see if he rejects me.

This is the worst idea I've ever had.

Why do I do this to myself?

The waiting feels like agony.

Dane: Then the answer is always yes.

A burst of energy flows through my body. *Always yes.* My pulse picks up until the blood is pounding so hard in my veins I might pass out.

Dane: When?

Wait, what? He just asked when. He wants to see me too.

Well, actually, he never said that, but it's implied . . . right?

My heart hammers in my chest.

What does this mean? It means nothing, dummy. He wants to sleep with me again. Nothing more. Stop getting worked up. This will never be anything more than a forbidden love affair I'll always have in my memory.

Josie: Today.

Dane: Tonight.

Josie: Okay.

Dane: I'll send you the address.

And he does.

This is a bad idea. I'll most likely get hurt, yet despite the impending doom that's settled in my gut, I can't find it in me to care.

I'd rather feel the pain than never feel at all.

chapter thirty-eight

Josie

HOURS LATER, I'M DRIVING TO THE ADDRESS HE GAVE me. The day went by pretty fast. I kept busy researching social media accounts for other sports teams to see what they were doing for marketing. I didn't limit myself to just hockey but did a deep dive into all sports—soccer, football, and hell, I even looked up rugby even though I know nothing about the sport.

After I was done, I read, my personal favorite being fantasy romances, usually with an ancient Greek twist.

A laugh bubbles, no time to think about that right now, I need to focus on tonight and not on the book I'm reading.

I'm wearing a short floral dress. It's innocent yet sexy, the perfect combo for a night in at his place.

For some reason, I'm nervous.

This isn't the first time we've been alone together, but it's the first time it's planned.

It's been spontaneous every time we've been together, but not this time. Will that ruin the excitement?

Or will he rip off my clothes?

My stomach tightens as his house appears in front of me.

It's a large, beautiful, modern white house with floor-to-ceiling windows and no soul.

It's so different from my father's house, the type of house where you can raise a family. A bitter barb jumps onto my tongue, but I push it back. Tonight isn't about my father.

It's about Dane and me, so despite my curiosity about the cold nature of his house, I push the thoughts away.

Once I've pulled up to where the front door is, I throw my car in park and head toward it.

The soles of my shoes click on the stairs as I go to knock on the front door. Hand raised, I don't even get to knock before it's being opened.

Dane stands in front of me, hair still wet from a shower, in a thermal shirt and jeans. I can smell the faint scent of soap . . . it smells so good; I want to burrow myself into his neck.

Damn.

He looks good.

Tall and handsome.

A five-o'clock shadow dusts his face.

Despite being in his house, he still appears grumpy, with no smile on his face.

He steps back and allows me to enter, and when I do, I let out a small gasp. This place is gorgeous. It's large and open.

Dane steps up to me, and I step back.

That makes him smirk, and I raise an eyebrow at him. "What?"

"Now that you're here, are you going to play this game?"

"And what game is that?"

"That you don't want to come all over my cock."

I open my mouth to say something, but before I can get the words out, he pulls me toward him. Then his lips find mine.

He kisses me as if I'm water and he's been in a desert. He

devours me. Plunders my mouth with his tongue. I sink against him, letting him take over and guide me.

I'm putty in his hands, and I wouldn't want it any other way.

He pulls away, taking a step back. "Let's get a drink and go over some ground rules."

I roll my eyes. "And there he is again."

"Who?"

"Mr. Grumpy Pants."

He throws his head back and laughs, a sound I've never heard before, and it warms my belly.

The sound is so beautiful I vow to always try to make him laugh. "Well, we can't all be hellfire, can we?"

"Nope. That's my job." I start to walk, placing one foot in front of the other, and wink at him. "I like Poseidon for you."

"Poseidon, ehh. Not sure it works?" He lifts his hand in my direction. "I seem to have lost my trident."

I lift my shoulder. "Well, he is the grumpy one."

"If I'm Poseidon, who does that make you? Aphrodite?"

"Don't you mean Amphitrite?"

He shakes his head. "No. Amphitrite ran from Poseidon to the mountains. Aphrodite *always* ran toward him. Always followed him."

"Are you saying I follow you?" I place my hands on my cheek, channeling my best Kevin from *Home Alone* face.

"If the shoe fits."

A laugh bubbles from my mouth. "I'm actually impressed. You know your Greek mythology."

"I bet you will find there's a lot I can do to impress you."

I arch a brow. "Such as?"

His lips tip into a sinful smirk. "I'll show you after drinks."

With that, he leads me toward a living room. He grabs the whiskey decanter and raises it for me to see. "Whiskey?"

"Interesting choice." I force a smile. "Do you ever drink anything else—"

"Now, why would I do a silly thing like that?"

"I don't know, maybe you wanted to live a little . . ." *I know I do.* "So what are these ground rules?"

I peer around the room, needing something to do with myself while he goes about making us drinks.

After he finishes pouring the two glasses, he hands one to me. I lift it to my mouth and take a sip. I choke at first, and he laughs for the second time tonight. I could die now, knowing I've made him laugh again. "Holy heck, that's strong."

He shrugs. "I guess it's an acquired taste."

"Yep. One I don't have." My eyes roll before becoming serious again. "What do you want to talk about?"

"This." He gestures back and forth between us. "Ground rules."

I look down at the glass in my hands, and then I look back up. "Okay."

"No one can know."

Despite knowing this was most likely how this conversation would go, it still makes my tummy hurt, which is stupid, seeing as it was my idea to embark upon a forbidden relationship.

Dumb girl.

Don't jump into the deep end if you don't know how to swim.

I puff my chest out and throw out my best fake bravado. "Obviously," I respond, rolling my eyes.

All lies.

Even as the words leave my lips, I can feel the lie in the way my heart hammers harder.

It's pathetic. I practically seduce the man with no-strings-attached sex, and he agrees. But then, what do I want?

Strings.

No. *You just want him to fight for you.* But of course, he doesn't want me for more than a quick lay.

No one wants me.

Not my mom.

Not my dad.

I bite the inside of my cheek, needing to ground myself.

"That it?" I add, my voice flat with no emotions despite the way my heart hammers in my chest.

"Yeah, I guess."

"Great, then let's get to it." I wink.

If I'm going to be his secret, I might as well play the part.

He walks up to me and takes the glass from my hand; he places both our drinks on the side table before he walks back over to me and sweeps me into his arms.

He walks us into his room and drops me on his bed.

"I want you to strip. All your clothes off."

I do what I'm told, pulling the dress over my head. Once I'm naked, I look up at him under hooded lids. The dress didn't allow for a bra, and well, I didn't have any clean underwear left because that would mean I would have to interact with Sherry.

"Very nice. Now I want you to lean back and spread your legs, Hellfire."

I do as I'm told. Leaning back on my elbows, I look at him.

He stares at me like a lion waiting to eat his prey.

As he approaches me, he licks his lips. The mere action is decadent. No one should look this sexy; I swear I almost come from just watching him.

He moves to the ground, right beside where my legs hang off the bed, and then he leans forward until his mouth hovers against my skin.

I wiggle my butt closer to the edge.

Giving him better access.

"Good girl." He slowly kisses up my thigh.

"I want to hear you tell me what you want," he says.

"Please," I whisper.

"Please what, Hellfire?" he taunts back.

"Do it now before I combust."

His steely blue gaze meets mine. "Where do you want me to touch?"

I lift my hips.

"Not good enough. I need to hear your words."

I close my lids and love and hate him for making me beg.

chapter thirty-nine

Dane

A GROAN ESCAPES HER MOUTH AS I PLACE A KISS ON HER UPPER thigh. She twists and turns, raising her pussy in the air, begging me to taste her.

I will, but all in good time.

The need to take her to the point of desperation is too strong to reward her right away.

The torture I'm doling out should be illegal. My lips dip, and her fingers grab my hair.

"Please," she begs again, and I smile against her skin.

I trail my tongue back up, drawing a line until I reach her pussy. She shudders when I make contact.

"Please what?" I ask against her damp skin.

"You know what I want."

My tongue skates over her clit, and she quivers again.

"Fuck you with my mouth or my dick?"

"Both," she moans. "But . . . one at a time. I don't want you injured."

I laugh, drunk with desire for this woman. "Good answer."

I close my mouth around her clit, my tongue circling it. The sounds coming from Josephine very well might be the most beautiful sounds I have ever heard.

I continue to eat her out, sucking harder and licking faster. Soon, I can feel her body tightening. She's so close.

I flick her clit again, and this time, it sends her over the edge, her hands tightening in my hair and pulling to the point of pain.

As she slowly comes down from her high, I move to a standing position, lifting my shirt over my head, then unzipping my pants and kicking them across the room.

Once I'm fully naked, I step up to the bed again.

"Get on your hands and knees. Ass up," I tell her, stroking my dick from root to tip.

She happily obliges, her body shaking as she waits for me to fuck her.

From this angle, I'll be able to see it all. Watching my dick inside her is my new obsession, and I can't wait. I line myself up and thrust inside, filling her to the brim with my cock.

Her breath comes out in a rush of air once I'm fully seated inside her, and I don't miss how her body clenches around me. It takes everything inside me not to come right now. Instead, I take a deep inhale and hold steady, willing my body to calm down.

"More. Move," she groans.

With my head tipped down, I grip her ass and pull her cheeks apart; then I watch as I slowly pull my now glistening dick out.

She squirms and moans, and then I slam back in.

"So good."

I retract and then thrust.

Fucking her harder, I drive into her with everything I have. She cries out with pleasure as her orgasm hits her hard. As she shivers around me, I feel myself careening over the edge, then collapsing forward, bringing Josephine with me.

It takes some time for us both to come back from our

post-orgasm high. Josephine flops to the right side of my bed, her blond locks fanning across my pillow. I stare at her for a minute, watching as her eyes flutter shut.

She looks peaceful.

I continue to observe her, and as I do, so many questions I wish I knew the answers to rush through my brain.

The need to find out everything about her has me perplexed. Since when have I ever cared to know a woman's backstory before? But with Josephine, I can't get enough. I want to know what haunts her because I know that something is going on. I watch the way she is with her father, and I wish she would confide in me. *Real rich coming from me. I don't even confide in Molly.* Nope, my secrets will go with me to the grave, yet despite the hypocrisy, I want to know everything about my little hellfire.

A part of me wants to ask Robert, but I know I can't.

The spot beside Josephine in my bed beckons me to join her. Pulling the duvet up, I cover her body before I slip under the covers and place a soft kiss on her forehead. She curls up beside me the moment I do, most likely sharing my warmth.

Having her here feels right.

With an inhale of my breath, I allow myself to relax. Tomorrow is the season's first game, so I need my rest.

Josephine's soft breathing lulls me to sleep, and I welcome the calm she brings me.

chapter forty

Dane

WITH EIGHT MINUTES LEFT IN THE FIRST PERIOD, THE ST. Louis Knights take the puck to the center line and then dump it into our zone as they make a full line change.

My gaze darts around the rink, landing on the puck behind our net. With a quick glance and a silent exchange, Mason stops the puck, setting it up for me to start our attack.

My stick darts out, and then I bring the puck around our net. Pivoting sharply, I pass it up the right side to Hudson, who's on our blue line.

It's up to him now to start our attack.

Hudson skates past the center line and decides to dump the puck into the Knights zone.

Aiden chases the puck deep into the zone while Wolfe and I skate to the blue line. My lungs burn, but I can't think about that now. This is our shot.

When Aiden gets the puck, he passes it to Wolfe at the right side of the circle, and then Wolfe passes to me for a one-timer.

Fuck.

The Knight's goalie makes a leg pad save.

Then I see *Hudson.* He's there, going for the rebound.

His arm pulls back, and he shoots, stuffing the puck in the net.

The crowd's noise is deafening. They cheer and chant as Hudson just scored the first goal of the game.

Fuck yeah.

Nothing beats this.

The excitement. The thrill. The team.

Sometimes, playing hockey is bittersweet, but never when I'm on the ice. When I'm on the ice, I feel like I found a home.

I search the crowd for her. Narrowing my gaze as I stare at a sea of faces.

Section by section, I look.

But I don't see any familiar faces. Not even Molly.

Where is she? All the details blend, and I blink my eyes.

Then, like a rope is tethered between us, my gaze lands on hers. The roar of the fans fades away as I watch her.

She smiles brightly. A smile so intense it reaches her eyes. I see nothing but pride, filling me with this strange feeling.

Happiness.

It's beautiful.

chapter forty-one

Josie

DANE SINCLAIR IS HARD TO READ.
The man is colder than ice.

To his teammates, he's granite, an impenetrable force. They need him like that to rely on him to protect them.

But behind closed doors, he's a man trying his hardest to fight his demons.

I see it in bits and pieces like a kaleidoscope.

The eager part of me, the part that refuses to back down from a challenge, loves that I'm the one who gets beneath his skin.

When his gaze found mine during the first period, right after Hudson scored, we had a moment, but then I didn't hear from him after the game. I knew he'd fight it and turn cold after. He can't help but retreat, but then I got a random text to meet him for brunch.

Which is where I'm off to now.

The location is in a neighboring town. It's far enough away that no one in our inner circle will see us, but still not far enough away that it won't be a problem if recognized.

I guess it's a good thing I work for the team because at least we can pretend that this is just business. At least, that's what I tell myself as we walk out of the diner.

I hate that I'm the coach's daughter.

I hate that he's like a son to my father.

I hate that I can't grab his hand and declare to the world that he's mine.

This is how it has to be.

I know in my heart that Dane's standing on the team would be jeopardized if my father found out about us.

But somewhere deep inside me, a part I don't want Dane to see, I wish he would own it. I wish he would fight for me. Come out and say he's with me, but what can I expect?

Of course, he will put his career first.

Is it wrong to just want someone, anyone, to fight for me?

Together, we walk farther into the restaurant. Our bodies are close together, fingers hovering near each other, but neither of us crosses the distance. *We can't.*

I stop my movements.

"Hellfire?" His gaze is locked on me as he waits for me to say or do something.

I study his face, sad that he's not smiling. Instead, small lines accent his forehead.

I wish we could laugh together. The small glimpses of happiness I've seen from him are apparently only allowed in the closed-off space of his house.

Maybe one day.

"Let's sit here." I point to a free table at the back before sliding into the booth, and Dane sits across from me.

After a second, he leans back in the booth, lifting the menu to his face to read. I do the same, settling on what I'll eat only a second before the server approaches.

"Hi, welcome to Barlow's. I'm Maryanne, and I'll be your server today. Would you like something to drink before I take your order?"

Dane lowers his menu and looks up at Maryanne. "I think we're ready to order. Josephine, are you ready?"

"I am."

Dane gestures for me to go. "I'll have the buttermilk pancakes and a coffee."

"What would you like with your coffee? Milk, cream?"

"Cream and two sugars, please."

She nods and then turns her attention to Dane, who orders three eggs and an array of veggies. When she leaves, Dane leans forward, placing his elbows on the table.

By the way he's looking at me, I can tell he wants to ask me something, but I'm not entirely sure I want him to.

"How did you end up here?" he finally asks, and I lift my brow in confusion.

"You asked me to meet you."

His lips twist up. It's not a full smile, but I can tell he wants to. "Not here, here, but in Redville."

Shit. I knew this moment would come up sooner or later, but I'm not sure I even want to tell him. If this isn't going to be anything serious, why bother?

His jaw is soft, and his eyes glisten at me with compassion. I guess I can tell him a little bit. The truth is, I barely speak to my father, so telling him much is out of the question anyway since I don't know anything.

My fingers twirl together in my lap. "My mom sent me." I try my best to disguise the annoyance in my voice, but I don't do a very good job, and by the way Dane's brows shoot up his forehead, he doesn't miss that fact.

"Well, that sounds like a long, complicated story."

Yep, just as I thought. I'm not good at schooling my features, after all.

I laugh. "Oh, it is, and we really don't have time."

Dane leans forward in his seat. "And you don't want to tell me anyway."

"Pot meet kettle."

He raises his hand in mock surrender. "You got me."

"I do. And I can ask you the same question."

"How I got here? Well, the short story is I never left." Dane rubs his hands together before placing one on the table.

"Exactly. How come? You were born and raised in Redville. Never left. And now play for the Redville Saints. You have this huge career. Have you ever considered moving somewhere else? There must've been offers."

"Not really." His fingers start to tap rhythmically. He's avoiding the question, and I'm going to call him out on that. Two can play this game.

"You aren't going to give me anything?"

"I couldn't leave."

A crumb. That's progress.

I lift my brow. "Why?"

"Sometimes I forget that I haven't known you for long. It feels like I've known you forever." Warmth spreads through my limbs at his words. It feels that way for me too, but at the same time, it feels like we're just scratching the surface. "Molly. I couldn't leave because of Molly. It's just us in this world, and she needed me."

It's a funny feeling when you can feel someone's pain as if it's your own. It radiates through every single layer of your soul, and all you want to do is reach out and comfort them. I don't need to know the story to know he didn't want to stay here. He did it for her. Still does it for her.

My heart breaks for him.

While I have no home, he's all the home she knows.

"When you're ready to talk about it, I'm here." He nods but doesn't meet my gaze. If I had to harbor a guess, he's lost in his own thoughts.

"Thanks, Hellfire."

chapter forty-two

Josie

"JOSIE, COULD YOU MEET ME IN MY OFFICE?" MY FATHER HOLDS up a finger when I try to bullshit my way out of any one-on-one time. "I have a list of potential brand collabs."

I frown. "Can you email it?"

"It's handwritten."

"*You* came up with it?"

I'm well-aware my doubt bounces from my face like a pop-up book, but c'mon. The guy probably thinks all-you-can-eat shrimp is the peak of advertising.

"Yes." He arches a brow. "Is that so hard to believe?"

"Well…" I make a show of checking the time, cringing internally. "We should head to your office now. I have a meeting soon."

I do not, in fact, having a meeting soon. I'm pretty sure I'm not important enough to have a meeting soon. After all, I put the un in unpaid intern.

My father leads me into his office and gestures to the chair. I sit on the very edge, taking in the place. Dozens of playbooks sit in militant stacks at the edge of his desk. Trophies line a floating shelf behind it, coupled with a photo of… I squint, trying to make out the contents of the gold leaf frame. Is that…me? No way.

When I finally return my attention back to my father, he has an unreadable expression etched across his face.

I cross my legs, playing it cool. "The list?"

"Doesn't exist." He has the decency to look sheepish. With a sigh, he removes his cap and tosses it in a wire basket beside his desk. "I needed an excuse to talk to you. You're avoiding me."

"I'm not."

"You are."

"No, I'm—"

"How many twenty-two-year-olds have kidney stones?"

"They were the size of my fist," I insist.

"Josie…"

He doesn't get to finish his sentence.

Hudson barges in the office, two palms up. "I swear I didn't do it."

I don't know what *it* is, but I certainly hope he did it, so he and my father can have a nice, long chat about it. Without me.

"Oh, what a shame." I jut out my lower lip, hopping off the chair. "This seems important. I'll let you two talk."

With that, I'm out of there before either of them can even blink. I'm halfway down the hallway when I see Dane.

"Where're you off to?" I ask.

He stops walking when he hears my voice. "Off to meet Aiden."

"Really? You guys going out—"

"No. Actually, he runs a youth group, and I agreed to volunteer over there."

"Seriously?"

"Yep. I realized I love helping the kids. I just hate fundraisers, so this felt like something I'd be into." He shrugs.

"Oh, you hate fundraisers. Is that so?" I lift my brow. "Was the last one so awful?"

He laughs. "No, Hellfire." He moves closer and lowers so his mouth is right next to my ear. A shiver works its way through my body at his proximity. For a second, I wonder what he's doing, and then I can feel a whisper of his breath against my skin. "It wasn't."

My lids close, and a small moan escapes my lips.

"Careful." He pulls away, acting like he's not the instigator today. Jerk. A damn sexy hot jerk, but still a jerk.

Dane starts to open the door, and my brain catches up with what's happening. "Wait, you're going now?"

He turns and peers over his shoulder. "Yeah, why?"

"Is it sketch if I come with you?"

He pauses, then a slow smile rises up his cheeks. "For marketing purposes."

"Of course. Haven't you heard? I'm the next Nick Naylor."

"Nick Naylor sold cigarettes to kids."

"How convenient. There will be plenty of kids at the youth league."

"Why not cigars? The ROI is higher."

"Have you seen the returns on e-cigs?"

He tosses his head back, roaring out a laugh before he sobers. "Seriously, though, make a show of taking pictures when you come. And not just of my ass."

"What?!"

"I know you look when I turn around."

"How could you possibly know that?"

"Because we work at an ice rink. Reflective surfaces are everywhere."

"It'll be hard not to take a picture of your ass, considering there's about six foot two inches and two hundred pounds of ass in front of me."

He frowns. "You think I'm only six two?"

Twenty minutes later, I'm stepping into the rink where the youth teams play. The cold air hits my face the closer I get to the ice.

Laughter and shouts echo around the children already on the ice, wobbling in their skates, hockey sticks in their hands.

Aiden must see me because he waves from across the rink. Dane, however, is already in full coach mode.

I wave back before approaching and pull out my phone to take candid pictures and videos.

Dane looks like a natural with the kids. Both boys and girls and their ages seem to be in a range. The one thing they all have in common is that their excitement is palpable.

They all laugh and giggle, and something infectious about it has me grinning as well.

I watch with heart-shaped eyes as he shows the kids how to skate, and the kids copy him.

He skates beside them, guiding them, and as the practice goes on, Dane teaches them how to handle their sticks. He then shows them different techniques and the best ways to control the puck.

He's phenomenal.

I can't get over it.

Needing a minute to rein my emotions in, I look down on my phone, but then the boisterous sounds of screams and giggles have me glancing back up.

Now he's letting them try to score on him.

It's adorable.

I could watch this all day. Seeing Dane interact with the kids is everything I didn't know I needed.

It's amazing.

He's amazing.

Seeing him today . . . *was everything.*

"Thanks, Coach!" one of the kids screams as Dane walks off the ice and approaches Aiden. Despite my distance, I can hear them as they speak. I should excuse myself, but I'm curious, so I don't.

"It reminds me why I originally fell in love with hockey. Thanks for inviting me, man."

"No problem, Sin. You better come back."

"Promise." He continues to walk, and I catch up to him. Together, we leave the rink.

"You're a natural, Dane. They loved you."

Dane shrugs, but I don't miss the smile that crawls up his face. Like this, he looks beautiful.

A man at peace.

If I'm not careful, this man is exactly the type of man who can break my heart because this is the man I can fall in love with.

chapter forty-three

Josie

ANOTHER DAY, ANOTHER CITY. THE SAINTS PLAY IN SEATTLE today, and we're already at the arena. Seeing as I work for the team, I'm just outside the locker room when I see Dane walking off. I have no clue where he's going, but something about the way he's stalking off has me concerned.

I follow him as he takes a back hallway, but I have no clue where it leads. How is this a good idea?

Something tells me that my father allows Dane extra wiggle room for the things he can do, and taking a moment before a game might just be one of those things. The game doesn't start for another hour, so where he's going is beyond me.

I watch as he opens a door, then follow him through it, but the door isn't even closed when he spins around and takes a step to cage me in against the wall.

My eyes open wide as my back presses against the brick wall.

"Following me, Hellfire?"

"Yes." There's no reason to lie. I tip my chin up. I'm owning it.

I'm friendless, parentless, and everything-less. He is the only source of entertainment in my life. He is also a willing victim.

"Why?" he asks.

"Because I'm *Aphrodite*. That's what I do. " I shrug playfully before growing serious. "And because, to be honest, you looked upset."

He narrows his eyes at me. "You're very observant, aren't you?"

"Only when something catches my attention."

He leans in and is now so close that his lips hover above mine.

"Sure it's a smart idea to be this close to me? Someone might *see*?" I mock.

"In the back stairwell? I think not."

"What are you doing here?"

"Catching my prey." He smirks.

"Come again?"

"Oh, that's the plan. Bait, Hellfire. I came here as bait. And it worked because here you are."

It hits me like a ton of bricks.

He lured me into this stairwell to be alone with me before the game. Butterflies take flight in my belly as my cheeks warm.

"So what's so important you lured me out here?"

"I can't kiss you in public, so private it is." His hand leaves the wall and grips my hip.

He moves closer, lowering his mouth to a mere inch away from mine. When he breathes, it tickles my skin.

"So do it."

Dane lifts my wrist, the one with my bracelet. "What's this?"

"Do you like it?"

"Did you get a trident charm to reminisce about our first night together?"

"How cute. You think this bracelet's for you. I'm simply cheering on the better team . . . The Seattle Tridents."

"Cute."

"I like to think so. Are you going to kiss me or what?"

He closes the distance, our mouths colliding in a frenzy of

pent-up passion. Mouths open, tongues battling for dominance, my hands wrap around his neck as he deepens the kiss before he pulls back. "I can't get enough of you," he says against my lips.

"That sounds like a you problem."

"Be careful with that smart mouth of yours."

"What are you going to do about it?"

Dane lifts my chin and stares into my eyes. "It's not me who's going to do anything about it."

"Oh, is that right?"

"Yes, Hellfire. Now get on your knees and show me what a good girl you are."

I do what he says, dropping down to the ground. My hand reaches out as I open the button of his pants.

Luckily, he's not in his hockey uniform yet because I'm not sure how I'd remove those.

Don't sell yourself short. Where there's a will, there's a way.

The zipper echoes through the small space, and once I slide it down, his dick pops out, long, hard, and ready to play.

I lick my lips, and Dane groans.

"Fuck, Hellfire. The way you're looking at my cock right now."

Leaning forward, I swirl my tongue over the head before wrapping my lips around him and sucking half of his cock into my mouth.

His hand wraps around my hair, fisting it, and he begins to thrust into my mouth.

"Just like that."

I continue to bob up and down on his length.

"Can you take me deeper? I want to fuck your throat." Since I can't answer, I nod my head and relax as his hands push my head into his groin. "Such a good girl."

His words drive me wild, making me feel warm and tingly. I squirm, and he chuckles. "Oh, you like that?"

"Mmm." That's all I get out before he pops his dick out of my mouth.

"Turn around and brace yourself against the wall."

I'm practically dizzy with need when I get into the position he wants me in.

With my eyes closed, I'm hyperaware of every movement, every sound. When he steps behind me, my heart threatens to beat out of my chest.

Slowly, he rubs the head of his cock up and down my slit. Dragging it through my drenched skin, he gets himself nice and wet. With one sharp thrust, he fills me to the brim. He's so deep I can barely breathe.

The feeling is divine. It feels like we are the only people in the world and that nothing matters but this.

I savor the moment for a second; we both do, and then he begins to thrust, his cock sliding in and out of me.

My head rolls back, and he grips me tighter, holding me in place.

"That's it. Take my cock."

I do. I take every inch, tilting my chest forward to let him get deeper. He fucks me in earnest until my thighs shake and my body trembles.

Time loses all meaning, and I'm unable to think of anything but us and what we're doing.

If I could live in this moment forever, I would.

"So good, " he groans, and electric waves zing through me until I can't hold back.

I'm falling over the edge. "I'm coming."

My words must set him off because I feel him throb, and his cock jerks inside me.

For a second, we don't move, then Dane pulls out of me while placing a kiss on my neck. "Thanks for following me, Hellfire."

"Always."

chapter forty-four

Josie

IT'S BEEN A WEEK SINCE I'VE HAD A MINUTE TO RELAX. I CAN'T wait to get into my bed and sleep. After today's game, I'm exhausted.

Believe it or not, taking pictures of hot hockey players warming up is hard work.

Do you know how hard it is to remember to click the capture button when someone is gyrating on the ice in front of you?

I deserve a raise.

When I arrive at the house, I park in my usual spot and bypass the house completely, heading to the guesthouse.

When I walk around the back and toward the deck, I'm surprised to see Dane and my father sitting there.

A part of me wants to walk right past them, not even acknowledge that they are there, but I know I can't. Well, if ignoring their existence isn't an option, I'll do the opposite.

Time to make Dane sweat.

With my shoulders pulled back and perfect posture, I stride in their direction.

From where I am, I have a clear shot of him perched on his chair, glass in his hand.

My father is beside him, and he turns his head in my direction just as I lift my hand to wave at Dane. My father must think it's for him because he waves back.

"Josie, come join us."

This should be fun.

"Oh, trust me, Robert, I'm coming." I smile big as I continue to walk toward them, and the closer I get, the more I know this is a bad idea.

As the sun ducks behind the clouds, ready to set into the night, the shimmery rays hit Dane at a perfect angle, highlighting just how handsome he is.

"What are you guys doing?" I ask, trying to turn my thoughts away from how much I want to kiss him.

Dane lifts his glass in response. "Having a drink."

"After today's blowout, I invited Dane over," my father explains.

"Do the other guys know you play favorites?" I retort before I can stop myself. My father chokes at my comment, and Dane looks like his eyes might bug out of their sockets. I've been at a point of disadvantage since I got here. I kind of like making Dane sweat outside the bed. As for Robert? Who cares how he feels?

"I don't play favorites on the ice," he responds, as if that makes it any better. "Why don't you pull up a chair and tell us how you like your new job?"

Dane jumps up from his seat. "I'll grab it for you," he says before darting in the direction of a chair and then bringing it back.

My cheeks warm, and I grin up at his hulking figure. "Well, aren't you the perfect gentleman."

I take the seat that he placed directly beside him. This close, I see how his Adam's apple bobs; I want so badly to touch it, to kiss him all over.

But that won't happen.

With both our hands on the armrest, we are practically touching, but we're not. It feels like torture.

If I move one inch . . .

No. I can't.

Dane coughs, and when he does, I swear I feel his pinky touch mine.

It's in your brain. He didn't touch you. He wouldn't risk getting caught.

As if he's reading my mind, his hand brushes my hand sitting right beside his chair.

When I don't pull my hand away, he touches my skin again. From where my father sits, he can't see us, and Dane knows it.

He's playing dirty, and I can't say that I hate it. I don't, I love it.

It feels like my heart will explode with each touch. The tension inside me is almost enough to make me shiver.

"So, Josie," my father asks, and I need to shake my head to remember what the question is.

"I like it. Well, I like taking pictures. The players"—I look at Dane and smirk—"are a bit much."

"Hey," he objects, and I smile bigger.

"What? You are."

"He's what?" my father asks.

"Grumpy. Dane is grumpy."

"That he is, but—"

"It's fine," Dane interjects, and I narrow my eyes at him and then at my father.

What was my father going to say? What don't I know about this man that *Robert* does?

"How long have you two know each other?" I finally ask. I have gotten bits and pieces of this story, but not enough to paint a picture.

"Since the beginning of my career."

"Really?"

"Yeah, actually, even before. Before my job at the Saints, I coached the University of Redville team."

"You did?"

"Yeah."

Dane is staring intently at me. I obviously can't decipher his thoughts, but it's clear as day that he's confused. He's realizing I know nothing about my father.

The man he regards as a hero in his life is merely a name and barely that in mine.

"I didn't realize that Dane played college hockey," I say more to myself than to anyone.

"Yeah, but not long. I decided to go pro soon after I started college."

"You were good enough," my father says proudly.

Is this what my father looks like when he genuinely feels proud of someone? The inside of my chest feels like someone is running a knife inside me. I hold back a sob as I will myself not to cry.

"You didn't finish college?"

"I didn't."

"I had no idea. Did you want a degree? Not that I use mine, but hey, maybe I will someday."

"College wasn't in the cards for me. I had other responsibilities and expenses. I needed the money only going pro would give me." Another small piece of the puzzle is given, yet no matter how hard I try, I can't seem to see the big picture. Who is Dane Sinclair, and what makes him tick?

chapter forty-five

Dane

Aiden: I have tea.

Hudson: I hear snake wine is better for fertility.

Mason: Aiden's trying to knock up Cassidy?

Dane: Makes sense. She's out of his league. He must be antsy to hold her down.

Aiden: We're already engaged, asshole.

Mason: Means nothing these days.

Aiden: Do you guys want the tea or not?

Dane: I thought you trying to knock up Cass is the tea?

Hudson changed the name of the chat to Nannies of Redville.

Aiden has left the chat.

chapter forty-six

Dane

It's been a few weeks since I started to see Josephine. It hasn't gotten any easier, yet I can't seem to let her go. My need for her can't be diminished, no matter how much I will it to be, which is a real problem.

Originally, I thought that she was an itch I needed to scratch—that once I had my fill, I'd be able to walk away—but I'm finding the opposite.

The more time I spend with her, the more I want her. Every time she's around, I tell myself this is the last time, that we are stepping deeper into dangerous territory, yet I can't stop myself from seeking her out. Even now, as I wait for her to arrive at my house, I look down at my phone and type a text to cancel our date, but I can't send it. I'm fucked for this girl.

It's not just about the sex either. No, that would be easy to call off. It's how she makes me feel weightless. Nothing can harm me despite all the concerns that hang over me when she's around.

I feel lighter.

I feel more like the boy I was before my parents died than the man I had to become after—scruples and all—so I could take care of Molly.

Changing the past can never happen, nor would I want to lose Molly, but I do miss the guy I was before I had to make a decision that changed the whole trajectory of my life.

A light knock raps on the door.

I drop my phone on the side table, abandoning the text calling this night off.

I stroll over to answer it, throwing the door open and looking at the woman who refuses to stop occupying my thoughts.

It's not her fault you're obsessed.

Before she can even speak, I loop an arm around her waist and drag her toward me, sealing my lips over hers. So much for all the good intentions of ending this.

Her slender arms wrap around my neck, fingers finding a home in my hair. We kiss with abandon. Like nothing in the world matters, and in truth, right here, right now, despite all the obstacles against us, it's the truth. Or at least it's our truth. I nip at her lip, pulling a moan from her mouth, and she giggles against me.

"Hungry?" her question tickles my skin.

"Ravenous."

When I pull back, Josephine whimpers a protest, and a laugh bubbles out from my mouth.

"I love that sound." She takes a step back, tilting her head up to meet my gaze.

I incline my head. "What sound?"

"When you laugh." She leans up on her toes and places a soft kiss on my jaw. "You don't do it often, and when you do, you get these cute little lines on your face."

"Are you saying I'm old?" My lip twitches.

"Oh, just do it already."

"Do what?" I feign ignorance.

"Smile. You know you want to."

"I don't." Another twitch. I start to turn around, but before I can, Josephine jumps up on the long bench that sits adjacent to the wall of my foyer.

"You sure?" She walks, and I shake my head at her antics. Even if I could stop myself, at this point, I won't. A full belly laugh erupts from inside me at how ridiculous she always looks when she tries to tightrope walk.

"Oh, Dane, aren't you forgetting something?" I lift a brow at her question. "I need help." She winks, wobbling, because if this were her actual chosen career, she would be fired right away.

She's awful at it.

I swoop in, bracketing my arms around her as she falls into me.

Now in my arms where she belongs, I carry her into the living room, depositing her on the large couch and moving in the opposite direction.

She huffs. "Where are you going?"

"To get popcorn."

"Um, okay, but why?"

"Because we're going to watch a movie."

"Are we now?"

"Yep." I head into the kitchen, grab a container of popcorn, and place it in the microwave. It's nothing fancy, but I don't want fancy right now. I just want to spend time with her. As I wait for it to pop, I grab a bowl and fill it once it's ready.

Would this be what it would be like if we could openly be together? Simple, easy, just two people lying on a couch, eating popcorn, and watching a movie. I head back in and find her sprawled out with her legs kicked up on the ottoman. She's grabbed a throw blanket and has it draped over her lap. The TV is already on, and it looks like she picked a movie.

"What did you pick?" I ask as I take the spot next to her, depositing the bowl on her lap.

"Something we'll both like."

Vague much? The sound of the TV has me looking up. Credits

rolling, it doesn't take me long to realize she picked the saddest movie on this godforsaken planet.

"Interesting choice."

"Who doesn't love *Titanic*?"

"I don't know, maybe Jack." As if my hands are possessed, I lift her legs off the ottoman and start messaging them. "Think if we watch it enough, Rose will share her door with him?"

"There wasn't any room."

"Note to self: never go on a boat with you."

She crinkles her nose. "Not on this salary, seeing as I'm an unpaid intern." She releases a yawn.

I pull her close, her head resting on my shoulder as the film begins. There's no way I'll be able to finish this movie.

Hellfire relaxes me.

With her in my arms, I fall asleep.

chapter forty-seven

Josie

WITH TODAY BEING AN OFF DAY, I SHOW UP AT THE practice arena to get some work done. The guys are practicing, and I'm supposed to take some videos of them. Nothing crazy, just hockey players training before a game to rev up the crowd. When I started working, despite Laurie's and my father's doubts, I started a TikTok page, and it has since gone viral. Fun fact: viral videos equal more sales.

Today, I'll be taking fun shots of the guys getting ready for the game against the Bulldogs. Apparently, they played them last year during the playoffs. I figure I can do some fun training montages and set them to music like they did in the Rocky movies.

As I approach the ice, I lift my phone and start to film them. A few videos of the team running drills should do. Nothing too crazy, but if I can get the right angle, it will work.

Hudson, of course, is showboating.

Currently, he's flexing his muscles in front of me while the rest of the guys are stretching.

"Cut that shit out, Wilde," Dane grumbles.

"She loves it. Don't you, Josie?" The smirk on Hudson's face is ridiculous. He looks like the cat that got the canary. Whereas Dane is more like a shaken can of soda . . . destined to explode.

"Wilde! Sin! Enough," my father barks at them. "Now split into three groups."

I watch as the guys move the puck quickly through each group, taking turns, each one eventually taking a shot.

The videos are longer than I'll need, so I'll have to edit, but I think it will be a really fun clip. And yes, I'll conclude it with Hudson flexing. The fans will get a kick out of it, even if Dane did not.

"Josie?" My father snaps a pen into the teeth of his clipboard, lowering it to his side. "A word, please?"

"Is it urgent? I have an appointment."

His brows furrow, and suddenly, he's aged ten years before me. "Is everything okay?"

Serves me right for blurting out the first excuse I could think of.

"A-ok. Just, ya know, girl stuff."

With that, I dart out of the rink and head to the back offices.

Ditching my father? Not my finest moment. Of course, the universe punishes me with a boatload of work.

I spend the rest of the day rewatching footage and marking timestamps for highlight worthy clips. When I can't put it off anymore, I make my way to my father's office to start editing on his computer.

I close the door behind me and walk over to his desk. Even though I've worked here for months, I've never actually looked around. Who am I kidding? This has nothing to do with looking around and everything to do with snooping. Despite my best attempts to want to know nothing about my father, I'm curious, so

I find myself rummaging through his stuff now. I start to thumb over the items lying haphazardly on the wood surface, leafing through the documents.

I'm not sure what I thought I'd find, but when I see the paper in front of me, I wish I hadn't snooped. DNA paternity papers. The words blur as tears fill my eyes. I didn't even know this was a question. My mother made it sound like it was a done deal that Robert was my father, but Robert must not have been a hundred percent certain.

Chatter outside the door breaks the silence, and I drop the letter. The letter shouldn't affect me as much as it does. Why does it anyway? It just confirms what I already know: he's my father.

But *I* never doubted my mom. Only *he* did. But that's not why I've been upset all this time. I've been upset because I thought he knew about me and never presented himself in my life.

Wait.

I grab the paper I discarded and look at the top right corner. One week after I was living with him already. He got the test when I was already in his house.

Why would he let me come live with him if he didn't know for sure that I was his daughter? And does this mean he was as blindsided by the turn of events as I was? My chest feels like it's caving in as I struggle to breathe. It's almost as if a hand squeezes my throat, each inhale more painful than the one before. Why does it have to be so complicated?

Talk to him.

The only answer is to ask the painful questions I don't want to ask, but if I don't, I'll never know. Could there be a chance that maybe I can have a family? I have my mom, but her lies have eaten away at me, leaving me utterly alone. Not true; you have him. Dane. My grumpy, forbidden lover. It's only temporary, though; he can only chase the pain away for so long.

The door flings open. Letter still in hand, I turn to face whoever has caught me in the act. There he is, in the flesh, the man I had only just been thinking about. The sound of the door closing echoes in the office. Then he steps farther into the room, crossing the small space that separates us.

"What are you doing in here?" I clutch the paper closer to my chest. His gaze flicks down to my hands as he slowly approaches me. "I followed you." There's a brief silence. "And before you give me shit about it, this is what *we* do. We follow each other."

He's right. We're really bad at boundaries when it comes to one another.

"Shouldn't you be in practice?"

"Yes," he says as his strides eat up the remaining distance between us until he's only a breath away. He should leave. I should tell him to leave. I don't, though.

For a moment, we don't talk, but then his hand reaches out and removes the paper from my hand. I close my eyes, tears forming behind my lids. I know he's reading it, and I feel naked before him and can't bear to see what the look in his eyes will be. The rough pads of his fingers lift my jaw. "Please look at me."

I shake my head.

"Hellfire."

"I don't want to talk about it." Unshed tears feel heavy behind my lids.

"And that's okay. We don't have to."

I take a deep breath and open my eyes. A lone tear runs down my cheek as I watch Dane place the paper back on the desk. "Come here."

"No."

"Please."

I scrunch my nose and shake my head again. He lifts his brow, but then he doesn't wait for me to move. Instead, he steps up and wraps his arms around me. It feels good to be encased in his arms. The comfort he gives feels real; it makes us feel real.

I shouldn't allow myself to think these thoughts, but as I exhale the pent-up emotion inside me, I fall into him. A wrecked sob escapes my mouth, and fresh tears fall, and he never lets me go. He holds me as my world crashes to the ground, and everything I thought was real disappears into a fog that has now lifted.

When my sobs stop, he pulls back and looks down at me. We stare at each other for a moment, and nothing matters at that moment but him holding me.

chapter forty-eight

Josie

It's been a long and draining week since I found the DNA test. When I said yes to coming over today, I felt fine. Now, standing at his front door, I feel like I'm dying.

I'm exhausted and to make matters worse, it's *that* time of the month.

We're supposed to be fun and casual, and now I'm rolling up feeling like shit. My stomach is cramping, and I'm miserable. It feels like I'm coming down with a cold or flu.

I should cancel.

If I turn around now and head back to my car, maybe I can text him from the car and let him know.

Right as I'm about to scurry back to my car, the front door opens.

"Planning on knocking? Or were you just going to stand there all day?"

"I mean, it's nice over here." I pretend to look around and

examine his front door. "Nice shade. Spacious. No one to interrupt me as I do some soul-searching."

He suppresses a smile. "The inside is even better. Come, I'll even make you hot chocolate."

Dane reaches out and pulls me into his arms and picks me up. "What are you doing?"

"Making the choice for you." He carries me into the house. His footsteps sound heavy with our combined weight, and I grimace from the sound.

Now my head hurts.

A groan slips out.

He halts. "What's wrong?"

"Nothing." There's no way he's buying what I'm selling since I sound like shit.

In his arms, I breathe in his scent. He smells delicious. Like the forest on a summer day. Crisp yet smoky.

My lids flutter shut as he walks us to his bed. Then he places me down on the floor. I expect him to kiss me, but instead, he pulls back the fluffy duvet.

"Get in."

I arch my brow. "What are you doing?"

"You don't feel good, so I'm tucking you in." He moves to the cabinet and opens it, rummaging through the drawer until he pulls a T-shirt out. "But first, put this on and get comfy."

I reach out and grab the soft cotton from him before slipping my sweater and leggings off.

Once I'm in his shirt, I slip under the sheets, and Dane then tucks me into his bed, taking great care to make sure I'm fully covered and comfy.

A feeling of comfort washes over me, and although my stomach hurts, I feel happy and at peace.

"What can I get for you?"

"I'm PMSing."

"Okay, well, I have plenty of experience with this. So let me handle it."

"Um—"

"Molly," he tells me.

"Oh, got it."

"Yeah, she's always had bad periods, so I'm an expert. I'll be back. Just close your eyes and rest."

I try to do what he says, but my mind is spinning a million miles per minute.

Is this really happening?

Here I am, a miserable wreck, and the man I'm supposed to be casual with is tucking me into his bed to make me more comfortable.

Shouldn't he be telling me to leave?

Isn't that what men do?

I wouldn't know. I've never had a boyfriend before. Obviously, I was no virgin when I met Dane. I've never had anything serious other than a college boyfriend, but he never would have tucked me into his bed when I was ill.

I close my eyes again, but my bone-tired body is not able to stay awake.

I'm not sure how long I've slept, but the sound of footsteps and rustling of plastic has me opening my eyes.

I blink a few times to clear the haze and find Dane standing beside where I'm sleeping.

"I brought you some necessities." His hands reach out, and he pulls back the duvet, slipping a heating pad over my stomach. It's already turned on and feels amazing.

"I also brought you some medicine and things."

"Things?" I smile.

He works his jaw as he hands me the bag, and I look inside. "I didn't know if you needed pads or whatnot or which you liked, so I brought—"

"The entire CVS store?"

"Hey, I stayed away from the nail polish and makeup section. It is a big black hole I never venture into unless Molly is really depressed." He grins. "I also made you hot chocolate with marshmallow inside, as advertised at my front door. Secret recipe."

Right on the nightstand, I find a huge, goofy ladybug mug with steaming hot chocolate and marshmallows. The man didn't leave anything up to chance. I take a sip and close my eyes. It's heaven. And he's right. It doesn't taste like a regular hot chocolate.

My brows knit as I try to figure out the secret ingredient. Cinnamon? No. No. It tastes like . . .

"Melted caramel candy." He helps me out, his voice hovering close by, his addicting male scent mixing with the cocoa smell. "Don't tell anyone. As I said, secret recipe."

"Now you'll have to kill me." I open my eyes, smiling.

The hungry possessiveness I find in his eyes brings me to a halt. "Kill you? Nah. I think I'll keep you."

"I love you—I mean." *Shit.* "Not love—you know what I mean."

Dane laughs. "Yes, I know. You love my superior hot chocolate."

"Yeah, I was talking to the chocolate."

There's also candy he bought from the drugstore. I grab a bar out of the bag and start eating it. Damn, that's good. There's crispy praline in each bite and creamy hazelnut.

It's to die for.

After I finish eating, I put the wrapper back in the bag, and he shakes his head. "I'll take the trash."

"Dane, you don't have to do that."

"Yeah, I do."

"No, really, this is too much."

"It's not nearly enough. Every girl deserves to be spoiled when she feels like shit."

I sigh, closing my eyes again. "I could get used to this." *But you shouldn't.*

Dane Sinclair is a drug.

One dose, and you're hooked for life.

chapter forty-nine

Josie

I ARRIVE EARLY TO OUR FLIGHT AND AM ALREADY ON THE PLANE when Dane and his sister arrive.

Molly sees me as she walks through the aisle to find a seat and smiles broadly. My stomach flutters. She seems so excited. *Maybe he talked to her about me.*

Excitement courses through my body as she approaches.

"Mind if I sit next to you?" she asks.

I gesture to the seat by the window. "Have at it."

"Great, thanks." She turns to face her brother. "I'm going to sit with Josie. Let me know if you need me."

When she steps past me, I get a clear view of him, and I feel my cheeks getting warm. When I left this morning, we hadn't spoken about this trip, but I assume after the past few days, he'll want me in his bed . . .

Maybe he'll even want to discuss us.

I open my mouth to say something, but he doesn't even look

at me. He just continues walking to another seat farther back on the plane.

My heart feels like it's going to explode from my chest.

Did that really just happen?

Maybe I'm reading too much into it. Perhaps he was preoccupied with finding a seat. Things always get a little nuts when you're on a plane.

Yeah, that's it. It's fine. *We're fine.*

"I'm so excited to go swimming."

I look over at where Molly practically bounces in her seat.

My brow furrows. "What?"

"The weather is still nice in Arizona, duh. I hate it when it gets cold in Ohio; all the pools close."

"Oh." Yep, that's all I got. I'm still thinking about her damn brother and what his behavior, aka the snub, means.

"There's a pool on the roof of the hotel."

"Ugh, I would kill for a skinny margarita on a rooftop pool."

"You should join me." The offer seems genuine, and a part of me wants to, but I'm also not sure what Dane has planned.

The past few weeks of the season, I've been sneaking out and meeting him when we're out of town, but who the heck knows. Once we take off, I'll find a way to talk to him and feel him out.

"Ugh, I want to. I'm slammed with that new Redville TikTok that's taking off, but let me see if I could escape for a bit," I answer as I recline back into the buttery leather seats.

Twenty minutes later, I find my opportunity. The plane has leveled out, and when I turn around, I see Dane standing by the bathroom, waiting to use it. If I pretend I'm also waiting, I can probably talk to him real fast.

Standing from my seat, I stroll casually toward where Dane is, trying not to make it obvious that I'm there to talk to him.

When he doesn't turn around to look at me, I lift my hand and move to touch his arm. His head turns, and our eyes meet.

They look glacial blue right now.

A chill runs down my spine, but it isn't the way he stares at me that has my stomach bottoming out. It's the fact that he just stepped away from my touch.

My arm falls to my side when there's nothing to grab on to.

My mouth opens and shuts. Did he really just evade me touching him?

"Dane?"

"Whoa, there, buddy. Personal space much?" He tries to chuckle, but I can sense there's more to unpack here. He doesn't want me here. "How can I help you?"

What's with the cold front?

Once again, I open my mouth to say more, but just as I find the words, the bathroom door opens. My father walks out, and Dane walks in.

I head back to my chair. No point in pretending anymore. I press the call button on my seat.

It's time for a drink.

chapter fifty

Dane

THE DOOR TO THE MAIN ELEVATOR IS ABOUT TO CLOSE WHEN a hand peeks through the small space. It instantly reopens, and when it does, my little hellfire stands at the opening.

Normally, I'd take the private elevator that only stops at the penthouse and pool deck, but for some reason, the damn thing wasn't working. Which I'm now happy about because I want to speak to her about what happened on the plane.

"Going up?" The side of her lips tips up into a smirk.

"I am."

Josephine stumbles forward as she enters the elevator. Great, my little hellfire is drunk. I step aside, allowing her to enter while holding out my arm to brace her so she doesn't fall. She has a tendency to fall even when she's sober. And knowing her, anything is possible.

"Oh, look, you're touching me in public." She scoffs.

This is what I was worried about.

My behavior on the plane was uncalled for, but seeing as Robert had just stepped into the bathroom, I wasn't sure when he'd be coming out or what he could hear in there.

Better safe than sorry, so I pushed her away, but the moment I did, I realized my mistake.

I hurt her, and I feel awful about it, which is why I understand her anger right now. She has every reason to be pissed at me.

The thing she doesn't understand is that it's not any easier on me than it is on her not being able to be openly affectionate, but with the season happening, the team can't risk any turmoil.

It would certainly be turmoil if the coach learned I engaged in a relationship with his daughter. After what I read, it's obvious that this relationship is new, and they're still trying to figure it out. Coach Robert seems more willing, and Josephine seems more reluctant, but again, it's not my place to put any extra stress on them.

"What floor, Hellfire?"

"The roof," she answers, and my back goes ramrod straight. The roof is where the pool is. There is no way that Josephine, in her current state, should be allowed anywhere near a pool.

A knot in my stomach forms, and I can't help the way my mind races with what-if scenarios of all the things that could go wrong if a drunk Josephine swims alone.

"I don't think that's such a good idea."

"Who are you, my dad?" She pushes my hands off her and moves to the other side of the elevator. Now, with her arms crossed at her chest, she levels me with a stare. "You might as well be. I've known you just as long." This is the first time that Josephine is openly talking about her struggles with her father. And while I know I should shut it down because she needs to be put to bed, I don't have the heart to stop her.

She uncrosses her arms, reaches for the button, and presses the top floor. I guess I won't be going to sleep after all. There's no way I'm letting her go up there alone. I need to be with her to make sure she's okay—not just physically but also emotionally.

The ride is relatively silent, except for a few audible sighs of annoyance coming from her. When we finally come to a stop, she doesn't wait to see if anyone is standing on the other side of the doors before she flies out of the small space.

The pool is empty. A sign on the wall says the pool has been closed for the past two hours.

I wonder if security will come up.

You never can tell. Sometimes, they turn a blind eye to the team's antics. I'm actually surprised Hudson isn't up here in the hot tub. But last I heard, he was busy with some local girl he met in the lobby. Didn't take him long to find his flavor for the night.

Before I can stop her, the little hellfire lifts her dress over her head and runs toward the pool.

Fuck.

Just what I need.

This is a disaster.

A part of me knows that I should be pissed about the way she's acting—that she's drunk or the fact that when we get caught up here, the ensuing drama will not be worth the view. But I can't be because I'm too damn concerned about her well-being to even care if anyone finds us here.

My heart pounds heavily in my chest. "Josephine."

She doesn't answer. Instead, she chooses to dive back into the water.

My left hand lifts, and I run it through my hair. What am I going to do with this girl?

She pops up for a second.

"Please don't make me come in and get you."

"Yeah, okay. I'm sure you're going to do that," she slurs.

"I will." I'd do anything to protect her. How can she not see that? *Because you're an asshole half the time, that's why.*

"No way you're going to ruin your fancy shirt."

Lies. I'd burn this shirt if it made her smile.

"Watch me."

Not waiting for another second, I walk to the edge of the shallow end, where she is now, and lower myself into the water.

I feel weighted down by the liquid clinging to the fibers of my clothes, but I keep trudging in her direction.

"Hellfire."

"Grump," she counters.

"Get over here," I growl. This woman tests my patience. My sanity, too. With each second I'm in this damn pool, the chances of her drowning grow greater.

This needs to end now. I need to get her out of here and make sure she doesn't hurt herself. But on the other side of the shallow end, Hellfire is having a grand old time, splashing around and doing what appears to be underwater cartwheels. She resurfaces with a giant smirk on her face. "Come and get me."

When I finally make it to her, she bats her wet lashes at me, and then she jumps, wrapping her legs and arms around me like an octopus.

I try to untangle her, but she's not having it. Why does she have to make everything more difficult, and why does she also have to be so damn enticing while she does it?

My dick, who apparently has a mind of its own, has come out to play, not that I'll let it.

"You might seem upset, but he doesn't." Her hand has found my hard dick in my soaked pants and has begun to rub me.

Great, just what I need.

If my dick wasn't hard enough, now it's sticking up practically to my belly, begging to fuck.

"Josephi—" I can't get her whole name out because halfway through, she's kissing me, all while stroking my shaft.

An idea comes to me, and I don't pass it up. I kiss her back, plundering her mouth. She falls deeper into the kiss, so deep she hasn't realized we're moving.

It isn't until the cold air hits us that she realizes we are no longer in the pool.

"Hey—" She pulls her mouth off mine.

"Shh—" I meet her lips again and render her speechless.

Then I head straight for the elevator. Pressing the button for my floor because the only way I can ensure her safety is if she's with me all night.

Consequences be damned.

chapter fifty-one

Josie

EARLY MORNING SUNLIGHT FILTERS INTO THE ROOM.
It's too bright. And way too early.

What time is it anyway?

I let out a groan, and when I do, something else hits me. My head is killing me. It feels like there is a pulse in my brain.

God, how much did I drink last night?

I blink my eyes open, squinting against the light. The moment the room comes into focus, I take in my surroundings.

Where am I? This isn't my room.

Hotel.

I'm away.

The Saints have a game today, so I stayed in a hotel.

Okay . . . I let out a breath, but as soon as I do, something else hits me . . .

This isn't my hotel room.

I jerk up, and I instantly regret the move as the room spins, which, in turn, makes my stomach churn.

Inhale. You're okay.

Once the sick feeling passes, I scan the room. It's much larger than mine. It's a suite. But whose?

Memories of the previous night rush over me.

Getting upset when Dane wasn't paying attention to me. Drinking.

Getting upset when my father tried to talk to me. Drinking.

Drinking for no reason.

Okay, well, that explains why my head is killing me.

What else?

There must be more to last night other than the booze that apparently kept flowing.

An elevator.

Dane in the elevator.

Oh my God.

A pool.

My hands lift, and I bury my head in them.

A groan escapes. "Did I really go swimming last night?"

"Yes."

Will the world please swallow me whole right now?

I turn toward the door as it flings open. The loud creak sounds like nails on a chalkboard, but it's the man who's prowling toward me that has my eyes closing in embarrassment.

"Open your eyes. It's not that bad."

I do and see he's holding a food tray.

When our gazes meet, he smiles. "Morning, Hellfire. How are you feeling?"

"Like I got hit by a truck," I mumble, pulling the covers up to my chin. "What happened?"

"I thought it was obvious? You got shit-faced." Dane sets the tray down beside the bed on the side table.

"But why am I here?"

"It was easier to take you down the private elevator for the suites than down the normal elevator you took from your room. Less chance of getting caught."

My cheeks feel like they are on fire. "Did I really go swimming?"

"Yes."

"Kill me now," I groan.

Dane chuckles. "No. I don't think so. Also, you won't get to eat the breakfast I ordered you."

"You ordered me breakfast?"

"Yep. And coffee. Creamer, two sugars."

"You remembered."

"I think you'll soon realize I pay attention when it comes to you."

If it were possible for my heart to beat out of my chest and explode, it would. Either that or I'd swoon until I melt.

After taking a seat beside me on the bed, he reaches over to grab the cup of coffee and passes it to me. I take a sip. "So good."

Once I've taken a few more sips, I place the mug down and look over the tray. A breakfast sandwich. I could kiss this man. I don't deserve his kindness after being such an ass last night.

"I really am sorry, Dane. Last night—I shouldn't have gotten that drunk."

"Why did you? What happened?"

I sigh, and the movement makes a small piece of hair fall over my face.

Dane reaches out and tucks it behind my ear.

"Josephine," Dane says gently, "you can talk to me."

I smile weakly. "I don't even know where to start."

"Sometimes, I find the beginning is the best place."

"It's a long story."

"I have time."

I shake my head. "No, actually, you have a game."

"It's six o'clock."

"Good point." After a few more bites, since I'll need my energy, I decide it's time to tell him.

I take a deep breath, looking down at my fingers currently twirling the sheet in my hand.

"I—last night, you were ignoring me—and when I tried to touch you—"

"I didn't mean to. I was—"

"Stop. You were right. You knew my father was in the bathroom, I understand, but then I started thinking about my father, and how much I don't know about him and how he's your family, and I just lost it."

He nibbles on his lower lip, most likely wondering if what he wants to say will upset me.

"There's a lot you don't know—and more that I don't know. The thing is, I only met my father the day after I met you. The first night," I clarify.

"I don't understand."

"My whole life, I never had a father. And then, one day, my mom shipped me off. She was done. The thing is, it's always been us. She's worked her ass off. Single mom. Low-paying job." I lift my hand to my head. "She's done everything for me, and I just wasn't doing what I needed to do, so she got fed up." And rightfully so. *I see that now.* I was a mess. "The same day she told me I was leaving, she told me about my father."

"I can't imagine that Robert would know about you and not want to be in your life."

"That's the thing. I stormed out and then left the next day. I drove to meet him. I was supposed to meet him at the party, but I chickened out. And you know the rest—"

He nods. "And then you came to work for him."

"Yep. I refused to talk to him. I don't know why. I still refuse. But that day in the office, I found the paternity test. The date on it. I don't think he knew about me either."

"There's only one way to find out."

"I know. But I'm not ready."

"I understand that. I can't begin to understand what you're going through, but I do know what it's like to have no parents."

"All you have is Molly."

"Yeah."

"You must think I'm an asshole for not wanting to talk to him."

"I don't, Hellfire. I'd never judge for that. Relationships are unique. It's not my place to judge."

We stare at each other for a minute, and then I lean forward, placing a kiss on his lips.

"Thank you."

chapter fifty-two

Josie

I SMOOTH MY SKIRT BEFORE I STEP INTO THE ROOM. IT'S PROBABLY not the smartest wardrobe choice, seeing as I'm near the ice, but I wanted to look cute today.

Drive him crazy.

"Hey, Josie." I turn to see Molly. I really like her. Whenever she's around me, she's super nice and always seems to be smiling. Well, that is, if Hudson isn't around.

She really seems not to like him for some reason.

"Molly." I smile back. "What's going on?"

Even though I know she's nice, I always feel a little awkward when she's around.

A part of me wonders if she can see through my act and knows I want her brother desperately.

Either way, if she does, she doesn't act on it, and I continue to play the part of indifference when he's around.

"What are you doing today?" she asks, and I lift my brow.

Besides trying to "bump" into your brother and seduce him, I have no clue.

"So much. I don't even know where to start." I laugh. "I have to come up with a content schedule for the week. Then I'm making graphics and scheduling the posts."

"I was thinking we should grab lunch, my treat. But you seem busy." She grimaces.

I hesitate for a second, wondering if I can juggle my day. Everyone gets a lunch break. Just because I don't always take one doesn't mean I don't get one. It could be fun. Plus, I really like Molly.

"Sure, sounds great." I flatten my skirt with my hand.

"Great. Let's say noon at the bistro. We can either walk together or meet there."

"Let's plan on going together. That is, if I'm done making my cute Canva montages of the players skating for the day."

Molly laughs. "I can't imagine Dane is happy about being in these videos. Hudson? Yeah. Dane? Not so much."

"He really doesn't have a choice. Plus, he doesn't even know I'm taking them half the time. I'm stealthy with my camera." I wink.

"Nice. Okay, well, I should go find that man. I have a list of one million things he needs to do, all of which he will protest. Bet you don't miss working with him."

Oh, but I do. Every single minute of the day. "Nope. Have fun with that list," I respond, biting back the real answer to her question.

Once Molly leaves the room, I head off in search of Laurie.

<hr />

A few hours later, I meet Molly at the exit of the practice arena. Together, we walk to a bistro a few blocks away. Molly chatters animatedly about her trip. How it was the best summer of her life.

The question on my tongue that I don't let out is, why did you come back early?

It only takes us a few minutes to walk to the restaurant, and when we get there, we find an empty table right away.

This area of Redville is much less crowded than the downtown area where the team plays their games. Plus, the ambience is adorable. It reminds me of a bistro you would see in the movies, like it belongs in France.

"I love this place." Molly beams as we approach the small, checkered table. The scent of freshly baked bread wafts in the area.

"It reminds me so much of France."

My assessment was right. "I wouldn't know. I've never left the Midwest. Well, not counting since I've started working for the team."

Molly stops walking and looks over her shoulder at me, brow lifted.

"Really?"

"Yep."

I can tell by her narrowed eyes that she has a ton of questions. *Get in line. So do I.*

Like why on earth did my mother never tell me about him? Or better yet, why on earth did she obviously never tell him about me?

While I haven't confirmed that, it's pretty apparent from the paternity test.

Oh well. One day, I'll get up the nerve to ask him.

Just not now.

Or anytime soon.

It's bad enough that my mom rejected me. I don't think I can handle another rejection.

"I haven't actually ever left Redville. To live, I mean. Obviously, I've left to go on trips and vacations. But I grew up here."

I slide into the chair, and she takes the one across from me.

"Really?"

"Yeah, I mean you might already know this from working with Dane while I was away, but our parents died, and well, he raised me."

I knew he raised her, but I never asked what that entailed.

"He mentioned it."

"Yeah. He became my legal guardian when I was eleven years old."

I close my mouth and nibble at my bottom lip. "He was so young. Dane was what—like eighteen?"

"He was."

"I can't imagine that was easy for either of you."

"It wasn't. Especially for him, but he doesn't like to talk about that. Or anything, for that matter." She laughs.

I incline my head and take her in. She's a beautiful girl with similar features to her brother. When she was eleven, I imagine she was most likely adorable, had a great personality, and was easy to deal with because of her sweet disposition. But still, that had to be hard at eighteen.

"Was he in college?"

"No. Actually, he was a senior in high school. It's why he stayed local, playing one year of college hockey, before Coach took him pro when he took over as head coach for the Saints."

I knew my father coached Dane in college, but I didn't realize my father was the reason he went pro so young.

It's bad enough that I know nothing of my father, but now it's even more heartbreaking.

I can tell right away there is a long story there, and of course, my father treats him like a son and vice versa; from what it sounds like, Dane was forced to grow up way before his time, and my father was the one who helped him.

Interesting.

Maybe I'm wrong about my father after all.

chapter fifty-three

Josie

A FEW DAYS AFTER OUR LUNCH, I'M PLEASANTLY SURPRISED BY Molly's invitation to join her for drinks tonight.

I glance around the bar, a nervous energy coursing through my veins. My heart races a mile a minute, and I'm not sure why.

Okay, that's a lie. I know why.

I just don't want to admit it to myself.

Dane.

He'll be here soon.

Not that it matters since he won't even speak to me when he's here, but just having him in the vicinity makes me jittery.

Maybe I'll be able to lure him away, sneak into the bathroom, and have my wicked way with him.

Looking around the bar, I spot the team. Hudson turns, and the moment he sees me, he waves.

I make my way through the crowd, and with each step I take, I search for Dane. Finally, as the crowd parts, there he is.

He doesn't see me at first, but then he tilts his chin up, and our gazes meet.

His features look tight, and his stare is unsettling, but then what looks like a small smile lines his face.

A rush of warmth fills my veins, and I'm sure my cheeks are crimson.

How does this man do this to me?

One look, and I'm a puddle on the ground.

When I reach the table, he turns to face Hudson, and my heart feels like it was stabbed with a serrated knife.

"How's my favorite intern?" Hudson teases, and a small, slender hand flicks his shoulder.

"Don't flirt with her. Not unless you want Coach to know, and you get benched or, worse, traded . . ." Molly says. I can't see her face, but since I've been spending time with her recently, I'd recognize the voice anywhere. "Actually—keep flirting." She leans forward until she's visible. "Sorry, Josie, but can you take one for the team? Hudson's a menace."

"Sure." I shrug. "Flirt away."

"Not nice, princess. I'm wounded." He raises his hands in mock defeat.

"Her name is Josephine." There's no mistaking the rough and gravelly voice. Dane isn't happy, not that he ever is.

"Jeez. You're even more of an asshole tonight than ever. What's up your ass?"

"Nothing. Just not in the mood for your shit tonight."

"Touchy. At least Molly—"

"Molly? Nothing," Molly chides. She stands up from her seat and heads in my direction, pulling out the chair directly beside me.

"With all this testosterone in the air, I figured us girls should stick together."

"Sounds good to me."

"Thank God, because it was either you or Laurie."

"Laurie isn't that bad."

258

"She isn't good, though."

I laugh because her assessment is spot-on.

It takes me a minute to get into the conversation. I'm pretty lost, seeing as I showed up late, but I try my best to mingle in a way that's not obvious.

Mason eventually returns to the table with a pitcher of beer, and I pour myself a glass. Unfortunately, when I do, a little dribbles out of the pitcher and gets on the table and my hand. I see a pile of napkins that I reach for, and when I do, I notice I'm not the only one who went for them.

Dane's fingers brush against mine. And although I know it was an accident, he lingers there. The moment stands still, voices fade away, and all that is in that room is him, and it feels like jolts of energy course through me as our skin touches.

"Sorry." Dane pulls away, and I want to beg him not to leave, but I really don't have a choice.

"It's fine," I respond, my chest pounding.

The touch is brief, but the effects linger. My face is warm and flushed.

This man does crazy things to me.

Dane moves to separate from me, and when he does, I get a clear shot of Molly.

She's looking right at us. Her eyes narrow, and her jaw clenches.

Shit. What did she see?

Does she know?

And if she does, what will she do with the information?

chapter fifty-four

Dane

ANOTHER GAME. ANOTHER CITY.
    Because of the distance and time of tomorrow's game, we're spending the night once again.

The plan is to go to dinner and then sneak Josephine into my room.

It's not ideal, but I can't imagine spending the night without her.

Her presence calms me, and I'll need that now more than ever, seeing as we are playing the Empires tomorrow.

They are a team to be reckoned with, but since we met them last year for the Cup, they are even more so.

Everyone thinks we're a shoo-in. Well, everyone except the assholes who are most likely betting against us.

Like all of New York.

I start to pace my hotel room; I'm having a hard time keeping still. Another reason I need my little hellfire. If she were here, I could work out my energy.

Fuck.

Now I really don't want to go to dinner.

Lifting my arm up, I check my watch. It's only seven, and dinner isn't until seven thirty.

I'm about to text Josephine to see if she's still with Molly when the hotel phone rings.

Strange. No one ever calls me on that thing. I walk over to the phone and pick it up.

"Hello." The confusion is most likely evident in my voice. Either that or I sound like a grump, as Josephine likes to tell me.

"Good evening, Mr. Sinclair. There's a package for you at the front desk."

My brows draw in. Why would anyone send a package to me? Especially since I'm in New York. But then I think about Molly. Maybe it was her. She does tend to drop off stuff I need; maybe she's too busy hanging out with Hellfire and gave it to the concierge.

She should have just given it to Josephine and made my life easier and a hell of a lot better.

Only one problem with that plan—Molly doesn't know about Hellfire and me. Second problem, she's way too observant not to see the signs if I asked her to have her bring it up.

Yep, nope. Bad idea.

"Can you have someone bring it up, please?"

"No problem, sir. It will be up shortly."

I hang up the phone and walk to the other side of the living room in my suite. Grabbing the whiskey decanter, I pour myself a glass and wait.

I'm halfway through my drink when the knock sounds against the door. I don't bother placing my glass down. Instead, I walk with it to the door and open it with my free hand.

An employee from the hotel is carrying a small, nondescript envelope. Interesting. Maybe not from Molly after all.

I reach into my pocket with my free hand, grab a wad of bills, and tip him before taking the envelope and shutting the door.

Even stranger is when I look at the white envelope, and the only thing written on it is my name. In neat uppercase letters.

I furrow my brow. The handwriting looks familiar, but I can't place it.

I place my glass down and rip it open. Inside is a single photograph. One from a long time ago.

I flip over the card. My breath catches in my throat. Memories of that night come flooding back, unwanted and vivid.

The handwriting. I know the handwriting, but it's the note scribbled that has chills running down my spine. *The past always has a way of haunting us.*

I drop the photograph as if it singed my fingers. My mind races a million miles a minute.

Who sent this? Do they know?

Maybe it's just a coincidence.

Anger and fear surge up, threatening to overwhelm me.

My heart pounds in my chest. It feels like I might throw up.

I flop down on the couch. The weight of it crushing me. Guilt and regret swallowing me whole.

"What the fuck do you think you're doing?" an angry voice booms from the now open front door of the house. I peer up and see my uncle Jim storming toward me. The man is a mean son of a bitch.

I sit up taller. "You're going to have to be a little clearer. I do a lot of shit," I respond, trying my best not to let him see fear. If my uncle sees blood in the water, he'll pounce.

"You know exactly what I'm talking about, you little shit."

From the corner of the room, the small face of my sister pops through the open door that leads to the basement. She was downstairs playing and must have heard the commotion. I meet her gaze and give my head a little shake, not large enough for Uncle Jim to notice, but enough that she knows what I'm telling her. To leave.

It would be bad if he caught her.

"You're a kid. There's no way you really think you're going to win."

"I will."

"With what money? You have no income." He sneers at me. "Don't fuck with me, Dane."

I stand from the couch, stalking over to where my uncle stands. "Get out."

"Big, tough guy. Let's see how tough you are when I make sure you get none of your parents' money." He laughs before turning around and leaving the house.

"Your uncle is an ass." I turn to see my friend Nick sitting there. Fuck. I forgot he was there.

"So what're you going to do?"

I bury my head in my hands. "I have no idea."

How the hell am I going to get the money to fight my uncle for custody of Molly.

"I might just have an idea that will solve all your problems . . ."

What am I going to do?

My whole life is based on a lie, and now—

No. This is just a coincidence. I shake my head back and forth, and if it's not?

My phone rings, and I see a text coming through.

It's Hellfire.

I can't see her.

Not now and, depending on if this threat is real, not ever.

If my secret gets out . . . life as I know it will never be the same.

What if Coach finds out? He'll never let me near his team, let alone his daughter.

The more I think about it, the more I know I need to break up with Hellfire to *protect* her.

And that leaves four problems.

First—I don't want to break up with her.

Second—I refuse to hurt her feelings.

Third—it's im-freaking-possible to break up with someone without hurting their feelings.

And fourth—I DON'T WANT TO BREAK UP WITH HER.

In the end, I know I need to be firm, or my persistent hellfire will scent out my weakness. She always does.

I stare at my phone, my hands trembling.

Do it.

Dane: Something came up. I won't be able to see you.

Hellfire: Are you okay?

Dane: Yes.

I bury my face in my hands. I did the right thing.

There was no choice to be made.

This is for the best.

chapter fifty-five

Josie

WE'RE IN NEW YORK TODAY. THE SAINTS ARE PLAYING THE Empires tonight, but since we have a few hours before the game, and Dane canceled on me yesterday, I've decided to take Molly up on her offer to go sightseeing with her.

"So, where to first?" I ask her as we step outside the hotel the team stayed in last night in New York City.

"You've never been, right?"

I shake my head. "Nope."

"Then today, we are tourists." She winks.

"And as tourists, where should we go?"

"Hmm, Times Square?"

"I saw it last night while we were driving in. Seemed crowded." I grimace playfully.

Molly laughs beside me. "It is, but isn't all of the city?" she deadpans.

She's right. Even now, this early in the morning, it's insane. I scan the street in front of me, and all I can see is an endless stream of cars and trucks passing us, honking taxis, and masses of people dashing by, all late for something. How they're already late when it's only seven in the morning is beyond me. Nothing is even open yet.

Hence, us meeting for breakfast before walking around. Duh. But alas, the city never sleeps apparently.

"Let's grab breakfast at the diner I saw a few blocks away when we arrived last night, and then after, we can walk downtown."

"Sounds like a good plan. I can always eat."

Together, we start to walk, Molly leading the way. "How do you like working for the team?" she asks, and I wonder if this is some sort of trick question. Molly seems observant. I've noticed her looking at me and her brother a few times, and I can't help but feel she knows.

I won't be the one to say anything. It's not my place, but it still makes me watch my words carefully. "I actually love it. I didn't know if I would, but I do."

"Social media marketing? Was that always what you wanted to do?"

"Isn't it what our whole generation wants to do?" I tease.

The light turns green, and we have to stop walking so we don't get run over.

Molly turns to face me. "Yep. Well, not me."

I narrow my eyes at her, wanting to know more. "Have you always wanted to work for your brother?"

"Hey." She laughs. "I asked my question first."

I roll my eyes playfully. "True, but I had hoped I could get out of answering."

"Ahh, there's a story there."

"Oh, there's a story." I laugh. "I was actually sent here because I had no clue what I wanted to do with my life. The Redville Saints was my punishment, believe it or not."

"And is it a punishment?"

I shake my head as I think about the past few months. "No. It's not. Honestly, I think it's probably the best thing that's ever happened to me. I love the energy of working for the team, and I love the marketing aspects too."

"Who came up with this punishment? I can't see Robert doing this."

"My mom."

"Maybe she was on to something."

I nod to myself, wondering if maybe she was. Perhaps she didn't send me away to punish me. Maybe she sent me away because she knew I lacked direction. I mean, I do love this. Creating content. Making people happy. It's a form of art, down to picking the music, the angles, and the fresh, original, funny content. It's cool to make engaging videos for something I'm not even that into. Hockey.

"We're here." Molly brings me back to the present, and I decide to table all thoughts of my mom for a later time when I can think about it. Right now, I'm in the city, ready to see the sights with a new friend.

chapter fifty-six

Josie

I T'S BEEN A CRAZY THREE DAYS SINCE I RETURNED FROM NEW York. I've barely had a moment to think. I'm creating a new TikTok campaign, so I've been running around the whole city interviewing fans and asking them what they love most about hockey. It's been amazing. The only downside is that I've been too busy to call Dane.

I figure he must be insane with his own stuff because he hasn't reached out either, so I decide to drop by his place before I head home to say hi.

I lift my hand and bang on the door, then follow by hitting the doorbell.

Maybe I should have called first?

That probably would have been the smart move, but I'm impulsive.

My fingers tap a rhythm on the wood as I wait for him to answer the door.

He might not even be here.

I didn't call or text, yet I expected him to be, what? Waiting for me at his home despite the fact I gave no inclination that I'd be stopping by.

This is not my finest hour.

I drop my arm.

Tap. Tap. Tap. This time, my fingers drum on my thigh. I'm about to turn around when the front door swings open.

"Josephine? What are you doing?" His voice sounds funny. Slurred. *Is he drunk?*

"Hi." I smile.

He steps closer to me until he stands in front of me. "What are you doing here?"

"You didn't call, so I figured I'd check in."

His body sways, and now I'm sure he's not sober. "And so you decided to just show up?"

I brush my hands against my thighs, wiping away a fleck of dust. Anything not to meet his stare.

"This is what *we* do," I remind him. "Bad day?" I ask. I reach my hand out to touch him, but he takes a step back before he crosses his arms at his chest, making it very obvious he doesn't want me to touch him.

I peer up at his face, taking him in. His eyes look unfocused, and his lips form a straight line.

The playful version I've grown to care about is long gone, replaced by a Dane Sinclair I don't even recognize.

"I wanted to be alone."

His voice is so foreign, it takes a moment to process his words. When I finally do, I have to force myself to stay upright. My vision starts to blur. He's reached into my chest and ripped my heart out. Even standing feels like fighting nature.

Breathe, Josie.

"Are—Are you okay?"

His chest rises and falls with jerky movements. Maybe it's

pathetic, but I narrow in on it, desperately seeking something to grasp. A weakness that'll tell me he's joking. Someone forced him into this.

"I need air," he blurts out, and hope blossoms in my chest.

"We're outside." I raise a brow. "If this is a joke, I'm not laughing."

"Shit." Dane winces like he didn't mean for me to hear his curse. He thrusts his hand through his hair with enough force to make the team stylist weep. "This isn't a joke. I'm serious. This isn't working, hel—Josephine. This isn't working, Josephine."

"Dane—"

"Just leave." He motions between us. "This isn't going to happen."

I open my mouth to argue. Something's clearly wrong. It's obvious he's keeping something from me, and knowing him, it's the same self-sacrificial bullshit that always ruins his life.

I refuse to let him make a choice we both know he doesn't want to make.

But then his face hardens. He nods to himself like he just gave himself the pep talk of a lifetime. And then he says something that manages to crush my hope into smithereens.

"Leave, Josie. You're not worth the fight."

I barely register his wince.

I barely register the tiny step he takes to me or the way his hands jerk forward to reach me.

The only thing I feel is sheer rage.

"You know what? Fuck you, Dane. This time, it *is* goodbye. Don't *follow* me next time you want to get your dick wet."

chapter fifty-seven

Josie

THAT MOTHERFUCKER.
You're not worth the fight.

His words ping-pong between my ears, back and forth, over and over again until I crank up the car radio to full volume.

I should have known. I should have left first.

He didn't pick me.

He picked my father.

I can't help but laugh at how cruel life is, giving me love only to take it away. My father, Mom, Dane. No one ever fights for me. I laugh and laugh and laugh until suddenly, I'm crying.

Fat tears race down my cheeks. It's ugly and wet, and anyone can see me losing my shit through the car window. I can't bring myself to care.

How the hell will I work with him? How can I see him and not feel the loss of us?

My heart is hollow.

This is what happens when you fall in love with someone who's off-limits.

Fall in love?

Shit.

Did I fall in love with him?

I did.

My fingers white-knuckle the steering wheel as I remember the moment it happened. That morning, I finally opened up to him and told him about my parents. He held me in his arms, and like an idiot, I fell.

Oh, who am I kidding? It happened the first time I saw him smile. The very first laugh.

I've always been Dane Sinclair's, yet he's never been mine.

My cries turn violent. All the emotions inside me pour out.

Tears rush past my lips, and my teeth rattle against each other as I shake.

It's like a dam has burst, and every single emotion I've pushed back is pouring out of me.

My sobs are the only sound in the car.

I reach my hand up and swipe the tears across my face. The moisture collects on my fingertips like blood pouring from a wound.

The drive to my father's house feels long and torturous. It's only about a fifteen-minute drive, but with hazy vision from swollen lids, it takes much longer, or at least it feels that way.

Finally, I pull up to his house and drive around back to my spot outside the garage.

I get out of the car and slowly walk toward the backyard. The night sky blankets me from above, and the only light comes from the stars that sparkle.

Reaching into my pocket, I'm about to pull out my phone when the side lights of the house come on.

"Josie? Is that you?"

Shit. It's my father.

For a second, I don't know what to say. If I talk, he'll hear the sadness in my voice. If I don't speak, he'll most likely come over to check on me. If he sees me, cheeks red, eyes swollen, there will be no hiding that I've been crying.

Unfortunately, the decision is taken from me as my father strides across the back patio and stops right in front of me.

"Josie." He steps closer, his hand lifting to touch my shoulder, but he stops right before he makes contact. "Are you—Are you okay?"

Another tear stains my cheek. There's no hope of pretending now.

"No. But I will be."

"I know we haven't gotten to know each other—" He sighs. "I know things are complicated, but Josie, I'm your father. I want to be your father. If you need me—"

A sob breaks from my mouth, and the next thing I know, my father's arms are wrapped around me.

Tears streak my cheeks as my body shakes.

He holds me tight, soft coos of comfort in my ear.

It's too much.

My head is spinning.

I feel like I'm drowning, and right now, I hold my father like he's the life raft keeping me afloat.

For the first time in my life, I have a dad; I have a safe haven, and I'm not alone.

I am not alone.

chapter fifty-eight

Josie

THE LAST RAYS OF SUNLIGHT CAST A SOFT GLOW OVER MY CAR as I pull down the long driveway.

I've been keeping a low profile since Dane ended things with me a few days ago. Right after the incident, I mentioned I wasn't feeling too well to Laurie, so she approved my request not to travel with the team last night for this morning's away game.

Are they back yet?

How awful would it be if my father invited Dane over tonight for one of their post-game meetings?

A shiver runs down my spine. No. That won't happen. Dane wouldn't do that to me.

I'm sure he knows I'm avoiding him since I wasn't on the flight yesterday. The only saving grace of this whole mess is that I got to work from the main marketing office, which was fun.

There's so much more to marketing than social media. These days, everyone thinks it's all about views and likes, but building a solid brand is the most important thing. I was able to watch the marketing team come up with a strategy for how to get more fans in the stands and not just steamy pictures of the guys warming up.

I park in my normal spot at the back of the house and walk toward the guesthouse.

The familiar sight disperses all the tension in my shoulders. It might have started as a prison, but the longer I'm here, the more it feels like a second home.

From the corner of my eye, I can see the lights are on in the kitchen, and it looks like someone is in the room.

I squint. It's Sherry, and by the way she's cutting vegetables at the sink, I'd guess she's preparing dinner.

My father must be home.

I halt my steps and continue to watch the main house. Just then, my father walks into the room and grabs a cup from the cabinet.

My lips tip up into a smile. Is he helping her set the table? Despite everything and the way I've acted, he held me and comforted me. I can't stop thinking about it.

I cried, and he was there for me. His concern for me was evident in the gentle way he held me and made sure I was okay. It's definitely a side to him I've never seen before, but to be honest, a part of me yearns for it now that I have.

For a second, my body freezes. I can't seem to will it to move toward the guesthouse. I'm locked in place, staring at them through the large bay window.

What would it be like to be included?

You are included.

They invited me every opportunity they got. I'm the asshole who pushed them away and said no. Maybe it's time to stop being afraid.

Taking a deep inhale, I make my decision, allowing my feet to carry me in the direction I want to go.

It's time to try.

My heart pounds in my chest as I approach the back door. I don't want to barge in, so I lift my hand and knock.

I can see them as they realize they aren't alone. My father's eyes go wide when he catches my gaze and dashes over to open the door.

"No need to knock." He steps aside to let me in. "You're always welcome."

For the first time since I got to Redville, I believe him.

It's as if a light switch went on the day he held me. I'm no longer dredged in darkness, trying to find my way. I'm able to see a light, and ironically enough, it's the father I never knew existed who leads the way.

"Are you joining us for dinner?"

I glance over my shoulder to look at him, and the softness and hope in his eyes make my chest lurch.

"I'd like that," I admit, realizing I would. This is not a lie.

"Fabulous. Sherry and I just finished setting the table in the dining room." He ruffles my hair like I'm five, and the knot inside me begins to untangle. "Come on in before Sherry eats everything. Never come between that woman and a peach cobbler."

From beyond the foyer, I catch someone shouting, "I heard that. Don't be surprised if we conveniently run out of chicken when it's your turn to be served."

Suddenly, there's nowhere I'd rather be than in that dining room, having dinner with my father.

Jittery nerves trickle through my system, twisting my fingers together. "Are you sure it isn't—"

"Yes, I'm sure." My father nods, leaving no room for discussion. "We want you here. Now let's go eat."

He ushers me into the dining room, where Sherry already is.

"Josie. Are you eating with us?" Her voice rises in excitement as she asks the same question as him.

My father steps forward, placing a hand on my shoulder. "She is."

Sherry smiles warmly at him and then pats the seat next to

her. "Sit beside me, then you can see your father better." I slip into the seat, stiffening when she leans in to whisper in my ear, "You'll need the vantage point to catch him stealing food off your plate."

I suspect she's joking on purpose to loosen me up, and it works…until I notice there's already a place setting in front of me. Sherry follows my gaze.

I fiddle with the placemat, suddenly overwhelmed. "It's set?"

"It is."

"Why?"

"For you, of course. It's been set since the day you came to live with us. " Her words bring water to my eyes.

I resist the urge to shake my head. How did I not notice before? Family isn't blood. It's commitment. It's being there in the small moments, so your loved ones feel comfortable turning to you in the big moments.

A second later, my father sits in his seat, and Sherry starts serving dinner. The dishes are simple—chicken Milanese with a lemon-parmesan arugula salad—yet, it's perfect.

"Did you have a good time working with the marketing team today?"

"I actually loved it. Don't get me wrong, I love influencer marketing, but I also loved the branding meetings. I love how everything is done for a specific reason."

"Maybe I can see if they will take you on for a few weeks. That will help your résumé tremendously."

"You'd do that?"

"For you? Yes."

Unshed tears cling to my eyes. "Thank you."

"Of course." He lifts his water goblet before taking a drink, and then he addresses me a little more seriously. "Are you okay?"

He's referring to the giant elephant in the room—me sobbing to him.

I can feel a lump growing in my throat.

A part of me wishes I could tell him and have him be the one to give me advice, but I know two jobs are on the line, and while I'm not as worried about me, I'm concerned for Dane. Something is eating away at him already, so I'd hate to rock the boat more.

"I'm fine. Really," I respond softly.

My father studies me for a second. The lines on his face have sharpened, telling me he's concerned, but thankfully, for everyone's sake, he doesn't push because I'm not sure I could lie if asked. I wouldn't want to.

"So tell me what you majored in?" Sherry asks. I'm surprised she doesn't know, but then again, I haven't really opened up to her or my father.

I really need to get to the bottom of everything because I feel like I'm in the twilight zone.

"I majored in folklore and mythology with a minor in communications, which is why this whole opportunity is so perfect. I guess, like all girls my age, I had hopes of being an influencer." I laugh.

"And now?"

"Now, I realize marketing is so much more than just going viral, and it all fascinates me."

"I'll definitely get you transferred to the main marketing office."

"That would be amazing."

"Bet you won't miss the stinky arena."

"I won't." *I'll miss a grumpy player.*

Stop.

No more thinking or talking about him. It's over. Time to move on and make a life for yourself.

An hour later, belly full, heart fuller, I stand from the table.

My hands are in front of me, my fingers twirling nervously. I know what I have to do, but why does it seem so hard?

"Josie? Everything okay."

"I was wondering—um, can I speak to you alone for a minute?"

"Of course. Sherry, do you mind?"

"Go ahead, guys. I'll clean up." She picks up a plate from the table. "Josie?"

"Yeah?"

"It was great having you tonight."

My nose tingles at her words, and I know without a doubt that if I let myself, tears would leak from my eyes. I don't allow them, though. I need my strength right now.

"Thanks," I squeak and then turn to look at where my father is going. We walk down a long hall that dead ends into a pair of pretty mahogany French doors. His arm reaches out, and he opens it for us, motioning for me to step inside.

When the door is shut, I stand still at first, then start to pace.

This is weird.

Awkward.

Do I just blurt it out? Maybe lead up to it . . .

Fuck it. I'm tired of overthinking my entire existence.

"When did you find out about me?"

Robert scratches the back of his neck. He looks as uncomfortable as I feel.

He gestures to the couch. "Sit."

Then he takes a seat in the leather wingback. "As crazy as it sounds, not until we made it to the finals this year, but when did I find out you were actually my daughter? After you moved here."

My pulse races as my heart rate accelerates and threatens to beat out of my chest.

Was it my mom?

Is she the reason I never had a father in my life? Did she keep him from me? Heat spreads across my face.

With my hands on my lap, I clench them into fists until the nails bite into the skin on my palm. Pain radiates through me, but it's nothing compared to the pain I feel in my heart.

I'll never be able to forgive her if she did this.

Wait, what did he say?

He let me move in with him before he knew I was officially his?

"What exactly happened?"

"I guess with all the hype of the playoffs, my picture was

shown on TV, and while I look older, I haven't changed much in twenty-two years. Your mom reached out to me. I'm still not sure how she got in touch, but she did. We didn't really know each other." He bites his lip, the implication pretty damn obvious. I'm the product of a one-night stand. "The thing is, I didn't remember her at first, and then when I did—"

"You didn't believe her?"

He nods.

"I can understand. The timing is sus."

"Yeah, a little. I asked your mother to have you take a DNA test."

As much as it hurts that he didn't believe her, I can't imagine how I would feel if I were in his position. Especially since he coaches a professional hockey team. For all he knew, my mom was some gold digger looking for an easy payday.

"Makes sense."

"I think you get your logical side from me."

"Don't get too ahead of yourself. It rarely comes out." I laugh, and he follows suit.

"I won't lie to you, Josie. I was in shock."

"So was I."

"I can't imagine. When I grappled with the notion that it might be true, I felt devastated by what I'd missed. I always wanted a family of my own, but it just wasn't in the cards for me. Sure, I've had Molly in my life since she was a girl, and I love her like a daughter, but I could have had you too." His voice cracks. "I missed so much . . ."

My eyes fill with tears. I can't imagine how hard this all must have been for him. My breath feels heavy and labored. All this time I wasted. If only I had been strong enough to ask these questions when I arrived. But no, I was hurt and wounded and afraid.

"I can't believe she called you and you let me come here. You didn't even know for sure that I was yours. Why?"

He sucks his cheeks in. "I might not have remembered her

well, but I could hear in her voice that she needed help. That you needed a place to stay and a job. I didn't hesitate. I told her to send you here immediately. I didn't know for sure you were my daughter yet, but in my heart, I did." He leans forward in his chair. "I'd never have allowed you to grow up without me if I knew."

A tear falls down my cheek. "I believe you. And I'm sorry."

"Why are you sorry?"

"For the way I've treated you. For avoiding you. For being so—" I bury my head in my hands, breathing in deeply to calm down. Once the pounding in my veins calms, I drop my arms. "I was horrible, and I have no excuse. Mom wouldn't talk to me, and my brain made up its mind about what kind of person you were. Growing up with her . . . it hasn't been easy, and—No. There's no excuse for how I've acted."

My dad takes my hand in his. "There's nothing to apologize for. I have you in my life now, and you have me. That's all that matters."

And just like that, he's no longer Sperm Donor, Coach Robert, or my father.

He's simply . . . *Dad.*

chapter fifty-nine

Josie

THE THING ABOUT A BREAKUP IS THAT YOU EVENTUALLY bump into your ex, which is why I am not looking forward to returning to the practice arena today to grab the few things I left behind. The team isn't always here, but seeing as there's no game today, there is a good chance I'll bump into Dane.

Rip off the Band-Aid.

Bumping into him is inevitable.

Since I'm working in the marketing department now, I'm not dressed in my typical casual attire. Today, I'm wearing a knee-length skirt, a pair of heels, and a lightweight sweater, and while my outfit fits in perfectly with all the high-level publicists, I do not fit in near the rink.

My heels click sharply against the concrete floors, and the familiar smell of ice permeates the air. Memory after memory attacks me the farther I walk into the space. If I'm lucky, I'll be able to go in and get out without being noticed, but something tells me I won't be so lucky. In the distance, I can hear chatter and try my best to make out who's talking, but I can't. Most likely, it's not Dane. He is often a man of few words.

It's fine. It won't be too awkward.

Can't be worse than some of the other embarrassing stuff I've lived through. Like the time I slipped and fell into a snowbank in front of my whole sixth grade class. I lived through that, so I can live through this.

This will be faster and far less painful, and I won't inherit a nickname. It took a while to get the kids to stop calling me frosty after I stood up covered in snow.

I don't think I've ever walked this fast in heels. My feet are going to kill me tonight. Well worth it if I can get out of here undetected. Of course, fate has other plans, as I see Hudson waving at me.

Great job, Hudson. Way to out me.

I take a deep breath and hope it ends with a wave, but again, no such luck on my part.

And since the Moirai sisters of fate seem to have it out for me, Dane walks off the ice when I pass him.

My guess is he's going to the locker room, and I'm going to the office beside the locker room.

Great.

"Josephine."

"Sinclair."

His eyes widen at the use of his last name, but if he's going to call me out, he doesn't. Instead, he stares at me for a long moment, almost like he's memorizing me.

"Take a picture. It will last longer."

"I didn't expect—"

"To see me again. Yeah, I got that."

"Look, I messed up. We both got carried away, and I let it happen. I take full responsibility. I'm the fucking adult over here."

And I wasn't? Good to know.

"At any rate," he continues, "we need to keep our distance now. We got too close to getting caught, and we both have plenty to lose. Turn around and walk away, Hellfire. There's nothing for you here."

chapter sixty

Dane

Hudson added Molly to the chat.

Hudson: Where's your brother?

Molly: Do I look like his keeper, asshole?

Hudson: Actually, yes.

Hudson changed the name of the chat to Dane Sinclair's Keepers

Molly has left the chat.

Hudson: Was it something I said?

Mason: ...

chapter sixty-one

Dane

I CAN'T BELIEVE THESE GUYS CONVINCED ME TO MEET THEM.

This is by far the last place I want to be. I trudge through the dimly lit bar, looking for my friends. After tonight, I might downgrade them back to teammates.

The music is obnoxious, and the walls practically rattle from the bass.

In the corner, in the usual spot, I find a way too happy Hudson, Mason, and, surprisingly enough, Aiden. Although I see him every day, he rarely goes out unless he's forced to or Cassidy has convinced him it would be good for him. I narrow my eyes as I approach, and I can tell something's up by how tight Aiden's jaw is. I glance over at Hudson. He's grinning like an idiot, but his demeanor isn't going to help me figure out what's going on. The man is always a juvenile child.

"There he is!" Hudson leans back in his seat, a shit-eating grin spreading across his face.

"Why are you so happy?"

Hudson shrugs. "I'm always happy. I give golden retriever vibes."

"Nah, just a horndog. And you." I turn to Aiden, suspicious. "What are you even doing here?"

Hudson claps his hands in front of his face like an excited schoolboy, and Aiden groans.

"Why did we invite him?" Aiden asks Mason while pointing at Hudson.

"Hey! It was my idea to grab a drink."

"He has a point." Mason shrugs.

"Plus, you both wanted to know what's up his ass—shit. I wasn't supposed to say that yet."

"*Yet*?" I quirk my eyebrow. What the hell did I just walk into?

"Yeah, sorry, man. Okay, let me start this again." Hudson stands from his seat and gestures to Mason, Aiden, and himself. "We're staging an intervention."

"*My* intervention?"

"Oh, boy. Pretty Boy is slow, but he is catching up."

"From *what*?" I barely drink. I don't do drugs, and none of them know about my relationship with Hellfire.

"You being a bigger asshole than normal."

"Are you fucking kidding me?"

"Case in point." Hudson reaches forward, grabs the pitcher, and pours me a beer. "Listen, man, we love you, but what the hell is going on with you?"

I take the glass from him, lifting it to my mouth. "I'm fine."

"You're not fine."

"Okay, I'm tired."

Hudson swirls the napkin in front of him. "Tired? That's the best you've got?"

"Is Hudson the official team leader?" I turn to look at Aiden. "And here I thought you were the captain."

"I'm just here for the beer. I thought this was a terrible idea. When you're ready to talk, you will." He shrugs.

"You're no help, Slate." Hudson turns to Mason next. "Goodie, are you going to sell me out too?"

"You have been a little more irritable than usual."

Hudson rolls his eyes. "Seriously, Goodie, that's all you've got? The man practically ripped the equipment manager a new asshole yesterday, and how about his fucking water bottle?"

Okay, he might have a point with that one. I did kind of lose my shit because the water in my water bottle was too high and started to overflow off the side, but in my defense, I had just gotten a letter from an unknown person basically telling me my life was over. Not that they know that, so I guess from their point of view, I have been kind of an asshole.

"Fine. I may be a little stressed, but I don't want to talk about it. Everything is fine, and while I appreciate you guys being concerned, I promise I have this."

Aiden nods, his expression softening. "I guess what we're trying to say, not eloquently 'cause Hudson's involved, is shit can get rough, and we all know that, but we wanted to remind you that you're not in this alone."

If anyone knows anything about keeping their secrets close to their heart, it's Aiden. While I am happy that he was able to find Cassie and no longer needs to hide anything, my issue isn't that simple. I can't ever have the girl I want in my life, as I know it could change if my secret gets out, but instead of saying any of that, I lift my drink and take a swig.

"Thanks, guys. And I know. I appreciate it. But I promise I'm okay."

"Fine, we're done. Now, let's drink." Hudson smirks.

"We already are drinking."

"I think what he's trying to say is let's get drunk," Mason clarifies.

"Yes, that!" Hudson agrees.

"I'll pass," Aiden and I say at the same time.

"I get him, but you, you're single. Where's your fun?"

Lost to a hellfire.

chapter sixty-two

Dane

THIS FUCKING BLOWS.

I'm in the penalty box, waiting for my time to end. All I want to do is get up from here.

My leg bounces against the bench as I watch the assholes from the other team get away with shit we're being called on for.

The longer I watch, the more pissed I become.

It's horseshit. That dick should have gotten a penalty for the last play, but no . . .

I pull my gaze away from the game. Needing to calm myself, I do the only thing I can. I search for her in the stands.

Stupid, yes, but it's the only thing that ever seems to work.

She's the only thing that makes me happy.

Not being with her is killing me.

I need to stay strong though.

The letter is a threat. I know it is. And until I know exactly who it's from and what their intentions are, I need to protect her.

She's not in her normal spot, which doesn't mean she's not here.

She could have gotten up for a second, but as I scan the crowd, I spot someone I haven't seen in years.

Fuck.

There, in the stands, in clear view as if it were planned, is my uncle.

The bastard I've been avoiding since I was eighteen. Even from here, I can see he's still a bastard.

My hands clench in my gloves. What is this asshole doing here? No fucking way is this a coincidence. He's here for me. But why?

The last time I saw him, we sat on opposite sides of the courtroom. After the judge awarded me custody of Molly, the dickhead scurried off like the weasel he is.

Finally, my time in the box is over. I shoot out, tearing across the ice, and drive my shoulder into the other team's defenseman with a sickening force. When he drops his stick and takes a swing, I toss mine, taking out all my frustration on this asshole. The crowd roars as we go head-to-head, punches thrown.

The refs, of course, are quick to break us apart, hauling me off him and sending me right back to the penalty box.

As soon as my ass hits the steel bench, I search for my uncle, but he's not there.

Did I imagine him?

I close my eyes, willing the game to end.

Behind my lids, I see his mocking face.

The way he went after Molly.

I did everything I needed to make sure she never ended up in his hands.

The man is a monster.

When the final horn blasts that the game is over, red-hot anger courses through me.

We lost, and I'm well aware it's partially my fault. I played like shit and was too busy fighting to defend my men properly.

But my head wasn't in the game, and now I have to change and find him. Despite my earlier assessment that it was all in my mind, I know, in my heart, he's here.

He has to be.

First—that monster never misses an opportunity to fuck me over.

Second—I wouldn't conjure him, of all people.

As I walk out of the locker room, dressed, a security guard approaches me.

"Mr. Sinclair, a man claiming to be your uncle is trying to see you."

Guess I didn't have to search long.

"Where is he?"

"By the entrance. Would you like me to bring him to you?"

Do I? Or do I want to come outside to avoid a public shit show? Both options suck.

I don't want to be openly seen with him. Who knows why he's here? That man was always after money. All those years ago, he thought Molly would be his payday. His intention to adopt her was never good.

Whatever he has to say to me is better said in private.

"Show him to the private room right beside the trainer's office. That should be vacant."

"Okay."

I head in that direction, opening the door and waiting.

It's not even two minutes later that the door swings open. He looks just as sketchy as the last time I saw him.

My father's brother.

A real piece of work.

He's just as bad as my dad, but this man never had the money my father did. Instead, he hated us for it.

When my parents died, he wanted the inheritance that their estate left behind and fought me tooth and nail to win custody of Molly.

An innocent pawn in his game.

I made sure that didn't happen and haven't seen him since.

When he walks into the room, there's no question he's still the same pathetic asshole, even after all this time.

The years haven't been kind to him.

Gray streaks paint his dark hair. The strands look greasy against his weathered skin.

"My favorite nephew."

"Your *only* nephew."

"That doesn't mean you aren't my favorite."

"Cut the shit." I shake my freshly showered hair, flinging droplets all over his cheeks. "Tell me what you want."

He smears the water off him. "Oh, I thought that would be obvious."

"And I thought the cigarettes would've killed you by now. Unfortunately, we can't always be right."

He scowls before it transforms into a smirk, sending ants crawling up my skin. "I'm sure you've gotten my letter by now."

Motherfucker.

He sent me the picture.

I move forward, ready to deal with him how I always wanted to deal with him. I'm not thinking straight. Without fail, he always manages to upend every ounce of my self-control.

He wags his finger, tsking, before he points up at the stadium camera above us. "I've always liked a good photo op, but something tells me this isn't your most flattering angle."

"I'm not that eighteen-year-old kid anymore, vying for any scrap of money I can to survive." I step forward, angling my lips down, so they can't be read. "I have resources to make your life a living hell, and I have absolutely no problem doing so. Cross me again, and I'll remind you why men five times your size run when they see me coming."

I don't know what's bravado and what's a promise. Can I do something to him? Sure. But can I do it without facing consequences? Doubt it. I've made too many mistakes. Left too many skeletons. It's already a miracle that my dirty secrets haven't been discovered yet.

My uncle smiles widely now, his tobacco-stained teeth showing. "I spoke to your good friend Nick."

A bomb detonates inside me.

He is not fucking around.

He knows.

"Nick? Good kid. Big imagination." I keep my face void of all emotion.

Always appear strong. Never show your weakness.

"You can pretend you don't know what I found out. It won't change a thing." He laughs. "You know, if you were a better friend, you'd send him to rehab. All it took was a few too many drinks, and he spilled all his secrets—and better yet, yours. He was a fountain of knowledge."

I will never understand how anyone can harm their own family.

He's an unwanted reminder that not all bonds are unbreakable.

I tip my chin up, feigning calm. "What do you want?"

"You know what I want."

"It always comes down to money for you."

"You wound me." He brings a hand to his heart, pretending to keel over. "What if I had cancer treatment I need to pay for."

"You don't."

"How do you know?"

"Because I'm never that lucky."

"Touchy, touchy. Fine. Money is the most important thing in the world." He lifts a brow. "I thought you, of all people, would know that."

The meaning is as clear as fucking day.

He knows what I would do for it.

Sell my soul.

"And how much buys your silence?"

His dark eyes gleam. "Haven't decided just yet."

"And if I say no?"

"You won't." He steps closer, and the scent of booze infiltrates my nose. "Because I will take away the one thing you tried so hard to protect."

"Touch a hair on Molly's head, and the only green you'll see for the rest of your life is the cemetary before I bury you in it."

"Now, why would I do that? She's the reason for all your troubles anyway."

I don't dignify that with a response.

"Fine." He waves a hand. "I'll leave Molly alone. She's nothing compared to the other girl, anyway. Anyone ever tell you that windows are clear?" A high-pitched whistle soars past his lips. "Who knew the coach's kid was so flexible?" He grins like a lunatic. And why not? He knows he has me. "I bet she tastes as good as she looks."

That's it.

I don't even feel the last of my self-control draining.

In an instant, I have him plastered against the door.

He flails in my hold, his legs dangling comically. "Careful there, nephew. You wouldn't want anyone to hear. How would the coach feel if I told him everything? Past. Present. I have pictures of that, too."

He wriggles his body until I let him out of my hold, knowing nothing good will come out of touching him.

With a grin, he flicks my hands off his chest and steps out from where I cornered him. "I'll be in contact."

The scumbag doesn't wait for me to respond.

He just walks out the way he came.

My skin buzzes with anger. Ribbons of rage loop around my throat, robbing me of my breath. I want to go after him, throw him against the wall, and pound the shit out of him within an inch of his life.

Fuck.

My fist flies out and punches the door.

The skin of my knuckles cracks, and red rivulets bubble to the surface.

I'm not used to this. Protecting people is wired in my DNA. Since I stepped into skates, Dad drilled it into me.

Protect, protect, protect.

Only this time…the person my loved ones need protecting from is me.

chapter sixty-three

Josie

I WAS LATE TO THE GAME, BUT I DIDN'T MISS HOW DANE PLAYED. He looked possessed by the devil. In all the time I've known him, I've never seen him like that. His whole demeanor was different.

Sure, he's always been grumpy, but this was different. He looked like he was breaking apart inside, and then when he fought with the other team, pounding his fists, the blood spraying across the ice . . .

Yeah, something isn't right.

I'm halfway down the corridor when my dad lifts his arm, waving me over. I head over to him. "Hey. What's going on?"

"Dane dropped his keys, but I have to meet with someone. Would you mind giving them to him?"

"Sure, no problem."

Big problem actually, but sure, why not.

Should be fun. Approaching Dane when he's in a mood is right up there with getting a root canal.

I turn toward the hallway that leads to the back door of the stadium. My pace is between a fast walk and a jog, wanting to get this over with.

He's already outside by the time I make it to the door and push it open. The cool fall air hits me in the face. I shiver, crossing my arms in front of my chest to lock in some heat.

"Dane!" I shout to get his attention. He turns over his shoulder and looks at me but doesn't stop. What the hell is wrong with him? I pick up my pace, jogging in his direction. Once I'm beside him, he finally stops.

I lift my hand, and he takes a step back. "You dropped your keys."

It might be dark out, but even under the canopy of a black sky, I can see his face. A face devoid of emotions.

His blue eyes look hollow, and his jaw is tight enough to snap. I search for anything else there—sadness, anger—but there's nothing. A chill runs down my spine. Is that even possible? But the evidence is clear as day. He's merely a body, a vessel, a soulless god.

His hand reaches out, and I meet him halfway, dropping the fob into his open palm.

I don't like this. Something is clearly very wrong with him.

I move closer, wary and unsure, but knowing I need to confirm he's okay despite everything. "I'm worried about you."

"You shouldn't be."

I lift my hand back out and touch his arm this time, but he pushes my hand off. It feels like my hand is sizzling from the touch.

"I don't understand what's going on with you."

"I don't have time for this."

A gust of wind blows. Sharp and fast. A storm is rolling in.

The loose strands of my hair whip against my face, blinding me for a second before I push them away. "'Cause you're so busy right now?"

"Actually, yes," he growls.

He continues to walk toward his car.

I keep pace with him, walking faster than my short gait can handle, but I refuse for him to get in his car and drive away.

The closer we get, the brighter it gets. There's a streetlight beside his car. The light flickers on and off like the bulb is about to blow.

My lids blink every time it momentarily shuts off.

Someone needs to fix that.

I catalog that in my thoughts as something I need to tell my father about, but right now, I have a bigger issue.

Like how to stop Dane and get him to talk to me. The man is a ticking time bomb, and it scares me to think of him in such a dark place.

From the corner of my eye, I notice the concrete ledge that runs along the side of the parking lot. It's not that high up, only a step up, but it will do the trick.

I jump up, and the heels on my ankle boots make a hammering sound.

Dane turns to face me, and I bat my lashes at him, hoping my antics will make him smile like it has in the past.

The man is a born protector. I see it every day from the way he plays hockey, how he took care of Molly, and how he never lets me walk on a ledge without his support.

This has to work.

"Josephine, I'm not in the mood."

Not Hellfire. I'm not Hellfire anymore.

"No, clearly you're not. But you need to talk to *someone*. Anyone. You can talk to me. Everyone needs help sometimes." To make my point clearer, I raise my hands to my sides for balance. "Everyone needs support. We can support each other, Dane. Let me in. Let me help you walk the tightrope."

I place one foot in front of the other and wait for him to stand beside me. To offer me his arm.

He doesn't. He doesn't even budge.

"Walk the tightrope with me, Dane." I take another step. His eyes are still hollow, dark obsidian holes. "Let me in."

Another step.

Motionless, he stands.

A statue.

A fortress I can't penetrate.

Another inch, and then another.

My upper body wobbles as I try to steady myself.

He'll reach out.

He always does.

Give him time. Help him break through the hurt that has him rooted in place.

One more step and my heel gets lodged, forcing my upper body to pitch forward.

He'll reach out.

He'll catch me.

But he doesn't.

chapter sixty-four

Dane

A SCREAM PIERCES THE AIR.
Time stands still. Everything happens exactly how they say it does in a movie. You see the moment of impact, but it can't be stopped.

That's how it feels as I watch Josephine careen to the ground. Her arms flail as she tries to regain her balance.

The ledge, which is only about two feet off the ground on one side of the concrete pavement, is actually higher on the other side, and that's the side where her body is falling.

In the dark, she couldn't see that the parking lot of the arena slopes back there. I thrust my arm out, trying desperately to stop her fall, but I'm too far away. My stubborn ass couldn't give an inch.

Gravity always wins.

How stupid could I have been? How could I not protect her?

Because I'm a selfish asshole who put myself first.

So lost in my brain that I didn't reach out.

But I can't think about that now. I can hate myself for failing her later. Right now, I need to get her.

A sickening thud echoes in my ears.

She's slipped through my grasp. I'm too late.

I dash over to where she's lying on the opposite side of the ledge. Carefully, I step over it and move to where Josephine is on the ground.

Bile collects in my mouth.

On the other side, golden-brown hair fans across the dark ground. I slip down, coming to her side. This close, I can see patches of hair are growing darker . . .

Blood.

"Josephine!" My voice is urgent.

My heart drops to my stomach as I notice a puddle of blood pooling beneath her head. Even though it's dark out, the streetlamp illuminates the night enough to see a stark contrast against her pale skin.

"Josephine, wake up." I place a finger on her neck.

Thank fuck. A pulse.

"Please, open your eyes." My voice trembles. "Hellfire."

I pull out my phone, hands trembling as I do, and fumble to dial 911.

My breath comes out in short, ragged breaths.

"Nine-one-one, what's your emergency?"

"My—my . . ." My voice cracks.

"Sir?"

"My friend, she fell and hit her head. I need an ambulance. I-I'm at Lancaster Arena."

"What's your location at the arena?"

"In the parking lot. The player parking lot," I say quickly, never lifting my gaze from Josephine.

"I'm sending an ambulance right now. Sir, can you tell me what happened?"

"She hit her head on the concrete."

"Is she conscious?"

"She's unconscious, and there's a lot of blood."

"Are you able to put something clean on the wound?"

"Yes." I unzip my jacket and pull it off, then look for where the blood is coming from. Without moving her, I place the jacket where the bleeding originates, making sure to apply pressure, hopefully to stop it.

"God, Hellfire. I'm so sorry. I need you to wake up. You have to wake up. I can't lose you."

With each second that passes, my heart pounds in my chest. It feels like it might explode.

Finally, in the distance, I hear the wail of the sirens. Then I see the lights.

Soon, two paramedics come rushing toward us.

The first one, a younger man, assesses her.

"Female, mid-twenties, head trauma, unconscious," he calls out to his partner.

His partner, a woman about the same age, nods and prepares her for transport.

Words ring out in the air, but it's hard to grasp them all. Low blood pressure. Loss of blood. Possible concussion.

Together, a second after securing her neck, they load her onto a stretcher.

"Is she—"

"We're doing everything we can."

They lift her into the ambulance. The doors are shut, and they speed away.

I'm still on the ground, my breathing still erratic, and the ambulance is no longer in sight. The red flashing lights are a distant memory.

My head drops, and when it does, a glint of something catches my eye.

What is that?

I reach my hand out and pick it up.

Josephine's bracelet.

My heart squeezes in my chest.

She needs to be okay. I don't know what I'll do if she's not.

Grabbing my phone, I dial.

"What's up, Sinclair? You ready to tell me why you were playing—"

"Robert." My voice sounds raw and gritty.

"What's wrong, Dane?"

"Josephine—"

"What about my daughter?"

"She had an accident in the parking lot. She hit her head."

"Is she okay?"

"I don't know. I called an ambulance. They've taken her to the hospital. I-I just thought you should know."

There's a second of silence. "What hospital?"

"Redville Health."

"Thank you, son."

His words feel like a gunshot in my heart. I hang up, but I want to tell him he shouldn't call me son.

I let him down.

But most importantly, I let down the one person who I truly ever felt peace with.

My hellfire.

chapter sixty-five

Dane

Hudson: What happened to Josie?

Hudson: Never seen coach take off like that.

Hudson: Hello?

Hudson: Anyone?

Hudson: Am I the only one who's here?

Aiden: I'll find out.

Hudson: Oh thank fuck, I thought you all left me.

chapter sixty-six

Dane

THE FLUORESCENT LIGHTS OF THE WAITING ROOM FLICKER A harsh glow above me.

I squint my eyes, a headache brewing behind my lids.

Who knows how long I've been sitting here, and I still haven't heard anything. Robert went back to see if he could find someone to give us news on Josephine.

The door swings open, and my heart lurches in my chest but then drops when an elderly man walks toward the exit.

Not him.

I wonder how much longer it will take for someone to come out here. My back hunches forward, and I lift my arm to knead the muscles tightened by my neck.

This chair is not the most comfortable.

I can't believe she fell.

I can't believe I failed her.

No matter how hard I try, her scream plays on repeat in my mind.

Over and over again, I hear the sound.

Over and over again, I see her fall.

Over and over again, I see her fall.

Every time I replay it in my mind, I can still feel the skin on her arm slip across my fingertips when I finally reached out for her.

None of this would have happened if I had only reached out when she first asked me.

I close my eyes, and there it is again.

The sound of the thud.

The blood.

All the blood.

My breathing feels choppy, and I pull in large gulps of air.

"You okay, man?" someone says beside me. "Sin?"

I open my eyes. Mason is there, and Hudson is barreling over in my direction.

Behind him is Aiden, Cassidy in tow.

Hudson's face looks red with rage. "What happened to our girl?"

"She fell."

"How the fuck did she fall in a parking lot, Sin?" he practically growls.

"She lost her balance. She was walking on the ledge. It wasn't that high, only about two feet off the ground, but she hit her head on a loose piece of concrete." Guilt makes my tongue heavy, but what else can I say? It's the truth; she lost her balance. She did something stupid and lost her balance.

You let her fall. It's all your fault.

It's always your fault.

Molly is the next to enter the room. Her eyes look red-rimmed like she might have been crying. She throws her arms around my neck when she sees me. "Is she okay?"

I shake my head. "I don't know. I haven't heard anything yet."

Molly is the closest thing to a friend as Hellfire has.

She had you.

I had no choice. With my uncle blackmailing me, I can't be with her. If I had reached out when she asked, she would have thought there was hope for us, but between my uncle and her father, we were over before we even started.

"There's no news at all?" Hudson asks.

I shake my head. "Nothing."

I sit back down in the cold metal chair. I'm happy to have my friends here, but they don't even know the half of my relationship with her.

"Why were you with Josie?" Hudson finally asks. "Alone in the parking lot?"

He eyes me in a way that makes me uncomfortable. Hudson is usually the playful one out of the bunch, but right now, his demeanor is anything but playful.

He thinks I hurt her.

And he is definitely not wrong in a sense.

"What are you implying?" Molly steps up into his space. Eyes colder than ice.

"Mind your business, pest."

I stand from the chair, moving Molly out of the way, getting up in Hudson's face. "Do not speak to my sister like that."

"Enough!" I look to my left to see Robert approaching us.

"There is no need to fight. We're a team," Coach Robert tells us.

"Not when he's speaking to my sister like that." I grunt.

Molly's small hand touches mine for a second, giving me a squeeze. "While I appreciate the big brother act, I can handle myself."

She can, but I've spent my whole life protecting her. I'm not going to stop now.

I finally nod and sit back down.

Aiden turns to Coach. "Any news?"

"Nothing yet."

"Well, maybe if we knew what happened," Hudson starts up again, and Molly practically growls at him.

"She fell. Want to know why? 'Cause we were arguing. But I didn't push her. She was on the ledge, walking, and she fell." I lift my hands and bury my head in them. "I couldn't get to her in time."

"It wasn't your fault." Robert places his hand on my shoulder, and I'm surprised he doesn't ask what we were fighting about. I'm surprised none of them do. Then again, they've always respected my space. "Accidents happen."

But it was my fault.

I'm the reason she was there.

I'm the reason she fell.

And if I were a better man, none of this would have happened. She would have been okay if I had just stayed out of her life.

I'm not good for her.

Just then, the ER door opens, and a doctor walks out.

"Father of Josephine Moreau?"

Robert moves to him quickly. "I'm Josie's father."

I move closer to hear, but I'm not sure I'll be able to make out his words with the way my heart pounds in my chest.

The doctor nods to Robert before speaking. "Your daughter suffered a concussion. She also has a pretty nasty gash on her hairline. That's where the bleeding came from. We ran a CT scan to check for any internal bleeding or swelling in the brain, and thankfully, everything looks normal."

"She's going to be okay?" Robert's body trembles.

"Yes, she has sprained her ankle, and we do want to keep her here for observation due to the blood loss and concussion, but I expect her to make a full recovery."

Relief floods me at first, but then it's soon replaced with a thick guilt that chokes me from the inside.

"Can I see her?"

"Of course. She's in room 505."

"Thank you," he says before he turns and nods a thank-you to us as well, then he follows the doctor to his daughter.

Now that I know she'll be okay, I can't stay.

"I have to go." I head toward the door.

"Dane, wait." Molly comes rushing at me.

"I can't."

chapter sixty-seven

Josie

TRY TO BLINK MY EYES OPEN, BUT MY LIDS STICK TOGETHER, NOT wanting to budge.

What the hell is wrong with them?

I lift my hand, rubbing furiously, but as I do, a sharp pain radiates through my body. An audible groan escapes my mouth, and wow, I sound like I've died.

What the hell is wrong with my voice, body, and eyes?

"Don't move. You have a head injury." I feel like someone told me that before, and I didn't remember. I also feel like my brain is floating like a balloon over my body, but that's another story.

"You have a concussion."

The voice sounds familiar, but it hurts to think.

I feel disoriented, and my head throbs. A concussion makes sense—my head does feel like it's been hit with a sledgehammer.

I blink again, and this time, my vision comes into focus.

Instantly, the fluorescent lights sting my eyes, and I cringe, wanting to recoil and hide under a pillow.

"The light."

My father is in the room, and the moment I speak, he switches off the overhead light.

Much better. While the room is still a sterile hospital room with white walls and no bells and whistles, at least I can see a bit.

The only light in the room is from the hallway, but it's enough to see his face.

He looks tired. Dark circles paint the underside of his eyes.

It's obvious I'm in a hospital, but why?

I try to think, and when I do, my brain hurts even more.

"What happened?" I ask. Maybe some guidance will help with the memories.

"What is the last thing you remember?"

"The game."

No, wait, that's not right. I remember the game. I remember watching Dane getting in it with a few players from the other team, and after the game was over—what? What did I do?

My dad asked me to give him his key.

"Are you okay?" My dad's voice has me looking in his direction.

"Yeah, I was just trying to remember."

"Take it easy. The brain is a complicated thing. After a concussion, simple tasks like even thinking too hard can cause confusion."

"Great."

"It will be okay, Josie."

"How did I get here?"

"You were in the parking lot. I guess you and Dane got into a fight, and you fell. He called an ambulance."

Mind racing. Pieces come together like a puzzle.

We didn't fight. He would have had to talk to me to fight. But that must have been the story he told my father.

What else did he tell him?

Did he tell him I wanted to make him smile? But he was too stubborn, too set in his own self-loathing to let me in.

That he said no.

He most likely told a lie, one where it was his fault I fell.

It wasn't.

I knew it was dangerous, and it was my fault for believing he would be there to catch me.

That's not on him; it's on me.

He said no.

And now I know where I stand.

My heart feels heavy, and I tremble with unshed tears. I want to cry. I can feel my heart wanting to break. I just don't want to break in front of my dad.

I want to be strong.

The tears win out and splash against my cheek.

My father rushes to my side, taking my hand in his. "You're okay. It's going to be okay," he says. "The doctors said you're going to be fine. You can go home tomorrow, and from there you just need to rest. A little R and R."

I can feel the tears welling in my eyes.

My father pulls up a chair and sits next to me. There's so much I want to tell him.

But can I?

As I move to open my mouth and unburden myself, a sound rings through the air.

A phone. *Not mine.*

My father rummages through his pocket and pulls his cell out, lifting it to his ear. "Hi, Vivian."

My mother.

Why is she calling him?

Me.

She's calling about me.

He doesn't have to say it, but I know it's true.

"Yes. She's right here. Yes, of course." He pulls his phone from his ear.

Before he even asks, I'm already nodding, a hand outstretched.

The moment I place the phone to my ear, I'm greeted by her soft cries.

"Mom."

It comes out before I can stop it.

I wanted to be tough—to stand up for myself and demand an apology for how much she's hurt me. But I can't help it. A tear rolls down my cheek.

"Josie. Oh my God. Your father told me. I'm getting in my car right now—"

You're better than this, Josie. Do not let anyone walk all over you. Not even your mom. Especially not your mom.

I suck in a breath, forcing myself to harden. "Mom. Stop."

"You're not okay. You have a—" A sob breaks from her throat, so I finish the sentence for her.

"A concussion. Oh, I know. People get concussions every day. It's really nothing for you to worry about."

"But you're in the hospital."

"And I'm being released tomorrow."

"I'm getting in my car now—"

"It's the middle of the night. You aren't driving here right now."

"But you need me."

That's rich, coming from her. I needed her when she kicked me out. I needed her to tell me who my father was, and she didn't do that either.

"Actually . . . I don't. I needed you months ago. Hell, I needed you years ago. But I don't need you now. Bye, Mom."

I hang up the phone before she can say anything else.

More tears threaten to spill. If I let them flow, I fear they'll never stop. So, I take in a deep breath and stare out the window.

Be strong, Josie.

Just because someone gave you life doesn't mean they need to be in yours.

chapter sixty-eight

Dane

I DON'T MAKE IT VERY FAR. I DON'T EVEN MAKE IT TO MY CAR.

Instead, I decide to walk around the hospital. I don't want to talk to anyone or see anyone, but I don't want to leave. I pace back and forth, and then finally, probably an hour later, I head back inside the hospital. I already know what room she's in, so I head in that direction.

When I make it, I find the door closed.

I knock once and hear the loud thud of footsteps. The door opens, and Robert is there. He looks at me, raising a brow. "I wanted to see if I could see Josephine."

"Let me see if she's up for visitors."

The door closes a second later, and his footsteps retreat. I can't hear anything, so he must be near her bed, but another second passes. When he opens the door this time, his face looks sunken in. I already know the answer before he even speaks. I nod my understanding.

"Dane."

I shake my head again.

"It's okay. I know it's my fault." I turn and leave, giving him no room to object.

chapter sixty-nine

Dane

I'VE BEEN HOME FOR ABOUT AN HOUR. WITH A GLASS OF whiskey in my hand, I sit on the couch. I know if anything happens to Josephine, one of my teammates will call me, but I can't help but think about her.

Why does everything have to be so complicated? First with coach being her dad, and now with Uncle Jim blackmailing me?

Why can't I get my shit together and just say fuck it to everything?

The sound of a knock on my door has me sitting upright. I don't move at first, but then I hear another knock, and a familiar voice says, "If you don't open your door, I will use my key."

It's Molly, and I know she'll use it, so I don't get up. I just sit there and take another sip of my drink.

It isn't long before I hear the telltale signs that she has entered the premises and is heading my way.

Her footsteps echo through the room, and then she stands in front of me with a hand on her hip.

She's going to lay into me.

It's about time someone yells at me for what I did to Josephine. It's about time someone tells me how it's all my fault and agrees that I'm a fucking asshole.

Coach wouldn't do it, but Molly will. "When are you going to get your head out of your ass?" *Here it comes.* "And just admit to me and yourself that you are madly, stupidly in love with Josie?"

For a second, I think she just said that she thinks I'm in love with Josie, but that can't be right. I open my mouth, then close it again. I must've drunk more than I thought because that's not what she said, right?

"Earth to Dane."

When I still don't speak, she lets out a long-drawn-out sigh.

"For my older brother, you're kind of stupid." That has me actually paying attention.

"What?"

"You heard me. You might be my older brother, but you are kind of dumb."

"Gee. Thanks, sis. Love you too."

"Okay, so here's how I see it. You've been lying to me. You and Josie are madly in love. You got into a lover's quarrel, and she stormed off and fell?"

"No, actually, that's not what happened."

"Then it's a lot worse than I thought. Let me see if I have it this time. You're in love with her. You were a complete idiot, most likely broke her heart, and told her you couldn't be with her . . . something to do with her father, and she approached you today because you were playing a crappy game and looked like you were miserable. Then you got into a fight, and she fell."

Now my mouth drops open because she actually nailed it. Well, she didn't mention the keys, but still pretty damn close.

She must see the look on my face and understand because,

again, she's my sister, and apparently, she's the smartest human being on earth.

"I nailed it, right?"

"Yeah, actually."

"Here's the thing, dear brother; things like this don't happen every day. It's not often you find someone who you care deeply for. Heck, look at Mom and Dad." I let out a large sigh. "No, I'm not gonna talk about Mom and Dad because I know how much you hate to talk about them, but don't think I don't remember the way that they were, though. How unhappy they were. What I learned from them is if she makes you smile and laugh, then who cares what Robert says?"

"I do."

"Robert is like a father to us. Dane, do you not think he'd be happy for you?" Molly stares at me. "He-he loves you like a son." Her words tremble as they come out, and I see the tears welling in her eyes right before they fall down her face. "We all love you so much, Dane. You've spent so much time putting me first; taking care of me, being the father that I needed because I had no parents, but one thing you haven't done is you haven't lived. I saw you that day when you touched her at the bar, and for the first time—"

She stops and sniffles as the tears cascade down her cheeks. "For the first time, I saw you happy. I don't remember the last time I saw you happy. Please don't give up. Fight for her. Fight for the person you deserve. Fight to be the man you're meant to be. This guy is a shell of a guy. That's not you, and I never would've wanted this for you. I never would've let you give up your life to take care of me. If I knew that this is who you were going to be—" She breaks down, her body trembling, and I stand from my chair, place my glass on the table, and envelop her in my arms.

"Please don't cry, Molly."

"I'm crying because I love you, Dane, and I just want you to be happy."

"I'll be happy."

"Promise me you'll go to her. Promise me you'll fight for your happiness."

I look at my sister, who is wiser than her years. "Okay, Molly. I'll fight for her."

chapter seventy

Josie

"DAD." MY SOFT VOICE IS BARELY ABOVE A WHISPER.
My father looks up, and when he does, shock is clear on his face. "Is it okay if I call you Dad?" My voice cracks at the question, unshed tears filling my eyes.

"Of course, it's okay, sweetheart. You can call me anything you like. As long as you're in my life." The moisture collecting in my eyes cascades down my cheeks.

"Okay, Dad. I'd like to." I sniffle, trying to hold back more tears.

"Then that's what you'll do." He smiles warmly, and I lie back on the bed and close my eyes. I'm not sleeping, but I'm resting.

I open my eyes a few seconds later, remembering that there was a knock on the door some time ago, and my dad was acting weird. I wonder if the doctor said anything. Maybe something is wrong. "Did I have any visitors?"

His eyes narrow, and I wonder what he must be thinking because he looks deep in thought. "Dad?"

"Are you calling me Dad to get a confession?"

"Um, no, but, um, is there something to confess . . . *Dad*?" I say his name in a mocking tone.

"Fine. You had a visitor. Actually, the waiting room was filled with the team, but one was more insistent that he wanted to see you."

"And the visitor?" I lean forward, anxious.

"Dane."

My heart pounds so hard it most likely will explode. "Why didn't you tell me?"

Is he mad at Dane? Does he know? No, he would have mentioned it to me, and he doesn't blame Dane, so why did he not tell me?

I shake my head. "I don't understand. Why didn't you tell me?"

"To be honest, it had nothing to do with you. I saw him, sweetheart. He wasn't in the right place. Emotionally, he was beating himself up. And he needed to cool down."

"Don't you think it should have been up to me to decide that?"

"Yes, and please forgive me, but you're my daughter, and he's like a son. He was hurting, self-loathing. I didn't want him to do or say something he'd regret."

"So you sent him home?"

"Yes and no."

"I'm not following."

"I sent him home, and then I sent him the one person at this moment who could get through to him."

"Molly," I finish for him. "That makes sense. I do wish you would have told me."

"And I promise, moving forward, I will tell you. I wanted to protect you because when I saw him, I saw the self-destructive boy I had met when he was in high school, trying out for the college team. I saw the same look in his eyes, and I knew he would self-destruct, and I needed to help him."

"I understand."

I understood more than he would ever know. It was the same

reason I fell, the same reason I stood on that ledge. It was the same reason I continued to walk, even though I had no balance. I saw something inside him that scared me, and I knew he needed to be centered again. And I thought I could help.

"I hope Molly gives him what he needs."

"I hope she does too." I settle back into the bed and wonder what Molly will say to him. I wonder if he'll let her in. My eyes close, and I feel weighted to the bed.

A few hours must pass, but my father remains by my side. A knock on the door has us both looking toward it. What time is it? Who would be here now? I look over at the clock and see it's four in the morning. My father stands and goes to answer it.

When I hear the sound of footsteps, I look toward where my father left, but my father isn't standing there when the shadow steps back into the light. It's Dane, and he's alone.

"Where's my dad?"

"He wanted to give us a minute . . . I, uh, promised to be on my best behavior."

"Why are you here?" My voice sounds foreign to me, gravelly and hoarse.

"I wanted to tell you how sorry I am."

"You made it clear how you felt about me. I was the idiot who thought I could help."

"And you can, and you did."

"Sure doesn't look like I did." I gesture to the bed and hospital room.

"Well, maybe not the way you intended, but it knocked some sense into me. Made me see things clearly."

"Oh yeah? And what did you see?"

"I realized I'm an idiot. I realized you're the best thing that's ever happened to me. That you make me laugh and smile. You give me peace, and it made me realize the most important thing."

"And that is?"

"That I love you." He steps toward the bed, taking my hand

in his. "You didn't just force me out of my comfort. You collided with me, twisting my world upside down." He brings it up to his mouth and places a kiss on my knuckle. "I love you, Hellfire. I love everything about you. And I'll spend the rest of my days proving you aren't a secret. You aren't an afterthought. You are the thought, the only thought that matters. You're everything."

I think my mouth is broken because, for the first time in like forever, it doesn't seem to work. It takes me a second to get my brain and mouth to work together, and I chalk it up to the fact I have a concussion.

"And my father?"

"We'll tell him."

"When?"

He smiles at me. "Now." I shake my head. "No?"

"Look, I'm done. Done being put last on everyone's list. I told my mother the same thing. From now on, you need to earn my trust. My love. My affection. And before you say anything about the fall, I'm not talking about the fall. I'm talking about the way you played with my heart and dumped me so fast, like I meant nothing. If I'm going to tell my father, it's because we're endgame."

"We are endgame."

"I'll decide that. And I'll decide it when I'm not laid up in a hospital bed with a concussion."

"Got it. You need some good grovel."

"That's not what I said."

"No, but it's what you deserve. You need to know I'm all in, and I'm going to give that to you."

He places one last kiss on my knuckle and takes a step back.

"Where are you going?"

"I'm going to leave before your dad returns. But don't fear, I won't be far away. I'll convince you I'm the man you need and that I'm worthy of your love."

chapter seventy-one

Josie

I T'S GOOD TO BE BACK HOME AND STAYING IN THE MAIN HOUSE.
I'm in a gorgeous suite Sherry prepared for me, which is even better.

The sound of my bedroom door sliding open has me turning
my head in its direction.

"What are you doing here?"

Dane takes a step inside.

"I call it Operation Grovel." He meets my gaze head-on, and
the sincerity of his stare does crazy things to my belly despite me
not wanting it to. What can I say? I'm only human, but that doesn't
change the fact that I need to put myself first.

I raise an eyebrow. "And where did you get a killer name like
that?"

A tiny smirk pulls at his mouth. "I googled it."

"Wow. I'm surprised you admit it."

His lips flatten into a straight line.

He's quick to correct himself, shaking his head once and then
taking a few steps forward, only stopping when his legs bump up

against the bed. "You'd be surprised by a lot of the things I'd do for you."

"Such as?" I prop myself up in the bed.

Dane's eyes soften. "Well, I'm here to take care of you today."

I glance around nervously. "Did anyone see you come in?"

"Well, seeing as you're staying in the main house." His brow pops up.

"Stupid question." In order to get into the house, someone had to let him in. *Duh.* I blame my lapse on how likable he is. Being in his presence makes my brain mush.

"Nothing you say could ever be stupid."

I roll my eyes, sighing loudly for effect. "I beg to differ, but okay." There's no masking my sarcasm, but I'm not trying to anyway. I say a lot of dumb things. Hell, our whole relationship stems from a night of me acting stupid.

He chuckles before pointing at the edge of the bed. "Can I sit?"

With a swift nod, he takes me up on my offer. "So grovel. What does that entail?"

His arctic-blue eyes twinkle. "Doing *anything* you want."

If this man could get a score for sex appeal, his score would be an A plus.

Endless possibilities dance in my brain. This could be fun. "Anything?" I raise an eyebrow.

"Within reason. I won't kill anyone."

Oh, wow, he went there.

"Pity." I shrug, biting my lip to hide my smirk.

"But other than that, everything is on the table."

"Would you TP the house?" This time, I can't help the mischievous grin spreading across my face.

"If you really want me to . . ."

I reach out and place my palm on his forehead. "Nope. No temperature."

He removes my hand and lifts it to his mouth, kissing it gently before placing it back on my lap. "I'd do anything for you."

"Did I get hit on the head, or you? Because you're acting weird."

"I'm acting like a man who was scared to death when I thought you were dead and realized I couldn't live in a world without you."

My heart thumps, and tears well in my eyes, but I push them away. "Back to the grovel. So. Um, what did you tell them?" I clear my throat.

"Tell who?"

"My father. Sherry."

"I told them I felt responsible for what happened to you and wanted to see if you needed anything. I'm pretty sure your dad hates me now." Dane shifts on the bed, looking down.

A piece of my heart breaks that he could ever think that. Doesn't he know how special he is? My father loves him.

Deep down, I know he does. He's only saying this because his mind remains clouded with the guilt of my accident.

"He doesn't hate you." I place a reassuring hand on his arm. "He loves you. You might not see it now, but I was so jealous for months. He looked at you and your sister the way I wanted him to look at me."

He glances back up, uncertainty still in his eyes, but there's also something else there: hope. "If you say so."

"I do." I squeeze gently.

For a moment, we both go quiet. A somber feeling is heavy in the room, but then Dane leans in closer. "How are you feeling?"

"Head still hurts." I grimace, rubbing my temples. "The doctor said I'd have a headache for a few days, but it still sucks."

Concern etches his face. "What can I do to help you?"

My fingers fidget with the hem of the comforter. "Nothing." I glance at the clock, then back at Dane.

His lips have formed a thin line. "Stop, Hellfire, let me help."

"Maybe I don't want you to grovel." I cross my arms, trying to stay strong. A part of me knows that, like Aphrodite, I'd always go to him. A gravitational pull between us can't be denied, but another part wants to be strong and hold out a little longer.

"You deserve the grovel." He brushes a strand of hair from my face, and I lean into his touch.

"I'm just tired. And everything hurts."

"So let me pamper you." Small lines crinkle the side of Dane's eyes as a hopeful smile tugs his lips up.

"Fine. A painkiller would be nice. And the super secret recipe hot chocolate?"

"Whatever you want. I'm here to serve you."

Despite my exhaustion, being taken care of sounds nice right now. I can't remember the last time anyone has taken care of me. My mom wasn't around much, and when she was, doting isn't a word I'd ever use to describe her behavior. Maybe I do deserve a little R and R with a side of being spoiled. "You win. What does the pampering entail?"

He raises his brow. "Foot massage."

"That's hardly pampering." I roll my eyes playfully.

"What would you do if you took a full *me* day?"

I shrug. "A massage, face mask, and then binge-watch my favorite scary movie franchise." Dane jumps up from the bed, springing into action.

"Done. Done and done. Give me five minutes." He pivots his weight from one foot to the other, and his face grows serious as if he's thinking. "Do you have a face mask?"

"Go look in the bathroom. That seems like something Sherry would have brought to the guest room; she was very thorough."

He strolls toward the bathroom, and then I hear the telltale sounds of a man rummaging. What does that sound like? It sounds like a toddler looking for their favorite toy—a loud hinge from opening a cabinet, the slam of closing said cabinets, a crash of lord knows what, and then a groan.

"Found it!" he screams, and I can't help but giggle. A second later, he strides back into the room with a few plastic packets clutched in his hand. He looks so damn proud of himself. Steps purposeful, the posture of a king.

The gleam in his eyes makes me melt when he gives me the packets. "I can't do it alone. Do it with me."

I hold one out to him, and he raises an eyebrow. "You want me to wear a face mask?"

"It would be a super good grovel," I tell him, biting my lip.

No way will he say yes.

His lips press together. "Please don't take a picture and send it to the team, no matter how tempting. Hudson won't let me live it down."

My mouth falls open. Did he really just agree to a home spa day with me? "You don't have to."

"Actually, I do." He takes the mask.

A few minutes later, we both have masks on—our faces covered in a layer of goo.

"You look very sexy in that," I tell him, giggling.

"Is this how you like me?" He tries to look serious but ends up laughing.

"Yep. All goopy."

An hour later, I'm tucked in my new big fluffy bed when there's another knock on my door.

Knowing Dane, he probably left something here.

I tuck some stray hair out of my face, hoping I don't look like I just ate myself into a contraband food coma and hid the takeout containers in the hallway trashcan.

"Come in."

The door creaks as it's pushed open.

"Oh, Josie."

That is not Dane's voice.

Nope.

It's the one person I told not to come, but it seems like with all things in my life, she's once again chosen not to listen.

She steps into my room, and my eyes widen at her appearance. My mother looks like shit—disheveled and exhausted. Like she drove all night. Did she sleep? Doesn't she have work?

327

"Why are you here? Don't you have someplace to be? Perhaps taking care of those bills you love to remind me about. The ones that are *all* my fault."

She winces, drawing my eyes to the deep circles rimming her lower lashes. "I deserve that. I took things out on you that I shouldn't have. I'm sorry for that. I'm sorry I made you feel like a burden."

"Want to know what I learned in my time away from you?"

She staggers away, probably taken aback by the raw fury in my voice. "Jos—"

I ignore her, carrying on. I need to get this out.

"I learned that people can only hurt you if you let them." I think about Dane and Molly, about Dad and Sherry, about everyone who welcomed me into their circles and made me feel wanted. "This is me saying goodbye, Mom. I no longer give you permission to hurt me."

"*No.*"

It's half-gasp, half-cry.

She drops to her knees and wraps her arms around herself. "How did it turn out like this? It wasn't supposed to be like this."

The words escape as a whisper as if she's chanting them to herself.

Still, I answer her, because I need her to know how much she hurt me. "How did you think it would turn out after you repeatedly reminded me that I'm a burden, never believed I could make something of myself, hid an entire father from me, and kicked me out of your home? Did you ever love me?"

As soon as I finish talking, I feel the weight soaring off me. For decades, I kept these words bottled inside me.

I stayed silent when she shook her head in disappointment at my grades, too scared she wouldn't show up on Sunday Date Night and I'd have to wait another week to see her.

I didn't say a word when she'd toss the utility bills into the shredder and complain about how much it cost to house a family of two.

Never once did I feel like she truly wanted me.

In fact, before Dane, I never knew what it felt like to be loved without strings attached.

"Of course, I loved you." Mom springs to her feet, determination lining every inch of her face. "I *love* you. I loved you the moment you entered the world, refusing to cry. Did you know that it took *minutes* for the doctors to get you to cry? I bawled for you, praying you were okay. I promised the universe that day that I would protect you with my life. That I'd give you everything you ever wanted and more."

I swallow, forcing myself not to sway.

I want to.

These are the words I've wanted to hear for years.

Too little too late.

"How would I know?" I turn away. "You never tell me anything."

"I won't lie and say being a single mom was easy. It's the hardest thing I've ever done, but I've never regretted it. I was just a kid myself, and there I was in the hospital, handed a child. I didn't know what to do. I promised you that I'd give you the world if you'd just breathe, and every time a bill came that I couldn't pay, I hated myself for it. You were never a burden, Josie. I just wanted to give you more, and I couldn't."

"I never asked for more." I thought of all those nights I tucked myself into bed as she worked two—sometimes three—shifts. "I just wanted you there."

"I know, and I fucked up. I don't know when it happened, but at one point, I couldn't see past my own failures. Instead of stepping back and reevaluating my priorities, I doubled down. I started taking on more shifts, spending more time away from you, chasing a better version of myself I thought would come if I could give you everything I promised I would."

"I already told you—" I start to say before she raises her hand to stop me.

"Please, Josie. Please let me get this all out."

"Go on, then." I motion for her to continue. "Explain."

"I should have told you about your father the second I discovered his name."

"You think." I roll my eyes, and the movement makes my head throb despite the headache medicine Dane gave me during his visit.

Then her words sink in.

Find out?

So…she didn't know?

Stupid, stubborn hope invades my chest, planting itself around my heart.

She didn't lie to me. Not really.

Chill out, Josie.

"When I met your father, I was a wreck. I didn't want to tell you about that night, because I was afraid you'd be embarrassed by me." Her head falls forward on a sob. "Until recently, I didn't even know who he was, Josie."

"What?" I hold my breath.

"The night I met him, I never got his last name." She swipes away her tears. "I was eighteen. I wasn't even in college yet, and I went to a frat party with a friend. I got drunk. Really, *really* drunk." She closes her eyes, sucking in a deep breath before opening them again on a groan. "This is so embarrassing."

I hesitate, not sure I want the answer to the question I'm about to ask. "He didn't…"

"Take advantage of me? God, no. We were *both* blasted. All I remember is that he introduced himself as Robert, we had this crazy connection, and I climbed him like a pole."

"*Mom.*"

"Sorry." She has the dency to turn pink. "We went our separate ways in the morning. By the time I found out I was pregnant, three months had passed, it was summer, and I didn't know where to find him. I returned to the frat house and asked around. The guys *laughed* at me, Josie. They *laughed*. It was like every mistake I made as a kid flashed before me in that moment. The booze, the sex, the drugs—"

My eyes widen. "Drugs?"

The mother I knew was always so straight-laced. I've never even seen her drink a sip of wine. Not even in pasta.

She groans, getting up and taking a seat on the empty visitor's chair. "So much drugs. That's why I got so scared when I found your stash?"

"Wait. Hold up." I shake my head, not following. "My *stash*? I don't do drugs. Never have, never will."

"Your stash. Of books."

"You mean my manuscripts?" I can't help the laugh that escapes me, even as my head threatens to split with a headache. "Oh, my God. When people say stash, they mean contraband, Mom."

A small smile makes its way up her cheeks. I didn't realize how little I've seen it.

"You called me Mom."

I look away, unsure how to answer that.

She sobers, scratching the back of her neck. "I snuck into your room when you didn't return that night and read one of your manuscripts. The ones you worked on for your creative writing class."

"Umm...okay?" I don't follow.

"*Devil Chalk.*"

"Oh. *Oh.*"

I wrote a short story on addiction for my creative writing final, which I turned into a novella the following summer as I debated pursuing a career in publishing. In the end, I realized it wasn't for me, but I couldn't bring myself to toss anything I'd written.

I shake my head. "Just because I wrote a book about addiction doesn't mean I've ever done drugs."

"It read like a diary."

"That's the writing style. *Bridget Jones* meets *Choke.* My professor thought it was cool."

"It felt so real. I saw myself in every page, Josie. You even knew how to cook meth."

"Yeah, because of a Google search. Couldn't you have asked me about it before, I don't know, kicking me out?"

"I messed up, didn't I?" She gnaws on her lower lip. "I just… am so embarrassed about my past and scared you'd found yourself on the same path. I thought it had to be my fault, and the only way to save you would be to get you away from me."

"So you sent me here."

"A few months before you graduated, I saw an interview on tv. Some sort of press conference, but there he was. Your father. It had to be him. Same first name and everything. I tracked down his number that very day, but I couldn't bring myself to call him."

"Why not?"

"When I found out I was pregnant, I cut everyone from that life out. I was too scared of meeting someone who knew the old me. I also didn't know how I'd tell you. Here I was, always telling you to be a good girl. Get good grades, don't sleep around, focus on your future. And I was—and still am—the biggest hypocrite. I didn't have the guts to call him."

"Until the morning you kicked me out."

"I got in touch with him a few weeks before, but that day was when I asked him to take you. I messed up. I was so focused on preventing you from becoming me that I pushed you away." She peers down at the floor before glancing back up. "I abandoned you when you needed me most. I'm so sorry, Josie. God, I'm sorry."

Tears stream down her cheeks. I bite down on my tongue, forcing myself to hold it together. But then Mom sobs, and I can't hold it in any longer. My own tears start to fall. Her words have opened up memories of my youth.

Scenes hit me in the chest like a ton of bricks. Every time she worked long hours to provide for me. When she tried to protect me from everyone, including myself.

Those are the moments that matter.

Yes, she should've talked to me. She shouldn't have sent me away. She should've told me about Dad the second I found out.

And she should've spent more time with me as a kid, making sure I never felt like a burden.

But she loved me.

She *loves* me.

She made so many wrong choices, but when it mattered, she did the right thing—she sent me here.

Working for Dad has been the best thing that's ever happened to me.

Mom sweeps me in her arms, brushing away my tears. "I know it's a lot to ask, but can you ever forgive me?"

"You hurt me. You hurt Dad."

"I wish I could take it all back."

"But you can't." I pull away from her, staring into her eyes. "I can't erase all the years I felt like you wished I was never born. I spent most of my life feeling like a burden, never having anyone to turn to for advice, and feeling inadequate in every sense of the word. But…"

"But?"

"But I know the truth now. I want to forgive you, but it will take time."

"So, you'll try?" Her voice sounds hopeful.

"Of course, I'll try."

I used to think I could never forgive her. But right now, right here, in this bed, in my new home, I know I can, eventually.

I thought I lost everything when she sent me away.

Instead, I found the most important thing—*myself.*

"Mom?"

"Yes, my love?"

"There's nothing wrong with becoming you." It's my turn to wipe her tears. "I've always looked up to you."

chapter seventy-two

Dane

WE HAVE A GAME TONIGHT, BUT THAT DOESN'T STOP ME FROM driving to Coach's house. After parking, I head to the door and knock.

Sherry answers the door with a large smile on her face. "Dane? Was Robert expecting you? He's not here."

"I'm actually not here to see Robert."

"Checking in on Josie again?"

I nod. "Yeah."

"She's in her room resting, but if you want to go up there . . ."

"I'll do that."

She steps out of the way, and I walk into the house and show myself to the room upstairs where Josephine is staying. I rap my knuckles on the door.

"Come in."

I take a step in and see Josephine sitting up in the bed. She looks so small among the giant fluffy pillows and large bed. It makes me want to scoop her into my arms and tell her I'll never let anything hurt her again, including myself.

"You're back." She tries to hide her excitement, but her eyes give her away. They shine brighter than usual.

I lean against the doorjamb. "That I am."

Her nose twitches, and I have to hand it to her. She's trying really hard not to smile, but there's no hiding it. She's happy I'm here. *Thank fuck.*

"Let me guess . . . more groveling?" she asks with the most serious face she can muster.

"I won't stop until you tell me you love me." I shrug. That's the plan, at least. "Want to know why? Because I love you, Hellfire, and I'll keep telling you until you believe me."

"Interesting angle."

"It's the only angle I have. I'll be here today, tomorrow, and every day until you smile at me and tell me I didn't fuck up the best thing that ever happened to me."

"I want to, but I have a hard time—"

"I know. You can't trust me yet . . . *yet* being the operative word. But you will. I'll make myself worthy of your trust."

"Don't you have a game to play?"

"I do, but I wanted to stop by first and check in on you."

I close the distance until I'm standing next to her bed, then point at the bed. Even though she let me sit with her yesterday, I still need her to give me the go-ahead. "Can I?"

She scoots over, leaving a free space.

I take a seat, then incline my head in her direction. "What's on tap for today's grovel?"

Her hand reaches out, and she rummages through the sheets. "Well, since you asked, today, I'm making Pinterest boards."

"You're doing what?"

She pulls her hand out, now clutching her phone. Her finger moves over the screen until she finds the app she's looking for, then she points the phone in my direction.

"Making boards. Like online, I have boards where I have out-fit inspos, favorite recipes, things like that."

"Interesting."

Not really, but I'll never admit that. If this makes my girl happy, then it's the best thing in the world.

She shrugs. "I think so."

I incline my head toward her cell. "Can I help?"

"Not really sure this is something you can help with."

"Try me."

"Fine." She moves over and gives me the spot right next to her in the bed so I can watch as she looks through images on the app.

After a few minutes of scrolling, Josephine stops. A pasta rec-ipe with broccoli rabe is what she's looking at. "Looks good, right?"

"It does."

"Great, that means I'll add it to my recipe board."

She taps on the saved board and then adds it.

"Can I see that?" I reach my hand out.

"Sure."

I take her phone in my hand and scroll through the pictures in the saved folder, noting in my mind the recipes and foods she's deemed her favorite. Perfect.

A plan forms in my mind of what I'll send her later today. She can't come to the game, but I know she'll be watching it from here, so I'll send her favorite snack, and by the looks of it, it's donuts.

"What are you smiling about over there?"

"Nothing." I smirk.

For the next hour, we play on her phone, and then, with a quick kiss on her cheek, I get up and head to the door.

"Kick ass tonight."

"I plan to."

I walk out of her room and let myself out of the house without saying goodbye. Once I'm no longer in earshot, I grab my phone and call Molly.

"Hey," she answers.

I press the ignition, and my car roars to a start. "Where are you?"

"Again. Hello, Dane. How are you? I am fine, thank you."

"Anyone ever say you're annoying?" I pull the car out of the driveway and start heading home to prepare for today's game.

"Anyone ever tell you that you have no manners?" She snickers into the phone. Gotta love my sister. Never one to bite her tongue.

"Yeah, a few times," I admit, most likely shocking my little sister.

She laughs. "What do you need?"

"I need you to find me the best donuts in town."

"You don't eat donuts."

"They aren't for me."

"Look at you, taking my advice and trying to win back the woman you love."

"Molly," I playfully scold.

"What? You're adorable."

"Will you help me? I kind of have a game to be at," I deadpan.

"What would you do without me?"

"Stop surviving."

"You're being too hard on yourself. I'm sure you could function for half a second, and if you convince Josie to forgive your sorry ass, she can handle you."

"Are you quitting on me, Molly?"

"Never. You'll have to fire me," she teases.

"That will never happen."

"Okay, so now that we have that settled, why don't I get to work? I don't have all day, after all. I'm supposed to go to this hockey game."

"Thanks, Molly," I say.

"My pleasure. And for what it's worth, I like her for you."

"I like her for me too."

I hang up the phone, smiling to myself. Making Hellfire happy makes me happy. I can't wait till she gets her package.

Hours later, and still sweaty, I meet Molly in the parking lot of the arena.

"You got the goods?"

She looks at me with slightly narrowed eyes. "Does this look like amateur hour?"

I raise my hands in the air. "Sorry, just had to ask."

Her mouth twists. "No. You didn't," she chides as she extends her arm and hands me the box. I decided that rather then have these delivered before the game, I'd deliver them myself after it.

I want to see Hellfire's face.

"Thanks, Mol."

"You're welcome, Dane."

Now, with the box in hand, I head to my car, and then get in and drive away.

My palms feel slick against the steering wheel from not showering after the game, but it's getting late, and I didn't want to miss Hellfire.

Traffic is practically nonexistent at this time of night, so I get to her house in record time, which is a good thing since every minute it takes means she could be sleeping.

The house is dark, and only a few small spotlights illuminate the way.

I park the car and step out, then head to the door. Once there, I hesitate. Coach might be home. How will I explain this? Fuck it.

I don't even care if he knows.

Hellfire will.

Good thing I think on my feet. I'll figure out something to say that will make sense.

My knuckles rap on the wood, and the door flies open a few seconds later.

"Hellfire, why are you out of bed?" I practically scold.

"'Cause you knocked." She rolls her eyes. "Who else did you think would answer? I'm the only one home."

Shit. I hadn't thought of that.

"What are you doing here, Dane?" She looks me up and down. "Did you come straight from the game?"

"Yeah."

"Why?"

That's when I remember the box of donuts in my hand. I thrust my hands up. "To bring you these."

"You brought me food?"

"Not just any food." I smile. "Only the best donuts in Redville."

A small laugh bubbles out of her mouth. "You didn't have to."

"That's where you're wrong, Josephine. I did."

And I'll keep doing it. For however long it takes for her to admit she loves me too.

chapter seventy-three

Josie

IT'S FUNNY HOW MUCH YOU CAN MISS SOMEONE DESPITE SEEING them only yesterday, but as I sit in my bed for another day of my recovery, I can't stop thinking about Dane.

Today, he's away for a game.

By the time he gets home later tonight, it will be too late for him to stop by, and I'd be lying if that thought doesn't make me sad.

This should be over soon, though. My ankle is feeling much better and my headaches are gone.

By next week, I should be approved to go back to work, hopefully.

Whether the team lets me come back is another story, but I'll think positively.

I flip on the TV and turn on the game. Obviously ready for the Saints to kick some ass. I watch as Dane effortlessly skates toward the puck, pulling back his stick to take a shot. He moves so fast it's hard to see. I watch with bated breath as the puck travels down the ice. The camera zooms in, and something catches my eye. There's something on his helmet. My brows furrow as I squint, trying to make out what it is. An actual snort leaves my mouth as I fall into a fit of giggles. A sticker. He has a sticker on his helmet. And what it says leaves me breathless.

I <3 Hellfire.

My door opening has me pulling my gaze away from the TV.

"Josie, it's me. Can I come in? I come bearing presents."

Presents? What kind of present does Sherry have? Maybe it's a milkshake. I could really go for one of those right now.

Dane did send me donuts, so anything is possible.

"Yes," I holler back.

A strange dragging noise has me shaking my head. What the heck is Sherry up to? But when I see what she's holding, I'm well aware she has nothing to do with this because this present can only be from one person.

Dane . . . *because who else would send me a six-foot trident?*

"Do you have any idea who would have sent this?" She places it against the wall.

"I have a pretty good idea." A laugh escapes me. The man is ridiculous.

"Care to fill me in?"

"You wouldn't believe me if I told you." And I can't really tell you without having to explain why he's sending me this.

"Say no more. Have fun with your . . . is it a trident?"

"It is."

This time, it's Sherry's turn to laugh. "Have fun with your trident."

"Thanks," I respond as she walks out the door.

The man is ridiculous, and I love it.

chapter seventy-four

Josie

OF ALL THE PLACES FOR DANE TO SURPRISE ME WITH AS AN outing, this wasn't what I expected.

But as I stand at the entrance of the vineyard, I can't help but smile.

I survey the little piece of paper in my hand, and I have to hand it to him. This is next-level grovel.

Dane Sinclair has created a scavenger hunt for me, and I love it.

In the early morning light, this venue looks nothing like it did that day. It's so lush with a sweeping view of the hotel, banquet hall, and vineyard.

It's absolutely beautiful.

Placing my hand on my hip, I look toward the location of the first clue.

Head to the scene where men cheer and scream, where Cups are on display, and you said no way.

A very pleased-looking Dane stands beside me, but of course won't help me. That would ruin all the fun. His words, not mine.

"Well?" He places his hands in his pockets, his eyes dancing with delight. He's really enjoying himself. Good, because he deserves it. He has spent every opportunity to be with me this week. He's bent over backward to make sure I'm okay.

"Has anyone ever told you that you're so annoying?" I stick my tongue out.

Dane chuckles while he inclines his head down. "Yep. You. But you love me for it."

I arch a brow. "Is that so?"

"Yep. And you know what?"

"No. But something tells me you're going to tell me," I chide.

"I love you." He's said it every day since the day in the hospital, and I love it every time I hear it. The words have slowly wound their way around my heart, filling me with hope.

Despite my heart knowing the answer, I push it off. Not ready yet. We still need to discuss some things before I make that commitment. Once I say the words, I'll give him my full heart to love and protect. He's still holding something from me, and while that's okay for now, since I need to concentrate on healing, he'll have to trust me enough one day. That's the only way we can move forward, but for now I'll enjoy this time together.

"Back to the clue," I say, needing not to think too much about the other stuff. Keeping it light until I'm better is my current motto.

"Any ideas?"

"There are two choices. One is the bar. The other is the banquet hall where I never went. My guess is the latter since the word Cup was specifically used, and since the Cup was there that night, I'm sure it is."

"Then lead the way." Dane extends his arm in the direction of the banquet hall.

As we walk down the gravel path, it feels like just yesterday when I chose not to go in this direction.

A fork in the road.

A fork? Or a trident?

A giggle escapes my mouth.

"What?" Dane asks from beside me.

I shake my head. "Nothing."

After a few more steps, we're standing outside the large mahogany doors. Dane pulls one open, and I step inside.

Looking around, I spot where the clue would be right away. He's not even trying to hide it, which makes this whole thing even funnier. On a large table in the middle of the room is a large and very fake replica of the Cup.

By the time I make it over and pull the next clue off it, my belly hurts from my laughter.

> *Where rendezvous start and guests arrive.*
> *A tired heart, a key they will find.*

"Off to the hotel." I hustle toward the exit and in the direction I need to go. Dane follows, letting me lead the way but staying close enough in case I need him.

This man is likely to make me a puddle on the ground before the day is out.

"Okay, spill. How did you make these clues . . . ? They don't exactly sound like you."

"I might have had help?"

"Molly. You really wouldn't be able to survive without her."

"I would if . . ." His unsaid words don't need to be said because the meaning is clear as day. He'd be okay if he had me.

Yep. Puddle, here I come.

By the time we arrive at the hotel, it's obvious that all the staff are in on today's events, because as I step up to the reception desk, a woman hands me a large iron key and a clue is attached.

> *You can find me at the fork in the road.*

I lift the clue in the air. "Did you even try with that one, Dane?"

"Um, yeah, Molly had to get off the phone, so no, Hellfire, I didn't."

I throw my head back at his words. "To the vineyard we go."

This time, when we walk, we're side by side, and every time I swing my arms, my fingers skim his. The touch of his skin makes my whole body hyperaware that in only a few more steps, we will be where it all changed. Where an innocent drink with a stranger became so much more.

Finally, we get to the path that leads to the vines. On the floor is an arrangement of tiny pebbles. The same ones we looked at that night.

"Funny, in the light of the day, it doesn't look like a fork or a trident."

"Are you sure?" Dane reaches out and grabs something sitting right next to the stones.

How did I not see that?

I narrow my gaze, but he's picked it up so fast that I didn't see what it was. That is until he dangles it from his finger.

My bracelet.

But this time, two charms are hanging from it.

Dane holds it out, and I take it in my hand, lifting it to look at what he added.

It's a small disc, and it appears that there are tiny letters or maybe symbols etched into the metal.

"What does it say?"

He shakes his head. "When the time is right, I'll tell you."

chapter seventy-five

Josie

TIME HAS A WAY OF MOVING FAST WHEN YOU DON'T WANT IT TO.
It's been two weeks since I fell. My ankle is healed, and my concussion is no longer an issue either. While I should be happy, and I am, of course, I'm also disappointed that Dane won't need to visit me as much.

Now that I'm officially *healed*, I can move back into the guesthouse again, and although I know Dane will still want to see me, he won't feel obligated to come over and "grovel."

Since I'm feeling one hundred percent better, I know where I'm going, and where I'm going is to watch the Saints play.

It's a home game, and I texted Molly to tell her I'm coming with Sherry.

"Thanks for coming with me," I say from the passenger seat as she drives us toward the arena.

"Are you kidding me? I'm delighted you asked me. Robert is always on me to go to a game, and I always say no."

"You do?"

"Yep, gotta keep them on their toes. That's my motto," Sherry says as she makes a right turn, going in the direction of the arena.

"That's funny. How long have you guys been together?"

"Seventeen years."

"Wow, really, that's a long time." The idea of a couple being together brings me hope. My mother never had boyfriends. Never brought any men into our house at all. I always assumed it was because of me, but now after everything, I understand it was to protect me. Being a parent must be hard. I pivot to look at her while she drives, my brain going a million miles a minute until I finally ask the question that has been on my mind for some time.

"You never thought about having kids?"

She shakes her head. "We tried, but it never happened."

"Sorry," I mumble under my breath. *Foot meet mouth.* I'm well aware you're never supposed to ask a woman about kids, but apparently, my curiosity won out.

"It's okay. I have everything I need . . . and that includes you, Josie. I want us to be a family. You, me, your father, and even your mom. Think you'd want that?"

My throat feels tight and my tongue heavy.

These are words I've always wanted to hear, and now I've heard them from more people than I ever imagined. The car around me blurs. From the dashboard to the window, everything becomes fuzzy with my unshed tears.

"I'd like that." As I blink away the water collecting, my cheeks grow damp.

Is this what it's like to get everything you've ever wanted?

I think it is.

───◦───

I'm a little late, but that's okay. I hurry to my seat but can't find Dane's number on the ice. Looking toward the penalty box, I spot him. With a quick glance at the board, I see that he has thirty seconds left in his penalty. Dropping my gaze, I try to catch his attention, my arm lifting in the air. It's as if he knows I'm here because his head tilts up, and our eyes lock. Instantly, his demeanor changes, and a smirk pulls at his lips.

I can't help but smile too.

The whistle blows, and after a few seconds with a quick nod in my direction, he's back on the ice. It's obvious to me that he's fueled up because he bolts toward a loose puck and takes control of it, skating with fury. There's only one member of the other team between him and the goal. The crowd roars with excitement as he approaches the goal. It's exhilarating to watch. I jump to my feet, cheering him on.

He pulls back his stick and fires a shot into the net. The entire arena erupts as the horns blare, music plays, and Dane just scored.

A couple of hours later, I continue to watch from the stands the rest of the game as the Saints kick ass. Dane is on fire. It's so exciting. I feel like I'm part of the game. My voice is hoarse when the Saints finally win.

Molly and I head down to the lockers, but before we get there, Molly stops in her tracks when she sees Dane talking to some man. Her eyes narrow, and she crosses her arms over her chest. Whoever it is, it pisses her off.

"I have to go," she says, storming off in the opposite direction before I can even stop her.

A second later, the man who was talking to Dane walks by. He has a smug look on his dirty face. The man looks like a creep. Once he's gone, I head in the direction he came from. When I get to Dane, his tight jaw reminds me of the day I fell. A shiver runs up my spine. I don't like seeing him like this. I hate it. Something is bothering him, and something tells me it was that man.

"Hey," I say.

He looks up at me and gives me a small smile. He's trying. I can tell. But it's like he's haunted by whatever they talked about.

"Let's get out of here."

We start to walk to the exit. I haven't been here since the

accident, and when I step outside, I'm transported back to that night. To the desperate feeling I had when he wouldn't talk to me, when he wouldn't let me in. As we step out into the crisp air, I take a deep breath in. It smells like burning leaves. I love it.

"Why are you smiling?" Dane asks.

"Just thinking about winter."

"It's almost here."

"It is, and I love it." I smile brightly.

Together, we walk toward his car. Neither of us has talked about if I'm going home with him. My car isn't parked here. I got a ride with Sherry, but I told her I would get a ride home with Molly. Of course, that was a lie. I always planned on asking Dane, but now I'm not sure it's a great idea. It's not that he's being mean, but he's being short and preoccupied.

When we are standing beside his car, I walk toward the ledge. The same ledge I fell from.

"Dane."

"Hellfire. Don't you dare."

I take a step up. My heart hammers in my chest. I shouldn't be doing this again, but I need him to know I trust him. I need him to be the man I know he can be. I need him to let me in.

"Help me walk the tightrope."

His eyes go wide. He looks at me like he's never seen me before, like he's having an epiphany. He crosses the space. No questions asked. No hesitation. He reaches out, his arms wrapping around me so there is no chance of me slipping.

"Why do you do it?" he mutters.

"Walk the tightrope?"

"Yeah, why?"

"For you. To show you how easy it all can be. All you have to do is put one foot in front of the other."

"And after everything, you still trust me?"

"I do. And do you know why?" I stop walking and pivot my

body to face him. The ledge isn't that high on the side he's standing on, so he still towers over me.

"Why?"

I reach my hand up to cup his cheek. "Because I love you, Dane Sinclair."

He pulls me toward him, picking me up until my legs are no longer on the ledge or ground. Then he walks us back toward the car and places me on the hood.

"Say it again."

"I love you, Dane Sinclair."

"I love you too, Hellfire. But can you make me a promise?"

"Depends what it is?" I challenge because I wouldn't be me if I didn't.

"No more walking the tightrope, okay? I'll be your gravity if need be." He leans in and places a kiss on my lips. I wrap my arms around his neck, and he deepens it.

"Take me home," I say against his mouth.

"Whatever you want, Hellfire. Whatever you want."

"I want you."

"Good, 'cause you're stuck with me now."

"And you're stuck with me."

chapter seventy-six

Dane

I DON'T HESITATE TO BRING HER BACK TO MY HOUSE. MY HEAD IS still spinning when we get there. I want to make this work with her, and in order to do that, I need to be honest.

Once out of the car, we walk into my living room, and I start to pace.

Josephine sits on the couch, watching me. She is most likely confused. Hell, I am, so I don't doubt that she is too.

She trusted me.

After everything that has happened between us, she trusts me. She got up on that damn ledge again and knew I would keep her safe.

Now it's time to show her that I trust her.

I continue to pace the room, working up the courage to tell her that one thing I have never told anyone. Once I'm standing directly in front of her, I come to a stop.

The air in the room feels heavier than normal, making it hard to breathe.

Will she understand why I did what I did?

With my head tilted down, our gazes lock.

Her large blue eyes are filled with nothing but love and compassion. She'll understand. I know she will.

"I need to tell you something." A nervous feeling weaves its way through my body. Despite knowing how she feels about me, I've never told anyone what I'm about to tell her.

Josephine fidgets with her hands in her lap. "Okay. I'm listening."

I clear my throat. It feels like I'm gargling rocks. "Fuck, I don't even know how to say this."

She stops moving her hands and reaches one out to squeeze mine. "It's okay. You don't have to tell me anything you don't want to."

"It's not that I don't want to." I sigh.

She cocks her head, brow raised. "Then what is it?"

"I'm scared," I admit.

Josephine sits forward on the couch but doesn't release me. "What are you scared of?"

"I am scared that once I tell you, you will never look at me the same again."

She gives my hand another squeeze. "Never going to happen."

"You don't know that."

"Then try me." She tucks a stray hair behind her ear. "But I promise nothing you ever say will change how I feel about you."

I shrug. "If you say so."

"I do." She pats the couch beside her. "Why don't you come sit down?"

With a shake of my head, I take a step back. "Let me get this out first." I close my eyes for a brief second, trying to find the strength inside me to tell her. "I guess I should start at the beginning."

"Seems as good a place as ever," she responds.

"When I was a kid, my father was really hard on me. He wanted me to be a hockey star. See, the thing was, he had tried, but an injury had crushed his dreams of playing professionally. Then he started to drink a lot." I draw in a breath. "Drinking ran in his family." I meet her gaze. "Being an asshole too." I gesture to myself.

"Stop," she says.

"I'm not just saying that to be funny. It's the truth. My father's brother was a complete degenerate, and while my father looked better on the outside, he wasn't. He just hid it well. He had a good job. Money. But it was never enough because what he wanted was the Cup. So he set out for me to live his dreams," I tell her. "Do you know the problem with living someone else's dreams?"

"No."

I stuff my hands in my pockets. "They're never your own."

"What happened?" She stares at me intently, but I can see the concern in her eyes.

Taking a deep breath, I find the words I've held on to for so long, and then on an exhale, I begin to purge myself of my secrets. "It was my senior year, and I was eighteen. I had gone to a party, and at that party, I got into a fight, but because it was Redville and I knew everyone in the town, the cops didn't arrest me. Instead, they called my father."

Josephine opens her mouth to speak, but then she shuts it, and I continue. "The problem was my parents had gone out that night. When they got the call, they were only a block from our house. I guess the sitter had to go home, so they got my sister and came to pick me up."

"What happened?" Her voice is low, almost scared to hear what transpired that night. I'm sure she knows; the bits and pieces I've told her probably make what happened that night obvious, but assuming and knowing are two different things.

"On the way to pick me up, they got into an accident, and well, my parents died."

Josephine lets out a tiny gasp, but I keep going.

"Molly was the only survivor. She had seen them take their

last breaths, and it was all my fault. I'm the reason my sister had to see that. I'm the reason she would grow up without a mother."

From where I'm standing, I can see the tears roll down her cheeks.

"It wasn't your fault, Dane."

I shake my head. "It was."

"I hate that you feel that way, and I'm sure Molly would too if she knew. You were a kid."

"I might have been a kid, but since I was eighteen, I needed to take care of my sister. I wanted to become Molly's guardian, but it wasn't easy, and my uncle stepped up. Things got dicey. The money our parents left us got tied up, and I couldn't access it right away. For a second, I thought my uncle would get her. I knew he didn't want her. He only wanted the money she would bring. I fought tooth and nail to keep her in the only home she knew. But the little money I did have access to ran out fast without a new income, and hiring a lawyer to get custody of Molly was an expense I couldn't afford," I say. "But I needed to find it, so I did."

"What did you do?" she asks.

"I point shaved a hockey game I was playing in. Then, through a shady friend, I bet on it."

She bites her lip, and I hear a pained noise from her mouth. "You did what you needed to do," she tells me.

Her words do little to comfort me. What I did was inexcusable and highly illegal. If the truth came out, my career would be over. I might not go to jail, as I'm not sure of the statute of limitations, but no one would work with me again. Still, for Molly, I wouldn't change one thing. I'd happily go to jail to make sure she was safe.

"You don't hate me?"

She frowns. "How could I? In your position, I'd have done the same. And your uncle?"

Removing my hands from my pocket, I run a hand through my disheveled hair. "He disappeared for a while until—"

"Until what?" she asks.

My jaw grows tight. "Until I received a letter. It was the night in New York when I canceled on you. That's why I did it. Why I ended things with you. I didn't want to, Hellfire, but I just thought I had no choice. I wanted to protect you. Then—he came to the game. You saw him. He claims to know what I did."

She squeezes her lids shut for a minute before reopening them. "Do you think he does?"

I nod. "Yes." There is no question from the smug look he gave me today that he does. The question is whether he can prove it, but from the desperate sound in his voice, I don't think he can. Of course, I'm not sure that's a risk I'm willing to take.

"Do you think he has proof?"

"No," I answer honestly. "Not that it matters. The scandal alone could ruin my career."

"It's your word against his. You're not alone, Dane." Josephine moves to stand. "We will come up with a plan." She takes my hands in hers. "Does Molly know?"

"Hell no," I answer fast. I never wanted my sister anywhere near that man.

She places a gentle kiss on my knuckle. "It's time you tell her. She's no longer a kid who needs protecting."

chapter seventy-seven

Josie

Y HANDS TAP NERVOUSLY ON MY THIGHS AS I WAIT FOR DANE to return. He went to call Molly. He needs to tell her.

I will never take the trust he gave to me today for granted. No matter how this all plays out, I will stand by his side.

Hopefully, it doesn't get to that, though.

Something tells me this man has zero proof and won't be taken seriously. However, I understand that it will be hard on everyone if it's brought to light, even if there's no evidence to corroborate it.

This will look bad for not only Dane but also the team and Molly.

There is no doubt in my mind that everyone who matters will take Dane's side. At the time, he had no choice. He needed to protect his sister, and he did what he had to do.

A minute later, Dane strolls back into the room. His head is tilted down, and his fingers twist together.

This man doesn't look like the man I know.

He looks weighed down by guilt.

I stand immediately and cross the space, throwing my arms around his body and pulling him into a tight embrace. We stand there for a long time, just holding each other. Then Dane leads me to the couch, and I lean my head to rest on his shoulder. The steady rise and fall of his breath calms me as he scrolls through his phone.

Time seems to pass slowly, my brain moving in a million directions, and I soon grow restless. My head tips up, and I see Dane frowning at his phone.

"What are you doing?"

"Just looking to see how long ago I called her." He's worried. I can understand. It can't be easy to tell her all these years later what he did.

I lift my hand and touch his jaw, slowly caressing his skin. "Everything is going to be okay."

"I hope so." He gives me a weak smile. He doesn't believe me.

I drop my hand from his face, and instead move to kneel in front of him. "Molly will understand."

He looks down at me, his gaze meeting mine. His eyes are glassy and tired. "How do you know?"

"She loves you. You do realize that she's an incredibly smart woman. She could do anything in the world, but she chooses to work with you, to help you, and she does that because she loves you."

"She does it because she feels indebted to me, which is insane."

I lift my hands and place them on his thighs. "Dane—"

"Now, what do we have here?" Molly's question cuts me off. When did she get to the house?

Shit.

I pull back, dropping my arms. Dane and I never spoke about what we were going to tell her. My mouth opens and shuts as I try to find words to explain why I'm kneeling in front of her brother, but Dane beats me to the punch and answers the question. "Josephine and I are together," he tells her as I stand and sit beside him on the couch again.

"It's about damn time. I'm happy you got your head out of your ass." She laughs, and I peer up at her. She's smiling broadly, and it makes my heart feel lighter. If she's happy about it, maybe my father will be too. It gives me hope. "Is that why I had to come? You need help telling Robert."

Dane shakes his head, and my body vibrates from the movement. "Unfortunately not. It's actually something else I need your help with, and it's bad."

"Wow, that's not too ominous."

"I think maybe you should sit." Dane gestures to the chair.

"Maybe we all should," I say.

With a sigh, Dane drops his arms from around me but takes my hand in his as he leads us to sit together on the couch.

He never lets go of me. Something tells me it's because he needs my added strength to get through this.

Fifteen minutes later, Dane finishes telling Molly everything. Tears stream down her face.

"It's not your fault. I don't blame you."

"How could you not—"

"Stop right there. Why did you get into a fight, Dane?"

"To protect a girl. I heard the scream and, well, just reacted. I had to get him off her."

"Exactly."

Dane shakes his head. "I don't understand."

"You were doing what you do. *You protect.* You're a protector, and it's why we love you. Listen to me right now . . . only Dad is to blame for our parents' deaths. I know you think I was too young, but I remember. I was in the car with him that night. He shouldn't have been driving. Mom wanted to drive. Did you know that?"

"No."

"Well, she did, and in his typical abusive way, he berated her, and ultimately, he drove. That's the reason they're dead. Not you. And as for the game, you had to. You have no idea what our uncle was like. The man was a bad man. He hated Dad. He hated you.

And the way he felt about me? You saved my life, and I will never fault you for what you did."

"What do you mean I saved your life?"

"He was abusive when he drank, which was always. He lost his temper. There is no question he would have hurt me if I had lived with him."

"Did he hurt you, Molly?" Dane grits out through clenched teeth.

Molly looks away from him, choosing to stare at the ground instead. "He did."

From where I'm sitting, I see Dane clench his fist. "I'll kill him."

"He only physically hurt me once, and I'm not stupid, Dane. I took pictures."

"That's not answering the question. There is more than one way to hurt a person."

"Fine. He hurt me."

"How did I not know?"

"Because, Dane, I knew how protective you were of me. And I knew I could never live with him, so I made sure to get evidence when he did lay his hands on me."

"Molly."

She shrugs.

"I can't believe how strong you are."

"You gave up your life for me."

"I'd do anything for you."

chapter seventy-eight

Dane

AFTER SPENDING THE PAST FEW HOURS WITH MY SISTER, SHE finally leaves. We have a plan for how we will deal with everything tomorrow, but for now, I'm going to enjoy my time with my little Hellfire. I'm going to worship her because she deserves no less than that. She stood by my side even though I was an asshole. She was there even after I walked away from her . . .

And when I let her down, she was still there. Now, with the shit hitting the fan, she hasn't left my side. The sound of the water in the bathroom has me walking to see what she's up to.

When I step inside, I find her brushing her teeth. An empty toothbrush container sits on the counter. She must hear me approach because she turns to face me after spitting out the water in her mouth.

"I hope you don't mind. I found a toothbrush."

"What's mine is *yours*, Hellfire."

She shuts the water off. "You ever going to stop calling me that?"

I take a step closer to her. "Do you want me to?"

"Nope."

"Good, 'cause I wasn't going to." I reach my hands out and place them on her hips. "I like having you here."

"I like being here."

"Then never leave."

She laughs. "One step at a time, Sinclair."

I raise my brows at the use of my last name. "Sinclair, is it?"

"Yep." She pops the *p*, and then lets out a squeak when I lift her and walk her to the shower. "What are you doing?"

"You're a dirty girl and need a shower."

"Alone?" She playfully pouts.

"Fuck no."

She makes quick work of undressing, and I turn on the water, then strip too.

Once we're both in the shower, I lather up her hair and her body. She deserves to be worshipped, and that's what I plan to do. I wash every inch of her, and when I'm finished washing her, I get on my knees and pull her legs apart.

"What are you doing?"

"Making you all dirty again."

I lean forward, swiping my tongue against her clit. "Any objections?"

"Nope."

Good, because I plan to devour her.

With my hands on her thighs, I spread her legs wider. "You taste amazing."

Josephine's legs start to shake, and I try to settle her, but it's nearly impossible with the way she vibrates as she falls apart on my tongue. I continue to suck her clit as she rides her high, and only stop when the trembling ceases.

"Let's go." I grab her and throw her wet body over my shoulder, and then step out of the shower. The cold air stabs at my skin. Josephine shivers in my grasp, but I doubt it's from the cold.

"You need to get us towels."

"Nope." I continue to walk, water pooling at my feet with each step I take.

Finally, when I'm in front of the bed, I drop her down and follow, laying my still wet body over hers.

With her legs bracketed around my hips, I bury myself inside her.

She feels amazing.

She is amazing.

Josephine gasps at the movement, and I hold steady, letting her adjust to my size. Then slowly, I pull back.

She wiggles her hips, slipping the head of my dick back inside her.

As she moans, my movement speeds up. Thrusting in and out of her. I want to draw this out, but I'm so close, I don't think I can. Having her come on my tongue has me already too close.

"I need you to wrap your arms around me, Hellfire," I command.

"Why?"

"I'm afraid I'll crush you, but I want no space between us." Her arms wrap around my back, and I bury my head in her neck. "I thought I lost you."

"I will always come back to you."

Like Aphrodite.

chapter seventy-nine

Dane

THE FOLLOWING MORNING, I LEAVE JOSEPHINE IN MY BED TO
meet Molly. She's waiting outside her apartment building when
I pull up to get her.

We drive in silence, but from where I'm sitting, from the corner
of my eye, I can see that she's just pulled a manila file out of her bag.

"What's that?" I ask.

"Everything we need to shut our uncle up."

"Okay."

"No more questions?"

"Molly, I trust you. If you say you have this, then I believe you."

"Thanks, Dane. You don't understand how much that means
to me." She rummages through some papers before she places the
manila folder back in her bag. "I'm happy for you and Josie. She's
perfect for you, you know?"

"She is."

"She's the perfect sunshine to your grumpy."

"Sunshine? Wait until you get to know her better, she's more of a hellfire."

"I can't wait."

I smile as I continue to drive to my uncle's house. He hasn't moved. He still lives on the outskirts of town, where he and my father grew up before my dad moved to the opposite side of town to start his own family.

When the familiar white house comes into focus, I slow my car. The place looks beat up. The years haven't been good to it. What was once crisp, newly painted white wood is now peeling and discolored.

The side window is boarded up, and the screen door seems to hang off the hinge.

No wonder he sees me as a payday, and the truth is, without Molly, he might just get it.

I roll the car to a stop, and then both Molly and I are out of the car and walking to the door. He must have seen us coming because the door flies open once we are on the front step.

"Look who finally came to visit." He looks at Molly. "And, Molly, you sure did grow up to be a looker, like your mama."

"Shut the fuck up and do not look at her."

"You have a temper." He snickers.

"You're one to speak," Molly jumps in.

"I don't know what you're talking about."

"Why don't you show us in, and I'll let you know."

My uncle pushes the door wider and lets us through.

The small room, which is the living room, smells like an ashtray. The smoke from that last lit cigarette still clogs the air. There's also the faint smell of weed. I look around, clocking a half-empty bottle of vodka.

Drunk and high, today should be fun.

"You here to pay?" He wipes his mouth with the back of his hand.

"Actually, I'm not."

"Oh, you're not?" He turns to Molly. "Did he tell you what he did? You both will have no place to live when I'm done with you. Actually, this one will. Jail."

"I don't think so, dickhead."

"Yeah, you don't think? What will your precious coach think when I tell him? Here's the deal; you pay me twenty grand, or I will go to the press with every sordid detail of your life. I will ruin you unless you pay me."

"I think you've got shit. You have nothing. And I called around. Your source? The bet . . . yeah, you don't have that source. Nick's gone. No one's seen him, and seeing as that's all hearsay, I don't think anything's going to happen to me, so why don't you fuck off with your threats?"

"Threats? You think this is just a threat?"

"No, I think it's blackmail. Which is highly illegal, and my sister here, she heard you—" I incline my head. "So this is how it's going to be. You're going to leave me and my family alone. And I'm going to live my best fucking life."

Molly steps forward, manila folder in her hand. I shake my head at her. I don't want her hands dirty; I never did. I wanted her here for support. I'd never let her put herself at risk. Whatever picture she has of the bruise he left on her, that's her story, and if she chooses to do something with it, I'll support her, but I won't let her dredge up the past for me.

She nods. She knows me well enough to know, but she does lift her phone. Then she presses the button.

On video is my uncle, clear as day, from thirty seconds ago, and all that's recorded is the blatant blackmail.

She smiles as we all listen. "Don't get any big ideas. I've already emailed it to my Dropbox."

"You bitch."

I take a step forward, towering over my uncle. "And you're a fucking loser. Stay out of my life. Anything I have ever done in my life was to protect my sister. I wouldn't change one minute of my life because when I look at her, I know it was all worth it to see the woman she's become."

Molly turns toward me and places her hand on my sleeve. "Let's go, Dane. He's no longer important."

"I don't think so. You don't get to win, not again."

"Yet you've never understood. It's not about winning; it's about love and family, and you have none. I wasn't going to do this, but just know you have skeletons in your closet, and we own them."

My uncle's brows pinch in, and he looks at Molly and then at me.

"My sister is resourceful when she needs to be. Don't test her or me. You understand?"

We don't wait for him to respond.

Once in the car, Molly turns to me. "Why didn't you let me use the evidence from when he hurt me?"

"Because that's your story, Molly, and only you get to decide if you tell it. I'll never make you do something you don't want to do or are not ready to do. When the time comes, and you're ready, I'll be here to support you, and if not, I'll still be here."

"Thanks, Dane."

"Anytime, Mol."

"Now, let's get you home to your girl." We both laugh before driving off into the future and closing the door on the past once and for all.

chapter eighty

Dane

Hudson: Daney boy have you been holding out on us?

Dane: I have no idea what you're talking about. And I don't want to know.

Hudson: My sources tell me you and coach daughter are an item.

Dane: Your sources are still searching for their two brain cells to rub together.

Hudson: Awkward. My source is your sister.

Mason: Backs out of the room slowly.

Aiden: Happy for you man. Josie is the real deal.

Dane: Thanks.

Hudson: Is it just me or has Aiden become a real sap since Cassidy and him got together?

chapter eighty-one

Josie

"WE NEED TO GO TO YOUR DAD."

"Do we really?" It's all I've wanted for so long . . . then why am I so nervous? Because the truth is, I have no idea how my father will react. Even though Dane thinks of me as a hellfire, I'm really not. Just for him.

"Yes. The whole team now knows. We have to tell him."

My nose scrunches. "Can't we stay in this bubble another minute?" *Please say yes.* What if Dad doesn't approve? What if he feels betrayed that we both lied? My stomach bottoms out, and I feel like I'm going to be sick.

Dad wouldn't do that, right?

"As much as I want to, the answer is no. Come on, Hellfire, I want to be able to show you off. I want to hold your hand in public. Kiss you in public, and I don't wanna sneak around anymore. I love you, and I want everyone in the world to know."

"Well, when you put it that way, how can I say no?"

"You can't."

"Fine, let's go," I groan.

Dane laughs, and the laugh sounds different. I never asked any questions the day he snuck out of bed. I knew he was going to see his uncle, and I knew Molly was going with him. I don't know what happened. All I know is he came back a different man. A lighter one. The dark circles under his eyes were gone, and he just seemed happier.

If he ever wants to tell me what happened, I'll be there to listen, but I'll never push him. I trust him with all my heart.

Fifteen minutes later, we park the car in the front of the house, and together, we walk around back to the door I always enter from.

"Hello, anyone here?"

"In my office," my dad calls out.

"You ready?" I whisper to Dane.

"Never been more ready for anything in my life."

We start walking, and as we enter the room, he takes my hand. I give him a nod, and we walk in together.

When my father looks up from his desk, he smiles at us both and then he clocks our joined hands.

He doesn't give any thoughts or feelings away. Just stares for a minute, then he picks up the phone and dials.

"Can you come to my office?"

Who did he just call?

Is it someone from the team that he wants to come to the house?

Or . . .

Footsteps sound from behind me, and I turn over my shoulder to see Sherry moving in our direction and into the room.

She walks past us and to my father's desk.

What is happening?

My heart feels like it's beating way too fast to be healthy.

Then my father stands, reaches into his pocket, and hands Sherry a twenty-dollar bill.

"Nice doing business with you, Robert."

"What is happening?" I ask.

"It seems these guys had a bet, and Sherry won," Dane responds.

Sherry bounces on her feet. "Sure did."

"I'm confused."

"Hellfire, we were the bet." Dane turns to my father. "How long have you known?"

"From the beginning."

My eyes go wide. Does he mean from the first night? Or the first day at work?

"How?"

"I saw the way Dane looked at you when you started working for the team. Yes, he was grumpy, but there was something else there, and for the first time since I've known him, I felt like he had a chance at happiness."

"So you knew that all the way back then, and you made her work for me anyway?"

"Hell, yeah, I did. Dane, you're like a son to me, and when I saw you happy, I decided—"

"To play Cupid?"

"I mean, I wouldn't say it like that."

"Matchmaker?"

"That sounds more accurate," my father says.

"You're not pissed?"

"Nope." My father walks up beside Sherry and puts an arm around her.

"And what exactly was the bet?"

"How long it would take Dane to get his head out of his ass and come here and ask for my blessing."

"I haven't asked yet, so technically, you haven't won yet, Sherry."

My dad's brow lifts. "Is that so?"

"It is, but you're right. I am here to ask for your blessing to date your daughter. I love her, and I can't go another day without the whole world knowing."

"Afraid Hudson might hit on her again?"

"Damn straight, but in all seriousness, I want to be with your daughter."

"You've always had my approval."

I drop Dane's hand and walk over to my father, hugging him. "Thank you."

"No need to thank me. I only want you to be happy."

I look around. Who knew when I got here that not only would I get a father, another mom, and now the love of my life?

Not me, that's for sure.

It's crazy how life happens.

I walk back to Dane, and then my father and Sherry leave the room, giving us a moment alone.

"I love you, Hellfire."

"I love you, too."

epilogue

Dane

Eight Months Later . . .

I SIT IN FRONT OF HIS TOMBSTONE, CUP IN HAND. IT'S BEEN A YEAR since I was last here, and since then a lot has happened.

The Saints won the Cup again, and I'm back here, but this time, I'm not alone. Sitting beside me is my little hellfire.

"Hey, Dad." I take a deep breath, and from beside me, Josephine places a small hand on my lap and gives my thigh a squeeze, letting me know she's here for me. "It's taken me a while to get here, but I wanted to tell you that I forgive you. I forgive you for everything, and I love you. You weren't always the best father, I know this, but you tried, you tried the best you could with the upbringing you had, and I forgive you." I look over at Josephine and she gives me a small smile. "This is Josie. Well, Josephine. Or Hellfire." I laugh.

"Hi," she squeaks out, probably not used to speaking to a tombstone.

I pivot my body a little and look at the gravesite right beside his. "Mom, it's been a while. I'm sorry I haven't visited for a long time. I was a dick, but I'm better now, and this woman is the reason. Mom, I want you to meet Josephine. She's everything you would have loved. She's smart, funny, and so strong. She makes me a better man, Mom, and I want to spend the rest of my life with her."

I hear a small gasp from beside me and move from where I'm sitting to kneel in front of Josephine.

Then I reach into the bag I brought, grabbing the little box I hid there.

"Hellfire, I love you more than life itself. You make me want to be a better man, a man who will make you proud. You are my reason for everything, and I want to spend the rest of my life with you." I open the box. "Will you marry me? Will you make me the happiest man in the world?"

"Hmm." She scoots back and slants her head, making a show of tapping her lip. "I'm not sure I can marry someone who keeps secrets."

"Secrets?"

The fuck?

I arch a brow, hoping she's messing with me because I cannot, under any circumstances, live without this woman. With a palm face down on an imaginary Bible, I hold up the other and declare, "I solemnly swear that I am not a serial killer. You won't find any bodies in my closet. Literally and figuratively."

"Pity. A body or two would be exciting." She lifts her wrist and wiggles her bracelet. "You never told me what this means."

"That knowledge is reserved for my future fiancée." I shift a little. "FYI—my knee is killing me."

Her eyes widen like she's just remembered I'm still on my knee. "Yes!" She can't help but jump up from where she's sitting, and then start bouncing on her feet. It's the cutest thing I've ever seen. "Of course, I'll marry you."

Standing, I place the emerald-shaped diamond on her ring finger, and she launches herself into my arms, showering my face with sloppy kisses. My cheeks, my forehead, the tip of my nose. And finally—fucking finally—my mouth.

She pulls away on a giggle. "Sorry, Mr. and Mrs. Sinclair."

I laugh. "I don't think they care." I pull out my imaginary Bible again and stick my other hand up, wanting to make this vow in front of my parents. "Josephine Moreau, from now until eternity, I will always be there for you."

"Even when I want to walk the tightrope?"

"Always when you want to walk the tightrope," I promise.

The last time I was here, I was a shell of a man. But through her, I've finally learned to love. Not just her but myself.

Life is ugly, and cruel, and twisted. All it takes is one moment to change your life. But it's when you're at your lowest point that you learn to appreciate the heights. My tragedies are beautiful because they brought me to her.

She tilts her head, a playful smile gracing her irresistible lips, and I know she's about to fuck with me again because she's hellfire. It's in her blood.

"Even if I have conditions?" she asks, still grinning.

I sigh. "Well, I've already committed one crime. What's another?"

"Why stop at two?"

With a growl, I yank her over my shoulder. "Just my luck to fall head over heels for the neediest girl on planet Earth."

"Don't think I didn't see the La Mer face mask in your bathroom. Two hundred bucks for a single mask? Are you kidding me?"

I set her down in front of a thick tree trunk and flatten my body against hers, letting her feel every inch of me. "I'll do you one better than a crime spree."

She arches a brow. "Oh?"

I lift her wrist and toy with a charm.

The charm.

"Really?" she gasps against my lips.

I graze my lips up her neck, teasing her jaw until I finally reach the shell of her ear. And then, I tell her what the charm says.

What I've known since we met, even before she told me she will always come to me.

"I will always look for you."

acknowledgements

I want to thank my entire family. I love you all so much.

Eric, Blake, and Lexi you are my heart.

Thank you to the amazing professionals that helped with Twisted Collide:

Jenny Sims

Marla Esposito

Crystal Burnette

Kelly Allenby

Champagne Formats

Jill Glass

Becca Hensley Mysoor

Anna Silka

Thank you to Lyric for bringing Twisted Collide to life on audio.

Thank you to my fabulous agent Kimberly Whalen.

Thank you to Michael Joseph and Hannah Smith for bringing the Saints of Redville to bookstores.

Thank you to my AMAZING ARC TEAM! You guys rock!

Melissa: Thanks for all your help and for keeping me sane.

Parker: Thanks for always being my sound board and helping me find the sprinkle.

Leigh: Thank you for reading and listening to me bitch.

To the ladies in the Ava Harrison Support Group, I couldn't have done this without your support!

Please consider joining my Facebook reader group Ava Harrison Support Group

Thank you to all the Booktokers, bookstagramers, and bloggers who helped spread the word. Thanks for your excitement and love of books!

Last but certainly not least...

Thank you to the readers!

Thank you so much for taking this journey with me.

Made in the USA
Columbia, SC
06 December 2024

48555765R00228